FIRE STORM

FIRE
STORM

Lauren St John

Orion
Children's Books

First published in Great Britain in 2014
by Orion Children's Books
This paperback edition first published in 2014
by Orion Children's Books
a division of the Orion Publishing Group Ltd
Orion House
5 Upper St Martin's Lane
London WC2H 9EA

1 3 5 7 9 10 8 6 4 2

A catalogue record for this book
is available from the British Library

Typeset by Input Data Services Ltd,
Bridgwater, Somerset

Printed and bound in Great Britain
by Clays Ltd, St Ives plc

ISBN 978 1 4440 1098 5

www.laurenstjohn.com
www.orionbooks.co.uk

For Catherine Clarke, who
routinely makes the impossible
possible, with love and a
thousand thanks

1

IN A CORNER stable at White Oaks Equestrian Centre, Casey Blue was experiencing an unfamiliar and distinctly unwelcome sensation – that of being crushed by a one-ton horse. For reasons unknown, Lady Roxanne had taken exception to being saddled and was expressing her displeasure by trying to paste Casey against the wall.

'Excuse me!' Casey panted indignantly after wriggling free. She massaged her ribs. 'That's no way for a lady to behave.'

In weeks to come Casey would discover that she was just one of a long line of people who routinely used that phrase – and worse – in connection with Roxy, but for now she was in the dark. She assumed that she'd inadvertently touched a sensitive spot on the horse's flank, or that Roxy was simply nervous in a new environment.

The 16.2hh bay mare had arrived the previous day when Casey was in London celebrating her father's birthday. It was especially important that she was with him because he'd only recently been released from prison for a crime he didn't commit. She'd asked her coach, Mrs Smith, to take care of things in her absence, but somehow that hadn't happened: when the lorry turned up neither Mrs Smith nor Casey had been there to welcome Storm's temporary replacement. Hardly surprising that Roxy was unimpressed.

Making encouraging noises, Casey reached for the girth. Roxy pinned her ears to her head, shifted her quarters and made a snapping noise with her teeth. She made it plain that if any attempt were made to fasten it, there would be consequences.

'Look, I know we've started out on the wrong foot, but I promise I'll make it up to you,' said Casey, leading the mare out into the yard where she was less likely to turn her new rider into a brick sandwich. 'You've obviously had a bad experience in the past, but it won't be like that here. I'm one of the good guys. Ask Storm.'

At the mention of Storm Warning, her champion horse, she felt a pang. She could see him in the far field, grazing peacefully with his friends. The other horses, mainly bays and a couple of chestnuts, blurred into one at this distance, but Storm's silver coat – the colour of lightning blended with thundercloud was how Casey liked to think of it – set him apart from the crowd even on dull grey days like this one.

Usually he'd be at the gate as soon as he spotted her, as eager to go out for a gallop as he was for treats and love, but today he was enjoying his holiday. Casey didn't blame him. Barely two weeks had passed since they'd won the Badminton Horse Trials and Kentucky Three-Day Event back to back – a feat that had earned Casey a place in the record books as the youngest rider in history to complete the double.

It wasn't until the British Airways horse transport plane landed at London's Stansted airport at the end of a long, gruelling journey from the US that Casey had realised how exhausted she was. She was in bed and fast asleep within hours of arriving home at Peach Tree Cottage and didn't surface for nearly two days. Storm had done much the same, lying flat on his side and dreaming like a foal.

When at last Casey did emerge from her bedroom, she took a well-earned break. For twelve glorious days she rose late, read books and spent time with her dad, who'd been warmly welcomed back to his old job at the Half Moon Tailor Shop. His boss, Ravi Singh, had never doubted his innocence. Best of all were the long beach walks and romantic picnics that she enjoyed with Storm's farrier, Peter, who also happened to be her new boyfriend. She was so besotted with him that even the thought of him made the blood practically fizz in her veins.

Rested and restored ('rebooted' she'd joked to Peter), she was now ready for the season ahead. Her primary focus was the Burghley Horse Trials in September. Victory there would hand her eventing's greatest prize: the Rolex Grand Slam.

So ferocious was the competition for this triple that only one rider had ever achieved it: Pippa Funnell in 2003. Hers was a feat that could never be repeated, because she'd won Badminton, Kentucky and Burghley in the days when the long format, which included a steeplechase and roads and tracks, was still an integral part of any three-day event. Even without the extra mileage, no rider had managed it since, although Andrew Hoy, William Fox-Pitt and Andrew Nicholson had come close.

Casey, who considered the 'short format' of dressage, cross-country and show jumping tough enough, considered Pippa to be some kind of superhero. At seventeen, she was years away from being anywhere near as good as Pippa, but miracles did happen – especially when you had a horse like Storm Warning. And Casey had the Badminton and Kentucky trophies to prove it!

The only cloud on the horizon was that Storm needed to have six weeks' rest before being brought back into training. Hence Roxy. Casey had imagined that, on the back of her success in Gloucestershire and Kentucky, she'd have her choice of top horses to ride for a couple of months, until Storm was once more ready for action. But with less than a week to go before she was due to resume work, nobody had come forward with a suitable mount.

Morag, White Oaks' acerbic manager, was unsympathetic. 'What did you expect? Your achievements this season are phenomenal, Casey Blue, and as a friend I'm in awe of you, but I wouldn't want you or Mrs Smith within a mile of one of my up-and-coming horses. Your unconventional – some would say downright batty – training methods are already the stuff of legend.'

'They can't be that batty,' protested Casey. 'Our results speak for themselves.'

'Yes, but not everyone wants their horse ridden flat out along a public beach without a bridle, or paddled in their neighbour's swimming pool. And those were among your more sensible experiments.'

Unfortunately, Morag was right. No one else was blunt enough to say it to their faces, but the end result was the same: a distinct lack of offers of shiny warmbloods with impressive CVs. That didn't bother Mrs Smith, because from the outset she was fixated on getting a youngster.

'In a perfect world what we need is a novice eventer who is still pretty green. Something to challenge us.'

'What *I* need,' said Casey, 'is a two-star, or even a three-star horse with a proven track record in show jumping and dressage so I'll be able to stay competitive throughout the season.'

'And what is this paragon of a creature going to teach you? What are you going to learn? Might I remind you that, Storm aside, you have only ever ridden one horse, and there'd be those who'd argue that Patchwork was at least three parts mule. The best riders on the circuit have ridden dozens of horses. They've also ridden and competed in many different arenas, from Pony Club competitions to local hunts and amateur racing. That's how great riders hone their skills. That's how they learn what makes horses tick.'

Casey, who was keenly aware that she lacked the riding experience that even the lowliest competitor on the circuit took for granted, said nothing.

Next day she was offered a couple of wildly unsuitable show jumpers by an ambitious couple who boarded their horses at White Oaks.

Just as she was beginning to despair, she'd received an email about Lady Roxanne, an Irish sporthorse who'd achieved reasonable results at intermediate level. Her owner, Jennifer Stewart, claimed that the mare had bags of potential but consistently underperformed. She begged Casey to consider taking her on. *As Badminton and Kentucky champion, you are among the world's best young riders and will undoubtedly help her to realise her potential,* she gushed in one email.

In another to Mrs Smith, she described Roxy as *gifted but challenging.*

Casey hadn't liked the sound of that at all.

'It has an ominous ring to it. Jennifer Stewart is like an estate agent describing a house as a dream home but needing a little work. I'll move in and discover that it's a crumbling ruin.'

Her teacher shook her head in wonder. 'Would you listen to yourself? Are you the same girl who, less than three years ago, paid a dollar for a bag-of-bones horse from a knacker's yard and shaped him into one of Britain's finest eventers? Now you're turning up your nose at a well-bred mare who has extensive competition experience just because her owner describes her as a little challenging?'

'She didn't use the word "little", said Casey, but she knew she was clutching at straws. And Mrs Smith did have a point. Taking on a mare who was a bit of a project could be both rewarding and educational. It might also distract her from missing Storm.

'You're right, as usual. I do need to ride more horses and this is the perfect opportunity for me to really get to know and understand a horse with a totally different temperament from Storm. Now that I think about it, I can't wait to get started.'

Recalling these words, Casey led Roxy to the hitching post in the yard. She stood for a moment admiring her new mount. The mare was the colour of toffee, with a shiny black mane and lustrous, intelligent eyes. When she wasn't scowling and snapping, she was pretty.

Distracted by the change of scene, Roxy stood perfectly still even when Casey adjusted the saddle. Her expression was positively serene. Casey relaxed. The crushing episode in the stable was obviously an aberration. Reaching for the girth, she started to pull it tight.

'Ow!'

Her screech of pain was so loud that it scared the birds from the nearby trees. Roxy had nipped her left arm, drawing blood.

As Casey swore beneath her breath and rubbed the purple flesh, she was shocked to see that Roxy's ears were pricked. The mare was staring into the distance as if the whimpering girl at her side was as inconsequential as a swatted fly.

Casey was relieved that the yard was empty and there was no one around to witness her humiliation. All the instructors were taking lessons and Morag and a couple of the stable girls were at a show. She glanced at her watch in annoyance. Where on earth was Mrs Smith? Her teacher had disappeared to Brighton the previous day on a mysterious errand and was now an hour and a half late, poor form when it was their first lesson back after a break and they had a tricky new horse to train. Casey had waited as long as she could before the delicious prospect of trying out her new mare had got the better of her.

If Mrs Smith had been a normal teacher, she could have rung her for an ETA, but Mrs Smith loathed mobile phones and had yet to answer the one Casey had bought her on their return from the US. That meant that Casey was on her own with the ironically named *Lady* Roxanne.

Adopting what she hoped was a stern but kindly tone, she explained to Roxy that biting, kicking and pasting riders against walls were all unacceptable behaviour at White Oaks. The mare ignored her. Casey lifted the saddle flap cautiously and put a wary hand on the girth. Nothing happened. But as she leaned in to tighten it, Roxy's head whipped round and she went for the kill, biting Casey so hard on the bum that she leapt into the air with a squeal.

An explosive laugh startled them both. Casey squinted into the shadows. A stranger was leaning against the stable-block wall. He was so close it seemed impossible that she hadn't seen him, and yet with his black polo-shirt, dark brown breeches and black long boots he was all but invisible in the shade.

He straightened unhurriedly and stepped into the sunlight. Casey caught her breath. He was shorter than Peter – perhaps by as much as two inches – and was as fair as her boyfriend was dark, but he had the kind of looks that teen magazines call 'heart-stopping'.

'I think you'll find that if you give her a carrot next time she does that, she'll be so surprised that it'll diffuse her temper,' he said in a friendly tone. 'She'll try to nip you again, of course, but if you respond by offering her another carrot, she'll soon learn that what she's come to regard as a negative experience is really rather fun.'

What he said made sense, but Casey's hackles rose. She didn't appreciate being told what to do by a boy she didn't know from Adam, especially a good-looking one and when she was in pain. 'Is that so?' she said coldly.

He flashed a grin and his hand came up and swept

streaky blond hair out of his eyes. 'But I'm sure you already know that. You don't get to achieve what you've achieved, especially with a horse as complex and brilliant as Storm Warning, without having rare gifts of communication with animals.'

Casey immediately felt silly for having taken offence over something so trivial when he'd clearly been trying to help. Besides, anyone who praised Storm was all right by her. She smiled. 'Oh, I wouldn't go that far. My horse-whispering skills are really not working on Roxy.'

'Wanna try the carrot trick?'

Casey hesitated, but her arm and right buttock were killing her and she didn't fancy being chomped again. 'Why not?'

When Roxy swung round with her teeth bared, Casey surprised her by popping a carrot in her mouth. Roxy was too busy crunching to worry about the girth or anything else. With the help of another two carrots, Casey was able to adjust the bridle unmolested.

'Need a leg up?'

Casey hesitated. The mounting block was at the far end of the yard. She'd finally got Roxy settled. Maybe it would be better to mount her now while she was quiet. 'Sure. Uh, thanks.'

As the visitor moved to cup his hands beneath her boot, his bicep brushed her chest. Casey felt a shot of pure attraction go through her, followed, almost immediately, by an inexplicable feeling of dread and guilt. The combined feelings disturbed her so much that she lost concentration and almost flew over the other side of Roxy.

'Don't mind me, I'm here for my first riding lesson,' she joked, struggling back into the saddle, red-faced.

'It was entirely my fault,' he said graciously. 'Don't know my own strength. Believe me, no one would ever mistake you for an amateur, Casey Blue.'

Casey gathered the reins. Now that she was gazing down on him, she felt more in control. It also occurred to her that there was something familiar about him. 'You obviously know my name. Mind telling me yours?'

'Apologies. I seem to have left my manners at home today. I'm Kyle. It's a pleasure to finally meet you. It's something I've wanted for a very long time.'

He said it as if he'd thought of nothing else for months.

'Why?' Casey asked before she could stop herself.

He grinned. 'Why not? You're the hottest young rider in the country.'

As he reached up to shake her hand, some sixth sense warned Casey that nothing good would come out of any association with him. She dragged her eyes away from his dark blue ones and glanced at the distant gate. Where *was* Mrs Smith?

Casey kept her voice cool. 'I'm hardly that, but thanks. You event?'

'Heavens, no. Not brave enough. On the whole, I find the ground a lot safer. Fewer broken bones. I teach a bit.'

It was then that the penny dropped. Casey hid her astonishment by allowing the restless mare to move forward a few paces. She could have echoed his compliment by saying, 'I know who you are. You're the hottest coach in Britain.' But there was something in the confident set of his shoulders that told her he already knew that. The previous October he had, at twenty, been the youngest person ever to be shortlisted for the Golden Horseshoe Riding Instructor of the Year Award, before being controversially beaten to the title. The eventing circuit had been abuzz with rumours about it afterwards. Since the winner was a close relative of one of the judges, the general consensus was that the result had been fixed and Kyle robbed.

She reined in Roxy. 'You're Kyle West?'

Again the laconic grin. 'Last time I checked.'

'Here to give someone a lesson?'

He stepped forward and pushed his blond fringe from his face as he looked up at her. 'Actually, I was hoping to see you.'

'Me?'

'Yes, I'd like a word with you if that's possible.'

Casey was as curious as a cat in a den of mice, but she didn't want to seem too eager. 'No problem at all, provided you don't mind hanging around for an hour or so. As you've probably gathered, Roxy and I are just getting to know one another and my coach, Mrs Smith, who should be here, isn't.'

Kyle kept pace with them as they left the yard. 'Sure

thing. Would it be okay if I watched you work? I mean, I don't want to intrude.'

'Be my guest,' said Casey, not knowing that those three words, so carelessly spoken, would change everything.

2

DESPITE THE LOW-SLUNG banks of cloud there was a brightness to the day, and the outdoor ménage, set against a backdrop of wildflowers, sheep and the five-hundred-year-old oaks that gave the stables their name, had seldom looked so inviting. Still Casey chose the indoor school, which afforded a little more privacy.

If Kyle thought it an odd choice, he made no comment. Without being asked, he settled himself on one of the tiered wooden benches that provided seating during winter competitions, sitting so still and silent that he was once again all but invisible.

At first his presence made Casey self-conscious, but the joy of being back in the saddle on a willing horse soon superseded that. Jennifer Stewart had not been exaggerating. Roxy had talent in spades. Her quarters needed serious work, but on the whole she was a beautiful mover. Tacking up aside, the only challenge so far had been staying aboard during a light-hearted bout of bucking.

As the session proceeded, Casey's confidence grew. She felt pleased that Kyle was there to witness her riding well and bonding with Roxy. It made up for the embarrassing scene in the yard. At the same time, it felt odd to be on a horse that wasn't Storm. Roxy didn't have Storm's power or fluidity or his almost psychic ability to read her mind, but she was responsive and there was plenty of pleasure to be had from her genuine paces. She had a good jump on her too, flying over a couple of low uprights as if she was at Hickstead. It was hard to believe that this was the same animal who, just minutes earlier, had drawn blood.

Kyle, for his part, said nothing. He leaned forward with a slight frown on his face, light rippling across his golden head as he turned to follow her progress. A couple of times she noticed him glancing down at his phone, but when she passed him again she appeared to have his full attention.

'Any comments?' called Casey as she slowed Roxy to a walk.

'You're doing great. Fantastic. I mean, there are a couple of tiny things but they're so tiny they're not even worth mentioning.'

Casey circled back. 'Mention away. What tiny things?'

'Really, they're nothing.'

'Then they shouldn't be hard to fix. Go on.'

'It's just – do you always do that thing with your foot?'

'What thing?'

'Put your weight on the outside of the stirrup so that you're leaning into your lower toe?'

For the second time that day, Casey felt like a beginner. 'What? No. I mean, I don't think so. Is that what I appear to be doing?'

He shrugged. 'It might not feel that way, but trust me, it is. It's so subtle that it's barely noticeable on the flat, but if you were jumping it would have the effect of destabilising your lower leg. Not exactly ideal if you're flying over the Cottesmore Leap at Burghley.'

Casey knew the fence well. She'd studied the television footage of it the previous year. It was the largest eventing fence in the world, its proportions exaggerated by the ditch that followed it, a yawning cavern so terrifying that, when walking the course prior to cross-country day, many riders chose to avoid it in case they lost their nerve before they'd even begun.

'Don't worry. It's easy enough to fix. Stand up in your stirrups until you feel balanced. See how your weight naturally inclines towards the inside? Now try it at a walk, trot and canter. There you go, you look better already. Feel any different?'

'Yes,' admitted Casey. She didn't want to say that in the entire three years she'd worked with Mrs Smith, her teacher had never spotted this apparently critical flaw.

'Try her over the oxer and see if it improves things.'

Casey did as he said and continued on over the upright. The difference was astounding. She felt so much more connected to Roxy, so much more secure. The mare seemed to make a better shape over the jumps too.

Kyle clapped. 'You're such a natural. Most of my pupils would take weeks to adopt a change like that.'

Casey halted in front of him. 'Anything else? You said there were a couple of things.'

He laughed. 'Oh, no, that's enough to be going on with for one day. I feel embarrassed to have said anything at all. You're the Badminton and Kentucky champion. You certainly don't need any tips from me. Really, Casey, I'm a massive fan.'

Casey found herself blushing. 'Thanks. Uh, if you bear with me for another ten minutes, we can have that talk you wanted.'

Elated, she urged Roxy into a canter. The mare popped neatly over the upright and turned towards the oxer. Her ears pricked and she put on a sudden burst of speed. At the last conceivable second, she slammed on the brakes.

Casey shot forward as if she'd been launched from a cannon, arms and legs flailing. She caught a brief glimpse of Kyle moving forward in slow motion and had time to cringe inwardly. Then she bellyflopped into the dirt, like a frog being dropped from a great height. For several minutes she was incapable of doing anything but gasp for air. Everything hurt, particularly her ribs and her bitten arm and buttock. But her primary sensation was humiliation.

Kyle came over with Roxy and helped her to her feet.

'Any advice?' Casey asked when she could finally speak.

Kyle grinned. 'Never get on any horse that hasn't first accepted you on the ground.'

After she'd tended to Roxy, who mercifully inflicted no further wounds, Casey walked Kyle to the car park.

'I'm sorry you had to see that. Deeply embarrassing.'

He laughed. 'Don't be daft. Even the best riders get taken by surprise now and then. She's a bit of a handful, Miss Roxy, but if anyone can take her to the next level it's you.'

Casey stopped. 'I wish I could share your optimism. Now what is it that you wanted to talk to me about?'

He looked down, dark lashes shadowing his cheeks. 'I ... okay, I'm now wondering if this is a terrible idea. You see, I'm here on the basis of a persistent rumour.'

'What rumour?'

'The talk on the circuit is that Mrs Smith is about to retire. I know it's presumptuous but I wondered if you'd do me the honour of letting me coach you. You're more than capable of winning the Burghley Horse Trials this year and I'd like to be the teacher who takes you there.'

Casey was stunned. 'I don't know what I expected you to say, but it wasn't that. I mean, I'm flattered that you'd offer to coach me, but you have it all wrong. People have always misjudged Mrs Smith because of her age, but if you knew her you'd know that, though she's in her sixties, she's smarter, stronger and more energetic and youthful than most twenty-year-olds ... '

She paused as a bus rattled around the corner and wheezed to a noisy stop in front of the riding centre.

'She's as healthy as an ox and would never dream of packing it in ... '

The bus door hissed open. Out stepped Mrs Smith. She stumbled slightly as her right foot touched the ground, tottered and almost fell. When she straightened, her skin was ghostly white and she looked every one of her sixty-three years. Her Indian cotton top and trousers, usually immaculate, looked crumpled, and it seemed to Casey that as she walked up the drive she wavered slightly in the breeze.

'Good morning all,' she called brightly. 'So sorry I'm late, Casey. Public transport nightmare.'

Kyle turned away to unlock a forest green MG sports car. His expression said all there was to say. 'Right, Casey, I'll be off. No point in troubling you further.' He pressed a business card into her hand. 'It's been a pleasure. Call if you need me.'

Casey avoided his eyes. 'I won't, but thanks.'

Perhaps it was the power of suggestion but as she gave

her teacher a hug it seemed to her that Mrs Smith felt thin to the point of being frail.

'Who was that?' Mrs Smith asked as the MG reversed smartly out of the yard.

Casey shut her ears to the thrilling growl of the sports car's engine as it powered away down the lane.

'Nobody important.'

3

CASEY WAS EIGHT years old when she first decided to become an eventer. She could recall the moment vividly. At the time, she was lying on the threadbare sofa at number 414 Redwing Towers, the East London council flat she shared with her father, re-reading a pony book for the zillionth time and breathing in the wafting delight of some soon-to-be-served vegetarian dinner. A small television crackled quietly in one corner.

'Five minutes till lift-off, Case,' called her father, which was her cue to stop reading and start laying the table. Casey didn't stir. She was in an exciting bit. She knew the outcome of the story, knew perfectly well that the foal would be saved from a snowy fate, but her heart still pounded.

'Casey Blue, where are you?' sang her father.

'Coming, Dad,' said Casey, eyes still glued to the page.

Two chapters later, she reluctantly set the book aside and hopped up. As she did so, another horse caught her attention – this one on the television. He was the fittest horse she'd ever seen and the same could be said for his rider. Galloping along a route lined with spectators, they were a perfect unit of power and grace. An enormous brush fence loomed. The horse popped over it as if it were nothing.

Casey sat down again.

As he rounded the kitchen bench with two plates of steaming lasagne, Roland Blue opened his mouth to chivvy her again. He shut it when he saw what had captivated her. Casey's mum had died when Casey was just two years old and ever since then horses – those in books and on television, those ridden by police in the street, and the shaggy cobs and ponies seen through the fence of the local riding school – had been her greatest comfort. As far as Roland was concerned, that was something to be encouraged. He grabbed some cutlery and a couple of napkins and sat down beside her.

'What are we watching? Oh, good, it's highlights from past Badminton Horse Trials. Don't know much about the event, but I do know that it's among the toughest sporting competitions on earth. Part of the reason is the death-defying fences. There's one of them right there! Did they really just jump over a house? Oh my goodness, when they clipped that log I was convinced they were going to come crashing down.'

'So was I,' gasped Casey.

'Yes, but from what I understand the real challenge of Badminton is finding a horse and rider that can multi-task. It's a mix of dressage, which is a bit like horse ballet, cross-country and show jumping.'

'Wow. You'd need a horse with wings.'

'Indeed you would.'

As if to prove her right, horse and rider flew over a rustic post and rails and dropped off a virtual cliff. The camera angle made it seem nothing short of suicidal. The pair plummeted to earth, freefalling.

'Good grief,' said Roland Blue.

But the horse not only lived to tell the tale, he did so with feet neatly aligned and ears pricked. As he bounded forward with a cheeky swish of his tail, his rider, who Casey would later learn was Lucinda Green en route to one of her six Badminton wins, patted him ecstatically, a wide grin on her face.

Casey had been so overcome that it was a couple of minutes before she could get it together to speak. When she did, it was with a degree of conviction only possible if you're an eight-year-old yet to be confronted with the harsh realities of life without money or connections.

'That's going to be me some day.'

That day had been close to a decade coming. Now, as she sat at her laptop in the kitchen at Peach Tree Cottage, browsing through fan mail, Casey wondered if she'd have quit and pursued a less brutal career path had she known the challenges before her. Perhaps she should have tried to get into art school or become a veterinary nurse.

But even as the thought crossed her mind, her gaze was drawn to an old photograph stuck on the fridge. It was of her thirteen-year-old self, beaming in charity-shop breeches and a Hope Lane T-shirt. She smiled at the memory. There was no better reminder that if horses had been her passion before she started volunteering at the run-down Hackney riding school nicknamed Hopeless Lane, they'd quickly become her whole world. After she and her father saved Storm, skeletal and crazed with terror, from certain death at a knacker's yard, Casey's destiny had been sealed. From that day forward she knew that the only life she wanted was one that had her beloved silver horse at its heart.

Three years on, Casey had everything she'd ever dreamed of and more. She'd won two of the world's greatest equestrian championships and moved from abject poverty to relative wealth in six months. Starting out on the circuit, she, Storm and Mrs Smith had travelled in a broken-down rattletrap of a van more usually used to transport three woolly donkeys. Casey had dressed in second-hand breeches, shirts and jackets, and Storm had to endure ill-fitting tack borrowed from Hopeless Lane.

These days almost every new delivery brought cellophane-packed clothes, gleaming boots and the very best in horse feed and tack from generous sponsors. Only that morning Casey had checked her email to find a letter from a company who wanted to provide her with a luxury lorry with her name on the side. Casey, whose usual mode of transport was White Oaks' functional but basic horsebox, had been overjoyed. Without consulting Mrs Smith, who was her unofficial manager as well as her coach, she'd pinged off an email to say, 'Yes! Yes! Yes! Thank you! Thank you! Thank you!'

So life was good, not least because on top of these achievements she had a boyfriend who loved her, an adorable cottage home and great training facilities.

And yet deep down she wasn't happy.

Something was wrong. Something was niggling at her. The kitchen had always been Casey's favourite room in Peach Tree Cottage because it was cosy and smelled comfortingly of apple pie, but that afternoon it seemed unnaturally gloomy and cold. Casey couldn't decide if it was Kyle's visit and the disquieting effect he'd had on her that had set her nerves on edge, or if it was something else entirely. Whatever it was, it didn't feel good.

She glanced down at her laptop. There were 181 unanswered emails. Most were from young fans inspired by her achievements. Some were so complimentary they made her blush. The rest were mainly appeals from would-be sponsors and journalists. All good news and reasons to celebrate, so why did she feel so uneasy?

Casey slammed closed her laptop and pushed back her chair. Locking the kitchen door, she set off across the fields. This was Kyle's fault. If he hadn't sent her into a flat spin by suggesting that Mrs Smith was on the verge of retiring, she'd be as dreamily content as she had been first thing that morning.

As soon as her teacher had put down her bag and had a reviving cup of chai, Casey had asked her outright if she was planning to quit for health reasons. True to form, Mrs Smith had laughed.

'My dear, I might have to change the habits of a lifetime and start wearing more make-up. Clearly I'm looking peakier than I'd supposed.'

Casey was annoyed. 'Can you be serious for once? Over the past few months, you've had quite a few headaches and bouts of tiredness and pain, plus there were a couple of days in Kentucky when you looked really unwell.'

Mrs Smith stared at her incredulously. 'Are you joking? It was sweltering in Kentucky. The Sahara Desert would have felt cool by comparison. And on top of that we were being targeted by blackmailers. Anyone could be forgiven for feeling under the weather. As for the tiredness, *you* had a break after Kentucky. I didn't. I climbed off the plane and got straight to work, with jetlag. For most of the past two weeks I've been tying up sponsorship deals, dealing with the media and organising your replacement horse. May I remind you that I am sixty-three. I'm fit for my age but I'm not superwoman.'

She had a point, but Casey was reluctant to let it go.

'Does that mean you're thinking of retiring?'

'Do you *want* me to retire? Is that what this is about – you thinking that I'm over the hill and should be replaced?'

'Don't be ridiculous,' said Casey. 'That's the silliest thing I've ever heard. I only worry that you've been working too hard, that's all. You, Dad and Peter are the most important people on earth to me. Your health means more than any event anywhere, including Burghley. Promise that you'll be honest with me if you ever get ill. Promise that you'll tell me if you have so much as a sniffle.'

Mrs Smith gave her a hug. 'My dear, you and Storm are my whole world and what a beautiful world it is. I give you my word that if teaching ever gets too much for me, I'll tell you. But I'm not about to retire, that I can assure you, and I can promise I'll be at Burghley in September to see you win. Now talk to me about Lady Roxanne. How did you get on with her this morning?'

Storm was waiting by the field gate, keen to have his dinner. He whickered joyfully when he saw his mistress. As Casey led him to the yard, she tried not to think about the fact that despite her assurances of wellbeing, Mrs Smith had disappeared to her room for a couple of hours that afternoon. She'd claimed that she wanted to research a few techniques that would help them in the coming weeks, but when Casey passed her door the total silence emanating from it suggested she was sleeping.

An image of Kyle's handsome young face swam into Casey's head. He had charisma and an energy that contrasted unfavourably with the picture Mrs Smith had presented as she'd stumbled off the bus that morning. Kyle hadn't had to research techniques. It was clear that, despite his youth, he had all the equestrian knowledge he needed at his fingertips. The tip he'd given her on tacking up Roxy had worked a treat, and she couldn't wait to jump Storm again now that her foot and leg position had improved. It was a subtle thing, but she had a feeling it would make a big difference, particularly over Burghley's cardiac-arrest-inducing fences.

She hadn't mentioned Kyle's impromptu lesson to Mrs Smith, let alone that he'd tried to poach her. What would be the point? Mrs Smith was her best friend, not just her teacher. It was inconceivable that Casey could ever be coached by anyone else. They were a team.

Storm nudged her. Casey blinked. She'd led him to his stable on automatic pilot and, rather than attending to his needs, had spent several long minutes staring blankly into space. She gave him a cuddle and immediately her mood lifted. Storm appreciated her, even if Roxy didn't.

She kissed him on his velvet muzzle. 'All right, impatient. One gourmet dinner coming up.'

She was smiling as she walked to the feed room.

Rounding the corner, she saw Roxy gazing imperiously from her stable door. Casey stopped to stroke her, but the mare ducked away, ears back. Casey's smile faded.

'Excuse me, Casey Blue?'

Casey turned to see a couple of little girls in grubby breeches and matching pigtails. The taller one thrust out a glittery pink notebook.

'Please may we have your autograph?' she asked shyly.

Casey wiped her hands on her jeans. 'Of course you can.' She took the proffered pink pen. 'What are your names?'

As she wrote, the girls kept up a running commentary.

'We're your number one fans!'

'We want to win Badminton before we're eighteen, like you!'

'And the Kentucky Three-Day Event and the Burghley Horse Trials! We want to win them all!'

'We'll take it in turns!'

'We think Storm is the most magnificent horse that ever lived. He's a magical colour too. He looks like horse-shaped lightning.'

Casey couldn't suppress a grin. 'That's a lovely way of putting it. I think that too. He does look good on the outside but it's what's on the inside that makes him special.'

'Do you have any riding tips for us?'

'I have two. Number one: love your horse and always do what's right for him or her. Number two: never give up on your dreams.'

As they hurried away, giggling excitedly, Casey was reminded of a conversation she'd had with Peter the previous week. She'd been describing the moment when, as a pony-mad eight-year-old, she'd fallen in love with eventing.

'Has it been everything you thought it might be?' Peter had asked. 'I mean, when you were volunteering at Hopeless Lane and trying to train Storm, is this what you wanted – to be considered one of the top riders and to experience all the fame and glory that comes with it?'

'Of course it is,' Casey responded, laughing. 'What kind of question is that? Of course this is what I wanted. It's what I *do* want. Wouldn't anyone? I'm the luckiest girl in the world.'

As she walked back to Storm's stable, a bucket in each hand, Casey told herself again that that was exactly what she was – the luckiest girl in the world.

Wasn't she?

4

CASEY HAD TAKEN it for granted that Roxy would improve upon acquaintance, but she was wrong. On the surface, the mare was a dream. She was superbly bred and had great conformation and elegant paces. If she was in the right mood, she was surprisingly bold over White Oaks' cross-country course and capable of performing a sweet dressage test and clearing a field of show jumps.

But therein lay the rub. She would only do those things if it suited her. If it didn't, there was no telling what punishment she had in store for Casey. After ten days of riding her, Casey was purple from head to toe. She'd fallen off six times, been bitten three times, had both feet stepped on and suffered a repeat of the wall-crushing incident. Her injuries had become something of a joke around the yard.

'Why don't you keep a first-aid kit in Roxy's stable and be done with it?' teased Morag. 'I mean, there are stuntmen who work on James Bond films with less aches and pains.'

Renata, a lumpen stable girl, was more blunt. 'I thought you and old Mrs Smith fancied yourselves as horse-whisperer types. Your methods don't seem to be working on Lady Roxanne, do they? She seems to have a grudge against you. Maybe you should give Kyle West a call. They say that what he doesn't know about riding and horses isn't worth knowing. And oh my *God* is he cute.'

She fanned herself, as if Kyle's heat was steaming her up from afar.

Casey ignored her. She'd never forgiven Renata for allowing two strange men to snatch Storm one bleak winter's evening in February. The men did have the correct documentation and it wasn't exactly Renata's fault, but Casey had never really got over it.

Nonetheless, her own failure to win Roxy over was galling and it didn't help that her teacher found the whole thing funny. For some reason, it amused Mrs Smith that the mare consistently outsmarted them. It wasn't that Roxy reared or went crazy in order to unseat Casey. She did none of those things. Ninety-five per cent of the time she was well-behaved to the point of being angelic.

No, what was really disconcerting was that there was a degree of cunning involved. She'd clear seven jumps in a row, ears pricked, cantering beautifully, and then on the eighth, stop dead. Launched into space, Casey would often clear the jump on her own. There seemed no way to predict or prevent it.

Roxy's other favourite trick was to wait until Casey was relaxed in the saddle, reins loose, as they returned to the yard. She'd then shy at some imagined menace, leaping sideways so hard and fast that there was no physical way of Casey remaining in the saddle. Like a character in a Thelwell cartoon, Casey would hover momentarily in mid-air before crashing to the ground.

Somehow the sight of Mrs Smith falling about laughing made the pain worse. 'I'm sorry,' her coach spluttered when it happened for the third day running. At the time, Casey was returning to the yard after a relatively successful attempt at the cross-country course. 'It's just that ... It's just ... '

'What?' Casey demanded, clambering to her feet and biting back a groan. The pain radiating from her rear brought tears to her eyes. Nearby, Roxy munched grass unconcernedly.

Mrs Smith sobered up. 'I'm sorry. It's just that it's been decades since I came across such an intelligent animal. She's toying with us. My guess is that she's been abused or treated poorly in her past – not necessarily by Jennifer Stewart, who seems terribly well-intentioned, but someone else further down the line. A groom, perhaps.

There is no doubt in my mind that she's been put in a situation where she's felt powerless. She's learned that the only way to get revenge is to use her wits to make humans suffer.'

'But can't she understand that we're not like that?' Casey said crossly. 'I mean, since she's arrived I've bent over backwards to be lovely to her, even though she's been a total minx at times. In return, I've been thrown, bitten, kicked and stamped on. Whatever she's been through, it's nothing compared to the abuse Storm endured and yet he understood from the beginning that we loved him and were doing our best for him.'

'First things first: Storm is not Roxy. Comparing them will get you nowhere at all.'

'Yes, but—'

'Secondly, you need to understand that Roxy is testing you. It's not a test you can afford to fail. There is no secret to passing it, but there is a shortcut. Kindness. No matter what question she asks you or how many times she throws you, you respond with love and gentleness. That doesn't mean you should be a pushover. You're a team and she needs to understand her part in that.'

'Okay, so tell me how to do that. Teach me the right way to handle her.'

'I can't. This is *your* journey. I can teach you technique, but you're going to have to figure Roxy out for yourself. Think of her as being a bit like a Japanese secret puzzle box. You'll solve one mystery and then find yourself facing another. The mistake many riders make with these types of horses is that they lose patience and force the issue. Try that with Roxy and it will backfire spectacularly. Attempt to dominate her and you'll make things a thousand times worse. You'll unlock the box with kindness, nothing else.'

Casey dusted down her breeches. 'That's all very well, but in a few days' time we'll be competing at the Salperton Horse Trials. If I haven't solved the mystery that is Roxy by then, we're going to be finishing last. Take what happened today. She shied at nothing. If she was afraid, I'd understand. But she's perfectly relaxed. It's all a game to her.'

She stopped. 'What is it? What's wrong?'

Her teacher's face, usually quite radiant, had gone puce. She clutched her side.

Casey dropped Roxy's reins and rushed over to her. 'Angelica, you're scaring me. Talk to me. What is it? Are you ill?'

Mrs Smith straightened up slowly, refusing Casey's arm. She smiled. 'Sorry about that. That sandwich we had for lunch didn't agree with me. I think the cheese might have been past its sell-by date.'

'I don't believe you. Are you ill, or aren't you? Either there's something you're not telling me or I'm dragging you to the doctor for tests.'

The colour had returned to Mrs Smith's cheeks. 'Oh for goodness' sake, Casey, sometimes you sound even more ancient than I do. Stop fussing. I'm not going to waste the doctor's time just because I have a spot of indigestion. At worst, I might be coming down with a cold.'

She scooped up Roxy's reins and handed them to her charge. 'If I were you I'd spend less time worrying about imaginary illnesses and more time focusing on Roxy. That's where your real challenge lies.'

Hobbling to the yard, rubbing her new bruises, Casey couldn't help noticing that Roxy's ears were pricked and she was stepping out keenly. The mare's mood always seemed to lift if she managed to unseat her new rider. Casey knew that Mrs Smith was right. The only way to change Roxy was to be patient and continue to try to bond with her. All the same, she would have appreciated some advice from the teacher she was paying to advise her. Kyle West had spent a sum total of forty minutes at White Oaks and yet he'd offered her several clear and helpful tips.

For free.

'Believe it or not, I am doing my best,' Casey told Roxy as she unsaddled her. 'Give me a chance and I'll prove that I'm worthy of your trust.'

She reached into her pocket for a packet of Polo mints. The mare hesitated for a long moment before gently lipping them from Casey's palm, brushing the girl's skin with her muzzle. As they stood together, a peaceful bubble enveloped them. In that instant Casey had no difficulty seeing through the mare's confident veneer to the vulnerable horse inside. Compassion welled up in her.

'You don't have to worry, girl. I'm going to take very

good care of you, I promise.' She rubbed Roxy behind her ears. For once the mare didn't sidle away as if Casey's touch was somehow repellent to her.

'Seen Morag, Case?' boomed Renata, leaning over the stable door. Infamously clumsy, she managed to kick over a bucket while she was at it. 'The vet needs to speak to her about the wormer she ordered and I can't find her anywhere.'

Roxy's ears flattened and she wheeled away from Casey as if she'd been struck.

Casey glared at Renata. 'If you could avoid scaring my horse half to death, that would be really helpful.'

The stable girl laughed. 'Oh, she's *your* horse now, is she? Thought she was on loan. Don't think the feeling's mutual. If you ask me, she doesn't seem too keen on you. Can't imagine why. Righto, if you see Morag, let her know I'm looking for her.'

As her footsteps faded, Casey tried to win Roxy round with another couple of mints, but the special moment had passed and they seemed once more to be on opposite sides of a wall. Not exactly adversaries, but hardly friends.

Casey thought about Salperton Park, less than three days away, and a knot formed in her stomach. There was a time not so long ago when she could have competed there invisibly. Now the eyes of the equestrian world were on her. Camera lenses sought her out. Sponsors held meetings about her. Fans expected miracles from her. Failure was a luxury she could no longer afford.

5

CASEY WAS NOT a fan of the 3 a.m. starts that were an inescapable part of eventing and tended to grumble and grouse as she yawned her way out of the bedroom. But once she'd splashed cold water on her face and downed a strong coffee, she was in her element. Rain or shine, there were few things she enjoyed more than preparing a horse to compete at its best.

It helped that Mrs Smith was a former dressage champion. Decades had gone by since she'd finished runner-up in the European Championships, but in the years she'd worked with Casey she'd impressed upon her pupil the importance of borrowing tips from the best dressage grooms. Casey had come to see her own pre-event ritual as part military operation, part art. Part science too because, as Mrs Smith often pointed out, a horse that isn't already in great condition is not magically going to look fabulous on the day. Good nutrition was critical to good looks.

For a horse who was borderline phobic about being touched, Roxy had proved surprisingly amenable to being made to look her best. She did not have the same objections to grooming or plaiting as she did to being tacked up, seeming actually to enjoy them, so Casey was able to work her way through an extensive to-do list with only a small nip for her troubles.

She liked to start the day with her own grooming routine. Before anything else, she wrapped the mare's tail in a damp bandage and ran a curry comb over her before backcombing the hair with a soft towel to remove any traces of dander. After using a soft brush on Roxy's face, legs and body, she trimmed the whiskers on her muzzle and under her chin. Mrs Smith had taught her to dab baby oil on the delicate skin around a horse's muzzle and eyes for added sheen. A polish with a dustcloth lent a burnished glow to the mare's coppery brown flanks.

Outside, the yard was still, the stars hidden beneath a blanket of overnight cloud. Wary of being kicked, Casey approached Roxy's tail with caution. Once the bandage was removed she used her fingers, not a comb, to untangle knots from the black hair.

'Nothing worse than a horse with a threadbare tail,' Mrs Smith always said. 'If every time you comb their tail they lose a few hairs, that adds up.'

Plaiting was an art in itself and one Mrs Smith had insisted that Casey master. She'd done so eventually, but only after much trial and error. Now she never went anywhere without her plaiting kit, which included brown, grey and chestnut elastics, waxed thread, large dull-tipped yard needles, scissors, a small metal mane comb, a seam ripper, hair gel and spray.

Once the last plait had been knotted to her teacher's satisfaction, Casey turned her attention to Roxy's feet, picking, washing and brushing them before applying dressing to the sole and wall of each. Finally, she cleaned and dried the mare's pasterns and the underneath of her fetlocks, an area prone to nicks and cuts. Some grooms liked to apply fly spray or show sheen to the body as a finishing touch, but Casey and Mrs Smith assiduously avoided any product that might inhibit sweating. As far as they were concerned, perspiration was an essential cooling mechanism for the horse.

By 4 a.m., Roxy was gleaming like a show pony. All that remained was for Casey to shower and pack everything she needed into the Jeep Wrangler they'd borrowed from Morag. Mrs Smith's elderly car was no longer up to the task of pulling the horsebox. Into the back of the Jeep went Casey's dressage and show-jumping jackets, three pairs of boots and breeches, two hats and four shirts. Saddles, bridles, rugs, bandages and eventing grease followed. The spare stall of the horsebox became a storage locker for horse feed, hay and bottled water.

Mrs Smith tapped her watch sternly as Casey scrambled to fill their ringside bag. It was a holdall that Mrs Smith liked to have on standby while Casey was warming up, in case of any last minute emergencies. Today, it contained a hoof pick, body brush, Polo mints, rain gear, a towel, a bottle of water, a couple of rags and a little pot of Vaseline, which Mrs Smith liked to rub on the bridle shortly before Casey's start time to make the silver bits gleam.

To keep Casey's energy up during the day, Mrs Smith also insisted that they pack a cooler box with protein drinks, homemade honey and oat bars and a lunchbox containing a quinoa, rocket, avocado, tomato and feta salad. In a separate container were rye bread sandwiches made with honey and crunchy peanut butter, which could be eaten at any time for an extra boost.

It was another half an hour before they were done. Frazzled and full of nervous excitement, Casey made her first attempt to load Roxy. The mare strolled into the horsebox without blinking an eye.

'Are you sure we have the right horse?' asked Casey as she hopped in to the Jeep. 'Not that I'm complaining or anything.'

Mrs Smith shrugged. 'She's clever. Perhaps, like us, she enjoys the adrenalin rush of going to shows.'

Minutes later they were on their way to Salperton Park in Cheltenham, Gloucestershire. As they drove out of the yard, Casey caught sight of Storm craning over his stable door, ears flickering uncertainly. It was only then she realised that he was probably bewildered that she was going to an event without him. She'd stopped in to say good morning as Mrs Smith groomed him, but she wished she'd had longer to reassure him.

She blinked away a tear. Without her horse she felt a little lost. Storm was her safety blanket. When she performed well it was almost always due to his courage, his talent and the almost mystical connection between them. As much as she was looking forward to the challenge of competing on Roxy, she couldn't shake the feeling that they were heading into a perilous unknown.

Once they were on the open road, however, Casey's nerves settled. Dawn came and went, a pink seam in the quilt of clouds. She drank coffee and half-listened to a country music CD as Mrs Smith drove. Ordinarily, she would have used the time to mentally rehearse the day ahead, but her mind kept returning to the previous night when Peter had come to Peach Tree Cottage for dinner.

The evening had started well. Mrs Smith had made a delicious curry with coconut milk and Casey had cooked a relatively successful rhubarb crumble. Afterwards, Mrs Smith excused herself and went to bed and Casey and Peter relocated to the sofa. One thing led to another and soon they were kissing.

The temperature in the room rose and not just because of the balmy summer air drifting in through the open windows. Casey slid her hands under Peter's shirt. She was running them over the muscles in his broad back and thinking how safe she felt in his arms and how much she loved him when her phone beeped.

'Don't get that,' murmured Peter and he bent his head to kiss her again.

But already Casey was wriggling away. 'Have to. What if it's urgent? Could be the event organisers texting everyone to say that Salperton's been rained off.'

'The only danger of that happening is if they've had an overnight monsoon,' Peter said wryly as he moved away and straightened his shirt. 'A week ago, they were in a panic because they hadn't had rain in a month and the ground was like concrete.'

Casey reached for her phone and a message flashed up:

Thinking about you. KW

She almost dropped it.

'Secret admirer?' Peter asked teasingly.

Casey felt the same rush of guilt and dread she'd had when Kyle West's bicep had inadvertently brushed against her in the yard. 'Don't be silly.' She jumped to her feet. 'How about a hot chocolate?'

He laughed. 'Now I'm curious. Who's texting you at 10p.m.?'

'Does it matter? Don't you trust me?'

"Course I trust you.'

'That's good to know, because I trust you too.' Their fingers entwined as Peter followed her into the kitchen. 'But if you must know, it was Kyle West. You know, the coach.'

Peter retrieved his hand casually. 'I do know. He has quite a reputation, and not all of it's to do with his talent around horses. I didn't realise you knew him.'

'I don't. I mean, he had some business at White Oaks a couple of weeks ago and while he was here approached me about taking him on as a coach. It was a two-minute conversation.'

'He was here and you didn't mention it?'

'I didn't mention it because it wasn't important. What's the big deal? Anyhow, I told him that Mrs Smith is the only coach I'd ever want or need. I'm not sure why he's contacting me again. I guess he's not used to taking no for an answer.'

'I guess not.'

Peter said no more about it, but it seemed to Casey that he held her extra close when she kissed him goodnight. As she climbed the stairs to her room her heart did little bunny hops of joy. It was the most amazing feeling in the world to love and to be loved.

But when sleep descended, the face she saw in her dreams was Kyle's. It was his blue eyes that hypnotised her and his golden head that bent to kiss her.

She woke in the early hours of the morning, sweating and absurdly guilty. Weren't dreams supposed to reveal the hidden desires of the dreamer?

44

But no, that couldn't possibly be it because she didn't desire Kyle in any way, not professionally and not romantically. It was true that on his visit to White Oaks he'd intrigued her and there was no denying that he was attractive, but his text had put her off. The arrogance of the man was beyond belief.

A blast of cold air and car fumes jolted her back to the present. Mrs Smith had pulled in to a motorway service station and parked in a quiet corner so that they could have breakfast.

When Casey climbed back into the Jeep after checking on Roxy, Mrs Smith was stirring boiling water into a lunchbox full of oats. She put yoghurt and cinnamon on top and handed it to Casey with a quizzical glance. 'You've been a million miles away all morning. I might as well be driving alone. What's preoccupying you? Is everything all right with Peter?'

Casey opened a pot of natural yogurt and added it to the porridge. 'Peter's perfect. I have a lot on my mind, that's all.'

'The only thing you should have on your mind is this morning's dressage test.'

'That is what I'm thinking about. Well, that and other stuff. Oh, I forgot to tell you, this company that makes horseboxes for quite a few of the top riders – Equi-Flow – wants to give us a free lorry. It's brilliant. It has space for four horses and luxury accommodation. There's a posh shower and toilet and the side opens out so you have a living area during the day and a room with a double and sofa-bed at night. Plus it has about six storage lockers for tack and feed. It's super-cool.'

'It would be cool if it were that easy,' Mrs Smith said drily.

'Meaning what?'

'Meaning there's no such thing as a free lunch. For every sponsor you take on, there's a time commitment. Pretty soon you'll find yourself with barely a minute in the day to do the thing that made you worth endorsing in the first place.'

'It's not like that,' said Casey, annoyed. 'They don't want anything from me. Obviously, I'll mention Equi-Flow if I talk to any journalists or do any magazine shoots, but basically all they're asking is that the Badminton and Kentucky champion is seen to be using one of their lorries.'

'But you're not going to be using it. *We* are not going to use it. Equi-Flow approached me after you won Badminton and I told them thank you but no thank you. Frankly, I think they have quite a nerve contacting you behind my back.'

Casey couldn't believe her ears. 'Are you crazy? Of course we're going to accept the lorry. Why would we turn down a free luxury lorry when it means we'll be able to stop borrowing Morag's horsebox? You know how it wobbles.'

'It was good enough to get you to Badminton,' Mrs Smith reminded her. 'Like it or not, we're going to continue to use it because there are no strings attached

46

and because the Burghley Horse Trials are less than four months away. Do well there and you'll be able to afford a decent lorry of your own – one that does not make you slave to a corporation.'

For a long minute they glared at each other.

'I don't want to wait till Burghley,' Casey said stubbornly. 'If I'm presented with an option that will make Storm or Roxy more comfortable and my life easier, why would I turn it down? Anyway, it's too late. I've already told them that we want it.'

Mrs Smith was incensed. 'Well, I'm your manager and I'm going to tell them again that we are absolutely not having their lorry – only this time I'll make my point more forcibly.'

'Don't you dare,' shouted Casey. 'You have no right to dictate to me what I should or shouldn't do. I've never signed any legal document giving you permission to run my life.'

As soon as the words were out of her mouth, Casey regretted them, but it was too late. They hung in the air like a speech bubble, hateful and cruel.

Mrs Smith went still. 'That's true. You haven't.'

'I'm sorry. That came out wrong.'

Casey felt sick. Ever since the two of them had bonded years earlier at the Tea Garden Café in the East End of London, where Casey was a teenage waitress and Mrs Smith was an enigmatic customer with a bohemian style that was all her own, Mrs Smith had been a shining light in Casey's life. Far more than a teacher, she'd been a friend, mother, psychologist, healer, personal trainer and font of wisdom on everything from reviving starving rescue horses to the finer points of Zen Buddhism.

And, yes, she'd also acted as Casey's manager, dealing with sponsors and setting Casey and Storm up at Peach Tree Cottage and White Oaks Equestrian Centre when they didn't have a penny to their name.

They'd never discussed a contract, because all the legal documents in England could never be as binding as the sacred bond of trust that had always formed the core of their relationship.

With a single sentence, that bond had been shattered.

Casey laid her hand on Mrs Smith's arm. 'I'm sorry. I didn't mean it. Of course you're my manager – and a million other wonderful things besides.'

But Mrs Smith didn't look round. She put the keys in the ignition and the engine shuddered to life.

'No, you're right. We've never had a signed agreement. Ironically, I've never pressed for one because I didn't want you to feel that I was trying to run your life. Perhaps that's just as well. We have a flexible arrangement that can be terminated at any time, and I think we should keep it that way. Who knows when one of us might fancy a change.'

6

THE FIRST PERSON Casey saw when she approached the warm-up area was Kyle West. He was wearing fawn breeches and a close-fitting blue jumper that hugged his finely muscled frame. It was hard to believe it wasn't calculated for effect. Yet there was something boyish and vulnerable in the way he swept his sun-streaked fringe from his eyes. He grinned at her as she reined in Roxy.

'Just the person I was thinking of. It's becoming a habit, you know – thinking about you.'

'Twenty-eight days,' Casey advised.

'What for?'

'That's how long it takes to make or break a habit. Twenty-eight days.'

He laughed. 'Are you honestly telling me that I haven't crossed your mind at least once since we met? Not even in your dreams?'

Casey's face grew hot. She leaned over the other side of Roxy and pretended to be checking a stirrup leather. 'I'm not telling you anything at all. I'm thinking about my horse and my test, nothing else.'

'Quite right too. If I was your teacher, I wouldn't have it any other way. Speaking of teachers, here comes yours. Mind introducing me?'

Perhaps it was just the washed-out light of the overcast day, but Mrs Smith's skin looked almost translucent as she walked up. She and Casey had barely spoken since the awful argument in the car. Casey had done her best to make up for what she'd said and Mrs Smith had been coolly professional, but they both knew that something had been broken.

Casey straightened in the saddle. 'Angelica Smith, meet Kyle West. Kyle, meet Mrs Smith. You two should have a lot in common so I'll leave you to it. I'm off to put Roxy through her paces.'

She glanced pleadingly at her teacher. 'Any last minute advice?'

'Plenty, but I'll stick to one simple tip. Roxy isn't Storm. Remember that and you'll be fine.'

As Casey rode away, Kyle turned to Mrs Smith. 'It's a pleasure to finally meet you. I've been curious about you for quite some time.'

Mrs Smith's gaze followed Casey. She gave no sign that she'd heard.

Kyle leaned nearer. 'I mean, as a teacher, you're in a dream situation. You have a pupil who is not yet eighteen and yet already she's breaking records that have stood since the sport was invented. With the right help, the world is her oyster.'

'And you're implying what exactly, Mr West?'

'I'm not implying anything. I'm only saying that Casey represents the future of eventing. Twenty-first-century riders need twenty-first-century solutions. Modern methods. Cutting-edge techniques.'

The wind was getting up and a gust came at them with unexpected force. Mrs Smith clutched at the paddock rail for support. The remaining colour drained from her face and she gave a little gasp.

Kyle frowned. 'Are you okay? Can I get you a chair?'

With immense effort, Mrs Smith recovered her poise. 'Whatever for?'

'So you can sit down. You seem ... faint or sick.'

'I'm perfectly well, Mr West. Never better. Would you like me to get you a trolley?'

'What for?'

'In case you need help with your enormous ego.'

He laughed. '*Touché.*'

Mrs Smith didn't smile. 'If you'll excuse me, I have work to do.'

As she moved away, a man took her place at Kyle's side. A childhood accident had left his face with a peculiarly mashed appearance, as if all the character had been pummelled out of it. Over the years, Ray Cook had learned that the best way to divert attention from his looks was to move, dress and talk in a way that allowed him to blend into the background. Being a nonentity had proved so useful that Ray had actively cultivated it. People could spend months with him and afterwards find themselves unable to describe him, other than to say that he was of medium height and build and had brown hair and eyes. They recalled that there was something odd about him but couldn't say exactly what.

Ray spoke seldom and when he did his voice was quiet and had no identifiable accent. 'I think you might have met your match in Mrs Smith.'

Kyle didn't turn his head. Anyone watching the pair from a distance would have assumed the men were strangers. 'Oh, please. If I thought I couldn't take on an old woman, I'd hang up my boots today.'

'Maybe you should. That old woman, as you so disrespectfully refer to her, has probably forgotten more about riding than you'll ever know.'

Kyle's eyes narrowed. He watched Casey practising her rein-back and noted that, despite the fact that a couple of former Olympians were warming up, a sizeable majority of watchers were glued to Casey's every move. Kyle wondered what Casey's opinion of him would be had she overheard the conversation he'd had with Ray on the way to Salperton Park earlier that morning.

Ray interrupted his thoughts. 'Come on, Kyle, let's not waste time winding each other up when we have business to attend to. Casey Blue is about to start the dressage and I don't want to miss it. After that, I'll buy you a coffee and we can figure out what to do next. Whether you like it or not, we need each other.'

Casey entered the dressage ring in a working trot and tracked to the right. In the lead-up to Kentucky a fitness trainer called Ethan Grange had taught her how to meditate prior to performing. Never had she been more grateful. Driving into Salperton Park, she'd been so stressed and upset about her row with Mrs Smith that she'd been tempted to withdraw from the competition. A five-minute meditation had helped enormously.

To her credit, Roxy had been as good as gold all morning. She seemed to thrive in a competition environment. Her enquiring mind enjoyed new challenges, faces and places. On the way to the collecting ring, she'd been on her toes like a dancer, spooking and feinting, but Casey had the impression that it was all for effect. Roxy wasn't nervous in the least. She was excited.

In Casey, those emotions were reversed. Part of her had imagined that after being tested at the highest level in CCI****four-star dressage, elementary dressage would be easy, but she'd reckoned without the difficulty of attempting it on a strong-willed young horse. During the four minute test, she found herself working overtime to contain the mare, especially when she changed the rein and circled right.

By some miracle Roxy halted and was immobile for two or three seconds, as required. She even agreed to a five step rein-back, albeit with ears flat. But as soon as she was given permission to transition from a trot to a canter, she expressed her glee by kicking up her heels and surging forward.

The judges were inscrutable in their cars, shielded from the buffeting wind. Casey could imagine them hunched over their scores, taking a dim view of her failure to deliver the 'balance, uniformity of bend and lengthening of stride and frame' called for on the test sheet.

Fretting over her mistakes, she forgot to think about her test. As she and Roxy drew to the close of a twenty metre circle, completed at a furious pace, her mind went blank. For the first time in her riding career, she had absolutely no idea what movement came next. Panic seized her. It occurred to her that when she rode Storm *he* remembered the tests better than she did. *He* anticipated her questions and was ready with the answers. They were one unit, working in sync. The problem with her and Roxy was that they didn't trust one another.

She stole a glance at Mrs Smith, who was beyond the

ropes, directly in her eyeline, but her teacher's expression was unreadable. Two more strides and a line of expectant faces came into view, one of which was Kyle's.

Casey thought: *This is going to be beyond humiliating.* Beneath her tweed jacket and yellow bib, she started to sweat.

Then Kyle did something or said something. Afterwards, Casey was never sure which. She only knew that he communicated the next move to her as surely as if he'd whispered it in her ear: *half circle right.* Casey remembered the rest herself. *Return to the track at E. Counter canter.*

A final transition to trot and it was over. Casey left the arena trembling as if she'd just done the cross-country.

Mrs Smith took Roxy's reins as Casey swung out of the saddle. 'You lost concentration because you were thinking about Storm, weren't you?'

'Yes,' Casey admitted. 'I was. I can't help it. I miss him.'

She took the packet of Polo mints from the ringside bag and offered a couple to Roxy.

'It could have been worse,' Mrs Smith said flatly. 'It could have been better too, but it wasn't a total disaster. Put it out of your mind. You barely have time to change before the show jumping.'

It was only as she led the mare back to the lorry park that Casey dared to glance over at the place where Kyle had been standing. The young coach was no longer there. The only person remaining was a man dressed in beige who was staring at her rather intently. Casey smiled at him but he didn't smile back.

She turned away and promptly forgot all about him.

7

I T WAS THE poorest excuse for a summer's day in memory and yet Salperton Park still managed to look idyllic. Every corner of the estate was lovingly tended and it showed. There were new roofs on the village houses, gardens bursting with flowers, and the rolling landscape through which the cross-country course threaded had the timeless loveliness of an impressionist painting. The house itself dated back to the seventeenth century and provided an imposing backdrop for the show jumping.

Casey's start time was 9.45 a.m., but that was delayed when a girl on an overwrought thoroughbred fell and fractured her arm in three places. During her extended warm-up, Casey had counselled herself very sternly to stop comparing Roxy with Storm. It was both pointless and unfair. Roxy's personality might leave a lot to be desired, but she was a first-class horse in her own right. It wasn't her fault if Casey lacked the experience to deal with her.

During the break Mrs Smith, who was obviously hurt by Casey's outburst in the car but making an effort not to show it, said something that stopped Casey in her tracks.

'Imagine it was Roxy who you rescued from the knacker's yard, not Storm. If that was the case, you wouldn't be getting frustrated with her. Nor would you be dwelling on her vices. You'd be the way you were with him – infinitely tender and patient. You'd know that she's a product of her past and it's up to you to understand her, not the other way around.'

These words stayed with Casey as she warmed up for the show jumping, shivering as the temperature plummeted to an unseasonal low and the wind strengthened. She tried not to be intimidated by the fact that Andrew Nicholson, one of the world's greatest riders, was sharing the collecting ring with her, along with an aggressive man with thinning hair and a large bottom who kept putting up the practice jump above class height, in violation of etiquette, as if they were competing in the Puissance at Olympia.

Casey shut him out of her mind and did her best to communicate kind thoughts to Roxy. Gradually, she felt the mare settle and calm. A key tenet in Mrs Smith's teaching was the importance of visualisation to success. Casey tried picturing threads of light bonding her and Roxy. She saw them flying over every jump and collecting a shiny trophy at the end of the day.

To a degree it worked. By comparison with those at four-star events like Badminton, the jumps seemed almost toy-like. But the whipping wind had brought a misty rain and it made for a challenging ride.

Roxy pulled hard, eager to take every fence at a gallop. As she soared over an upright flanked by two giant parrots, clearing it with air to spare, Casey had an insight into the untapped potential of the mare. She jumped with energy and confidence and she jumped cleanly. She was in her element.

They were unlucky to have one pole down, but Casey could not have been more pleased. She stood in her stirrups as Roxy cantered over the finish line, patting the mare and waving to her cheering fans. She hoped that Kyle was watching. It would be good to have him witness her putting in a decent performance.

That was her last thought before Roxy did her trademark sideways shy. It happened so suddenly and violently that Casey hadn't a hope of remaining in the saddle. She landed flat on her back, unable to do anything other than wheeze. There were groans of sympathy from the crowd.

Casey felt a surge of resentment towards the mare. She thought: *Why am I even surprised? She hates me. Her sole aim in life is to embarrass me.*

Kyle's concerned face loomed above her. 'Have you

broken something or are you just winded? Blink once if you have a serious injury or twice if the only thing wounded is your pride.'

Since sinking into the ground wasn't an option, Casey blinked twice. Kyle waved away the St John's ambulance crew who were rushing over with a stretcher. Without consulting her, he lifted Casey into his arms and carried her from the arena.

'I kind of like it when you're winded,' he remarked with a grin. 'It means you can't protest or come out with ridiculous lines about twenty-eight days. I can assure you that if you actually were to become a habit, it would take me a lot longer than that to get over you. What's that? Oh, you want me to put you down. Well, if you insist, but don't do it on my account.'

Casey was scarlet when he finally set her on the ground and not just because of her fall. She was in love with Peter but her body betrayed her whenever Kyle came anywhere near her. Being pressed against his chest, close enough to breathe in his sexy boy smell, had sent her blood pressure through the roof.

'Thank you for helping, but you shouldn't have done that,' she said, scowling to hide her confusion.

He laughed. 'Oh, but I did. You were holding up Andrew Nicholson.'

Suddenly shy, Casey looked away. 'You must be wondering how I've ever managed to win a single event. Every time you see me I'm either falling off or making an idiot of myself, or both.'

His blue eyes were twinkling. 'I'm not thinking anything other than it's a normal part of the process of adjusting to a new horse. My father says he's learned more from bad horses, or horses behaving badly, than he has from good horses.'

'So your dad's a horseman too? Does he teach?'

'My dad's dead,' Kyle said curtly. 'Sometimes I forget and use the present tense.'

Casey was mortified. 'I'm so sorry. I—'

'Don't be. He went a long time ago. I miss him, but I've made my peace with it. It is the way it is.' His smile was sad. 'Anyway, we were talking about you. I was about to say that you should look at the positives. Lady Roxanne has a pretty amazing jump on her. I'd like her in my yard. She has a couple of personality issues, but we could iron those out very easily.'

'And how would you do that?'

'Casey! There you are. What happened?'

Mrs Smith hurried up to them, wet and flustered, with bright spots of make-up on her cheeks. Tendrils of her silvery fair hair had pulled loose from their ponytail mooring and her multi-coloured Tibetan jacket contrasted bizarrely with Kyle's immaculate blue jumper and pale breeches. She paused to get her breath.

'Laura Collett's groom brought Roxy to me. She said you'd taken a tumble and been carried out of the arena. I had visions of you being carted away in an ambulance. Thank goodness you're okay. I'm afraid I missed seeing

61

you jump because I was in the bathroom. With the delay, I got confused about your starting time.'

Casey was annoyed. 'You were in the bathroom?'

'Yes, I was. Is that a crime?'

'No, it's not, but it would have been helpful if you'd seen Roxy's performance and could give me some advice. That's why you're here, isn't it? Kyle was just telling me that he believes she has a couple of psychological issues which could easily be resolved.'

Kyle lifted his hands in mock surrender. 'Hey, don't put me in the middle of this. I was only venturing an opinion.'

Mrs Smith regarded him coolly. 'I bet you were.'

Kyle shook his head as if he couldn't understand why she was being so petty. 'Casey, if you're feeling all right, I'm going to head to the members' tent for a quick bite to eat. I don't suppose you'd like to join me?'

'We have a quinoa salad waiting in the car,' Mrs Smith interjected.

'I've had a fall,' Casey said sarcastically. 'I think I need something a bit more substantial than a quinoa salad. Kyle, I'd love to join you if that's okay. I'll take care of Roxy and be right there.'

If Mrs Smith was offended, she didn't show it. 'Don't worry about it. It's all in hand. I'll look after Roxy. You kids enjoy yourself. See you in good time for the cross-country, Casey. If it happens, that is. According to the forecast, a storm is moving in.'

Back at the horsebox, Mrs Smith tended to Roxy before tipping both salads into the bin. Under normal circumstances she couldn't stand waste, but her stomach heaved at the thought of food. After allowing Roxy to munch some grass for a few minutes, she returned the mare to the horsebox. To her relief, Roxy boxed easily. But when she went to move away, the mare whickered softly. Mrs Smith smiled a weary smile. She pressed her cool cheek to Roxy's warm silken one and for a long moment the pair drew comfort from one another.

'Don't tell Casey how well we get on,' Mrs Smith said softly. 'She might take it personally.'

Unable to stay upright for another second, she sank to the floor in the other stall and lay stretched out in the semi-darkness, a wet cloth covering her eyes.

No matter how much she tried to distract herself, she ceaselessly returned to the same thought. What preoccupied her wasn't Casey, Kyle or even the cross-country. It was the two remaining Nurofen in the pocket of her Tibetan coat. She wanted them with the desperation of an addict, but she knew she needed to hold off until shortly before the drive home. If she didn't get the pain under control before she sat behind the wheel, she could put them all in a ditch.

Mrs Smith had lied to Casey when she claimed she'd got confused about her start time. She'd known to the

63

minute when her pupil would be jumping. But shortly before Casey entered the arena, Mrs Smith had been swamped by an avalanche of agony so horrific it had sent her rushing to a Portaloo to throw up. When she emerged, she'd been so white and shaky that she'd had to down a fizzy drink – normally anathema to her – in an attempt to raise her blood-sugar levels in a hurry. Catching sight of her reflection in the glass counter of the burger van, she'd been shocked to see how wan she looked. When Casey fell, Mrs Smith had been sitting in the Jeep repairing her make-up.

She'd always known there would be a day of reckoning, but she'd convinced herself it would be a long way off and certainly after the Burghley Horse Trials. Now, it seemed, it was not to be. Angelica Smith's devotion to Casey, Storm and Roxy was total, but the pain that crashed with hurricane force through her body had become so debilitating that it made it impossible for her to do her job. Worse still, it was making it difficult for Casey to do hers, and that Mrs Smith would not tolerate.

But the idea of being without Casey and horses, her reasons for breathing, was almost as excruciating as the cancer eating her up inside. And Mrs Smith was in no doubt that that was what it was: Cancer with a capital C.

Five or so months earlier, Mr Andrew Mutandwa, an oncologist, had sent her for a battery of tests. Even before she left his office, he'd been frank in confiding that he feared the worst. For that reason, she'd deliberately given him a false address to which to send the results.

When at last a hospital letter did reach her, it was two days before the start of the Badminton Horse Trials. She'd been faced with a stark choice. If she opened the letter, the news might be a death sentence. At the very least she would have to undergo a course of radiation and/or chemotherapy which would compel her to abandon the girl and horse she loved at the hour they needed her most. Either way, life as she knew it would be over.

But there was another option. She could burn the letter without reading it and hope that the whole thing would simply go away. Out of sight, out of mind. So that's what she chose and in doing so incinerated her only chance of stopping the monster in its tracks.

Her promise to herself was that she would quit as Casey's teacher after Badminton and return to the hospital. But when Casey won the championship, she was immediately invited to compete in the Kentucky Three-Day Event. At that stage, Mrs Smith's pain was still manageable and there was a more pressing issue than her health. Casey and her father had become the victims of a vicious blackmail plot and once again Mrs Smith was needed. Then Casey won in Kentucky too and suddenly the Grand Slam was in play. And here they were.

And all this time Casey had no idea that she'd taken on a terminally ill coach.

Mrs Smith had hoped to keep the truth from Casey until after Burghley, in three months' time, but her encounter with Kyle West had changed everything. It was what he'd said about Casey being the future of eventing and needing 'modern methods' and 'cutting-edge techniques' that had really got her. With a few blithe sentences, he'd reduced Mrs Smith to the status of an ancient relic. Listening to him, she became conscious that her clothes were wrong, her teaching was wrong, *she* was wrong. If he'd stabbed her in the heart, he could not have wounded her more. She felt as if the lifeblood was leaking from her body.

Footsteps sounded outside the horsebox. Mrs Smith sucked in a breath, whipped the rag from her eyes and hauled herself to her feet. 'In here, Casey,' she called. 'I was about to grease Roxy's legs.'

Her brief rest had eased the pain enough that she could make a good show of tacking up Roxy for the cross-country while Casey changed into a red and white polo-shirt, air jacket and clean breeches. Lunch with the handsome Kyle seemed to have cheered her up considerably and she was clearly making an effort to be nice after her biting comments of earlier.

'Just enjoy yourself,' Mrs Smith counselled as they headed to the start of the cross-country. 'You and Roxy are still getting to know one another. Salperton is a lovely galloping track with lots of big, bold fences. It goes without saying that they don't have the degree of difficulty of those at Badminton or Kentucky, but Mike Etherington-Smith is one of the best cross-country course designers in the world so don't make the mistake

66

of underestimating them. Give Roxy room to breathe and let her stretch her legs.'

She squinted at the seething black clouds overhead. In the distance thunder growled. 'Let's hope the storm holds off until you're done.'

As it happened, the weather was irrelevant. Roxy ran out twice at the second fence, the incongruously named Savage Selection Tasting Table, incurring forty penalties. Casey retired her at once.

Every rider suffered run-outs. Even veteran jockeys like Pippa Funnell and Zara Phillips lost championships because their horses baulked unexpectedly at obstacles, but that didn't lessen Casey's frustration.

As she hosed Roxy down and Mrs Smith used loading the Jeep and horsebox as a cover for swallowing her painkillers, the entire lorry park came to a collective halt. In through the gate came a lorry so vast and shiny that it cut through the gloom of the afternoon to dazzle all who gazed upon it. It was painted in blue and silver and emblazoned in scarlet lettering: EQUI-FLOW, PROUD SPONSORS OF CASEY BLUE AND STORM WARNING, WINNERS OF THE BADMINTON HORSE TRIALS & KENTUCKY THREE-DAY EVENT.

The pain in Mrs Smith's head and abdomen increased exponentially the closer the lorry came. Two photographers appeared out of nowhere and took pictures of its arrival.

'Tell me you didn't authorise this,' she said to Casey.

A broad grin spread across her pupil's face as she

secured Roxy's lead rope to the old horsebox. 'I'm afraid I did and I don't regret it one bit. Isn't it gorgeous? Isn't it the coolest lorry you ever saw? It's easily as smart as William Fox-Pitt's. It might not be as big, but it's perfect for Storm, Roxy and I. And you, of course. Come on, even you have to admit that it's fab.'

Before Mrs Smith could summon a response, the lorry braked beside them, closely followed by a Land Rover the size of a tank. The Land Rover disgorged an ebullient man with a pleased red face and spiky grey hair, two blondes in ludicrously high heels who looked like swimwear models, and a further two men wearing gaily coloured T-shirts and expensive suits.

'Casey Blue, what an honour to meet you!' cried the first man. 'Allow me to introduce myself. Edward Lashley-Jones at your service. Ed to my friends. I hear that you've had a bit of a disaster in the cross-country, but no matter. You'll be back to your winning ways very soon, I'm sure, and in the meantime it's fantastic that you're here to greet us and take part in the photo shoot.'

He gestured in the direction of his companions. 'Allow me to introduce my business partners, Rupert Pinkney and Tony Hampton and their ... partners, Candi and Mandy. Girls, would you like to show Casey around her new home, as it were?'

'Great to meet you all,' said Casey excitedly. 'Thank you so much for doing this, Mr Lashley-Jones – Ed. I'm over the moon. Can I introduce you to my coach, Angelica Smith?'

Ed Lashley-Jones' eyes slid over Mrs Smith and dismissed her. 'Excellent, excellent. Now we need to get on if we're to get the pictures done before the rain moves in. All right, Casey? We must have a little something for Her Majesty's Press.'

Casey gave her teacher an imploring glance. 'Come on, Angelica, let's explore our magnificent new lorry.'

Mrs Smith stood firm. 'There's no way I'm getting in to that thing.'

Casey blanched. 'Would you excuse us a moment?' Steering Mrs Smith away, she whispered: 'What are you doing? Why are you trying to ruin this for me?'

Mrs Smith was in too much pain to be diplomatic. The Nurofen had yet to kick in. 'Casey, I'm telling you for the last time that you're making a mistake. These people will bleed you dry and use your bones for soup. They're parasites.'

'And you know that for certain, do you? You have a crystal ball? You're unbelievable. You've met them for all of two seconds and you've already judged and condemned them – something you're always telling me not to do. Well, I'm sorry, I'm doing this, whether you like it or not. It'll be good for me and even better for the horses. Who cares if I have to do the occasional photo shoot. I'll be travelling in the lap of luxury and all for free.'

Mrs Smith inhaled an agonising breath. It took every ounce of willpower she possessed to remain standing. 'Casey, I'm only saying these things because I care about you and don't like to see you being used. Believe me when I tell you that this lorry will come at a price. If you do this thing, you can do it on your own. It's me or the lorry.'

'Everything all right, Casey?' called Lashley-Jones. 'I think I just felt a spot of rain. We must get these photos done now. Heaven forbid the girls' hair gets messed up. We'll never hear the end of it.'

'Your choice,' Mrs Smith said again. 'Either the lorry goes or I do.'

Casey's mouth set in a mutinous line. 'You go, Angelica. I choose the lorry.'

8

YOU GO, ANGELICA. I choose the lorry.

Three days after the Salperton Park debacle, Casey sat in the passenger seat of the lorry in question, sipping a cappuccino made by the state-of-the-art coffee machine in the lorry galley and watching the Wiltshire countryside unfurl before her. A banner of blue sky lent the scene a fairytale quality.

She was thankful that Mr Farley, the driver assigned to her by Equi-Flow, was the silent type. His conversation had so far been limited to asking her which address he should programme into the sat nav. Mr Farley was not included in the Equi-Flow package. Already, she had been billed for his services.

'You understand that Equi-Flow can't possibly chip in

for a chauffeur?' Ed Lashley-Jones had told her. 'I mean, we're giving you a quarter of a million pound wagon. Don't get me wrong, we're delighted to do it and you'll be a superb ambassador for our company, but we have to draw the line somewhere.'

Personally, Casey would have preferred it if the line he'd drawn was on his own consumption of champagne in the members' tent on Saturday night at Salperton Park. But in the end a drunken sponsor was only one of the many horrors she'd had to endure that day, and paled beside the events that followed.

After she and Mrs Smith had argued in the lorry park, Casey had been forced to paste a smile on her face and act as if nothing would give her greater pleasure than to pose for an excruciating number of pictures in front of her flash new 'wagon', as Lashley-Jones insisted on referring to it. The impromptu photo shoot caused a certain amount of derision and merriment among the passing riders and grooms. It also attracted many more autograph hunters.

While Casey was being shown the interior of the lorry by Candi and Mandy, Mrs Smith had slipped away in the old horsebox, taking Roxy with her.

To save face, a furious Casey had had to pretend that had been the plan all along. Unluckily, she was then at the whim of Lashley-Jones, who was providing the driver who would take her back to White Oaks in the new lorry. He and his cohorts headed straight to the members' tent, where they proceeded to put away as many seafood platters and glasses of champagne as they could manage. The only thing that saved Casey's sanity during the long evening that followed was thinking about Kyle, who'd come to her rescue for the third time that day, during the afternoon photo shoot.

Just as Rupert Pinkney was suggesting that she change into a tight-fitting Equi-Flow T-shirt and perch on the bonnet of the Land Rover with Candi and Mandy, the storm that had been threatening all day descended. In two minutes Casey was drenched to the skin. Abandoned by the Equi-Flow tribe, she was rushing for shelter when Kyle appeared out of nowhere with an umbrella. They took refuge in an officials' cabin, empty but not yet locked.

Kyle glanced at the goose bumps on Casey's arms.

'You're freezing, Casey Blue. Is it compulsory to suffer when you're doing fashion shoots or would you like me to escort you to your car before you catch pneumonia? This wind is absolutely wicked.' He squinted into the deluge. 'Where is the horsebox, anyway? Or have you already moved everything into the new one?'

Casey was shivering uncontrollably. 'It's gone. Mrs Smith's taken Roxy home. We ... we had words.' To her embarrassment a tear rolled down her cheek.

Unexpectedly, Kyle hugged her. 'I'm sorry.' He didn't probe. 'I'm guessing that you don't have a change of clothes?'

'I'm f-fine.'

'You're about a million miles from fine. Unfortunately,

73

I haven't brought any spare clothes with me, but you're welcome to my jumper.'

Ignoring her protests, he unzipped his brown leather jacket and pulled off the blue jumper that she'd admired earlier in the day. Beneath it was a white vest that emphasised every contour of his flat stomach, narrow hips and slim, strong arms. Casey's eyes dropped to his breeches and worn, mud-splattered boots. He was quite devastatingly attractive.

She swallowed. 'I have a boyfriend.'

Kyle's face was unreadable. 'This is not about whether you have a boyfriend or I have a girlfriend. This is about stopping you from catching your death of cold. If your boyfriend was here, I'm sure he'd be doing the same thing for you.'

He handed her his jumper. 'It was clean when I put it on this morning, but I can't vouch for it now. If you're willing to take your chances, it'll keep you warm till you can find something better. Keep the umbrella too. I think I have another in the car.'

He shrugged into his jacket and moved to the door. His gaze met and held hers. 'See you down the road, Casey Blue.'

Since her only other option was hypothermia, Casey stripped off her soaking polo-shirt and put on the jumper as soon as he was out of sight. It was still warm and smelled faintly of cologne and clean sweat. The soft cashmere enveloped her in a hug. As much as she tried to tell herself that it was a practical solution to the damp clothes problem and that anyone would have done the same, wearing it felt like a betrayal of Peter.

And for the rest of the evening she had to sit in the members' tent and listen to the merry chatter and inane questions of the Equi-Flow bunch, while the jumper clung to her like a second skin.

It was midnight when Casey finally crawled into bed at Peach Tree Cottage. Despite her exhaustion, she tossed and turned. Shortly before six, she gave up on sleep and crossed the fields to the stables. Roxy seemed disappointed to see her, which was good for neither her ego nor her spirits. As she opened the stable door, the mare looked past her hopefully as if she were expecting Mrs Smith.

'Just me, I'm afraid,' Casey told her with a sigh, wondering, for the thousandth time, what she had to do to win Roxy's approval.

She wondered too how she was going to win back Mrs Smith's. She felt ill about the things she'd said. They played in her head like a stuck record. Passing her teacher's bedroom door a little while earlier, she'd debated whether to take her a cup of chai and a bunch of wildflowers as a peace offering. She planned to apologise and promise to make an appointment with a lawyer that very week to have a contract drawn up making Mrs

Smith her official manager. Waiting for the kettle to boil, however, she'd decided that Mrs Smith might be in a more receptive mood if she'd had a decent night's sleep and some breakfast. With that in mind, Casey decided to deal with the horses first.

Peter turned up as she finished grooming Storm. He'd spent the previous day and night in Norfolk, shoeing Arabians for Lord Lavington. Casey, who was in the midst of a flashback featuring Kyle in his white vest, nearly had a heart attack. To compensate, she kissed Peter with a little too much enthusiasm. He laughed.

'I was worried about telling you what I'm about to tell you, but if this is the effect that my absence has on you maybe it won't be so bad.'

'Not planning to leave me, are you?' Casey asked with a smile.

'Leave you? You must be joking. You're the best thing that's ever happened to me. But I may have to go away for a while.'

He drummed his fingers on the stable door. 'Case, I don't know how to tell you this ... '

'You're making me nervous, Peter. Just say it, whatever it is.'

'All right, I will. Last night I had a phone call from the manager of the Lone Pine stud near Mount Juliet in Ireland. You've heard of Alejandro Hall?'

Casey had. He was the Argentinian farrier whose wizardry with the feet of horses had been directly or indirectly responsible for some of the greatest horse-racing triumphs of all time. It was said that he could take a donkey with laminitis and, after only three treatments, make it run like Nijinsky.

'I've dreamed of taking one of his courses for years, but he only selects a handful of people and the waiting lists are a mile long. I put my name down for one before I ever met you but until last night I'd never had a response.'

'And now you have?'

He looked sheepish. 'Now I have. There's an eleventh-hour cancellation. Only trouble is, the course starts tomorrow.'

Casey looped her arms round his waist. 'And that's a problem why? Surely that's the good thing about having a dad who's a farrier too? Evan can take over some of your work.'

'Yes, he can. It's not work that I'm anxious about; it's you, Casey. I don't like it when we're apart.'

'I know that, and I feel the same way. But this is the opportunity of a lifetime, Peter, and it's important. It's also your passion. You've gone to the ends of the earth to support me and help me pursue my dream. I'd be the most selfish girl ever if I didn't do the same for you.'

Peter's shoulders sagged with relief. He put his arms around her, letting his fingers find the hollow at the base of her spine, hot and damp after her efforts with the horses. 'Thank you. That means everything. I promise I'll call, text and email so often that you'll be totally sick of me.'

Casey ran a hand over the fine stubble on his jaw. Peter would never turn heads the way that Kyle did, but to her he was gorgeous and the kindest, most wonderful boy she'd ever met. That he also had the sort of body that adorned the cover of men's health magazines didn't hurt either.

She kissed him again. 'I love you.'

Conscious that it had taken her far too long to say it in the year before they got together, she now said it as often as she could.

He grinned. 'I love you too. You really don't mind that I'll be out of the country for ten weeks?'

'*Ten weeks?*' Casey pulled away from him. 'You didn't say anything about ten weeks. I thought you meant that you'd be gone five or six days. The Burghley Horse Trials will be starting by the time you come back.'

She wanted to scream, 'You can't go. I need you. Without you at my side every step of the way, I'll never win Burghley.' But she couldn't, for all the reasons she'd already said. Over the past few months, Peter had constantly put her career first, regardless of his own feelings. There was no way that she was going to deny him this chance.

Instead she took his warm hands between hers. 'What I meant to say is that the best thing you could possibly do is go away for a few months. You'll be spared all of my usual pre-event stress and angst and be back in time to use your newfound knowledge to fit Storm with the perfect shoes to help him with the Grand Slam.

It couldn't be better. I'll miss you like crazy, but I'll be happy knowing that you're doing something that makes you happy.'

'Really? Well, since you put it like that.' A smile spread like sunshine across his tanned face. 'Oh, Case, I'm so excited. I've wanted to meet Alejandro Hall for years. I—'

Footsteps rang on the cobbles. 'Hey, Casey, you've made page five of the *Daily Mail* today,' cried Renata, arriving at the stable like a small tornado, brandishing the newspaper. 'Boy, are you going to be breaking some hearts ... Ah, sorry, didn't realise you had company. Hi, Peter. Never mind, I'll pop back later.'

Peter reached for the paper. 'Don't be daft, Renata. Give it to me. If Casey gets hold of it first she'll decide she looks terrible and I'll never see it.'

'Okay, but don't shoot the messenger.' She beat a hasty retreat.

Peter opened the paper and went stiff. Casey had to bite back a squeak of horror.

Beneath the headline, FEELIN' KINDA BLUE, was a photograph of Kyle carrying Casey from the ring at Salperton Park. Casey's eyes were closed and her face was nestled into Kyle's shoulder. He was wearing the blue jumper that was presently tucked from view beneath Casey's pillow in her bedroom. To anyone unfamiliar with the situation, they looked like lovers in an intimate embrace.

TOP EQUESTRIAN COACH KYLE WEST, 20,
COMFORTS 17-YEAR-OLD CHAMPION EVENTER
CASEY BLUE, AFTER A FALL AT THE SALPERTON
PARK HORSE TRIALS YESTERDAY. A SOURCE
CLOSE TO THE PAIR INSISTED THAT THEY ARE
'JUST GOOD FRIENDS'.

Peter said quietly: 'Is there something you'd like to tell me, Casey?'

'No,' cried Casey. She snatched the newspaper and tossed it over the stable door. 'I mean, yes, there is something I'd like to tell you. It's not what it looks like. I had a fall. I was winded. While I was on the ground trying to breathe, Kyle scooped me up and carried me out of the ring because we were holding up Andrew Nicholson. That's it. That's all there is to say. Typical tabloid to read something more into it.'

Peter's arms were folded defensively across his chest. 'But why him? When he texted you the other night, you told me you barely knew him.'

'I don't. We've had two or three brief conversations and that's it. But what was I supposed to do? I was in pain and couldn't breathe. He kindly came to my rescue because he thought the first-aid people were taking too long to reach me. I'm afraid I was incapable of gasping, "Put me down! My boyfriend wouldn't approve."'

'Okay, okay, it wasn't your fault, but you have to admit that it looks bad. The whole country is going to think that you and Kyle West are an item. It's the last thing

I need to see when I'm about to go away for months on end.'

So don't go, Casey wanted to say. *Stay here and protect me from Kyle.*

What she needed protection from she wasn't sure. Perhaps herself. She felt guilty even for having the blue jumper. It was as if a little piece of Kyle was hidden in her bedroom.

She put her arms around him. 'Peter, I'm sorry about the photo. If the positions were reversed I'd be mad too. But it's you I love. That's all you need to know.'

His dark eyes bored into hers, seeking reassurance. 'I believe you. I also trust you. Don't ever think I don't. But you're famous now, Case. Look at your new lorry. Everyone will want a piece of you. People are going to be throwing money and temptation at you all the time. It's not always going to be easy to resist.'

He left soon afterwards. His plan was to drive home to Wales to collect a few things he needed for his course before flying directly to Dublin from Cardiff. He and Casey had walked arm in arm to the car park, smiling again and teasing one another, but both knew that the incident with Kyle West had cast a shadow over things.

Returning to the stables, Casey bumped into Morag.

'Nice wheels,' she said, nodding towards Casey's new lorry. 'Fit for a queen. Lot to live up to, but I'm sure you'll learn to deal with the pressure, especially if Kyle West has taken a shine to you. It's a shame that it's all got a bit much for Mrs Smith. I saw her climbing into a taxi last night with two suitcases.'

Casey's blood turned to ice.

Morag was watching her closely for a reaction. 'Bit of an odd time to take a holiday, isn't it, with only months to go till Burghley and Storm about to come back into work?'

Casey found her voice. 'Mrs Smith has not had a break for as long as I've known her. I'm not about to begrudge her a little time off. Now if you'll excuse me, I have a million things to do.'

As soon as she reached the field gate, she broke into a run. Her limbs felt weak. All she could think was, please God, let this be some terrible mistake.

She flew into Peach Tree Cottage and up the stairs. Mrs Smith's bedroom door was still shut. Casey paused, lungs burning. She wanted to hold on to the last moment when things were still the same. She wanted to believe that Mrs Smith was having a lie-in – perhaps reading *The Tao of Love* or a biography of the Dalai Lama. Casey would say sorry and give her a hug and they'd laugh about how silly it was to fall out over a lorry. They'd have breakfast together and plan the day.

There was no reply when she knocked. Inside, Mrs Smith's room was spotlessly clean, the bed stripped. Not a trace of her remained.

On the bed was a note. Casey's knees gave way and she sank onto the mattress. The paper shook in her hand.

Dearest Casey.

Please don't blame yourself for my going. To be honest, it's been a long time coming. Loath as I am to admit it, I'm not getting any younger and things that used to be effortless for me are now a struggle. Yesterday, things came to a head. It wasn't so much because of our disagreement, although I admit I was hurt. Rather it was because I came to the reluctant conclusion that I can do no more for you. You're a beautiful, talented young woman and I could not be more proud of you, but you represent the future of equestrianism, the 21st century, and I am about the past. You need a dynamic young teacher who can take you to the next level. You need modern coaching and cutting-edge techniques. Mine would only hold you back.

One of your many wonderful traits is that you are loyal to a fault. You'd never end our relationship, even if you agreed with any of the above. For that reason, I think it best to leave now, before you come home. Our time together has been the most precious of my life and I'm proud to have played a part in helping you to flourish and grow. In return I ask only one favour of you. Don't try to find me. Focus on your own life and on your preparation for Burghley. Be happy. Above all, be true to yourself.

Your loving friend always,
Angelica Smith

For what seemed like hours, Casey sat in the echoing silence, too heartbroken to cry. She was roused from her misery by her phone buzzing in the pocket of her jeans. The call was from an unknown number. She prayed it was Mrs Smith.

'Casey, it's Kyle.'

'Oh.'

'I can't imagine what I've done to generate such enthusiasm,' came the dry response. 'Unless you're cross with me about the photo in the *Daily Mail*. Personally, I rather like it. It's already pinned on my office wall ... Joke. That was a joke.'

'Kyle, what do you want?'

'Want? I don't *want* anything. When I last caught a glimpse of you, you were being dragged in the direction of the champagne tent by the Equi-Flow piranhas. I'm only calling to check that you made it home safely and that you're feeling okay after your fall. I also wanted to tell you that you rode much better than your results, if that's any consolation.'

Casey pulled herself together. 'I'm sorry. I didn't mean to be rude. Thank you so much for the loan of your jumper. It was a lifesaver. Unfortunately, something awful has happened.'

It all came out then. The arguments with Mrs Smith. The devastating note.

Kyle listened without a word. Finally he said, 'Would you like me to help you find her? I know a man who knows a man who might be able to track her down.'

'NO!' Realising that she sounded slightly hysterical, Casey took a deep breath. 'Thanks, Kyle, but no thanks. If Mrs Smith doesn't want to be found, the least I can do is respect her wishes. Anyway, she's better off without me.'

'Maybe *you're* better off without her.'

'That isn't true. Mrs Smith is the best person I've ever known. I've always needed her far more than she's needed me. Everything I've ever achieved is because of her. I depend on her utterly. I don't know what I'm going to do. I'll be lost without her.'

'Casey, you've achieved the things you have because of your talent, passion and hard work, not because of Angelica Smith. I'm not denying she's a good teacher, but don't underestimate your own ability – or Storm's.'

'Thanks, but—'

'Casey, I know this situation is hard for you, but I don't want you to worry about a thing. I'm going to take care of you.'

'You have reached your destination!' chirruped the sat nav, startling Casey from her reverie. 'You have reached your destination!'

'Blasted machine,' barked Mr Farley, speaking for the first time in two hours. 'Always says we've arrived when we obviously haven't. Don't see no horses around here.'

They'd come to a halt in a shadowed lane overhung by the intertwined branches of oak, sweet chestnut and yew. On the left side of the road an overgrown track wound through the trees and out of sight. Craning out of the window, Casey spotted a faded wooden sign obscured by the vines and purple flowers of a deadly nightshade plant: Rycliffe Manor.

'I thought your Mr West had one of the best yards in the country,' grumbled the driver. 'The entrance doesn't look promising.'

Casey, who was thinking much the same thing, said primly: 'He's not *my* Mr West.'

They bumped up the track, grass brushing the underside of the lorry. Casey grew increasingly nervous. Perhaps they should turn back before it was too late. She could always say she'd changed her mind.

'Mr Farley ... ' she began.

The lorry gave a final, defiant surge and burst from the trees. Sunlight flooded into the cab. Stretching before them were three hundred rolling acres of exquisitely pretty parkland. A manor house, partially obscured by a high hedge and trees, looked grandly on, while a smart granite signpost directed visitors to the Rycliffe Manor Equestrian Centre along an immaculately graded gravel road.

'This is more like it,' said Mr Farley as they passed white-fenced paddocks in which sleek, glossy horses nibbled at waving emerald grasses. 'Now what were you saying?'

'Nothing.'

Casey gripped the edge of her seat, palms sweaty. As they neared the stables, she saw a girl with short auburn hair lunging a chestnut horse. Sparks of sunshine bounced off his hide. Beyond them was a field of professionally designed show jumps. It could have passed muster at Hickstead.

In the car park, Casey climbed stiffly from the lorry. She inhaled deeply. The air was fragrant with the mingled smells of horses, wood shavings and jasmine. As she approached an iron gate set in an archway, Kyle appeared on the other side. His face lit up at the sight of her. Hurrying forward, he slid open the bolt and let her in. 'Welcome to Rycliffe Manor, Casey. I'm so glad you could make it.'

'It's good to be here.'

'Great. Let's show Roxy her new quarters and then I'll give you a quick tour.'

As she led the mare to a light, airy stable in a block made of creamy Cotswold stone, Casey had to stop herself from gasping out loud. It was simply the most stunning training facility she'd ever seen. The stables themselves lined two sides of a manicured grass courtyard, in the centre of which was a tinkling fountain. Roses bloomed in beds of blazing colour.

An indoor school flanked the third side of the courtyard and signposted paths at each corner led to a horse therapy pool, two ménages and a cross-country course. Order and cleanliness reigned. Not a wisp of hay was out of place.

Kyle was watching Casey's expression. 'Do you approve?'

'Approve? I love it. It's magnificent.'

Kyle grinned. 'See, I told you I was going to take care of you.'

9

THE FIRST SHOCK to Casey's system was Kyle's teaching style. Whereas Mrs Smith's approach was heartfelt, spiritual and intuitive and as likely to involve scraps of wisdom she'd gleaned from *The Way of the Peaceful Warrior* as it was techniques picked up when she was a dressage champion, Kyle was all business.

'I have one hard and fast rule,' he told Casey as he led her to what he called his 'video suite' above his office. 'I never discuss training or give advice outside a lesson. Don't ask me because I won't respond. The way I see it, you wouldn't go to a doctor or a lawyer on the street and expect them to give you free medical or legal advice. Why is a riding expert any different? It's no problem if you want me to work with you at an event, but it needs to be organised in advance.'

He smiled. 'Fair enough?'

'Of course,' Casey said hastily, thinking about Mrs Smith, who'd been happy to discuss technique and plan strategy twenty-four seven and who couldn't have cared less about money. Casey had paid her ten per cent of her winnings and, since her victory at Badminton, taken over the rent payments at Peach Tree Cottage. But that was nothing compared to the fortune Mrs Smith had secretly spent supporting her in the early days of their relationship. Casey had tried to pay her back, but Mrs Smith claimed to have lost all the receipts.

Kyle ushered Casey into a small room filled from desk to ceiling with the latest computer and audiovisual equipment. As they entered, a man stood up quickly. His thinning hair and the sallow skin of his strange, squashed face were more or less the same uniform beige as his chinos and polo-shirt.

'Casey, let me introduce you to Ray Cook, my right-hand man,' said Kyle, patting him affectionately on the back. What Ray doesn't know about horses isn't worth knowing and the whole place would go up in smoke if he left. Ray, I'm sure Casey Blue needs no introduction. Badminton and Kentucky Three-Day Event champion. One of the most talented young riders in the country. I've asked that she give us forty-eight hours to prove to her that we're worthy of helping her win Burghley, so we all have to be on our best behaviour.'

Ray smirked but made no response.

'Pleased to meet you,' Casey said. He looked familiar but she couldn't place him.

Ray shook her proffered hand and left the room with nothing but a muttered, 'Great. Well, I'll be off then.'

Kyle shrugged. 'As you can tell, I don't employ him for his personality.'

They sat down at an oak bench weighed down by an X-box, a professional video camera, a couple of computers, a television and two banks of monitors showing CCTV footage of the indoor and outdoor schools, the cross-country course and a couple of roads on the estate.

Kyle pulled over a laptop. Three videos were cued up on it. He hit play on the first. It was Casey's dressage test at Salperton Park. She watched herself battle to contain Roxy as the mare kicked up her heels before plunging into an energetic and uneven canter, ears flattening when she was asked to transition into a trot.

Next came the show jumping. Casey squirmed in her chair as she watched herself fly from the saddle when Roxy shied. The part where Kyle carried her from the ring in his arms had, mercifully, been edited out. The third video showed Roxy run out at the second fence in the cross-country.

Kyle pushed back his chair. His polo-shirt, breeches and long boots were all black, which somehow emphasised his golden skin and hair. Casey thanked her lucky stars that he was being so business-like. It didn't

91

lessen his attraction but it did help keep her mind on the task at hand.

'Looking at those, what do you feel went wrong?'

'Everything,' Casey said at once.

'Not at all. You did most things right. Your problem is one of concentration. Each time you lose focus, Roxy senses that and reacts badly. Watch again.'

As the video played, Casey saw immediately that he was right. Here was the moment when she thought about Storm. Here was when she relaxed and allowed her mind to drift to Kyle and Peter. Here was when she thought about fence three when she should have been thinking about fence two.

'Come,' Kyle said, 'let's go and visit Roxy.'

On the way downstairs they passed Ray, who was returning to the video suite. Casey smiled at him, but he looked past her as if he hadn't noticed.

Roxy was munching hay in her spacious stable. Her ears went back when they appeared at the door and she made no move to come over to them.

Kyle took what looked like earplugs from his pocket. 'Hearing aid,' he explained. 'I find it helps me when I teach. My pupils don't have to shout when they talk to me.'

Casey smiled. 'Makes sense to me.' She opened the stable door. 'You told me at Salperton Park that Roxy had a couple of issues, but that they could easily be fixed. What are they?'

Kyle leaned against a pillar. 'I'll begin with a question.

I've no doubt that you've worked incredibly hard on getting to know Roxy and trying to make her feel comfortable, but have you found that she's continued to be a menace? Is she prone to biting, kicking, bucking or shying, mostly for no apparent reason?'

Casey was amazed. 'Are you psychic? That's exactly how she's been.'

'What was Mrs Smith's advice?'

'She told me to be infinitely patient and said that horses like Roxy are like Japanese Puzzle Boxes. As soon as you solve one question, you're presented with another.'

Kyle laughed. 'That's one way of putting it. Another is to understand that in Roxy you have a horse with huge potential but one who is as intelligent as she is insecure. Her "vices", for want of a better word, come out of boredom or fear. That's why she responded so badly when you lost concentration at Salperton Park. She's so sensitive to your mood that she felt abandoned. Deal with these factors and you'll have a champion.'

'Great. How do I do that?'

'It starts right here. She needs to spend as little time as possible in the stable during the day. When she is inside, I'm going to have Ray pipe classical music and BBC Radio into her stall so she feels she has company. We'll also give her a specially designed hay net that requires the horse to use ingenuity in order to get at the food. But in the summer I'd prefer her to spend most of her time outdoors where she has lots of natural stimuli to keep her amused.'

'What about training?' Casey asked. 'How do I keep her entertained or feeling supported when I'm working with her?'

'You have to keep finding new challenges and make her use her brain. With a horse like this, I'd advise keeping lateral work to a minimum. Work on a few specifics, make a big fuss of her when she gets something right, then take her out for a hack or a cross-country gallop. How long have you had her on loan?'

'Nearly a month.'

'Good. So you've had plenty of time to bond with her. Go over to her and give her some attention.'

Reluctantly, Casey approached the mare and rubbed her neck. Roxy's only response was to show the whites of her eyes and stamp a foot.

'When you show her affection, does she normally respond in a hostile way?'

Casey was forced to admit that she did on most days. 'Although she's better at events.'

'So it's safe to say that you've failed to bond with her? Then that's our number one priority. Until the two of you connect, she's not going to do her best for you. In fact, she's going to expend most of her energy trying to hurt you or get one over on you. The problem is, we don't have a lot of time. We'll need to come up with something pretty dramatic if we want to change her response quickly.'

He grinned. 'Don't look so crestfallen. We'll get there. And when we've sorted out Roxy, we'll move on to Storm.' He glanced at his watch. 'It's lunchtime. Let's grab a sandwich and coffee. I want to talk to you about your riding.'

Casey crawled into bed that night. It was a wonderful bed, a snowy expanse of Egyptian cotton sheets and duck down, which was especially welcome because she felt as if she'd been beaten all over with a baseball bat.

Kyle's first lesson had been entirely abstract. No physical riding was involved. Over lunch he'd informed her that her biggest weakness was her lack of experience with other horses and that it was critical that she addressed it. He presented her with a list of ten horses. She was to spend an hour working with each during the two days she was at Rycliffe Manor.

'Would you like me to work on anything in particular?' she had asked and was told to use her imagination.

Midway through the meal, a helicopter landed noisily in the field outside. Kyle dashed off to give a wealthy client a lesson. As instructed, Casey spent forty minutes schooling Roxy on her own before turning the mare out into a field. For the remainder of the afternoon she rode, in succession, a 17hh piebald cob with a sluggish stride, two jumpy ex-racehorses and a black gelding who pulled like a train. By 6 p.m., her arms were in such pain she could barely lift her fork to her mouth at the dinner table.

It was strange, and strangely thrilling, to be going to sleep in such close proximity to Kyle. His double-storey house, constructed from the same honey-coloured stone as the stables, was only a stone's throw from the equestrian centre's guest quarters.

Lying in bed, Casey checked her phone apprehensively. One message was from her dad, who was very excited to have been whisked to Florence at short notice on a cloth-buying mission with Ravi Singh. Two messages were from Peter – one to say that he'd landed safely in Dublin and missed her already, and a longer one raving about the breathtaking landscape of the Lone Pine Stud in Mount Juliet, where he'd be spending the next couple of months.

He added a P.S. *Hope you've had a good time at Rycliffe Manor. Do what's best for you, babe, and don't worry about anything else. Pxx*

Casey texted him an account of her day with lots of kisses on the end and pressed send. She felt much better. Before he left Wales, she'd called him with the news about Mrs Smith going. Peter had been stunned. He adored her teacher and found it difficult to comprehend that she would walk out on Casey with the Grand Slam in sight purely on the basis of a couple of heated exchanges.

The trickiest part of the conversation had been

breaking it to him that she was thinking of taking on Kyle West as a coach. There'd been a series of muffled curses. Finally, he'd come back on the line. 'Why him, Casey?'

And she'd had to attempt to explain that she didn't have time to shop around for coaches – not with Roxy being impossible and Storm about to return to full training. Kyle was one of the best. If he was keen to take her on, she had to go with him. Apart from anything else, she had obligations to her sponsors.

To his credit, Peter had been great about it once he'd had a chance to digest the news. 'I understand why you're doing it, but that doesn't mean I have to like it. I'd even go so far as to say that Kyle might do a better job than Mrs Smith. I'd just prefer it if the bastard wasn't so good-looking.'

Propped up in the pillows, Casey flipped through the latest issue of *New Equestrian* magazine, which had a cover story on Kyle. She too would have preferred it if he was less attractive, but wishing it wasn't going to change one hair on his head. Thank goodness he was so professional around the yard. It was only when he'd escorted her to her room that she'd caught a glimpse of his customary charm.

'Sorry it's been a bit mad around here today. I haven't been able to give you as much attention as I'd have liked. I did ask Ray to keep an eye on you and he was impressed. That takes some doing, I can assure you. Said you handled the racehorses like a pro.'

Casey had taken the opportunity to return his washed and folded jumper. Kyle took it from her with a rueful smile. 'I was hoping you'd keep it. I liked the thought of you wearing it.'

Casey had been so flustered that she'd practically shoved him out the door. Kyle was dangerous. No matter how much she tried to fight it, he got under her skin.

Judging from the article, she was not alone. The journalist called it the 'West effect'.

What everyone would like to know is how a high-school dropout whose only contact with horses was the beach donkeys in his seaside hometown became guru to the stars before he was out of his teens. The answer is elusive. West is the definitive International Man of Mystery. Even his former riding teacher is bemused.

'Kyle went from being the boy most likely to fail his BHS Senior Equitation and Coaching certificate to getting a distinction and wowing everyone who knew him,' said Terry Bond. 'It was as if suddenly, overnight almost, he was brushed with angel dust. I'm proud of him. He has everyone from Saudi princesses to former Olympians queuing for a sprinkling of that Kyle magic and I'm delighted to have helped him along the way.'

Part of the reason for West's meteoric rise is his state-of-the-art equestrian centre at the sumptuous Rycliffe Manor, home to multimillionaire Steve Remington. Before they fell out Remington was a business associate of Lionel Bing, father of West's former star pupil, the now disgraced Anna Sparks ...

At this, Casey stopped reading in shock. Anna Sparks had once been her most bitter rival. In the years leading up to Casey's Badminton win, vain, beautiful and prodigiously gifted Anna had reigned supreme as the best young rider on the eventing circuit. Along the way, she'd made it her mission to humiliate Casey and poke fun at her East End background and cheap clothes at every turn.

When, in spite of everything, Casey rose through the ranks, Anna tried to snatch Storm away from her and destroy her chances. But her maniacal obsession with winning at all costs backfired spectacularly. In a karmic twist, she was banned from eventing for five years for whipping a horse at Badminton. Millions of television viewers witnessed the horrific incident. No one had seen or heard from Anna since. There were rumours that she'd moved to Dorset to live with her mother, a music teacher.

Casey flung down the magazine, feeling ill. Kyle had coached her sworn enemy. There was no way that she could take lessons from a man who'd had anything to do with Anna Sparks. He must have known she was hideous. Casey glanced at her watch. She should pack her suitcase and leave immediately.

But how? Mr Farley had gone for the night. The chances of her getting a cab to collect her at 10 p.m. and drive her from the wilds of Wiltshire all the way to Kent were slim at best. Plus it would be astronomically expensive.

Distraught, she picked up the magazine. She might as well hear what Kyle had to say in his own defence.

What she read next changed everything. Kyle, it turned out, had almost had his fledging career destroyed by the fallout over Anna Sparks.

'It's human nature,' West says now. 'People always want someone to blame. With Anna out of the picture, it was me. That's okay. I understand that. But it hurt my clients, cost me business. Some felt tainted by association. It was painful because I love horses and it sickened me that people might think I in any way sanctioned that kind of behaviour. Anna disappointed me just like she did a lot of other people.'

Before he could recover, fate struck another blow. Philippa Temple, head of the Equestrian Centre at Rycliffe Manor, who'd taken West on as assistant manager after he finished runner-up in the Golden Horseshoe Riding Instructor Awards, was killed in a freak car accident. The brakes failed as she drove home alone from a show. A devastated West almost gave up on teaching altogether, but was persuaded by friends and clients to continue.

'I felt I owed it to her,' he says.

Casey slumped into the pillows. She'd read about Philippa's death at the time, but never having heard of her before hadn't really taken it in. Poor Kyle. That explained the little boy lost look that sometimes sneaked through his confident, sophisticated exterior. He'd been through hell. Well, she for one was not about to desert him. He'd condemned Anna Sparks' actions. That was good enough for Casey.

She turned off the light and lay in the darkness listening to the night creatures. Sleep descended so suddenly that it caught her in mid-thought, but it was a sleep plagued by dreams in which Mrs Smith was at the wheel of a runaway car. Over and over Casey tried to save her in the new lorry. Over and over she failed.

10

THE HAPPIEST ROBIN in the world woke Casey at the crack of dawn. As a shaft of orange sunlight slanted across her pillow, she dragged herself upright. Her muscles still ached from the previous day, but she wasn't tempted to go back to sleep. On the bedside table was the list of horse names given to her by Kyle. Her task today was to 'work on something different with every one'.

Walking stiffly to the stables a little while later, Casey wondered if a massage counted – for her, that is, not the horses.

Fortunately her first ride of the day was an easy one. Poetic was a twelve-year-old brown mare with a sweet, kind temperament. She was eager to please and much loved by her owner, a young girl. Casey did some light dressage work with her and was quite sorry to return her to her groom. She pined for Storm.

Looking in on Roxy, she found that the mare had already been fed and groomed and was leaning contentedly over her door while Taylor Swift sang country songs to her. She ignored Casey, as usual, but seemed cheerful enough.

'We tried her with Mozart and Beethoven, but she didn't take to them at all,' said the auburn-haired girl Casey had seen lunging the chestnut.

'Can't say I blame her,' Casey responded with a laugh. 'A lot of classical music stresses me out. I'd choose Dolly Parton over Wagner any day. I do like Bach though. My coach sometimes plays *St Matthew's Passion* on the way to events and it's amazingly soothing.'

The girl frowned. 'I didn't know that Kyle was into classical music.'

Casey's face grew hot. 'I meant my old coach – I mean, my last coach, Mrs Smith. Umm, I'm Casey Blue.'

'We all know who you are,' the girl said drily but not unkindly. She shook Casey's hand. 'Hannah. I'm a junior instructor here. Apologies, I thought it was a done deal, you and Kyle. Professionally, not romantically, I mean.' She giggled. 'I hear you have a boyfriend, which is nice. Peter Rhys, is it? Storm's farrier?'

'Uh, yes,' responded Casey, bemused by this segue.

'Anyway, Kyle likes you as a rider, you know. You're all we've heard about for weeks. Casey this and Casey that.

Ray approved of how you handled the thoroughbreds yesterday and believe me, it takes a lot to impress Ray.'

'That's what Kyle told me. What's he like?'

'Ray's all right. A man of few words but he's pleasant enough and he knows how to run a business. Kyle's a genius at what he does so it's best for him not to be distracted with the boring day-to-day things. Ray keeps the centre ticking over nicely and that works for everyone.'

She glanced at her watch. 'Please tell me that's not the time. I was supposed to meet someone in the indoor school ten minutes ago.'

After breakfast and a hair-raising attempt at the show-jumping course on a highly strung Arabian the colour of whipped cream, Casey went in search of Kyle. He'd been rushing about all morning, but he'd promised to analyse some video footage of her riding Roxy and a couple of other horses.

Kyle had told her to meet him in the video studio at ten, but Casey was early. Unable to control Adonis, the Arab, and fearful of falling off or injuring one of the most valuable horses in the yard, Casey had returned him to his stable after just thirty minutes. As a result, it was 9.48 a.m. when she reached the office building. Halfway up the stairs she heard raised voices.

'No!' yelled Kyle. 'No, no, no. It's too risky. It's the craziest thing I've ever heard and I don't want anything to do with it.'

'That's because your emotions are involved,' Ray said silkily. 'It's business, pure and simple. It's about what works.'

'The way it worked with Mouse, you mean?'

There was a silence. 'I thought we agreed not to talk about that again. That wasn't my fault. The girl was out of control.'

'Yes and on this occasion so are you, Ray,' snapped Kyle. 'What if something goes wrong? Do you really want that on your conscience? Try anything and you and I are going to have a serious problem.'

A floorboard creaked. Casey darted into the bathroom on the landing. She flushed the toilet and ran the water in the basin, emerging in time to see a scowling Ray going by. She smiled and was astonished when he quickly wiped the cloud from his face and smiled back.

'Morning, Casey. How did you get on with Adonis?'

'He, h-he's a handful,' stammered Casey.

'Yes, he is, but we're working our magic on him. In a month's time he'll be a different beast.'

With that, he was gone. Shaking her head in puzzlement, Casey went up to the video studio. Kyle was bent over his iPad, playing a video game where he hacked angrily at bits of fruit with a machete.

'Sorry,' he said when he saw her. 'Guilty secret.'

Casey pulled up a chair. 'Actually, it's quite endearing. You'd be too perfect otherwise.'

His hands stopped moving on the screen. A bleak look flitted across his face. 'Casey, if you knew me, you wouldn't say that.'

So suddenly that afterwards she wondered if she'd imagined everything that came before, he gathered himself and gave her one of his usual heart-melting smiles. 'Right, let's look at some of the footage from yesterday.'

There were three short videos – one of her working with Roxy and a couple of her riding the lazy cob and the first racehorse.

'We'll start with you and Roxy,' said Kyle.

Casey waited expectantly.

'So there you are. You're in the ménage with Roxy … Looking good. We need to address some of the issues we talked about yesterday, but otherwise you're doing fine. Better than fine, in fact.'

'Which particular issues?'

'What I told you yesterday. Concentration and bonding and stuff. Let's take a look at these other videos. Here you are with Barnaby, the cob … ' They stared at the video together. 'Great,' said Kyle. 'I wouldn't change a thing.'

He closed the lid of the laptop with a bang. 'What I'd like you to do this afternoon is take Roxy around the cross-country course. Stretch her legs and give her something to think about.'

He was up and out of the video room before Casey had time to ask another question, leaving her bemused and wondering whether Kyle blew hot and cold with all his pupils or if it was something unique to her.

By the time Casey had schooled three other horses and grabbed a sandwich for lunch, it was almost five o'clock. Her body was tired and ached all over, but it was perfect weather for a gallop: overcast and warm without being hot.

The cross-country course wound its way through the most glorious part of the estate. Roxy seemed to appreciate it as much as Casey did. Her head was up and she was relaxed but bouncy. Casey was tensed to hang on in case she shied at a fleeing rabbit or the blackbirds, finches and robins rustling in the hedgerows, but Roxy seemed fascinated by her new environment, not afraid. Her big lustrous eyes were popping out of her head.

As Casey let herself through the gate that opened onto the cross-country course, she had to pinch herself. Though small, the fences were close to Badminton quality, imaginatively designed and built by experts. If she signed Kyle's contract that evening, all of this would be hers – not literally, but it would mean that she could train here any time.

It helped allay the doubts that had crept into her mind

after the argument she'd overheard and the vague way in which Kyle had analysed the videos. Ray was an odd character and she could imagine him being difficult to deal with at times. Following their heated exchange, Kyle had obviously been in no mood for picking apart her riding faults. But one bad day didn't make him a bad teacher. Ninety-nine times out of a hundred he'd be the star coach everyone said he was.

With that final thought, she urged Roxy forward. The mare settled into a smooth gallop, clearing the first brush fence with room to spare. Balanced lightly in her stirrups as Roxy effortlessly negotiated flowerbeds, logs, oxers and even a mini water jump, Casey felt a surge of happiness that their working relationship was improving. It frustrated her that they were still business acquaintances rather than friends, but she supposed Mrs Smith was right. Bonding with a horse took time and patience. There were no shortcuts.

At the thought of Mrs Smith, Casey's stomach gave a lurch. She wished that there was a number she could call so that she could at least check if her teacher was all right. Quite apart from the guilt she felt over the awful things she'd said, she was plagued by fears that Mrs Smith had been hiding the true state of her health and could in fact be grievously ill. She might be sick, scared and alone and Casey would never know.

Tears blurred the next fence. Roxy lost impulsion and refused an easy post and rails. After circling back and coaxing the mare over it, Casey told herself off. Hadn't

Kyle told her that losing concentration was one of her biggest faults? She couldn't expect miracles from Roxy – or Kyle – if she didn't deliver as a rider. The buck stopped with her.

Roxy's performance, on the other hand, was exceptional. When they flew over the final fence, which was adjoined to the first, the mare was barely out of breath. Casey made a big fuss of her as they slowed to a walk.

She was about to dismount to open the gate when she noticed it was padlocked. This was problematic for two reasons. One, because she'd left her phone behind and couldn't call the equestrian centre for assistance, and two because Hannah had expressly told her that on no account should she use the only other gate, which was situated close to fence ten. 'Two crazy horse-hating dogs live along that lane and trust me, you do not want to run into them.'

For that reason, Casey spent twenty minutes leading an increasingly agitated Roxy up and down the fenceline in the hope of spotting a passing worker or rider who might rescue them. She was sure that Kyle, Hannah or one of the grooms would notice that she'd been gone for ages and come in search of her. But apart from a faraway tractor and a distant speckling of sheep the landscape stayed depressingly empty.

In the end Casey had no choice but to try the other gate. Such was her desperation that she was profoundly grateful to find it unlocked. Before allowing Roxy to go through it, she listened carefully. The lane ahead appeared to be a peaceful avenue of mossy trees and musical birds. If any horse-hating dogs did pop out of the bushes, she made up her mind to do her best to keep Roxy to a walk and not to do anything to provoke them. If they did get aggressive, Roxy was fast enough to outpace them.

Nevertheless, her heart was in her mouth as she set out along the green tunnel. Once inside it the birdsong was muffled and the air smelled of rotting leaves and moist, fertile earth. Roxy's appreciation of the estate's flora and fauna evaporated as they proceeded. She spooked at every squirrel and leaf. Casey tried soothing her, but she was on edge herself and it didn't work.

'In ten minutes we'll be back and I'll be hosing you down and giving you a nice dinner,' she told Roxy. 'This will all seem like a bad dream.'

They drew level with a cottage hidden behind a high hedge. There was a sign on the white gate: *Beware of the Dogs. Enter at Own Risk.* Casey laid a nervous hand on Roxy's shoulder. 'Easy, girl. We're going to be just fine.'

Her ears strained for a bark or a growl, but her only warning was the clink of a chain. Like a vision from a nightmare, a Rottweiler and a Doberman Pinscher hurdled the gate and came at them on silent paws.

The Rottweiler attacked first, springing at Roxy's neck, only narrowly missing her jugular. The mare screamed in terror, rearing so high that she almost overbalanced. Somehow she righted herself and came crashing down,

110

landing a glancing blow on the Doberman. With Casey clinging petrified to her neck, Roxy wheeled and bolted along a track cut through the trees.

Casey's one hope – that the dogs would lose interest when their territory was no longer under threat – was in vain. Their determination to hunt down their prey increased with every bound. The rough track didn't help. Roxy was galloping at breakneck speed, but the ground was pocked with rabbit holes and fallen branches and each step was a disaster waiting to happen.

We're going to die, thought Casey. *We're going to die or suffer a horrific accident and there's not a thing I can do to stop it.*

A five-barred gate appeared in front of them. Roxy hesitated, took two extra strides and then it was too late. She was too close to make the leap. As she came to a plunging stop, Casey saw that the dogs were almost upon them.

They were trapped.

Flinging herself to the ground, Casey snatched up a stick. Over her dead body would they hurt Roxy. She ran forward brandishing her weapon. 'Get away!' she screamed. 'Leave us alone!'

They paused, snarling. The Rottweiler charged first, retreating with a squeal as she landed a blow. The Doberman darted around her to try to get at the mare. Casey tried to strike it but missed. It sprang at Roxy's flank, drawing blood. The terrified mare cowered against the gate, neighing wildly.

Casey swung at the Rottweiler as it lumbered forward to join the game, and hit the Doberman a crack on the nose as it moved in to attack Roxy again. Enraged, the dogs now turned their attention to her. The Rottweiler sank its teeth into her boot, shocking Casey into dropping the stick. It gripped her ankle like a vice. She was defenceless as the Doberman, his pointed ears pricked and yellow fangs bared, crouched to spring.

A piercing whistle blasted through the trees. The dogs looked crestfallen. White-eyed and whining, they melted into the undergrowth.

Casey ran sobbing to Roxy. Taking careful hold of her bridle, she stroked the mare's quivering neck. 'I'm sorry. I'm sorry. I made a mistake and I could have got you killed. Oh, God, Roxy, I'm so sorry.'

She expected the mare to wrench away or try to bite her, but Roxy did none of those things. She buried her nose in Casey's shirt, hiding her eyes like a frightened child. Casey put her arms around her and held her close. The mare's coat was dripping with white foam and blood. How long they stood there she didn't know.

'You're okay, I take it?'

Girl and horse started violently. Ray was striding towards them.

'I-I think so.' Casey's voice shook. 'I'm not sure. Roxy's been bitten.'

Ray moved closer. 'It's a scratch. It'll heal in no time.' His dull brown eyes were lit with a strange fire. 'What are you doing here? You could have been killed. The dogs are not pets. They're guard dogs. I told Hannah to be sure to warn you not to use the second gate on the cross-country course. If she forgot, I'm going to fire her on the spot.'

'It's not her fault,' Casey said hastily. 'She did tell me not to use the gate *and* she warned me about the dogs.'

'Then why—?'

'Because the main gate was locked,' cried Casey, her voice rising as the full horror of the situation started to sink in. 'I didn't have my phone and I waited for ages in the hope that someone would come by. Nobody did so I decided to chance the lane. When she said that there were crazy dogs along this road, I didn't know she meant Cujo and the Hound of the Baskervilles. *What? Why are you looking at me like that?'*

'Because,' Ray said grimly, 'you and your horse nearly ended up as dog meat for nothing. You made a fatal error. The main gate doesn't lock. It's always open.'

'What are you talking about? I saw the padlock with my own eyes. It was a big brass one.'

But Ray was already striding down the track. 'Show me. We need to walk right past the gate on our way back to the stables. I'd like to see this phantom padlock. And don't worry, I've chained up the dogs.'

Casey was so furious at being disbelieved that she had to bite her lip to stop herself saying something she regretted. 'Fine. Lead the way.'

They were approaching the gate when Kyle came roaring up in a pickup truck. He was out of the vehicle almost before it came to a halt. His face was full of panic.

'When they said you hadn't returned, I thought you might have had a fall. What happened? Are you okay? Why is Roxy bleeding?'

'Despite being explicitly warned not to do so, Casey took the back gate,' Ray told him. 'It's not her fault. She wasn't to know the dangers. I'm afraid the dogs—'

A look of naked fury flashed across Kyle's face. A vein pulsed frantically in his jaw. 'The *dogs*?'

'I'm sorry,' Casey said miserably. 'The main gate was locked. I couldn't get out. I was getting desperate.'

Kyle stared at her. 'But that gate is never locked. It hasn't been locked once in the eighteen months I've been here.'

'I'm sure Casey knows a locked gate when she sees one,' Ray said in the tone of someone who thought the opposite. 'Let's take a look.'

'At the phantom padlock, you mean?' jibed Casey, still smarting from his earlier remarks.

He had the grace to look ashamed. 'Apologies. I spoke rashly in the heat of the moment.'

With Roxy following so closely that her muzzle was in constant contact with Casey's arm, they walked over to investigate. When they reached the gate there was a long silence.

'But it was there,' Casey insisted. 'There was a brass padlock. It was glinting in the light. How could I have imagined something like that?'

Ray held up his hands as if he, too, was mystified. In

reality, he was probably thinking she was an idiot.

'Forget about it. No real harm's done. You handled yourself well. You put your horse first and she thanks you for it.'

Roxy was so intent on being close to Casey, she was practically leaning on her.

'Thank you for saving me, Ray,' said Casey, trying not to sound ungrateful. 'I hate to think what would have happened if you hadn't come along when you did.'

The fire had gone from Ray's eyes and they were once again veiled and dull. 'No problem. I hope it doesn't colour your view of Rycliffe Manor. It's usually pretty peaceful around here. '

With a nod to Kyle, he struck off across the fields without a backward glance.

Casey looked pleadingly at Kyle. 'The padlock was there, I promise. I'm not making this up.'

He put an arm around her shoulders and she could feel the heat of his skin through her shirt. 'I believe you, Casey, don't worry. I'll make some enquiries. I'm sure there's a simple explanation. Maybe one of the temporary estate staff mistook this paddock for one of the sheep fields. Try to put it out of your mind. The main thing is you're not injured. Now let's get Roxy to the stables. I'll walk with you and send someone back for my truck.'

Casey managed a weak smile. 'I'm fine, really. You go. I'll see you there.'

She tried to move away, but Kyle moved with her

and kept his arm around her. 'Are you kidding? On my watch, you and Roxy have been frightened half to death. I feel responsible. I'm not letting you out of my sight until I know you're safe and sound.'

11

CASEY SLEPT IN Roxy's stable at White Oaks for the next two nights. She'd called Morag on the way home to ask if there was any chance that the mare could move into the stable beside Storm's. Morag's approach to horses and training was the polar opposite of Casey's and they hadn't always seen eye to eye, but the stable manager had a big heart. Casey was only midway through recounting an edited version of the dog attack when Morag interrupted.

'Consider it done. Anything you need, hon, anything at all, I want you to call. Seriously, I mean it. Night or day, don't even hesitate. We're here for you.'

Casey was deeply touched. She clicked off her phone,

put her arms around Roxy and they stood like that all the way home.

When the lorry was finally parked in White Oaks' familiar driveway and Mr Farley was on his way to a local pub for the night, Casey unloaded Roxy and led her to her new stable. It was piled extra high with the best bedding and had a bucket of water and hay net already installed.

After settling the mare in, Casey nipped next door to say hello to Storm. He was ecstatic to see her and she clung to him as if he was a life raft in high seas. In a way, he was. For the moment, he was all that remained of her support team. There was no one else that she could talk to and nobody at all who she could ask for advice about Rycliffe Manor Equestrian Centre. Peter was too biased against Kyle, her father knew next to nothing about horses, and Morag would have made some cutting comment about 'celebrity teachers'.

But Storm always made her feel better. He was so intelligent and his love was so constant that just being around him reminded her that by saving him, she had done something right once. And on that day, she'd relied on her own judgement. She'd made a decision to rescue him, regardless of the consequences, and she'd changed both of their lives for ever. Casey sighed. She wished she could stay longer, but the purple twilight was turning black and she knew she had to prioritise Roxy.

Still traumatised, Roxy grew anxious when she was left alone for even a moment. Casey virtually sprinted across the fields to Peach Tree Cottage to fetch a sleeping bag, pillow and blanket. She'd barely been gone for forty-eight hours and already the air in the house smelled stale. Passing Mrs Smith's bedroom, she saw again the stripped bed and the coat hangers dangling forlornly in the empty cupboard.

Down in the kitchen it occurred to her that she hadn't eaten since lunchtime. But there was no bread for toast and the milk was sour. Mrs Smith usually ordered the groceries and she was gone. Dejected, Casey tried calling Peter but his phone went straight to voicemail. She wasn't in the mood to leave a message, nor did she want to think about where he might be or who he might be with. Desperate to hear a comforting voice, she rang her dad, but his phone was switched off. She supposed he was still in Italy. She was glad for him, but it added to her sense of isolation.

Roxy whickered a welcome when Casey returned and watched with interest as the sleeping bag was unrolled on the stable floor. Before turning in, Casey put another application of manuka honey on the small puncture wound on Roxy's flank. The mare barely flinched. She made no attempt to nip Casey or crush her against the wall, simply gazing at her with adoring eyes.

The thing that kept coming back to Casey was Kyle's comment about how they needed to come up with something dramatic to bond Roxy to her, and how quickly that had come to pass. She stopped the thought there. She didn't want to think about the padlock, glinting in the light. And she definitely didn't want to dwell on the dogs and their yellow killer eyes and snarling savagery and what would have happened if Ray hadn't arrived when he did – Ray who, it had turned out, was responsible for the feeding and training of the guard dogs.

Casey snuggled into her sleeping bag. At least she had two friends in the world – Storm and Roxy. Four if you counted Peter and her father, and five if you added Mrs Smith. Mrs Smith would be her friend always, she knew, but Casey had not been a very good friend to Mrs Smith. Not at all.

And what of Kyle? Was he a friend?

Either way, he was her new teacher. She'd signed the contract before leaving Rycliffe Manor that evening. The office secretary, a briskly efficient bottle-blonde named Joyce, had lent her a fountain pen to fill in her address and other details. As Casey scrawled her signature a bubble of ink had oozed from the nib and run down the page. It was blue ink, but for a split second Casey's brain had turned it red so that it resembled blood.

Tucked up in her sleeping bag, she was scared to shut her eyes in case the dogs returned in her nightmares. When at last she did drift off, she didn't have a single dream. Neither did Roxy. All night long, the mare watched over her, her delicate nostrils fluttering as she breathed in the scent of the girl who'd saved her.

Next morning Casey started riding Storm again. He was fat and full of beans after his long holiday, but it was heavenly to be riding him. Since all she planned to do was hack him across the fields at a walk or slow trot, she took Roxy along on a lead rope. Morag thought she was mad and said so, but it couldn't have gone better. Storm and Roxy had made eye contact over their stable doors and had taken a liking to each other. Before the end of the ride, they were firm friends.

At the beginning of July, Casey entered Roxy in the Westwood Classic in Winchester. So inseparable had the mare and Storm become that Casey was tempted to bring him along to keep them company, but she was reluctant to unsettle him. She wanted to ease him back into training and keep him relaxed and content for as long as possible before the pressure starting piling on.

The new lorry was the last word in luxury. Every surface had a mirror shine and the seats smelled of new leather. The galley kitchen had everything the champion rider could possibly need and the foldout bed was so comfortable it almost swallowed Casey when she tried it out. In the back, Roxy had room to spare.

But with only the taciturn Mr Farley to share it with, Casey found it hard to enjoy the lorry on her own. It was like being a child left alone in a giant toyshop. The best toys in the world were no fun if you had no one to play with.

Added to which, her sponsor, Ed Lashley-Jones, was already becoming insufferable and she was only weeks into her contract.

'Congratulations on appointing Kyle West as your coach,' he'd rung to say when the news broke. 'Smart move. Handsome young man at the top of his game. Much better for your image as eventing's youngest superstar than that Mrs Smith who—'

'Careful, Ed. I'd like to remind you that it was Mrs Smith's coaching that got me where I am.'

Perhaps sensing that he'd strayed into a danger zone, Lashley-Jones backtracked smoothly. 'Of course, of course. I only meant that West is the man of the moment and you couldn't have made a better choice.'

He hung up after reminding her to promote Equi-Flow to any reporter, sponsor or top rider she came across. 'But only if you do well. If you have a meltdown, the way you did at Salperton Park, it's best not to mention us.'

With that vote of confidence ringing in her ears, Casey arrived at the Westwood Classic. The lorry park was already humming with grooms checking plaits and doing last minute touch-ups and riders on their way to the collecting ring. Casey saw nobody she knew. She couldn't ever remember feeling so lonely at an event. Lots of people said hi or stopped to talk to her, but many were strangers or acquaintances keen to be associated with her only because of what she'd achieved. She did have lots of friends on the circuit, but they were all away or busy.

To distract herself, she took her time putting on white breeches, a smart tweed jacket from another new sponsor and highly polished brown boots. As always, the last thing she did before she rode was put her mum's rose brooch in her pocket, only now she kissed it first. In the absence of everyone else she loved, it was infinitely soothing to know that her mother at least was always there.

She also texted her father.

How's Italy, Dad? Hope u r having a fab time. Envious. Seems ages since we spoke. Would love you to come on the road with me some time. Miss you. Cxx

No sooner had she sat down than she was up again. Caffeine always made her restless. She'd breakfasted on a motorway-service-station croissant and three cappuccinos from the lorry's fancy coffee machine. It was the kind of breakfast Mrs Smith would have heartily disapproved of, but, Casey told herself defiantly, Mrs Smith wasn't here. Kyle was.

He came striding up as she swung into the saddle. Casey noticed right away that he had in his hearing aid. He was wearing his blue jumper again, this time with faded black jeans that hugged his hips.

'For luck,' he said with a grin, tugging at the jumper. His blonde fringe flopped endearingly across his face.

'I'm not sure about that,' said Casey wryly. 'When I last wore it I had to spend an evening in the champagne tent with Ed Lashley-Jones and Mindy and Cindi. Or was it Candy and Bambi?'

Kyle laughed. 'Look at it this way. You did survive. That's saying a lot. And this teacher is here to stay.'

'Speaking of which, do you have any advice? What should I think about in the dressage?'

'Actually, the thing I want you to think about is what you do *before* the dressage. I noticed at Salperton that your collecting-ring strategy leaves a bit to be desired. You want to make sure that you have Roxy's attention and that she's relaxed. Try a few transitions – trot to canter and vice versa – and then bring her back to a walk. Next time ask her for a halt. Keep her guessing.

'As for you, your main task is to stay in the moment. There's nothing you can do about a mistake you made thirty seconds ago. It's gone. What you can do is focus on making the following movement as flowing and beautiful as possible. Oh, and Casey ... '

'Yes?'

'Don't forget to have fun.'

12

COMPETING IN THE intense, electric atmosphere of Badminton and Kentucky had been the most exhilarating experience of Casey's life, but she'd forgotten how much she enjoyed the buzz of the smaller events. Eventing was a great equaliser. The rigorous qualifying system ensured that the giants of the sport had to bring their young mounts on alongside those of policemen, bricklayers and nurses riding every shape, breed and colour of horse.

At times it made for chaos in the lorry park and collecting ring, but the risk factor in horse trials meant that it attracted as many genial cowboys as it did women who were fazed by nothing. Most people took most things in their stride.

Despite her achievements, Casey always got an attack of butterflies before competing. More so today because she didn't have Mrs Smith standing on the sidelines with her ringside bag full of emergency items. Casey especially missed her homemade granola bars. The croissant had not been a good idea. It had left her feeling bloated and lacking in energy.

Kyle caught her eye and smiled reassuringly. Besieged by a steady stream of fans – pretty girls, potential sponsors and the relatives or partners of riders who wanted to know if the 'West effect' could boost their rankings, he dealt charmingly with each. But his focus never left Casey. He made her feel special.

Gradually, her nerves steadied. Roxy was keyed up but responsive and Casey entered the dressage arena feeling confident. She intended to do her best, but all that really mattered to her was that she and Roxy were a team. Day by day the bay mare was learning to trust and accept her, just as Storm had. That alone was like winning the lottery.

The previous week Casey had called Roxy's owner, Jennifer Stewart, and asked if she could buy the mare. After their ordeal at Rycliffe Manor and the relationship they'd built since, Casey already knew that she would not be able to bear parting with Roxy in two or three months' time. She also believed that Roxy was a star in the making and her price would soon shoot up. When that happened she'd quickly be out of Casey's price bracket – if she wasn't already.

But Jennifer Stewart was a canny bird. It turned out she was a lawyer. Casey had opened the conversation by apologising for their dire performance at Salperton Park. She'd hinted that Roxy might have personality issues. But Jennifer Stewart cut her off in mid-sentence with a breezy, 'Now that you're working with Kyle West, I'm anticipating a drastic improvement. It would be rash of me to part with the mare at this stage. As she moves up the rankings, she'll leap in value.'

Depressed, Casey had ended the call. She couldn't lose Roxy, had to find a way to keep her. For a minute, she'd contemplated riding badly on purpose for the next few events so that Jennifer Stewart would decide that the mare was a no-hoper and be glad to part with her, but she'd banished the thought almost immediately. It was selfish and wouldn't be fair to Roxy. Roxy had a talent. Casey would be letting both of them down if she didn't encourage the mare to shine.

And shine Roxy did. The finer points of dressage were still new to her, but she was razor sharp and learned quickly. She also had wonderful natural balance, a critical ingredient in a dressage horse. Those qualities, together with her newfound affection for Casey, helped her to an assured performance that morning.

It was sheer bad luck that mid-way through, Roxy spotted a Rottweiler panting behind the ropes. It was on a lead, but that made no difference. Before Casey could stop her, she'd bolted halfway across the dressage court.

It was a measure of how much they'd bonded that

Casey was able to pull her up within a few strides. Gently, she persuaded Roxy to continue. Bearing Kyle's words in mind, she put the incident behind her and focused on making the rest of the test perfect. Her heart was pounding, but she softened her hands and did everything she could to communicate calm to Roxy.

Kyle was quietly pleased.

'There's work to be done, especially on her quarters, but the change in you both is extraordinary. I'm still embarrassed about what happened at Rycliffe Manor. When I said that we needed to find a dramatic way of uniting the two of you, I didn't have a mauling by rabid dogs in mind. You'll be glad to hear that we're reviewing our safety measures. The second gate is now locked and chained so that nobody else will ever make the same mistake you did.'

Casey didn't want to think about the dogs ever again and said so. After that, she blocked them from her mind so effectively that she and Roxy managed a clear round in the show jumping with only two rattled poles.

She'd changed out of her show-jumping gear and was making herself and Kyle a cappuccino in the new lorry when she heard raised voices outside.

'I don't believe it,' Kyle was saying in an agitated tone. 'That's impossible. There must be some ghastly mistake.'

When Casey went out, he was talking to Sam Tide's girl groom, Marsha. He looked quite shaken.

'What's going on?'

Marsha hesitated but Kyle snapped: 'Oh, for goodness' sake, tell her. She'll find out soon enough.'

'Find out what?'

'Anna Sparks.' Marsha's small brown face twitched with righteous indignation. 'Your nemesis. You'll never believe it, but she's here. Right here at Westwood Park. It's disgusting.'

'I'm surprised that she's brazen enough to show her face at an event, but there's no law against it,' said Casey. 'Just because she's banned from competing, doesn't mean she can't watch. She'll be a pariah, though. No one will speak to her.'

Marsha was hopping with indignation. 'You don't understand. She's not watching, she's competing. The ban has been overturned on appeal. They're reporting on Sky news that she claimed that some pills she was taking – diet pills, would you believe – made her act irrationally and violently. She told the appeal panel that that was the reason she attacked Franz Mueller's poor horse at Badminton.'

Casey was stunned. 'And they believed her?'

'There'll be an outcry, but yes they did. You're not going to want to hear this, Case, but she's competing in the same Intermediate class as you. Like a villain in a soap opera, she's back. Anna Sparks is back.'

When Roxy burst from the D box in the cross-country a little while later, Casey had only one goal and that was to vanquish Anna Sparks. She rode like a girl possessed. Every hurt that Anna had ever inflicted, every slight and every time she'd ridiculed Casey for having ill-fitting charity-shop clothes, or the wrong tack, or horsebox, or a knacker's-yard horse added fuel to the fire of Casey's loathing.

But the thing that really drove her on was what Anna had done to Storm. After Lionel Bing, Anna's wealthy father, had tricked his way into stealing Storm (money had changed hands, but as far as Casey was concerned it was theft), Anna had attempted to ride him – with disastrous results. The injury he'd sustained at their yard had caused him a huge amount of suffering and nearly cost Casey her career. Yet evil Anna Sparks was back competing as if nothing had happened.

'Whatever it takes, you have to beat her today,' Kyle had told her grimly. 'I don't care if you finish fortieth and she finishes forty-second. I just want you to finish ahead of her.'

'Oh, I will. You can take it to the bank.'

Whether it was because the Rottweiler had stirred up memories of the attack at Rycliffe Manor, or purely because she picked up on Casey's recklessness and rather liked it, Roxy responded with everything she had. They flew around the cross-country course as if they were at Badminton. Fruit tables, skinnies, ditches and a water jump featuring real flamingos – Roxy took them all in her stride. Sometimes she leapt so high and so boldly that Casey, expecting a more modest jump, was almost unseated.

Once, she thought she saw Ray in the shade with a video camera, unsmiling and dressed to blend with the crowd, but when she glanced back there was no one there. She decided she must have imagined it. If his right-hand man was at the Westwood Classic, surely Kyle would have mentioned it.

The crowd at the event was tiny in comparison to that at Badminton or Kentucky, but their enthusiasm more than made up for it. The applause swelled as Casey rode. If Roxy hesitated, Casey urged her on with a passion that was almost manic. The finish line flashed by all too soon. Then it was over and Casey, still high on adrenalin, was out of the saddle and hugging Roxy. Roxy's legs were trembling with effort, but her ears were pricked and she looked as if she was smiling.

'Did we do it?' Casey demanded as Kyle came rushing up and threw his arms around her. 'Did we crush Anna Sparks?'

Kyle grinned. 'I told you this blue jumper was lucky. You annihilated her, baby! Not only that but I think you might have won. *We* might have won – Team West. There are two riders who could still get past you, but I have it on good authority that neither is particularly strong on the cross-country phase.'

He was right. Team West had won the Intermediate class. An overjoyed Casey collected her prize to great cheers.

When she returned to the lorry, she found to her astonishment that it was the most popular in the park. The living area had been extended, the mini bar was open and music was blaring. Kyle was serving drinks to an ebullient crowd, most of whom were strangers to Casey. There were wolf-whistles and more cheers when she walked up. Michael Edge, a former Badminton champion, came over to tell her how well she'd ridden. Lots of people asked for her autograph.

The phone rang constantly. First it was her dad, who she'd texted to report that she'd won. 'Casey, I'm so proud. I can't talk long because I'm in Italy – back tomorrow … but what is this about you changing coaches? How could you possibly break it off with Mrs Smith?'

Annoyed that he immediately jumped to the conclusion that it was she who had done the leaving, Casey pretended she couldn't hear him and told him she'd call back when she had a chance.

Ed Lashley-Jones called next. 'Casey, you little beauty. I knew you had it in you. I wanted to remind you that you're obligated to mention Equi-Flow if you speak to any journalists. I don't want to put words in your mouth, but if you could say something to the effect of, "My Equi-Flow lorry, the best on the market, played a big part in my success today," I'd be most grateful.'

'Mr Lashley-Jones—' began Casey.

'It's Ed to you, Casey Blue. I also wanted to give you a nudge about looking in your diary to check your availability for a paintball contest and a polo outing. I did email but haven't heard back. As per your contract, we have a string of corporate days coming up. You'll be expected to entertain our clients, give lessons and pass on tips. Motivational speaking is what we want.'

Next it was Jackson Ryder from *New Equestrian* magazine. 'Congratulations, Casey. That's quite a turnaround from your performance on Lady Roxanne at Salperton Park. Has changing teachers had anything to do with it?'

Kyle came over with a glass of champagne. Casey almost never touched alcohol but she took it from him gratefully. A few sips of fizz and she felt invincible.

'Has changing teachers affected my performance? Absolutely. Kyle is a magician. For us to achieve what we have in a matter of weeks is phenomenal.'

'Best decision you ever made,' Kyle whispered in her ear.

'Best decision I ever made,' Casey told Jackson Ryder laughingly. As soon as the words left her mouth she wished she could take them back. After all Mrs Smith had done for her, how could she say such a thing? It was as if fame was going to her head just like the champagne.

'So you fancy your chances at the Burghley Horse Trials in two months' time?' Jackson Ryder asked.

Casey wanted to tell him not to print her previous

comment, but Kyle was so close she could almost feel his body heat and she didn't want to offend him. 'Burghley? I'm feeling great about it. Storm Warning is back in training. Provided he stays fit, we'll be going for the Grand Slam with everything we've got.'

'You'll have heard by now that Anna Sparks' ban has been overturned on appeal,' Jackson pressed. 'Any comment?'

Casey opened her mouth to start ranting but decided against it. Better to be gracious. 'None.' She clicked off the phone before he could ask any more awkward questions about Mrs Smith.

Kyle was smiling.

'Reporters. They're the same the world over. Have a drink, Casey. Enjoy yourself. You deserve it. You wiped the floor with Anna Sparks. You're a much better rider than she could ever be. Burghley, here we come.'

'Thanks, Kyle.' Casey raised her glass and smiled back. 'I could get used to this – the high life.'

Kyle let out a groan. 'Trust her to rain on our parade.'

The partying folk spilling out of the lorry had all stopped in mid-sentence, drink or gesture. They were riveted by a lonely figure walking dispiritedly across the busy lorry park. She was wearing a white polo-shirt with a grass strain on the back and leading a skewbald gelding.

Casey was puzzled. 'Who is she? Why is everyone staring?'

Kyle was incredulous. 'You don't recognise her? That's Anna Sparks, your old rival.'

Casey gave a snort of laughter. 'You're joking?'

'She got what was coming to her. She treated everyone like dirt on the way up and now she's having to eat it on the way down.'

As the girl drew nearer, Casey saw that it was indeed Anna Sparks. She'd piled on weight. Her heart-shaped face was puffy. She was still pretty and smartly dressed but she was not the ravishing beauty she had been when she ruled the circuit as one of the finest young riders in the world.

Her skewbald was fit and lean and had a quality look about him, but he hardly compared to her previous horse, Rough Diamond. He was caked in mud and rather poorly turned out. Despite this, his head was up and he looked quite pleased with himself.

'Seems as if a large part of Ms Sparks' success was her daddy's millions,' said Marsha, appearing at Casey's side with a beer. 'Now that they're not speaking and she doesn't have the best horses money can buy and an entourage to take care of them, she's discovering that eventing isn't quite so easy. Today she started last and finished last.'

Anna's pale gold hair, once a cascading mane, had been cut shoulder-length. Her fringe fell messily across her face. As she passed the lorry, she lifted a hand in a small wave. Nobody waved back, although a few people giggled and one of the riders shouted: 'It's the great Anna Sparks! Quick, somebody call the RSPCA.'

'Don't worry, it looks as if she's off the diet pills,'

Marsha said in a loud voice. 'That means there'll be no outbreaks of violence. Not today, at any rate.'

Everyone laughed, including Kyle. Casey was about to join in when Anna glanced up and their eyes met. Anna was the first to drop her gaze. She hurried away, pulling her painted horse behind her.

'The funniest part,' said Casey when she talked to Peter on the phone later, 'was when she went over to this funny little horsebox. It was so unglamorous and out of character. We all laughed till we cried. Do you remember when she used to have that huge luxury lorry that was the same make as Andrew Nicholson's? How the mighty have fallen.'

There was silence on the other end of the line.

'Are you still there?' asked Casey. 'Peter? Hello?'

'I'm here.'

'What do you think? Isn't it hilarious?'

'Do I think it's hilarious that a girl who is plainly suffering is turned into a laughing stock? No, frankly, I don't. Can you not see that what you did to Anna Sparks this evening was an exact replay of what she did to you at Brigstock two and a half years ago when she made fun of you and Storm and the donkey van you travelled in?'

'No,' Casey said coldly. 'I can't. That's different.'

'In what way is it different?'

'It just is. Whose side are you on, anyway? You haven't even congratulated me. We won, Peter. You're supposed to be happy.'

13

BARBARA MACCLESFIELD, HEAD nurse at the Primrose Valley Hospice, followed Mrs Smith into room 312 and watched as her newest resident deposited her meagre luggage on top of the chest of drawers. If you could call it luggage. Not counting an ethnic rucksack that doubled as her handbag, Angelica Smith's worldly possessions consisted of one large carpetbag, Kashmiri in origin, which had faded over time. She looked as if she'd recently disembarked from a ship originating in the Far East. Her clothes were equally exotic. In spite of the summer heat, she was wearing, over her Indian cotton dress, a coat that made her look as if she was auditioning for a role in *Joseph and the Amazing Technicolor Dreamcoat*.

'It's from Tibet,' explained Mrs Smith. 'I went there with my father as a teenager. Divine place.'

Beneath the window was a bed covered with a white sheet, pink blanket and pink candlewick cover, all made with military neatness. The remainder of the cramped room was taken up by a chest of drawers, a cupboard, a chair and a pale blue rug to match the walls. A television with an extending arm was bolted to the wall.

The only personal touch was a freshly picked daisy sitting in a glass on the chest of drawers. A pair of disposable white slippers, still in cellophane, sat on the mat beside the bed.

'You're an economical packer, I must say,' remarked Nurse Macclesfield. 'Most people bring everything but the kitchen sink when they come here – grandfather clocks, cats and enough books to fill the British Library.'

Mrs Smith smiled. 'This is it. Didn't think I'd need anything else.'

The nurse gestured towards a painting of a ship battling a gale in a tumultuous green ocean. Just looking at it made Mrs Smith feel seasick. 'Knocking nails into the wall is not permitted, but if you'd like to take down that picture and replace it with one of your own, feel free.'

Mrs Smith opened her carpetbag and lifted out a photograph of Casey. When choosing which to bring, she could have selected any number of shots of Casey soaring over fences, doing dressage, or kissing the Badminton trophy. But the one she loved most was a black and white one taken about a year after Mrs Smith had started working with her. Storm was still on the thin side and lacking in muscle tone, and Casey's collar was sticking up and her hair awry but, to Mrs Smith, they were beautiful in their innocence.

The photograph had been taken by Peter in the days when he and Casey were only friends, but the feelings he had for her were evident in the framing of the image. He'd captured horse and girl leaning together, forehead to forehead. Unaware that she was being photographed, Casey had her arms around Storm's neck and her eyes closed.

It was a picture of love, taken with love.

Whenever Mrs Smith glanced at it she was struck by how impossibly young Casey looked. Placing it on the bedside table, she wondered for the thousandth time whether it had been a mistake to agree to teach a naive young girl how to compete with the best in such a high-risk sport. Perhaps it had all been too much, too soon.

'What a wonderful photo,' cried Nurse Macclesfield. 'Is that your granddaughter?'

'No, that's Casey. She's my best friend. The horse's name is Storm Warning. He and Casey were the youngest ever Badminton champions.'

'I do enjoy a game of badminton,' said the nurse, misunderstanding. She'd never heard of eventing and would not have known a Derby winner from a Clydesdale. 'I'm not much good at ball sports on the whole, but I find that shuttlecocks are more visible and travel slower. Not at the Olympics, of course, but generally.'

She tailed off. 'You must have led a terribly exciting life.'

Mrs Smith looked away. 'Casey and Storm were my life.'

'Will she be coming to see you – your friend?'

'She doesn't know I'm here. I didn't want to worry her. She's busy, you see. She has Burghley coming up and the pressure is immense.'

Nurse Macclesfield pursed her lips. 'I understand. They're all busy nowadays, the young ones. However, I'm sure she'd want to know that this is where you'll be, you know, from now on. I can set you up on email and you can get in touch.'

'No!' said Mrs Smith with a finality that brooked no discussion.

Not wanting to upset a resident on her first day, Nurse Macclesfield said anxiously: 'I do hope you like it here. We'll do our best to take care of you.'

Suddenly weary, Mrs Smith sank down on the chair. It seemed a shame to disturb the crease-free bed. 'Are all of the patients at Primrose—?'

'We prefer to call you residents,' interjected the nurse.

'Residents – is this really where they come to die? Do people simply sit around waiting for the curtain to descend on their lives?'

'I wouldn't put it in quite that way. We'll do our best to help you to continue to enjoy life for as long as you

140

can. How long that is, varies so much from individual to individual. Every now and then, we see a miracle and it's lovely when it happens, but it's best to be prepared. For some people, sadly, there really is no hope.'

'There's always hope – if not in body, then in spirit,' Mrs Smith said with feeling.

Nurse Macclesfield perked up. 'Of course there is. That's our philosophy too. For that reason, we have a full programme of activities. There is ballroom dancing, bridge, Pilates, chess and the perennially popular knitting club. I know it might not feel that way right now, but you still have a lot to live for.'

As the door shut behind her, Mrs Smith shuddered.

Somehow she survived a glutinous dinner and a screening of *It's a Wonderful Life*, followed, next morning, by a breakfast of watery scrambled eggs and tinned mushrooms. But by 10.38 a.m., she was climbing the walls. So far she'd turned down an early morning Pilates class, two card games and an invitation to knit a Highland terrier.

For people who are supposed to be on their last legs, these Primrose Valley residents have way too much energy, Mrs Smith thought uncharitably.

Temporarily freed from the pain that had crippled her, she found her restless mind returning constantly to

141

Storm and Casey. Casey, she knew, had already moved on. Mrs Smith detested technology and could barely operate a mobile phone, but the guilt she felt at abandoning Casey and jeopardising her career had driven her to an internet café. With assistance, she'd managed to access *New Equestrian* magazine's online site. What she read had devastated her.

When Mrs Smith looked up Casey's results, she'd hoped to find that her former pupil was doing reasonably well. Discovering that Casey had cruised to victory on Roxy barely a month after Mrs Smith left her was a blow. But the killing part had been Casey's words. It was bad enough that she attributed her success to the arrogant Kyle West and described him as a 'magician'. But then she added insult to injury by saying it was the 'best thing I have ever done'.

The agony Mrs Smith experienced as she digested the implication that she'd been a negative force in Casey's life was worse than anything the cancer had thrown at her.

And it was cancer. That much had been confirmed by the oncologist, Andrew Mutandwa, when she'd walked into his office the day after walking out on Casey.

'*Why?*' he kept asking her, near apoplectic with distress over her new test results. 'Why did you do it, Angelica?'

She shrugged. 'I had no choice.'

'Everybody has a choice. What I fail to understand is why yours was not your own health but mad, neck-breaking horse competitions. If you'd allowed us to start chemotherapy or radiotherapy five months ago, we would be looking at a very different outcome. I'm not saying that we'd have been able to save you. But with the right treatment we could have extended your life by years. Now you have months.'

'How many months?' Mrs Smith asked calmly. He wasn't telling her anything that she didn't expect to hear.

Mr Mutandwa looked more ill than she did. Originally from Zambia, he found these types of conversations almost more distressing than his patients did. Before answering, he retreated behind his desk and drew comfort from the wood-framed photo of his wife and children.

'I can't sugarcoat this for you, Angelica. You don't have much time. It is not an exact science and I don't like to put a number on it, but if I were you I would start saying goodbye to my loved ones.'

Mrs Smith emerged from the hospital feeling curiously relieved. For months she'd been unable to give a name to the monster destroying her from within. Now she could. Not only that but she had a shopping bag full of pills designed to eliminate the worst of the pain. All her life, Mrs Smith had spurned conventional medicine in favour of alternative treatments. Overnight that had changed. Now as she swallowed the tablets that stopped the spasms that sometimes ripped through her body with hurricane force, she felt that no amount of gold could compensate the sainted humans who made painkillers.

'By refusing to acknowledge my letters and face up to the truth about your disease sooner, you've effectively launched a grenade in your abdomen,' the specialist had bluntly informed her. 'Now you're going to have to endure the consequences.'

Mrs Smith had decided that she didn't like Mr Mutandwa after all. A little sugarcoating never hurt anyone.

Sitting on the fluffy bedcover at Primrose Valley, she paged through her red notebook. She had five such notebooks. They contained every detail of Casey's training schedule going back to the first morning at Hope Lane Riding Centre, when Storm was still a bag of bones and Casey a gawky fifteen-year-old in stretched breeches.

Mrs Smith opened the red notebook to a fresh page. During the night she'd had a flash of inspiration. For some time now she'd been very much on the side of those who believed that the removal of the steeplechase and roads and tracks sections at CCI****four-star events had unintended consequences for the horses' performance. The long format was too long but the short format was too short. Unable to sleep, Mrs Smith had come up with a way to redress the balance. Feeling more alive than she had in weeks, she urgently jotted down key points.

Mid-sentence, her pen paused.

'What are you doing, Angelica?' she asked herself. 'Casey no longer has any use for you or your eccentric ideas. You're a sad old fool. Read a book or take up knitting. Forget eventing. It's history.'

In the corridor outside her room, there was a squeak of wheels. Mrs Smith had been at the hospice less than twenty-four hours but already she was familiar with the sound of her neighbour's oxygen trolley. There was a timid knock at the door.

Mrs Smith set aside the notebook. If her room hadn't been on the second floor, she would have hopped out of the window and made a run for it.

'How about joining us for a 3 p.m. game of Monopoly?' rasped Irma Irving, trailing more tubes than an octopus.

Mrs Smith hesitated but it wasn't as if she had anything better to do. Board games were her new Badminton. 'Love to,' she said. 'Thanks for asking.'

14

O N   A   H O T   summer's night in Gloucestershire, Casey sat on a garden bench watching fireworks scream into the starry sky and explode in a dazzle of scarlet. The man paying for both the party and the light show was Casper Leyton, multimillionaire owner of one of the biggest eventing studs in the United Kingdom. His daughter was a protégé of Kyle's and it was through Kyle that Casey had received an invitation. She'd jumped at the chance to go. Leyton's parties were legendary.

'You lucky thing,' cried Marsha, Sam Tide's groom, when Casey told her. 'Last year I spent so much time begging Sam to take me that in the end he agreed to pretend I was his date. I saw three Hollywood stars, half a dozen top riders letting their hair down, that delicious boy who won *The X Factor*, two Olympic rowers and a Russian gymnast. I could have died of happiness.'

The smoke from the fireworks mingled with smoke from the barbecue and swirled around the beautiful people dancing and chatting on the terrace. Stone steps led down to a heated swimming pool. Already that evening a couple of bikini-clad starlets had leapt into the water. The barbecue had been set up on a raised deck at the rear of the pool. There were platters of lobsters and langoustines, a hog on a spit and every kind of salad, vegetable dish and dessert imaginable. An ice sculpture of a unicorn, melting in the heat, regarded the scene imperiously.

Before Casey had won Badminton, she'd always wondered what it would be like to be part of the elite echelon of riders who were invited to the best parties and events. Their lives seemed impossibly glamorous. Now she was among them. Not that many of them knew who she was. A couple of people had congratulated her on her success and a drunk had offered her an obscene amount of money to part with Storm, but most guests looked past her or through her. The women were universally thin, tanned and coiffed. The men radiated power and assurance. Their Rolex watches winked in the lights. One lady, assuming Casey was a waitress, had asked her to fetch a drink.

Kyle had barely spoken to her since they arrived. Each time she spotted him, he was with a different girl and they were all stunning. 'Don't get any ideas about fancying Kyle,' Hannah had warned her. 'You'll only get hurt. Girls are all over him all the time and he's very polite and charming to them, but they make the mistake of thinking he's interested in them. Take it from me, they're dead wrong.'

Casey had laughed off this speech, putting it down to Hannah's fairly obvious crush on Kyle, but now she wasn't so sure. From this angle, it looked a lot like flirting.

She did her best to convince herself that it didn't bother her. Their relationship was purely business. Strictly speaking, they weren't even friends. She didn't want to think about the chemistry that had swirled around his sports car as he drove her to the party earlier, or the feeling she'd got when he put the top down and the wind blew through his hair.

All in all it had been a week that would have once been beyond her wildest fantasies. Thanks to Equi-Flow, she'd been invited to spend a day watching the Duke of Essex Polo Grand Prix in Hylands Park and enjoying a gourmet picnic. Ed Lashley-Jones had been cock-a-hoop about her weekend victory and had introduced her to lots of stylish aristocrats and celebrities, not one of whom she recognised. They didn't recognise her either, but such was Ed's enthusiasm that they dutifully fawned over her and bared sparkling white teeth.

The problem had come when Casey refused to agree to give a course of riding lessons to Candi's whiney teenage son.

'I'm sorry,' she said. 'I would if I could, but I'm in the midst of preparing for the Burghley Horse Trials and I'm working flat out. It's crucial that I focus.'

'But you have time to attend parties,' Lashley-Jones said pointedly. 'Might I remind you, Casey, that sponsorship is not all take, take, take. You have to give back some time, otherwise our shareholders will start to ask questions about why we're investing in you.'

He'd apologised later, but Casey was unnerved. Mrs Smith had been right. Ed and his cronies were parasites.

Watching a rocket curve into the night sky and burst into pink stars, she wondered what Peter was doing. Was he missing her as much as she missed him? Or was the Irish girl on his course, the one he'd described as 'so pretty that nobody could believe it when Orla also turned out to be a wickedly good farrier,' keeping him company?

But no, Peter wasn't like that. She'd trust him with her life. He loved her. With Peter she'd never once felt inadequate, the way she did now. Quite the reverse. He always, always made her feel good about herself.

Well, mostly. She hadn't felt good since he'd had a go at her over Anna Sparks. Quite why he'd stuck up for Anna, Casey couldn't fathom. Ms Sparks had treated him appallingly in the days when he used to shoe Rough Diamond and her other horses. But then that was one of the things Casey loved about Peter. He always looked for the best in people.

That said, he would not have enjoyed this party. It

wasn't his scene at all. Peter was the grandson of a Welsh sheep farmer and he was resolutely down to earth. If he'd been here now, he'd be wanting to leave. 'What's happening to you, Casey?' she could hear him saying. 'These are the kind of people you used to despise.'

'Enjoying yourself?'

Kyle loomed out of the darkness and flopped down beside her. He was wearing an open-necked white shirt, black trousers and Italian shoes. By some distance, he was the most gorgeous guy at the party. Casey inched away surreptitiously. The closer he came to her, the faster her heart skipped.

'I'm having a fabulous time,' said Casey in a bid to convince herself that she was doing just that. 'How about you? You seem to be flavour of the month.'

Kyle leaned forward, his tanned forearms resting on his thighs. His gaze was on the increasing revelry at the swimming pool.

'Is that what I am – flavour of the month? What happens when it's someone else's turn?' He said it lightly but there was a bitter note in his tone.

'Sorry. It was a flippant thing to say and not what I meant at all.'

'No, it's true. One slip-up and all this could be snatched away.'

He straightened and put an arm along the back of the bench. Casey's skin tingled as his hand brushed her shoulder. His face looked boyish and vulnerable in the moonlight. 'Ever get imposter syndrome, Casey?'

'If you're asking do I ever worry that someone is going to tap me on the shoulder one day and tell me that there's been a giant mistake – girls like me don't become eventing stars – then the answer is yes. All the time. I look at riders like Mary King and think I must be delusional to imagine I might ever be in their league. Competing at this level was my dream, but now that I'm here I worry that I don't deserve it.'

A firework popped and crackled, scrawling champagne-coloured graffiti across the night sky.

'Yes, you do,' Kyle assured her, 'and you have the results to prove it. I can relate to how you feel though. Sometimes I wake up in a cold sweat, convinced that my pupils will realise that there are other, better coaches and one by one they'll leave me.'

Casey laughed. 'I think we should both agree that we are where we're meant to be and enjoy it while it lasts. Anyway, you've convinced me that you're going to help me and Storm win the Grand Slam. They'll have to give you the Golden Horseshoe Award after that.'

He grinned and the arrogance returned to his body language as if he were donning a cloak. 'They will. Hey, don't pay any attention to me. I'm having a moment, that's all. Happens sometimes. Wanna get out of here?'

151

Two days later, Casey moved Storm to Rycliffe Manor for a week of intensive work. At White Oaks she'd been doing interval training with him and had been astounded at how rapidly her big silver horse shed pounds and regained his fitness.

Even Morag was impressed. 'I guess it's something to do with muscle memory. You've done so much work with him over the past year that I suppose six weeks off is nothing to a horse like him. His champion genes were simply lying dormant, waiting for a chance to burst forth.'

As much as she tried to talk herself out of it, Casey had reservations about taking Storm to Rycliffe Manor. It was a breathtakingly lovely estate and the facilities were second to none, but the incident with the dogs had tainted the place for her. Whenever she thought about the cross-country course, the dogs came bursting into her imagination and pounced on Storm, fangs bared.

But move to Rycliffe Manor she did, because Kyle was her teacher and he and the estate came as a package. She was also keen to get working with Storm because it would take her mind off Roxy. A week after the Westwood Classic, Jennifer Stewart had rung to say that she'd sold the mare and would be coming to pick her up the following morning. Casey had been gutted. She'd come to adore Roxy and had convinced herself that Jennifer would realise that she, Storm and Roxy belonged together. Parting them would be cruel.

Sadly, like many people who viewed horses as

investments rather than intelligent, feeling beings, Jennifer never let sentiment get in the way of a good deal.

'But we've bonded,' Casey told her, as she led Jennifer to Roxy's stable and demonstrated the transformation in the mare. 'Look how gentle and amazing she is. She's a pleasure to work with. When she arrived here, she was a biting, kicking menace. She tried to crush me against the wall when I attempted to saddle her. Now look at her.'

She gave Roxy a couple of Polos. 'She's only just settled in and found her feet. It seems such a shame to move her. Besides, she's besotted with my horse, Storm. They're like two lovebirds. Give me another couple of months and I'll try to find some more money and give you a better price for her.'

Jennifer, who'd come straight from the office and was wearing a power suit in grey and cream, ran an appraising hand over Roxy's shining bay coat. She gave her a slap on the rump that made the mare jump with fright.

'I hear what you're saying but I can't do it, Casey. I have a buyer in hand and that's worth two in the bush. But I do agree that she's improved beyond all recognition. That Kyle West is a wonder. I don't know how he's transformed her in such a short time. Please thank him when you see him.'

Irritated that Jennifer had immediately leapt to the conclusion that the change in Roxy was down to

Kyle's influence, Casey made a big show of cuddling Roxy and kissing her goodbye after loading her in the horsebox.

'She's always been an odd one, Lady Roxanne,' said Jennifer as they lifted the ramp and bolted it shut. 'That's what I told the journalist who called, doing an article on you. I said Roxy's character had been affected by what happened at the home of the people who bred her. They had these great big dogs. I'm not sure what breed they were, but something scary. Unbeknown to their owners, these mutts had dug a hole under the fence and would routinely go into the paddock where the yearlings were kept and terrorise Roxy.

'Apparently, the family had a teenage son who didn't like horses who found this funny. He used to sit on the fence and laugh. The parents went berserk when they found out. Roxy was sold twice before I bought her as an investment horse. At that stage, I was ignorant of her background and had great hopes for her, but her problems soon became too much for me. I have a demanding job and didn't have time to deal with her. I was in a quandary as to what to do when I read that you were looking for a ride while Storm Warning was resting. I'm glad it worked out so well.'

Absorbed in her story, she didn't notice that Casey had stopped listening. Vicious dogs had terrorised Roxy as a yearling and it was vicious dogs that had triggered the chain of events that had led to her transformation. If it was a coincidence, it was a striking one.

'Who was the journalist?' Casey asked casually. 'Which publication were they from?'

Jennifer Stewart jingled her car keys. 'Do you know, I'm not sure. *Horse and Hound*, I think, but I may be mistaken. It was weeks ago now.'

It was a warm day but Casey was suddenly freezing. She tried to remember the timeline – what had happened when. 'Before I won the Westwood Classic?'

'Oh, well before. I don't recall the woman's name either. She did tell me but I've forgotten.'

She drove away with Roxy neighing desperately, bewildered that she was being wrenched from Casey and Storm, her new best friends. Casey didn't stop crying for an hour.

Lonely in the guest room at Rycliffe Manor that night, she tried calling Peter. She needed to reconnect to him. He might have been only a few hundred miles away in Ireland, but it felt as if he was on the moon.

Peter would tell her that she was letting her imagination run away with her. He didn't like Kyle, but he was man enough to put that aside and reassure her that she was doing the right thing bringing Storm to Rycliffe Manor. That, of course, people didn't go around engineering dog attacks as a training method. That nobody would do that unless they were psychotic.

The phone was answered on the second ring not by her boyfriend but by a girl with a huskily sexy voice and an Irish accent.

Casey was thrown. 'Umm, I think I might have dialled the wrong number. I'm trying to reach Peter Rhys.'

The girl said breathily: 'This is Peter's phone. He forgot to take it with him when he went out. Who may I say called?'

'My name's Casey.' Then she added for good measure, 'His girlfriend.'

There was a giggle. 'His *girlfriend*? Oh, how sweet. He hasn't mentioned you. I'm Orla, by the way. We're doing Alejandro Hall's course together.'

Casey digested the information that, after a month in Ireland, Peter hadn't told the prettiest girl on his course that he was in a relationship.

'Peter will be back soon,' the husky voice was saying. 'He's only nipped out to get us a pizza.'

Us?

'Everyone else went off to the pub, but he and I felt like a quiet night in. I'll tell him that you rang.'

Casey switched off her phone and for a brief, angry moment wondered why it was that she was trying so hard to resist Kyle when her boyfriend was getting cosy with Orla.

15

*H*ELP ME, CASEY! *Help me!*

Casey sat bolt upright in her bed at Rycliffe Manor Equestrian Centre. She'd forgotten to shut the window and the room was like the Arctic but she was bathed in sweat. It wasn't a dream, she was sure of it. She'd heard Mrs Smith call out to her as clearly as if she'd been standing before her.

With shaking hands she dialled Mrs Smith's number. Mrs Smith rarely, if ever, answered her phone, and would never dream of doing so at 2.45 a.m., but if she was as desperate as she sounded perhaps she would. Her hopes were dashed when it went straight to voicemail.

Casey debated whether to call her dad, who was back from Italy, but decided against it. If she rang him in the dead of night and said she was hearing voices, he'd think she'd lost her mind. Better to at least wait until he'd had breakfast.

She lay back down and did her best to convince herself that the voice had been a product of her own guilty conscience. She was haunted by the way it had ended with Mrs Smith, haunted by not knowing what had become of her. Mrs Smith had never done anything that was expected of her and could at this moment be at a yoga retreat on a mountaintop in Kerala, but again and again Casey returned to the worst-case scenario – Mrs Smith desperately ill and alone.

Her alarm rang, blasting the thought from her tired mind. In an effort to increase her riding experience, Kyle had entered her in the Aston-le-Walls Horse Trials in Northamptonshire. She'd be riding a big black bruiser of a horse called Assassin's Code. Casey had set her alarm for 3 a.m., even though she wasn't actually required to do anything. Rycliffe Manor's star clients were not required to do any pre-event grooming. All plaiting and preparation would be done for her by a groom and Assassin would be boxed and ready to leave at 5 a.m. sharp.

Casey had at first been so taken by the novelty of not having to get up at the usual unearthly hour that she'd agreed – albeit with a twinge of conscience. Mrs Smith was a firm believer that the pre-show routine was an essential part of the rider-horse bonding experience. Now she was glad she'd changed her mind. It meant that she could do an hour's lateral work with Storm and ensure that he was settled and happy before she left him for the day. It would also take her mind off the question of Mrs Smith until she could ring her dad. She planned to ask him if the Hackney grapevine had any news of Mrs Smith's whereabouts.

'Well, this is very upsetting,' said Roland Blue, who was making scrambled eggs when she rang him from a motorway service station en route to Northamptonshire. 'It's bad enough that the two of you have parted company and you know my feelings on *that* subject. But I didn't know you weren't in contact.'

'Don't give me a hard time, Dad. I feel awful enough as it is. Can you please just do me a favour and try to find out where she is? I'm worried about her.'

Pans clanged in the background. 'I'll see what I can find out, Pumpkin, but it's concerning that she's simply vanished. As a matter of fact, I was going to text you to ask for her new contact details. The other day I passed her old flat and there was a For Sale sign out the front. What happened between the two of you, anyway? I thought you were the best of friends.'

There was a knot of fear in Casey's gut. Where was Mrs Smith? Somehow Casey had convinced herself that she was back living in her Victorian apartment in London's East End, feeding strays and drinking chai at the Tea Garden the way she had when Casey met her. 'We were friends. We *are*. Dad, I have to go. We're on our way to Aston-le-Walls and everyone's waiting for me.'

'Sorry,' she said to Kyle as she clambered into the lorry. 'I needed to speak to my dad about something.'

When Kyle had first suggested that he travel to and from the event with her, Casey had been thrilled at the thought of having company in the big lorry. But so far that morning he'd hardly said a word. He'd been sweet to her when he did speak but for the most part he seemed moody and distracted.

Now he frowned. 'Your dad? Do you get on with him?'

Casey was surprised that he was surprised. 'I adore my dad. He's all the family I have in the world. Well, apart from Mrs Smith, but she—' She broke off. She didn't want to go there.

Kyle didn't appear to notice. 'Can I ask you a personal question?'

'Depends.'

'You don't have to answer if you don't want to. Your father – he's a convicted burglar, right?'

Casey tensed. 'Yes, he is. But he did his time and now he's a successful tailor.'

'Do you mind if I ask what he did?'

Casey took a deep breath. She rarely talked about it and it never got any easier when she did.

'About five years ago, he fell in with a dodgy crowd. They convinced him to join them on a job to rob a multimillionaire. We were battling to make ends meet and it wasn't hard for them to persuade Dad that this man would hardly miss a few thousand. But on the night of the robbery, everything went horribly wrong. The owner of the house woke up and ended up attacking Dad with a poker. The police came just as Dad knocked the man out with a lamp in an attempt to defend himself. His so-called mates escaped scot free. Dad got eight months. Volunteering at a local riding school and my friendship with Mrs Smith were about the only things that got me through it.'

Kyle was watching her intently. 'And you forgave him?'

Casey wondered where this was going. 'He's human. People make mistakes and he paid for his. I was angry with him for a long time, especially when the tabloids got wind of what he'd done and it was all over the papers. But eventually I forgave him. He's tried so hard to rebuild his life and make it up to me. Added to which, he helped me rescue Storm from the knacker's yard. I'll always love him for that.'

Kyle opened his window and let a blast of cold motorway air into the lorry's cab. 'You're amazing, Casey Blue. I could never be like you. If I found out that my father had committed a crime, I could never forgive him. It's not that I'd cut him off or anything. I'd stay in touch with him or even stay with him. But the horror of what he'd done, the ruined lives, would stay with me till my dying day.'

It was not the most cheerful conversation Casey had ever had and she was relieved when Kyle excused himself not long after they arrived at Washbrook Farm and went off to see another client. She was making herself the first of many cappuccinos and reading the names on the start sheet when she heard a muffled sob.

Outside, she saw nobody in distress. It was a blustery blue day, perfect for riding, and the lorry park was already packed with immaculately turned out horses and riders and grooms in various states of anxiety or excitement. Casey was about to return to her cappuccino when she heard the sound again.

The lorry beside hers was temporarily deserted. Walking round to the other side, she was startled to see Anna Sparks in tears. The reason was obvious. Her skewbald's plaits were sticking out in all directions. He looked like a pony punk rocker.

When Anna glanced up to find Casey watching her, she was mortified. Recovering, she wiped her eyes roughly and glared. 'Enjoying yourself? Bet you are. What could be more entertaining than watching Anna Sparks finally getting her comeuppance? She's so used to having an entourage that she can't even plait a mane. Well, Casey Blue, it's your lucky day. You're about to see something even more amusing. Very shortly I'll be disqualified as a no-show because I have no hope of being ready for the dressage. The person who'd promised to help me hasn't shown up. Happy now?'

'Don't be ridiculous,' said Casey, striding over and

162

taking the elastics and thread from Anna's unresisting hands. 'If I wanted to make you suffer all I'd have to do is ride better than you. Now shove over and let me redo your plaits. You're going about it all wrong. Watch and learn. Mrs Smith taught me and she's a genius at it. She's also a perfectionist. When I first attempted to plait Storm's mane, she made me redo it about eighty times. In the end my hands were so sore I could barely hold the reins.'

She undid the botched plaits, combed out the horse's mane and started again. 'What's his name?' she asked more kindly.

'Chocolate.'

'You're kidding?' Casey caught herself mid-giggle and told herself off. Anna was an evil wicked girl who'd injured Storm and gone out of her way to mock and deride Casey. She was not to be trusted.

'If I'm going to do this for you, I've got to concentrate,' she said huffily. 'Why don't you go and do some stretches or something? Mrs Smith always says that it's as important for the rider to be warmed up as it is for the horse.'

If, an hour earlier, someone had told her that she'd be plaiting the mane of her sworn enemy's horse and offering her advice, Casey would have fallen on the floor laughing. She'd have said that she'd rather walk barefoot on hot coals. But faced with Anna's distress she found herself incapable of hating her. Odder still, she felt a perverse pride when Anna posted a good dressage result, despite having only had five minutes to warm up.

Kyle was not pleased that Casey almost made herself late for the dressage in the process.

'Where were you?' he demanded. 'I came looking for you and you'd disappeared. I'll be very annoyed if Assassin performs poorly in the dressage. It's his best discipline. What were you doing?'

'I'm sorry,' said Casey, reluctant to admit to helping Anna. 'I got talking to someone and lost track of time.'

Fortunately, she performed well in the dressage, finishing a couple of places ahead of her old rival. The show jumping was less of a success. Assassin had a habit of accelerating after every jump. He'd fling up his head and almost bash Casey in the nose, making it difficult for her to keep him on line. Impossible to slow, he completely misjudged the wall and ended up crashing through it.

'There were one or two good bits but on the whole it was a mess,' Kyle said when Casey exited the arena. 'Don't blame Assassin. It was your fault. With horses like him, the key is to work on problem areas in the collecting ring. When you ride circles, be disciplined about them. Don't drift. Ask him to lower his head and gradually you'll find that he takes the contact down, freeing up his back. Because he feels more secure, you'll find his canter much easier to ride.'

Casey was so relieved that Kyle was no longer upset with her for being late to warm-up for the dressage that she didn't like to point out it would have been helpful if

164

he'd told her that when she still had time to do something about it, and not after the event when she didn't.

She found Kyle's teaching good but inconsistent. It puzzled her that he could be lucid and insightful one minute and stubbornly blind the next. Take what happened in her lunch break, for instance. Casey was making them both cappuccinos in the back of the lorry and plotting how to improve her performance in the cross-country. She might have helped Anna Sparks – currently six places above her after only four faults in the show jumping – but she was fiercely determined to finish ahead of her.

'How would you feel about changing Assassin's bit?' Casey asked Kyle, who was sprawled on the lorry sofa in black breeches, Ariat boots and a white polo-shirt, looking impossibly attractive. His blond hair flopped over his face as he pored over *Eventing* magazine.

He didn't look up. 'Case, let's talk about this when we get home. I don't think it's a good plan to start changing things mid-event.'

'But what's your opinion? I have a feeling that his bit is making him unhappy and that's why he's pulling. He's desperate to escape it.'

Kyle tossed aside the magazine and took the mug of cappuccino from her. When she sat down beside him, he pushed his fringe from his blue eyes and gave her one of those looks that made her feel as if she'd developed a heart murmur. 'Did I ever tell you I think you're beautiful?'

'No, but I—'

'I know, I know. You have a boyfriend. Where is he? That's what I'm curious about. If you were mine, I'd never let you out of my sight.'

Casey jumped up and pretended to be looking for the sugar. She didn't want him asking probing questions about Peter, who still hadn't called her back. He knew she was competing at Aston-le-Walls and yet she'd not had so much as a text from him since leaving a message with the ravishing Orla. That was how Casey pictured the Irish girl: ravishing. She'd have silky dark tresses, a permanent tan and a stunning figure. Together with the seductive voice and Irish accent, she'd be hard to resist – especially on a quiet night in with a pizza.

'Peter's on a farrier's course in Ireland. With Alejandro Hall. He has to be away. He doesn't have a choice.'

'Everybody has a choice,' said Kyle. 'But don't worry. I'm not hitting on you. Well, maybe a little. Really, I just wanted you to know that I think you're very pretty. You're kind too, which is a lot more important.'

He glanced at his watch. 'Gosh, is that the time? I'm supposed to be meeting someone for a bite to eat. See you before the cross-country, Casey.'

It was only after he'd gone, leaving his untouched coffee cooling on the table, that Casey realised he'd evaded the conversation about the bit.

Without a change in tack the cross-country was, if anything, a more hair-raising experience than the show jumping. Assassin's owner was a farmer who had bigger biceps or more authority than Casey did. Either way, she was unable to do much more than steer as he flew around the course as if he was pursuing the leaders at the Grand National. By the end Casey was so drained that she was like a ragdoll in the saddle.

She had hoped that Kyle might be there at the finish, but he was nowhere in sight. 'Probably watching it on the monitors with some of the officials,' Assassin's groom consoled her. 'Easier to watch several riders at once.'

Casey had planned to help cool Assassin down, but the groom waved her away. 'Get yourself a cold drink. You look as if you need it.'

Casey found a stand selling milkshakes and sipped a strawberry one as she studied the scoreboard. There were still five or six riders to go, but barring a disaster she'd finish twenty-ninth. Anna Sparks was two places behind.

She was crossing the lorry park in search of Kyle when Anna came running up. 'Casey, wait. I don't know how to thank you. After the way I treated you, I wouldn't blame you if you hated me.'

Casey stopped. 'Let's get one thing straight. I did what I did for your horse, not for you. I wouldn't help you if you were the last girl in England.'

Anna's face fell. 'That's okay. I totally understand. If I were you, I'd feel the same way.'

'Great,' said Casey. 'At least we've cleared that up.' Then, as Anna continued to stand there, 'Look, no offence, but some things are hard to forget. See you around.'

Anna followed her. 'Casey, please. Let me say one thing. I'm sorry about Storm. You don't know how much. My father bought him without telling me, but that's no excuse. I knew that it would kill you to part with him and I went along with it anyway. I rode him and it was my fault that he was injured.'

Casey couldn't believe what she was hearing. For so long, she'd raged at Anna in her head. Never did she imagine that her arch-enemy would one day apologise to her in person or appear to show genuine remorse.

'I want to try to make it up to you and the only way I can think of is to warn you.'

'Warn me about what?'

'Whatever you do, don't let Storm go to Rycliffe Manor. Nothing is what it seems there, not even Kyle.'

Cold fury surged through Casey. She had to restrain herself from physically shaking the girl. 'Do you know that just for a moment you had me fooled? Idiot that I am, I was starting to believe that you'd changed. I guess I was wrong. You're the same stuck-up jealous liar you always were. Once a bitch, always a bitch.'

Anna went white. 'Casey, I'm not saying this to hurt you. I saw what they did to Mouse. He was never the same after he went there.'

Casey had a flash of déjà-vu. She was standing on

the stairwell at Rycliffe Manor listening to Kyle say accusingly to Ray: 'The way it worked with Mouse, you mean?' And Ray had responded: 'That wasn't my fault. The girl was out of control.'

'Casey, I'm not saying this out of jealousy. You have to believe me.'

Before Casey could think of a suitable retort, her phone buzzed in the pocket of her breeches. She snatched it out, hoping it was Peter. To her delight, Mrs Smith's number came up.

'You have no idea how happy I am to hear from you,' she cried joyfully.

But the voice on the line was not Mrs Smith's. 'Am I speaking to Casey Blue?'

A chill rippled through Casey. 'Yes, you are. Who is this?'

'Casey, my name is Barbara Macclesfield. I'm head nurse at the Primrose Valley Hospice in North London. I apologise for disturbing you – I understand you're very busy – but I wasn't sure who else to call. Angelica Smith has no next of kin and she said ... well, she described you as her best friend.'

'She ... she did?'

'I'm afraid I have bad news. Mrs Smith is gravely ill. She collapsed last night and is not responding to treatment.'

'What treatment?'

'For cancer. You do know she has cancer?'

The lorry park blurred before Casey's eyes. Dimly,

she was aware of Anna rushing forward to put an arm around her.

She said faintly: 'I'm in Northamptonshire but I'll be on my way as soon as I can find someone to drive me to a train station. Is she in hospital?'

'Sadly, it's much too late for that. I'm sorry to be blunt, Casey, but if you're going to come, it needs to be now. Angelica is dying.'

The phone fell from Casey's hand. She collapsed on the ground, sobbing uncontrollably.

Suddenly Kyle was there, lifting her into his arms. 'Get away from her,' he yelled at Anna. 'Haven't you caused enough damage? Casey, sweetheart, what's wrong? Sorry I couldn't get here any quicker, but don't worry. I'm here for you now.'

16

THE FIGURE LYING motionless beneath a pink duvet at the Primrose Valley Hospice was paper-white and birdlike, unrecognisable as the charismatic teacher who'd taken a penniless teenager and a knacker's yard horse and made them champions. She was hooked up to a drip and heavily sedated. On the bedside table was a black and white photograph of Casey and Storm.

At the sight of it Casey almost burst into tears, but she knew she had to stay strong for Mrs Smith's sake. 'How long has she been here?'

Nurse Macclesfield was rarely surprised by anything, but the slender, athletic girl regarding her with serious, storm-grey eyes was unlike any other teenager she'd come across. She had been brought to the hospice by a startlingly beautiful boy wearing black breeches and fabulous boots. As thrilling as it was to have a character who looked as if he'd stepped straight from the pages of a Jane Austen novel cross her path, Nurse Macclesfield had been thankful when Casey had sent him on his way with barely a backward glance. Several of the residents had weak hearts.

'Ten days,' she told Casey. 'Angelica has been with us for around ten days. At first she made an effort to join the other residents in card games and Pilates, but she became increasingly restless. She seemed obsessed with visiting book shops and libraries. I worried that she might be overdoing it, but she didn't want advice. There was nothing I could do. Primrose Valley is not a prison. Residents can come and go as they please, unless they have dementia or Alzheimer's. But in the case of someone like Angelica, how they choose to spend their last days is up to them.'

Casey looked up sharply. 'You mean, their last years?'

'No, I don't. We care for the terminally ill in the final stages of life. In most cases, that means months or weeks.'

Casey stared at her, not understanding. 'Are you saying that when Mrs Smith came here, she already knew she was dying?'

Nurse Macclesfield felt for her. She'd seen it before. Friends and relatives who were so caught up in their own frenetic lives that they didn't see what was in front of them until it was too late. 'She did know she was dying, yes.'

Casey sank onto on a chair. 'I don't understand why she didn't call me.'

'She said that you were too busy, that you had a horse event to prepare for. The Burghley Horse Trials, is it?'

A wave of nausea enveloped Casey. She'd shouted at Mrs Smith and told her that she'd never signed a document making her manager. Like a spoilt, selfish child, she'd raged: 'I choose the lorry!' She'd thoughtlessly compared Mrs Smith's increasing frailty with Kyle's youthful vigour when all the while Mrs Smith must have had the strength of ten lions to keep teaching and keep giving when her body was being ravaged by a killer disease.

Casey went over to the bed and gazed down at the woman she loved like a mother. She took Mrs Smith's hand in hers. 'How much time has she got left?'

'It's hard to say. Her specialist, Andrew Mutandwa, told her she had months, but it could be weeks or even days. Between you and me, I think it would help if she had a reason to go on living.'

It was then that Casey saw, poking out of Mrs Smith's rucksack, a red notebook. She knew what it was immediately. Throughout their time together, Mrs Smith had never gone anywhere without a journal. She kept meticulous records of every nuance of Casey and Storm's training programme, as well as nutritional notes and other critical information. They'd often paged through these diaries together, recalling particular sessions or looking up cross-country-course diagrams or measurements, so Casey didn't feel she was violating Mrs Smith's privacy now.

Opening it, she fully expected the last entry to correspond with the date Mrs Smith had left White Oaks. But the red notebook was virtually full. Page after page was filled with detailed plans for Storm's training schedule right up until the Burghley Horse Trials in September. That was astounding enough, but it was Mrs Smith's radical new theories on preparing for CCI**** four-star events that blew Casey's mind.

She closed the journal with a snap. 'Nurse Macclesfield, how long would it take you to get Mrs Smith's things together? She's coming home with me.'

'I'm afraid that won't be possible. She's too ill to be moved. Casey, I know it's hard to accept but she's dying.'

'That's exactly why I want her with me. If she stays here, she'll die quietly and quickly, surrounded by strangers. If she comes with me, I'll give her a reason to live. Whatever happens, she'll be with me and Storm. We're the ones who love her most.'

Nurse Macclesfield opened her mouth to object, but in the face of Casey's steel-eyed determination she knew she wouldn't get far. Besides, if her brief acquaintance with Angelica Smith had shown her anything it was that she was a free spirit whose flame had burned brightest when she talked about being on the horse circuit with Casey and Storm. If she were to survive, they might be the miracle she needed.

'Give me ten minutes,' she told Casey. 'I'll speak to the doctor and organise some transport for you. Now would you like a cup of sweet coffee? You're rocking on your feet.'

17

THE RUSTING GATES had been given a lick of paint and a climbing rose was blooming on a trellis outside the office, but in all other ways Hope Lane Riding Centre – known to all but Mrs Ridgley as Hopeless Lane – was unchanged. The same motley crew of learners bumped around on the same leaden-footed horses. Casey stopped to give a Polo to Patchwork, the woolly piebald cob she'd long ago attempted to coax over piles of junk in a bid to pretend she was riding at Badminton. She had hoped that Patchwork might remember her fondly, but he merely crunched the mints and stared vacantly into space.

'Humbling, isn't it, the way they move on and forget all about you,' said Mrs Ridgeley with her usual lack of tact. Unnoticed, the stocky, yellow-haired owner of the riding school had come up behind Casey as she walked along the line of horses. 'Fame means nothing to them. Doesn't mean a lot around here either.'

Casey met Mrs Ridgeley's gaze without flinching. Few people could have done a better job of running a riding school in one of London's roughest inner-city neighbourhoods and for that the woman had her respect, but Mrs Ridgeley had thought that Casey was out of her mind to rescue Storm and she'd made their lives much more difficult than was necessary. At the same time, Casey would be for ever grateful to her. Without the loan of Mrs Ridgeley's storeroom, which became his stable, Storm would have had to be put down or returned to the knacker's yard to be slaughtered.

She summoned a smile. 'Believe it or not, I didn't come here to gloat. I came to see how you were all doing and to find out if you needed a hand. I'll be staying with my father for a week or two. If you wanted me to give some free lessons or even muck out, I'd be glad to do it.'

'Casey Blue!' cried Gillian, Hopeless Lane's best instructor and one of Casey's favourite people. 'You haven't forgotten us. We miss you. We especially miss the entertainment factor provided by you and Storm in the early days. Remember that time he cleared a stack of show jumps and the water trough as if he were a scrawny Pegasus?'

'We definitely do not miss those days,' Mrs Ridgeley said firmly. 'Gillian, Casey here seems to think that the

177

customers of Hope Lane might benefit from her free services. She has even offered to muck out. What do you think?'

Gillian whooped with delight. 'Are you serious? That's made my day. Casey, you're on. How soon can you start?'

For Casey, it was comforting but also deeply unsettling to return to her roots. She realised with a sense of shame that she had not spent a night in her old home at No. 414 Redwing Towers, a council block every bit as grim and grey as she remembered, since she and Mrs Smith had moved to White Oaks in the lovely Kent countryside in spring the previous year.

As she walked the streets of her childhood, including the cacophonous, sometimes deadly 'Murder Mile', everything she'd done and achieved fell away. She felt anonymous. None of the immigrants, artists or city workers who flowed like a human tide through Hackney knew or could have cared less about Badminton or the Kentucky Three-Day Event. It was liberating.

Her father was beside himself with happiness to have her home, but he fretted constantly about Mrs Smith, installed in Casey's bedroom. Surrounded by Casey's old horse posters, she spent most of each day sleeping. Casey took her bowls of homemade minestrone and tried talking to her, but all she did was lie staring at the ceiling. She either couldn't speak or didn't want to.

'Surely she should be in hospital?' worried Roland Blue. 'She's depressed and terminally ill. She needs professional help.'

'Give her time,' said Casey. 'We're all the help that she needs. Well, she needs to be with horses too, but first she needs to be well enough to move.'

On the fifth day, when Mrs Smith seemed worse than ever, Casey took a bus to Dalston. It was a while since she'd been to the house of Janet, Mrs Smith's healer friend who'd twice saved Storm, but she remembered the number.

'*Cancer?*'

Janet, a voluptuous woman in an embroidered white kaftan, jingled her bracelets in agitation. She was sad but not surprised to hear of Mrs Smith's diagnosis or what had followed.

'Never did like being told what to do, Angelica. Always liked to take things one step too far. But I can't criticise her because I'm the same way. Even so it seems tragic that in choosing to embrace life in all its glory she must now pay the highest price.'

Casey fought back tears. 'So help her. If anyone can save her, it's you.'

'Oh, no,' said Janet. 'No, no, no. Cancer is beyond my scope, I'm afraid. Casey, I know it's hard but you'd probably do best to take Angelica back to the Primrose Valley Hospice. They're the experts with this sort of thing.'

Casey jumped to her feet. 'You don't believe a single word you've just said,' she said furiously. 'You believe quite the opposite. You're reluctant to step in because you're afraid of it going wrong. You think I'm expecting you to cure her. I'm not. But I am asking you to put yourself in her position. Given a choice between a slow death in a stifling hospice room, where the most dramatic thing that happens in any day is a game of Scrabble, or going out on a high, which would you go for?'

She took the red notebook from her bag and handed it to the older woman. Janet flicked through it in silence. 'She's written all of this in the time since the two of you parted?'

'Yes, and it's pure genius. I want to use it. Her strategy: I want to use it to train for Burghley.'

Janet's eyes widened. 'Are you suggesting what I think you're suggesting?'

'Uh-huh.'

'Far be it from me to question your sanity, but ... Oh, all right, I will question it. Have you lost your mind?'

Casey grinned. 'Probably, but you have to admit that I'm right.'

'It's risky.'

'I know.'

'You need to understand up front that I can do nothing to cure her cancer or slow the spread of the disease. All I can offer is something – a potion – that might, for a time, make her feel a little better.'

'Worked for Storm,' said Casey. 'Made him a champion.

No reason at all why it shouldn't do wonders for Mrs Smith.'

She slept in a sleeping bag beside Mrs Smith's bed that night, as she had every night for the past week. Or at least she would have slept if she could. Mostly she stared into the darkness, worrying first about Mrs Smith, who had swallowed Janet's green potion without comment and immediately dropped into a coma-like sleep, and next about Storm, alone at Rycliffe Manor.

Nothing is what it seems there, not even Kyle.

What if Anna hadn't been speaking out of envy or bitterness? What if she'd genuinely wanted to keep Casey from making a terrible mistake?

Regardless of Anna's motivation, Casey couldn't bear being apart from her precious horse. Since the day of his rescue he'd only ever been taken care of by her, Mrs Smith and, occasionally, Jin, a Chinese friend of Casey's from Hopeless Lane. Now he was alone in a strange place being looked after by Assassin's competent but rather vacant groom. It didn't exactly fill Casey with confidence.

She'd phoned Kyle twice to check on Storm. Kyle insisted he was fine.

'Like me he's missing you, but otherwise he's doing well. We've turned him out in the field so he can stretch his legs, but if we're going to have any chance at winning the Burghley Horse Trials he needs to get back into training asap. Ray has offered to ride him or lunge him. He feels that Storm has grown a little spoilt and accustomed to getting his own way and might benefit from someone with a different approach to yours in your absence.'

Casey had only just managed to stop herself from screaming: 'Don't you dare let that freak touch my horse!'

Controlling herself with difficulty she said, 'Under no circumstances is anyone to ride, school or do anything other than groom and feed Storm. I'll be back in a few days and we'll get to work.'

'Great. Let me know if you need anything in the meantime. How's Angelica?'

'She's making a great recovery,' Casey lied. It irritated her when Kyle referred to Mrs Smith by her first name and in such a familiar way.

'That's good to hear. The sooner you're back in the saddle the better. Oh, by the way, Joyce in the office said that Peter called, looking for you. She didn't know he was your boyfriend so she told him that you were away for a couple of weeks and couldn't be contacted. But I expect that by now you've told him where you are.'

Casey had murmured something unintelligible into the phone and hung up as soon as she could. That was another thing she was worried about – Peter. She'd sent him two texts about Mrs Smith and left a message saying that she was at her father's flat and would love to talk to him. Agonisingly, she hadn't received a single response. But if he'd tried to ring her at Rycliffe Manor, surely that meant he still loved her?

Scrolling down to his number, she'd pressed call. His phone went straight to voicemail. The temperature in Casey's heart sank to zero.

Lying on the floor beside Mrs Smith, she struggled to get comfortable in the sleeping bag. Everything hurt. When sleep finally came, it was fractured by images of Orla clinging to Peter with her long red nails, and Ray lunging a terrified Storm.

And all the while Anna's warning was stuck on repeat in her head. 'Whatever you do, don't let Storm go to Rycliffe Manor ... I saw what they did to Mouse. He was never the same after he went there.'

Who was Mouse?

She was woken by a sliver of sunlight sliding under the blind. Even before she opened her eyes, she knew that something had changed. The energy in the room felt different.

She hauled herself upright. Mrs Smith was sitting in the armchair watching her. The colour had returned to her cheeks. She was desperately thin, but her eyes were bright.

'God, how I've missed you, Casey Blue.'

Casey burst out laughing. Jumping out of her sleeping bag, she flung her arms around Mrs Smith. 'Not half as much as I've missed you.'

She pulled back and said sternly: 'Don't ever do that to me again – vanish and not tell me where you are.'

'I won't, I promise.'

'I'm sorry,' Casey said. 'I'm sorry for being so selfish and self-absorbed that I didn't notice you were ill. How you kept it from me for so long, I can't imagine. You must have been in agony. And on top of everything you had me behaving like a brat. I lost the plot for a while. Fame went to my head.'

'Oh, I wouldn't go that far,' murmured Mrs Smith. 'Casey, I'm sorry too. The reason I hid my illness from you – and from myself, I might add – was that I didn't want it to get in the way of everything you've ever dreamed of and worked so hard for. I knew that you'd do what you've done now – drop everything to take care of me. The irony is that in keeping it a secret and not dealing with it, I've made the situation a thousand times worse for both of us. I'm wracked with guilt that I've caused you so much stress and worry at such a crucial point in the season. If I've done irreparable harm to your chances, I'll never forgive myself.'

'Then make it up to me,' implored Casey. 'Teach me again.'

'Casey, I can't. That life is over for me. Thanks to Janet's potion, I feel better this morning than I've done in six months, but you know as well as I do that it's not going to last. No, what I need to do as a matter of urgency is return to Primrose Valley. It's not such a bad place, you know, once you get used to it. The menu leaves a lot to be desired but apart from that ... '

'If that's what you feel you should do then I won't stop you,' Casey said. 'But in that case, would you mind if I borrowed your red notebook? I mean, you won't be needing it at Primrose Valley.'

Mrs Smith tensed. 'Why would you want to do that?'

'I'd like to use it as a training manual for Burghley.'

'Casey, the notes in there are nothing more than the ramblings of an eccentric pensioner.'

'No, they're not. They're brilliant.' Casey cast a cheeky glance at her teacher. 'What's it going to be, Angelica? Do you want to do the sensible thing and return to your room at the hospice, or would you like to do the insane and completely inadvisable thing and join me on a wild quest to do the miraculous? I haven't a hope of winning Burghley without you, you know.'

'Yes, you do. You have the handsome Mr West at your beck and call. You told the *New Equestrian* that leaving me for him was the best decision you ever made. I have to confess I was hurt.'

Casey was shamefaced. 'I don't blame you, but I swear I didn't mean it. It was an idiotic, off-the-cuff comment. Kyle told me to say it and I was still on a high from my win with Roxy so I repeated it. Look, I'm not going to deny that I think Kyle is great. He's a lovely guy and he is, as you say, very handsome, but his methods are not really working for me. If you won't agree to coach me for Burghley then I'm going to withdraw.'

'You wouldn't!'

'Try me.'

'You can't blackmail a sick woman,' said Mrs Smith in a scandalised tone, but there was a twinkle in her eye.

Casey grinned. 'I can and I will, especially if I think that taking on the impossible challenge of the Grand Slam will give you a new lease of life.'

'You're sure about this?'

'I've never been more sure in my life.'

Mrs Smith drew her silk robe more tightly around her thin shoulders. Her voice shook with excitement. 'I'm not going to travel in that horrid lorry, you know.'

'Don't worry, you won't have to. As from next week, the lorry will be no more. Ed Lashley-Jones is taking it away and threatening to sue. You were right about everything. He's spitting mad that I didn't turn up for an Equi-Flow motivational day on Monday – a paintball contest in the New Forest. I was supposed to spend the morning talking about my rags-to-riches rise to Badminton champion and my afternoon crawling through the undergrowth trying to avoid being shot by Equi-Flow clients. I sent Ed a text asking what part of "I have a family emergency" was so hard for him to understand and he took grave offence.'

'He'll get over it,' said Mrs Smith. 'Wendy or Cindi or whatever their names are can mop his fevered brow.'

'So will you do it – teach me?'

Mrs Smith gave her a radiant smile. 'Try stopping me.'

18

CASEY CAUGHT THE train to Wiltshire early next morning. She felt it only fair that she tell Kyle as soon as possible and in person that she would no longer be requiring his services. How he would take it was anybody's guess. Casey had a feeling it wasn't going to go well. She hoped she was wrong because she liked him a great deal and didn't want to upset him, especially after he'd told her his fears about his clients leaving him. But there was too much at stake. She cared about Kyle, but not a fraction as much as she cared about giving Mrs Smith a reason to live.

But as the train sped through the Wiltshire countryside, the image that stuck in her head was of ink dribbling, like blood, down the contract. What if he held her to it? Lawyers would get involved and there could be an ugly and expensive fight to get away from him.

She caught a taxi from the station to Rycliffe Manor. The first time she'd visited, Mr Farley's sat nav had sent them to the rarely used back entrance. The front entrance was much more imposing. Iron gates, flanked by sculpted bronze stallions, glided open as they approached. A sign set into the redbrick wall announced Rycliffe Manor Estate as the 'Proud Home of the Kyle West Equestrian Centre'.

The first person Casey saw when she walked into the yard was Hannah. The junior instructor was sitting on the edge of the fountain reading a thriller. 'Between lessons,' she said in explanation.

Not that Casey had asked. Around the yard she'd heard whispers that Hannah was the least popular of the teachers and struggled to win clients. Casey couldn't understand why, although she could see that Hannah had a jealous streak. Madly in love with her boss, Hannah's attitude towards her had gone from lukewarm to extra frosty as Kyle's interest in Casey had increased and her supposed boyfriend had failed to put in an appearance at Rycliffe Manor.

'If it's Kyle you're after you'll have a long wait,' Hannah said pointedly now. 'He's with an important client.'

Casey did a mental eye roll. Mr Farley would be arriving with the lorry at any moment and she wanted to speak to Kyle and be on her way with Storm as soon as she could. But she wasn't about to confide in Hannah.

'No problem. I'll wait for him in the office.' She was dying to see her beloved horse, but she wanted to get the Kyle speech over first.

She was halfway to the cool stone building that housed the video suite, office and guest quarters when she remembered Anna Sparks' words. Turning suddenly, she was startled to catch Hannah staring after her, a peculiar expression on her face.

'Everything all right, Hannah?'

'What? Oh, yes. I was miles away. I was thinking about the plot of my novel. It's a murder mystery set in a racing stable.' She shoved the novel into her bag as if that would make it less scary. 'Did you want something?'

'Who's Mouse? A friend of mine mentioned that he used to come here.'

Hannah laughed. 'That's one way of putting it. Mouse was the stable name of Anna Sparks' horse. You remember, the one she drove mad – Rough Diamond.'

Casey thanked her and hurried away to the office before Hannah could ask any awkward questions about which friend had talked to her about Mouse. She was in turmoil. The majority of people who'd witnessed Anna's attack on Best Man at Badminton would be of the same view as Hannah – that if anyone was to blame for Rough Diamond's breakdown it was Anna Sparks herself.

Yet at Aston-le-Walls, Anna had claimed that Rough Diamond was never the same again after what 'they' did to him. Did 'they' mean Kyle and Ray or someone else altogether?

190

Casey slowed as she reached the office. Joyce was on the phone, arguing with someone over the non-payment of a bill. She didn't notice Casey start up the stairs.

On the landing, Casey paused. She needed to pull herself together and formulate a plan. In the conversation she'd overheard, Kyle had snapped: 'The way it worked with Mouse, you mean?'

'That wasn't my fault,' was Ray's snarled response. 'The girl was out of control.'

Was the girl in question Anna Sparks? If so, who had been responsible for harming her horse?

More urgently, where was Storm? Was he okay?

A voice cut into her thoughts. The door of the video suite was open and she could hear Ray talking in a low, urgent tone. Casey crept up the final few steps. If Ray was on the phone perhaps she could get a sense of the man behind the mask.

But as she approached the door, she saw that he wasn't chatting to some remote caller at all. He was speaking into a microphone. On the television monitor before him an elegant woman was schooling a horse.

'If she wants her horse to lengthen his stride during the trot, she needs to drive him forward so that she has a more consistent connection. His ribcage will feel a lot looser,' he was saying.

There was a crackle as Kyle's disembodied voice relayed the instruction to the rider as if it was coming from him.

'That's better,' Ray said into the microphone, 'but

remind her to keep leaning on the inside of her stirrup. The more she does that, the closer she'll be to her horse's centre of gravity. That's the final tip. Lesson's over.'

'Okay, Steph, we're done for the day,' said Kyle. 'Keep leaning on the inside of your stirrups. It'll keep you nearer to your horse's sense of gravity.'

Casey felt as if she had fallen into a shaft with no bottom. The whole operation was a scam. Every last bit of it. Kyle was the suave, charismatic front for the centre. He was customer- and media-friendly and looked good gracing the covers of magazines. Ray was the expert, but he was not a people person. His battered face and surly manner gave the wrong impression. Worse still, he had contempt for the clients. He made it obvious that he knew far more about their horses than they did.

In that instant Casey was certain that whatever had happened to Rough Diamond was Ray's fault. Kyle had been involved in the deception of the riders, but it was clear that Ray alone manipulated the horses.

Casey began to shiver. If they were capable of a deception on this grand a scale, what else were they capable of? She had to get Storm away from here.

Her mobile beeped. Mr Farley had arrived with the lorry. She grabbed her phone to silence it, but it was too late. Ray was at the door. He knew immediately that she'd seen and heard everything. Reacting with a boxer's speed, he barred her escape route, fists clenched at his side. 'If you breathe a word about this, you'll be sorry.'

From far away, Casey heard Kyle's voice in the office

downstairs. He was saying something to Joyce. Ray stepped back and folded his arms.

Kyle came rushing up the steps, his face alight. 'Hey, Casey, Joyce said you were back. Sorry to keep you waiting.'

He stopped when he saw her expression.

'What's going on?'

'Casey knows everything,' said Ray. 'She heard me talk you through the lesson.'

Kyle covered his face with his hands. 'No.' When he lifted his head, Casey saw again the little boy that lived inside him. 'Casey, I can explain. It's not what it looks like. I—'

'Save it,' snapped Ray. 'This is not something you can sweet talk your way out of, Kyle. The game is up. But don't worry. She's not going to tell anyone, are you, Casey? Not if she wants to get to Burghley in one piece.'

'Don't you dare threaten her,' yelled Kyle.

'Or what? What will you do about it? I told you that you were making a mistake choosing this girl. I told you it was a bridge too far. It was obvious you were half in love with her before you even met her. I told you that you'd ruin everything if you didn't get your emotions under control.'

'And I told you that by trying to live your dreams through me you'd destroy my life. Congratulations. That's what you've done. Well, it's over. You and I and this whole charade, it's over.'

For a second the two men's faces were in profile and

that's when it clicked. Casey gasped. 'Now I get it. You're father and son.'

Ray gave a short laugh. 'I wondered how long it would take for someone to cotton on. Incredibly, you're the first to figure it out. That's what happens when you're the ugly father of a beautiful son. People don't make the connection. Kyle takes after his mother, you see.'

'But why the secrecy? Who cares if you're related?'

Ray glanced at Kyle, who was slumped against the wall. He opened his mouth as if to say something then thought better of it. 'Seemed better that way.'

Picking up his car keys, he gave Casey a warning look. 'Remember what I said. Mind you watch your mouth.'

As his footsteps faded, Kyle jerked to life like a statue becoming real. 'Casey, I don't know what to say.'

'Don't bother saying anything, Kyle. I'm going to get my horse and go. I'm not interested in your excuses or your lies. Oh, and don't worry, I won't be telling anyone. Just leave me and Storm alone. You owe us that much.'

She flew down the stairs and out into the yard, almost knocking over Hannah, who'd heard shouting and come to investigate. When she reached Storm's stable and saw that he was leaning over his door, ears pricked, whickering with joy at the sight of her, she could have wept with relief. With shaking hands, she put on his headcollar and rug.

'We're going home,' she told him. 'You're safe now and we're going home.'

Never had she been so happy to see the monosyllabic

Mr Farley. As quickly as she could, she loaded Storm and ran back to the tack room to collect her saddle and bridle. She was hunting for her girth when Kyle appeared in the doorway.

He looked so utterly crushed, his handsome face drawn, that Casey's heart went out to him. She hardened it at once, but he'd seen her weaken and was already moving forward.

'Casey, there's nothing I can do or say to make up for what's happened. Believe me, I feel like the lowest person on earth. But I couldn't let you go without some explanation. The whole coaching thing, it was Dad's dream. I—'

'Oh, so it's Dad now, is it? Not Ray. You told me your father was dead, Kyle. In the grave. How could you lie about something like that?'

He reddened. 'It's a long story. You see, Dad – Ray – always had a gift for working with horses and riders. As a young man his goal was to teach the top horsemen in every discipline, but although he achieved phenomenal results he was always passed over in favour of teachers with a fraction of his talent. Because he looks and sometimes talks like a prize fighter, no one ever took him seriously. It frustrated him so much that he became bitter and angry. Like your father, he made a series of terrible decisions and we all had to suffer the consequences.

'One day it occurred to me that I could make him proud and at the same time make up for some of his disappointments if I became an instructor myself. It wasn't what I wanted to do with my life, but I love horses so I thought it would be easy. I enrolled on an instructor course. Within days it was obvious that I was hopeless.'

'So you came up with a plan to combine your talents?'

'It was Dad's idea. He convinced me to try it for an exam. It was so easy and worked so well that he became obsessed with doing it for real. I was reluctant to go along with it at first. I was sure that we'd be caught and the fallout would be horrific. But somehow we never were. Money started pouring in and reporters started writing about me and before I knew it the whole thing had snowballed out of control. Initially I was eaten up with guilt, but I justified it as a short-term solution. I persuaded myself that as soon as I'd learned as much as Ray, I'd be able to teach on my own. But it didn't work out that way. The more successful I became, the more pressure I was under to be this miracle-working guru. I didn't dare tell riders like you my own theories in case I was exposed as a fraud. Every day I felt as if I was walking a tightrope without a safety net.'

'But that first day at White Oaks. How did you know what to say to me then?'

'Some of it was improvised. I've watched Ray deal with biting horses for years, for example, so that part was easy. Some of it he'd told me to say in advance. He'd watched you ride at Badminton so he had a few theories that applied in any situation. Casey, I'm sorry.

196

More sorry than you can possibly imagine. Things just snowballed. They got out of hand.'

Casey spotted the girth hanging over a different saddle and snatched it up.

'I'd like to sympathise with you, Kyle, but right now I'm shattered. You and your dad – what you've done is fraud. I trusted you, Kyle. *You.* Not Ray. Most alarmingly, I trusted you with Storm and my career. Never in a million years would I have willingly put either my horse or my future in the hands of Ray. Don't compare him to my dad. My father is a caring, decent man. He's not perfect but he would never, ever harm an animal. How could you let Ray ruin Rough Diamond?'

She stared him in the eye, willing him to tell the truth. 'It was Ray, wasn't it? Anna got the blame but it was your dad's fault.'

Kyle was grey with misery. 'He didn't ... I wasn't sure ... Anna was behaving like a princess and someone had to take control. Ray understands horses. He said that Mouse was too arrogant and that he'd perform better if he was made to understand who was in charge ... '

All of a sudden Casey felt exhausted beyond words. 'I think I've heard enough. I'm going. Storm's already loaded and I need to get him home.'

She moved to get the saddle, but Kyle grabbed her arm. 'Casey, wait. Please don't end it like this. Don't you understand that the reason I'm so devastated is because it's you I've betrayed? I love you. I think I've loved you from the moment I saw you ride at Badminton. Don't tell me you feel nothing for me because I won't believe you.'

Before Casey could move or resist he kissed her.

A shadow fell across the doorway. 'Now I see why you haven't been returning my calls.'

Casey tore her lips from Kyle's and sprang back. Peter was staring at her in horror.

'I heard about Mrs Smith and came as soon as I could, but nobody seemed to know where you were. Finally, I got hold of your father and he told me you were on your way to Rycliffe Manor. I was reluctant to come here but I thought you might need me. I guess I was wrong. You've found a different shoulder to cry on.'

Without another word, he strode away across the yard.

Casey gave Kyle a furious glare. 'Now look what you've done.'

She sprinted after Peter, but when she reached the car park his van was already halfway across the estate. The love of her life had gone.

19

O N A STIFLINGLY warm afternoon in mid-August
Angelica Smith sat in a deckchair and watched
Casey work with Storm. By her calculation the silver
horse was a couple of weeks away from reaching prime
condition, but then hers was the opinion of a perfectionist.
To a casual observer, he was a majestic sight, a virtual
equine machine. His break from competition had done
him a power of good, as had the intense fitness regime
of the past few weeks, especially the steeplechasing. He
was hungry again, burning to gallop and jump.

Casey was a different matter. On the one hand, her
work ethic could not be faulted. She was completely
focused on getting herself and Storm in the best possible
shape for the Burghley Horse Trials in the third week of

September, less than a month away. The bad habits that had crept in while she and Mrs Smith had been 'on a break' (that was how they jokingly referred to their time apart) had been jettisoned. No more lying on the sofa eating microwaved pizza or takeaway chips. No more chocolate or multiple cappuccinos. Nothing but raw egg, yogurt and spirulina smoothies and wholesome vegetarian cooking with lots of brown rice.

To anyone who didn't know her, Casey looked incredible. Her dark hair was thick and glossy and her grey eyes clear and bright. Her enviably tanned slender limbs were those of a professional athlete. But those were all physical things. Psychologically, she was lower than Mrs Smith had ever seen her. Peter had returned to Ireland and was refusing to take her calls. She was putting on a brave front but Mrs Smith knew a broken heart when she saw one.

'The worst thing about it is I brought it on myself,' Casey had said in their only conversation on the subject. 'I never stopped loving Peter, but I allowed myself to be seduced by Kyle's looks and the whole glamorous package that came with him – the sports car, the beautiful estate, the sophisticated parties. I can't blame Kyle if he thought I was flirting with him. At times, maybe I was. And now I've lost the best thing that ever happened to me.'

'Give Peter space,' Mrs Smith had counselled. 'He's wounded but he'll come round.'

Privately she wasn't so sure. Peter was passionately in love with Casey but he had a stubborn streak. He also had a strong sense of right and wrong. If he thought she'd cheated on him, he wouldn't easily be won over.

As Casey transitioned to a walk Mrs Smith called out: 'Storm had too much bend in his neck during the shoulder-in. On the next corner I want you to let him think he is going into the diagonal but ask him to shoulder-in down the long side instead.'

Shortly afterwards she waved for her pupil to come in. They'd been training hard for forty-five minutes and Mrs Smith didn't believe in pushing a horse any harder. There was nothing to be gained from turning Storm sour.

Casey's skin had a fine sheen of sweat, but neither she nor Storm was remotely puffed as they came to a halt. 'It's working, isn't it?' she said excitedly. 'Your red notebook plan; it's doing everything we hoped it would.'

Mrs Smith had been so close to death at Primrose Valley that she now felt as if she could actually taste life. To her, every extra hour was a gift, not merely because she was alive but because she was with Casey and Storm, doing what she loved. That the red notebook plan was indeed working was a bonus.

'I can't take all the credit,' Mrs Smith said modestly.

Casey laughed as she slid off Storm and rewarded him with Polo mints. 'I know, I know, it was Lucinda Green, six times Badminton champion. She's the one who sowed the seeds of your brilliant strategy.'

Mrs Smith handed her a bottle of water and poured herself a mug of chai from a flask. 'It's true, she did.

It was a comment she made when we had a brief conversation during the Kentucky Three-Day Event. We were discussing the Grand Slam and why no one but Pippa Funnell has won it. Lucinda felt that Burghley presented a unique set of challenges because the ground was extremely undulating. In terms of terrain, it's far tougher than Badminton and the Kentucky Three-Day Event. That's why horses that train on all-weather surfaces are the ones who suffer most in terms of exhaustion. To her, the key is to get a horse fit on as many types of terrain as possible.'

Casey undid Storm's girth and took off his saddle. 'Is that how you got onto the subject of the long format of eventing versus the short format?'

'Basically, yes. Like a lot of people, Lucinda feels that since the FEI did away with the roads and tracks and steeplechase section of four-star events, horses aren't as fit as they used to be. I agree. A tired horse is a horse that can misjudge a fence. And when you're riding one of the most treacherous cross-country courses in the world, the smallest error can lead to disaster.

'It doesn't help that the format of CCI four-star events means that you go from the sedateness of dressage to the speed and high risk of the cross-country. Previously, you had the roads and tracks and steeplechase phase in between to get a horse thinking. Research shows that there were fewer rotational falls in those days because the long format took the edge off the energy of the hottest horses and enabled them to arrive at the cross-country

202

with their mind on the job. There are also statistics showing that it led to fewer stress-related injuries such as bowed tendons.'

Casey turned on the hose and ran cool water over Storm. He wrinkled his muzzle as she washed his head and neck. 'So you thought you'd adapt the format to suit Storm and me?'

'Exactly. The long format takes too much out of the horse. The short format is too short. So I thought we might do something in between. In our training, we'll include the steeplechase, as we've been doing for the past few weeks. But on cross-country day at Burghley, we'll only do roads and tracks – perhaps with a few hedges and other natural obstacles added in. I've spoken to the farmer who owns the land adjacent to Burghley Park. He has no problem with us using his farm as an extension of the cross-country course.'

Casey switched off the water. 'Are we really doing this, Angelica? Are we really going to attempt the impossible?'

Mrs Smith's heart skipped a beat. 'Yes, Casey, we really are.'

20

THAT EVENING, CASEY made them both a vegetarian cottage pie topped with liberal quantities of grated cheddar. Mrs Smith was the better cook, but Casey was determined to ease her workload. She'd arranged for a cleaner to come twice a week and insisted on doing all the shopping and chores herself.

Ignoring her teacher's protests, she'd also insisted on having a legal agreement drawn up making Mrs Smith her manager.

'There's no point. I don't know how long I'll be around.'

'I don't care if you're here for one day or ten years,' said Casey. 'Well, I do, but you know what I mean. I want you protected and I want you to know that, along with Peter and my dad, you're the most important person in my life. You're family to me. You're something more than that too. You're my mentor and my best friend. Anything I've ever achieved or ever will achieve is because of you.'

'Thank you, Casey. That's quite enough compliments to be going on with,' Mrs Smith said sternly. Praise always made her uncomfortable. 'You might want to check on the cottage pie. There's smoke pouring out of the oven.'

As Casey raced to rescue the dinner, Mrs Smith watched her with a smile. It was good to have the old Casey back, and fairly wonderful to be back herself. Thanks to Janet's special potion and Mr Mutandwa's painkillers, she felt better than she'd done in months. She could function. She could walk and think and she had hope.

Janet's magic mix had come with only one condition.

'This concoction is packed full of stimulants to keep you going, but in your fragile state I can't vouch for the consequences. Will you promise me that you won't exert yourself too much or do anything that radically raises your heart rate? Keep calm and don't do anything silly.'

Mrs Smith had laughed. 'Janet, my dear, I think my aerobic days are behind me. I don't think I've jogged anywhere since I ran a five kilometre race for charity in my forties. Have no worries on that score.'

As Casey scraped the burned bits off the cottage pie, Mrs Smith sat at the kitchen table deep in thought. Knowing that she'd never breathe a word, Casey had confided to her every detail of the Rycliffe Manor scam.

The problem was what to do about it. What Kyle and Ray had done was not a crime. At worst, they were guilty of misrepresentation. And Kyle had said he would no longer be part of the charade. Nothing good could come of exposing them.

They couldn't even warn other riders on the circuit – people like Sam Tide, the Australian rider, one of Kyle's star clients, in case there were repercussions. Despite Ray's threat, Casey was convinced that he would never risk actually harming her, but she was afraid that he would find a way to get to Storm.

Mrs Smith, however, was not one to do nothing in the face of injustice. Casey's description of the dog attack had chilled her to the marrow. She was certain that it had somehow been engineered, probably by the sinister Ray. She was equally sure that anyone capable of such a heinous act had done similar things – or worse – before. With that in mind, she'd contacted Detective Inspector Lenny McLeod, the policeman who'd helped Casey deal with a blackmailer a few months before.

McLeod owned a Morgan mare and was officially horse mad. Having read dozens of articles on Kyle West, he was surprised when Mrs Smith asked him, in confidence and as a friend, to run a background check on Ray Cook, manager of the Rycliffe Manor Equestrian Centre. Three days later he rang her with the results. Ray's record was squeaky clean.

'Not even a parking ticket,' he told her. 'Why, what were you expecting me to find?'

'I'm not sure. I suppose I was mistaken. Thanks for looking into it.'

'No problem. There are a couple of other searches I could try. If I find anything I'll let you know.'

Casey set a plate in front of Mrs Smith. 'One gourmet serving of chargrilled cottage pie. Jamie Oliver eat your heart out.'

As she sat down her phone rang. 'Mind if I get it?'

Mrs Smith shook her head. She knew that Casey was hoping it was Peter.

The voice on the end was confident and well-spoken. 'Casey Blue? This is Casper Leyton. You attended one of my parties a while back.'

Casey was thrown. 'Uh, yes, Mr Leyton. Thank you. It was kind of you to invite me. I had a great time.' Raising her eyebrows at Mrs Smith, she put him on speakerphone.

'Call me Casper. Casey, I have a proposition for you. I have a four-star horse named Incendiary who is on form and more than capable of winning the Burghley Horse Trials. That's not just my opinion. That's the verdict of some of the best experts in the business. His pedigree has to be seen to be believed. He's been competing in New Zealand this season and has blown everything out of the water. Mark Todd tried to buy him but I got in first. I was hoping to persuade a friend of mine to ride him at Burghley but it turns out that he has already entered another two horses. He recommended I ring you.

'I'll be truthful, my initial response was that you were

far too young. But your track record is impressive. Added to which if you pull off a miracle and make history, it would give my business the kind of publicity boost that money can't buy. So how about it? Fancy a second ride? It would give a massive boost to your chances.'

Casey was reeling. Many of the top riders rode one or more horses at four-star events for the simple reason that it doubled or tripled their chances of grabbing eventing's most glittering prizes. If the first horse performed poorly or was injured, there was always the hope that the other would save the day. If Incendiary was as good as Casper claimed he was Casey's chances of winning the Grand Slam would increase dramatically.

'I'm flattered that you'd consider me, Mr Leyton. I – well, I'm not quite sure how to respond. Thank you. It's an amazing offer. Would it be okay if I discussed it with my coach before giving you an answer?'

'Kyle West?'

'Angelica Smith is now my teacher.'

'Oh.' There was a pause. 'Sure. Take as long as you need. Write down my number. Give me a ring when you've made up your mind.'

Casey clicked off the phone and looked across the table at Mrs Smith. 'What do you think?'

'I think that it's a decision only you can make. What I can tell you is that I read an article on Incendiary a couple of months ago and he's the real deal. If God designed an event horse, it would be him. His conformation and balance are quite exceptional. If you rode well, you'd be in pole position for the title. Of course, you might have to accept that the horse that helped you get there isn't Storm Warning. Storm is a champion and the bravest horse I've ever known, but Incendiary is in a different league.'

She covered Casey's hand with hers. 'Do what feels right, my dear. I'll support you either way.'

Casey nodded slowly. She tapped in Casper's number. He answered before it rang.

'That was quick. So what's it going to be? Are we going to go for the Slam together?'

'Mr Leyton, I can't thank you enough for giving me this opportunity. To be honest, I'm blown away by it. But I'm going to have to turn it down.'

'Turn it down?! Am I hearing you correctly? Maybe I haven't done a good enough job of explaining that this is the chance of a lifetime.' Casper Leyton was unaccustomed to taking no for an answer.

'Please don't think that I'm in any way ungrateful. I just don't feel that I'm the right rider for your horse. If he's as special as you say he is, you need a rider who is dedicated to Incendiary alone and not someone with divided loyalties, as I would have with Storm. I hope you understand.'

Casper Leyton gave a grudging laugh. 'I don't, but I appreciate your frankness and I admire your devotion to your horse. Doesn't mean that I think you're any less crazy for turning mine down, but I respect your decision. If that's your final word on the matter, I should tell you that there is another rider in the frame. You were my first choice, but I'm going to move to Plan B and you're not going to like it.'

'I doubt I'll have an opinion. Who you choose to ride your horse is your own business.'

'From what I hear, you will have an opinion about this rider. I'm going to give Incendiary to Anna Sparks.'

Casey almost dropped the phone. 'Anna Sparks? But … but … '

'That's the reaction I've had from everyone. "Anna Sparks …!" Cue stammering and apoplexy. My own advisors think I've lost my mind. I know she's a risk but it's a risk I am prepared to take. It is true that she lost her temper at Badminton and lashed out at Best Man, but if you watch the video on YouTube, you'll see that she only once made contact with him. Most of the time she was just hitting out in a blind rage.'

'And that makes it okay?'

'No, but I'm confident Anna is no longer the same person. She's learned some painful lessons. She's lost every friend and every sponsor and been pilloried by the newspapers. She's changed. People do. If she's guilty of anything it's of letting fame go to her head. Speaking from experience, she's not alone.'

'No,' Casey said, 'she's not.'

'Everyone deserves a second chance,' said Casper Leyton.

After he'd hung up, Casey switched off her phone and picked up her fork. Her cottage pie was cold.

Mrs Smith was watching her in puzzlement. 'When Leyton told you he was giving the horse to Anna Sparks, why didn't you change your mind? You could have stopped him. This is a girl who, only a few months ago, behaved monstrously towards you. She was your sworn enemy. Now you've handed her the ride of a lifetime. It could mean the difference between you winning or losing.'

21

THREE-DAY EVENTING first became a recognised sport at the Olympic Games in Stockholm in 1912. Its governing body, the Fédération Equestre Internationale (FEI) describes this multidisciplinary competition as one in which the aim is to 'show the rider's spirit, boldness and perfect knowledge of his horse's paces and their use across country, and to show the condition, handiness, courage, jumping ability, stamina, and speed of the well-trained horse.'

In the days when riding so much as a gymkhana on the intransigent Patchwork seemed like reaching for the stars, Casey had committed this passage to memory. It came back to her now, in a nostalgic wave, as she crossed the courtyard to Burghley House for the annual

Thursday night riders and owners cocktail party.

In the driveway outside, the most famous names in horse trials were alighting from SUVs and sports cars in tuxedos, evening gowns and little black dresses. Since eventing requires a degree of physical fitness unheard of outside horse racing, most looked like models or film stars, but it was odd to see them out of their riding gear. Like Casey, most preferred breeches and boots.

Walking in alone in her short black dress and high heels – bought for Casper Leyton's party – Casey felt like Cinderella wrongly invited to the ball. Then Marsha joined her, which was worse. Casey had decided she didn't particularly like Sam Tide's groom, who was only at Burghley House because she'd again posed as Sam's date. Unless they were wealthy and made regular appearances in *Tatler*, *Vogue* or *Horse & Hound*, Marsha seldom had a good word to say about anyone.

'It just goes to show that money doesn't buy common sense,' Marsha was saying as she sipped at a blue cocktail with a cherry floating in it. 'Casper Leyton must have a screw loose. Why else would he allow a dangerous lunatic like Anna Sparks to ride a horse like Incendiary at Burghley? Sam is livid. He could have done with a second ride. Obviously, he'll be one of the favourites to win here no matter what, but Incendiary would pretty much have guaranteed that he'd walk away with the title. Depending, of course, on Michael Jung. One can never rule him out.'

She fished the cherry out of her drink and crunched

it up. Interestingly, it didn't occur to her to include Casey and Storm among the list of potential winners. It shouldn't have mattered but Casey was irritated by the omission.

'You can blame me,' she told Marsha. 'It was because I turned Incendiary down that Casper decided to offer the horse to Anna.'

Marsha almost spat out the remains of the cherry. 'Come again? You did what? Are you mental?'

'I'm not sure. Probably. Sam already has a horse to ride at Burghley. Anna will be focused on Incendiary and she'll give it everything she's got.'

The expression on Marsha's face as Casey walked off was well worth the sleepless nights Casey had had since reading an outraged editorial in the *New Equestrian* about Casper Leyton's controversial decision to hire eventing's *enfant terrible* to ride his horse at Burghley.

And what a horse Incendiary was. Casey had seen the stallion for the first time earlier that afternoon. He was the colour of Mocha coffee with muscles that coiled and rippled beneath his satin hide. But the most striking thing about him was his balance. As Anna transitioned from a canter to a medium trot, he seemed to float like a mythical being. Watching him, Casey knew immediately that she'd made a potentially catastrophic miscalculation. If Anna was at the top of her game, the pair would be a significant threat.

Still, Casey didn't regret doing what she'd done. It was Storm's courage and power that had carried her to victory at Badminton and Kentucky. If she was fortunate enough to have glory come her way at Burghley, she wanted it only if Storm was part of it and could share in it. The idea of riding a horse that might beat him was intolerable.

Casey had been about to return to the lorry park when Anna came after her. 'Casey, wait, please. I need to speak to you.' Pulling up the stallion, she patted him delightedly before dismounting.

'Isn't he the most heavenly creature on earth? Well, he is to me anyway. I suppose you feel the same about Storm Warning. Casey, I can't begin to thank you. Casper told me that it was only because you didn't want to ride any other horse but Storm that he hired me. Casper's read me the riot act, of course. If I damage so much as a hair on Incendiary's head I might as well emigrate to Brazil.'

'Then don't,' Casey said. 'Treat him like gold.'

'Oh, I will.'

Casey studied Incendiary. He seemed relaxed and kept nuzzling Anna's pockets for treats – surely a positive sign. 'Have a good Burghley, Anna. See you on the other side.'

'Same to you. See you on the other side.'

At the cocktail party, Casey left Marsha looking thunderstruck and retreated to a corner of the room where she felt less exposed. Along the way, people patted her on the back and wished her luck for the championship. Casey found a shadowed spot and stood there nursing a glass of elderflower. She wished she hadn't come. The face she most wanted to see was absent. As a farrier, Peter hadn't been invited. Even if he had been, he wouldn't have come. A cocktail party in a stately home wasn't him at all.

Casey checked her watch. Very shortly she'd make her excuses and return to the hired lorry where Mrs Smith was waiting. She only had to make it through another ten minutes.

Peter was at that moment checking Incendiary's shoes. Casper Leyton had asked him to fit them the previous week. It was at Leyton's stables that he'd learned that Casey had refused the offer of the stallion out of loyalty to Storm.

Peter had been thrown by this news. It had forced him to revise his opinion that Casey was no longer the girl with whom he'd fallen in love, but it still wasn't enough to make him call her. He'd caught her red-handed with Kyle. Who knew how many times it had happened before? She'd not only broken his heart, she'd trampled on it, and he wanted nothing more to do with her.

On his return to Ireland, he'd gone out of his way to

kiss Orla at the first opportunity. It had only happened the once because he found that kissing someone other than his girlfriend had nauseated him. He realised then that he loved Casey in a way that was infinite. If he moved to the ends of the earth, she'd still inhabit his whole heart and soul. She'd ruined him for every other girl.

As if that weren't bad enough, he'd misjudged Orla. Sucked in by her beauty and ample charms, he had been appalled to discover, on the last day of his course, that she'd hidden his phone beneath the cupboard in his room. He couldn't prove it was her but he knew it was. On it were at least a dozen missed calls, texts and messages from Casey. It was some consolation but it wasn't enough. Nothing could make up for the agony he'd felt when he saw her kissing Kyle.

'How do they look?'

He stood up. Anna Sparks was in the doorway, wearing jeans and a polo-shirt. He almost didn't recognise her. She'd cut her hair and put on weight and bore no resemblance to the princess who'd once ruled the circuit. In Peter's opinion her new look was an improvement but then he'd never liked over-made-up fashion victims.

'His feet are perfect. How has he ridden since I shod him? Any tenderness?'

'None at all. His paces are fantastic. Lighter than air. Thank you, Peter. You've done a brilliant job, as usual.'

Peter stared at her in astonishment. In all the years he and his father had spent shoeing the Sparks' horses, he didn't ever recall the word thanks leaving Anna's mouth. She and her ghastly friend 'V,' a girl conspicuous now by her absence, had spent most of their time making fun of him.

'You're welcome. How are you? Not going to the cocktail party with the other riders?'

There was a split-second of hesitation before she responded: 'Not this year. I wanted to check on Incendiary and go over my test for tomorrow's dressage. How about you? Why aren't you with Casey?'

'We broke up,' Peter blurted out before he could stop himself.

She circled Incendiary and nodded approvingly at his new shoes before answering. 'It's none of my business, but are you nuts? The two of you are made for each other.'

'You're right. It's none of your business. But if you must know, she prefers someone else.'

'I don't believe you,' said Anna. 'Who is this person she supposedly prefers? Is it a rider? If you're talking about Kyle West, you're barking up the wrong tree. Kyle is every girl's dream man—'

'Thanks!'

'Can I finish my sentence? He's every girl's dream in terms of looks, but he has issues. I don't want to get into it, but there are armies of ghosts in his past. Something to do with his dead father. To make up for it, Kyle has this overwhelming need to make everybody love him. He did it with me and Casey wouldn't have been any different.'

218

'If you're trying to make me feel worse than I already do, you're doing a great job.'

'Anna gave an exasperated sigh. 'Will you be patient and let me finish? I was going to say that whatever feelings he may or may not have had for her, they weren't returned. My father's former business partner owns Rycliffe Manor. He called me recently about something to do with my dad. We got onto the subject of the equestrian centre and he told me that Casey ran out after a blazing row with Kyle about six weeks ago and they haven't spoken since.'

Hope flickered in Peter's heart. 'How do you know they haven't been in contact?'

'Because Kyle left the country on some undisclosed mission at around the same time. For all I know, he might still be abroad. Ray has been teaching all his clients. They were furious at first, especially Sam Tide, but now they've decided that he's even better than Kyle. He's an oddball and his methods are unusual but he does know horses inside out. Or at least he thinks he does. Personally, I think that the two of them ruin as many horses as they fix, but I'm not sure that anyone apart from Casey would share that view.'

'Why are you telling me this, Anna?'

'Because I owe Casey. Don't be a muppet, Peter. Casey worships the ground you walk on. Go to her before the championship starts and make her smile.'

'I don't know. I'll have to think about it.'

With a flash of her old imperiousness, Anna said:

'Peter Rhys, are you honestly saying that you've never made a mistake in your life?'

Peter went crimson.

Anna rolled her eyes. 'Exactly.'

After she'd gone, Peter leaned against the stable door. He felt oddly exhilarated. Anna was right. If he didn't fight for the girl he loved, he'd regret it for the rest of his life.

But how could he get to her? She was at the cocktail party at Burghley House. Later, she'd join the other riders at the members' enclosure dinner. She'd be surrounded by admirers. He had no invitation to either event, nor did he have the right clothes. Faded black jeans and a creased denim shirt with a missing button hardly qualified as correct dress for a black tie party. If he went bursting into Burghley House like a lovelorn character in a film, people would fall down laughing.

No, he'd have to wait until after Casey had finished her dressage test on Friday and try to find the right time to approach her then.

He was about to leave the stables when it occurred to him that there was one thing he could do for Casey that evening. He could check Storm's feet. If there were any shoeing problems that might hamper the horse in the dressage, he could secretly put them right.

Peter started in the direction of the block where Storm was stabled. As he approached he thought he saw a shadow move. Seconds later, a door banged shut. Peter quickened his pace. There'd been break-ins and horse tampering at other events in the past. Burghley had superb security, but one never knew. It only took a second.

When he reached Storm's stable, he was relieved to see the horse munching on his hay net. Rarely had he looked better. His silver coat had a mercurial gleam and his condition was superb.

'Hello, champ. How's it going?'

Peter let himself in and Storm whickered with pleasure. He was pining for Casey and Roxy, but his favourite farrier was a welcome substitute. Lifting his feet happily, he allowed Peter to examine his shoes.

A door squeaked open and heels came tip-tapping along the corridor. Storm's ears pricked.

'Hello, gorgeous,' said Casey. 'Couldn't stay away. I was missing you.'

She didn't notice Peter until he stepped out from behind Storm and gave her a lingering look that took in every detail of her sexy black dress, long, shapely legs and the dark hair she'd tried unsuccessfully to tame.

'That's good to hear,' he said with a grin, 'because I've missed you too.'

22

CASEY PULLED HER long black boots over breeches as white as fresh snow and zipped them up. Thanks to Mrs Smith, they'd been polished to a military shine. Over her white shirt, she put her navy-blue coat and tails, hand-stitched for her by her father, now a qualified tailor. On the cuffs he'd embroidered a delicate rose design. It was a tribute to her mum, as was the rose brooch Casey carried in her pocket. Having it with her always made Casey feel as if her mother was riding with her like a guardian angel, sharing in every high and low.

Unlike the Equi-Flow lorry, the back of the hired one was cramped, but Casey didn't mind in the least. This one came without strings attached. Opening the narrow closet, she checked herself in the mirror. She looked a lot more poised than she felt.

In under an hour she would be competing for the ultimate prize in eventing. It was hard to take in. Many experts were of the opinion that the Burghley Horse Trials had taken over from Badminton as the toughest Three-Day Event in the world. If she won . . .

But, no, Mrs Smith had told her to put both victory and the Grand Slam completely out of her mind. As far as she was concerned, Casey had enough on her plate without ratcheting up the pressure even further. Casey was inclined to agree. Today was about posting a decent dressage result, nothing more, nothing less.

Putting her top hat over her short, neatly gelled dark hair, Casey stepped out of the lorry. Mrs Smith and Peter were waiting with her horse. Storm's head went up and his ears pricked when he saw her. Nothing got his blood racing like competition. He pranced on the spot, showing off. Mrs Smith, who'd had rather more sleep than Casey, had insisted on plaiting his mane. Needless to say, his turnout was of Grand Prix quality.

Casey felt a rush of love when she saw him. In a way, it was because of Storm that she and Peter were back together. There'd been no dramatic scenes. As soon as they saw one another, they'd rushed to embrace.

When at last they separated, Casey said, 'Peter, I'm so sorry about what happened with Kyle. It really wasn't what you thought. He—'

Peter put a finger to her lips. 'Stop. I'm sorry too. I'm

no good at being away from you. I hate it. I want to always be with you. If you'll have me, that is.'

'Oh, I'll have you,' Casey responded cheekily.

There'd been chemistry between her and Kyle, but like everything else it was based on an illusion. When he kissed her, she'd felt only guilt. Peter's kisses sent an electrical storm crackling through her veins. As he held her to him, they fitted together. There was a rightness about Peter that went to her core.

Putting her arms around his waist, she looked up at him. 'Wish me luck in the dressage?'

'I do, but you won't need it.' Leaning down he whispered: 'You look devastatingly beautiful, by the way.'

Turning to Mrs Smith, Casey held out her hands. Her teacher gripped them. 'Just do your best, my dear. Nothing else matters.'

Casey's eyes were suddenly bright with emotion. 'Thank you for everything and especially for being here.'

'Wouldn't miss it for the world. I love you, Casey, and I'm more proud of you than you'll ever know.'

'Love you too.'

As Casey swung onto Storm, boosted by Peter, Detective Inspector Lenny McLeod hurried up. He'd been on a health kick since she'd last seen him and was almost unrecognisable as the podgy policeman who'd accompanied Peter to Kentucky. He'd traded caffeine, fast food and lonely all-nighters for the gym and more days out with his Morgan mare, Montana. It suited him.

His grey hair was neatly trimmed and he was fit and slim in his plain clothes – a white shirt, grey blazer and jeans.

The only thing that hadn't changed was his razor-sharp gaze. It raked the faces of the passing crowd like a scimitar, daring them to commit a crime and get away with it. Casey could imagine it acting as a truth serum on any criminal who stood before him.

McLeod was at the championship as a friend, but also on unofficial business. After Mrs Smith's phone call about Ray Cook, he had done some investigating into the staff at Rycliffe Manor. He knew that she'd never have contacted him unless she had serious cause for suspicion. While he'd found no specific evidence of wrongdoing, there was enough smoke for him to be convinced that a fire was either about to start or already smouldering. One person in particular had a background that set all sorts of alarm bells ringing. Gut instinct had driven him to Burghley. He saw no harm in keeping a close watch over Casey Blue.

'Why do I feel as if you're guarding me?' Casey said teasingly as the detective accompanied her and Storm to the collecting ring. 'I'm not complaining. I like having my own personal bodyguard, but I'm wondering if you know something I don't. Should I be worried?'

McLeod grinned up at her. 'Casey, as you are perfectly aware I'm only pretending to be your minder in order to get up close and personal with the stars. How else would I get a ringside seat to see you and Storm?'

Casey smiled back but he saw doubt flicker across her face.

'What is it? What's wrong?'

She pulled up Storm. 'Lenny, can I say something to you in confidence?'

'Of course.'

'Mrs Smith told me that she'd spoken to you about Ray Cook. I'm not sure how much you know about what went on at Rycliffe Manor but to cut a long story short I was threatened when I left. I've tried to push it out of my mind to focus on Burghley, but now that I'm here it's like a shadow hanging over me. Last night Peter caught a glimpse of someone creeping around Storm's stable-block. I haven't said anything to anyone but it's been eating away at me. I wouldn't put it past that man to try to hurt us – hurt Storm.'

McLeod put a hand on Storm's neck. 'Casey, this is the last thing you should be thinking about when you're about to do dressage. I'm not dismissing your fears. Far from it. I hear you loud and clear. At the same time, I want you to relax and trust that I have your back. Can you do that?

This time Casey's smile was genuine. 'Yes, I can.'

'Good. Now go out there and do what you do best.'

It was 2.55 p.m. when Casey entered the arena. The stands were packed with thousands of people and millions more were watching her live on television and yet as she cantered into the dressage court she'd seldom felt more nervous. It was only after halting and saluting the judges that she remembered Mrs Smith's words. Nothing mattered but the here and now. Nothing was more important than connecting to Storm.

Casey and Mrs Smith had taken a gamble with Storm, not entering him in a single event in the lead up to Burghley. They'd reasoned that it was more important that he arrived at the event completely sound than with extra competition experience. As she changed the rein in a medium trot and guided him into a shoulder-in-left, Casey knew they'd done the right thing. Storm was one of those rare horses who rose to the big occasion. He drew energy from the crowd. His ears were pricked and he felt elastic.

Mrs Smith had gone through the test with Casey so often that she could almost hear her teacher narrating each movement as she rode. *Half pass left. Track left. Collected trot. Extended trot.*

The crowd melted away. Nothing existed beyond Storm. *Shoulder-in right. Circle right, eight metres. Medium walk. Change the rein in extended walk. Halt. Five step rein-back. Proceed in collected canter right.*

A dog barked. Casey felt a rush of panic. The Doberman and Rottweiler were at Storm's heels. She saw again their slavering jaws, the blood dripping from the gash on Roxy's flank.

Storm felt her snatch at the bit and was confused. He forgot about the flying change. When the contact came on again, he was relieved. They moved into a serpentine of three loops. They were bonded again, horse and girl, a spiritual centaur. Applause rippled around the arena. The board flashed Casey's provisional score in red – 45.3, putting her in twelfth place. For today, at least, it was over.

23

ANNA SPARKS SHRUGGED into her air jacket and slipped her bib over the top of it. There was a time when she'd have felt invincible in the lead-up to the cross-country, especially if she'd posted a personal best of 40.3 to lie third behind David Powell and Sam Tide after the dressage, but today nerves roared through her system like ocean waves, building and crashing. Anna didn't mind them. Every rider had them. In a way, they were necessary.

She'd once read an interview with the great Mary King, who'd said that she was never afraid as she waited to start the cross-country. If you were, she told the journalist, you shouldn't be eventing. What she feared most was making a stupid mistake that might let her horse down. 'I think what we're doing is so ridiculous ... '

In spite of herself, Anna laughed. She knew exactly what Mary had meant, but it was good to hear it from a gold medal-winning Olympian. Her own anxiety was all to do with Incendiary. She was petrified of doing him harm, either physically or results-wise. The horse was a champion from the tips of his ears to the finest hair on his glossy tail. The onus was on Anna to bring out the best in him.

She was also nervous of the crowd. The reaction to her dressage performance on Friday had been muted in some quarters and downright hostile in others. Leaving the arena, she'd been subjected to loud booing and catcalls. She hoped that the antipathy towards her didn't spill over during the cross-country and in some way endanger Incendiary. If he was injured and it was her fault, she'd never forgive herself.

Hopping down the steps of the lorry that Casper had loaned her, Anna hurried over to Incendiary. He was tacked up and waiting impatiently with Niall, his groom. To be on the safe side, Anna checked her horse over for the umpteenth time. Running her palm across his muscled chest, she drew comfort from the rhythmic thud of his heart. He was feeling confident about the day ahead even if she wasn't.

Riding to the collecting ring, Anna caught a glimpse of a scoreboard. She felt a stab of guilt. Casey Blue had passed up the opportunity to ride Incendiary and now Anna was nine places ahead of her.

'My advisers think I've lost my mind,' was Casper Leyton's opening remark when he'd called her. 'Having been turned down by one seventeen-year-old rider well known for acting on her emotions, I'm offering my finest horse to another, recently banned teenager. Luckily for you, I happen to believe in second chances.'

Since then, Anna had spent a substantial portion of each day trying to come up with a way to repay Casey. So far she'd failed. Perhaps she always would.

From time to time, she rehearsed a conversation in which she asked Casey if she'd consider going for a coffee or a meal when she was next free, but the chances of it happening were remote. Anna had worked hard to become a better person than the spoiled, ego-maniacal brat she'd been before she was banned, but she couldn't forget Casey's words. 'Once a bitch, always a bitch.'

Maybe Casey was right. Maybe leopards never really changed their spots.

Behind the ropes, Niall signalled to her. Five minutes until her start time for the cross-country. Anna's pulse rate doubled. Incendiary began to bounce like a racehorse. It was an overcast day but quite muggy and his neck was already soapy with sweat. He had the ideal temperament for an eventer. Calm and collected on dressage day and all fire when it came to the cross-country.

As he jogged past the milling crowds, snatching at the bit, Anna couldn't repress a grin. Some riders were scared by hot horses, but not her. Their passion for speed thrilled her.

She was moving towards the start when a woman in a blue baseball cap and olive green Barbour jacket crossed her vision. Her cap was pulled down but her profile and something about the way she moved triggered a memory. As she neared, she threw a glance in Anna's direction. There was something so cheerfully malevolent in the look that a bolt of fear that had nothing to do with the fences to come went through Anna. An instant later the woman was gone, swallowed by the milling crowd.

A strange numbness came over Anna. The scene swam away. In a flash, she was back at Rycliffe Manor. She was in the office, throwing a fit because she was positive that she'd left her diary in her bag behind the desk and it was no longer there. It wasn't valuable, but it contained contact numbers and intimate details that she definitely didn't want shared. On a previous occasion her favourite T-shirt had disappeared from her room in the guest quarters.

After raging at Kyle about the missing items Anna had demanded that the police be summoned. Kyle had listened very patiently and soothed her in that infuriatingly reasonable way of his. He'd promised to replace the diary. At the same time, he'd managed to imply that she was being quite petty, considering that she was a millionaire's daughter and the combined cost of the journal and T-shirt was the cost of a couple of coffees. He also implied that she'd more than likely lost them somewhere else.

Ray had been much more scathing. 'I'm not being funny, but who would steal your diary? Isn't it just an endless stream of lunch dates and shopping sprees?'

In the midst of the row, Anna had noticed Hannah watching her from across the courtyard. The junior instructor was sitting on the edge of the fountain with a book in her hand, the picture of innocence. Right then Anna knew – was a hundred per cent certain – that it was Hannah who'd taken her diary and T-shirt. The girl was obsessed with Kyle. The theft of the diary would presumably give her ammunition by allowing her to pry into the life and secrets of a perceived love rival.

Of course, there was no proof that it was her, and Anna had been so creeped out by the brazen way in which Hannah stared her down that she'd dropped the matter then and there.

But it was the final straw. She'd grown increasingly worried about the effect that being at Rycliffe Manor was having on Rough Diamond. Her gifted chestnut horse seemed to have lost the fiery pride that had made her insist that her father bought him for her. His stable name, Mouse, had once been ironic. Now it summed him up. But who or what was responsible for the change, Anna had never figured out.

With hindsight, she realised that she was equally culpable. Had she cared more about the wellbeing of her horse and less about the pursuit of fame and glory, it might be Rough Diamond she was riding at Burghley and not Incendiary, who belonged to Casper Leyton and would never be hers.

At the time, however, the thing she kept returning to was a comment made by Ray soon after Rough Diamond arrived at Rycliffe Manor. 'He has the potential for greatness, your horse, but he needs to be taken down a peg or two.'

Following the stolen diary incident, Anna had made plans to tell Kyle that she was changing teachers. Tragically, that came too late for Rough Diamond, who melted down the following weekend. That, for Anna, had been the beginning of the end – in more ways than one. Such had been the catalogue of woes that followed that Hannah and her stalker tendencies had been the least of her concerns.

' … Anna Sparks riding Casper Leyton's Incendiary,' the Burghley announcer boomed.

The clock was ticking. Anna's limbs were weak. She was in no condition to manage the stallion plunging beneath her.

The look that Hannah had given her … it was triumphant. More than that, it was evil. What if it hadn't been Ray who was responsible for robbing Rough Diamond of his confidence and driving him to a breakdown? What if it had been Hannah, the person who routinely exercised the horse? What if it was all part of her plan to rid Rycliffe Manor of her perceived rival? If so, it had worked. She'd destroyed Rough Diamond and driven Anna away. Those two things had set in motion a chain of events that had ultimately almost ended Anna's career.

Could she be planning to come after Anna again? But no, why would she do that? Anna was no longer a threat to her. Casey Blue, on the other hand, was. If there was even a hint of a flirtation between her and Kyle, Hannah's paranoia would magnify it. Anyone capable of stealing, lying and destroying a horse in order to rid Rycliffe Manor of one rival for Kyle's affections, would have no qualms about doing it to another girl, especially since she'd never been caught. Casey was about to compete in one of the most dangerous events in the world. If Hannah decided to try something wicked, the consequences could be catastrophic.

The countdown had started. 'Five, four, three ... '

'Niall!' screamed Anna. 'Niall!'

The groom flew to the ropes. 'What the heck's going on? You're about to be eliminated.'

Anna leaned down. 'This is a matter of life and death. Get an urgent message to Peter Rhys or Angelica Smith. Tell them that they need to stop Hannah Morley. She's on the cross-country course and I think she's out to get Casey. They'll know what to do.'

Giving Incendiary his head, she was gone in a blur.

24

ELSEWHERE IN THE genteel environs of Burghley jazz musicians in boaters and candy-striped jackets entertained the crowds, oblivious to the unfolding drama. Beneath a pewter sky, armies of horse-crazy teenagers in a uniform of polo-shirts, skinny jeans and brown Ariat boots scoured the tented village for tack and clothes. Anyone over the age of eighteen tended to dress in identical tweed and Barbour jackets, with assorted spaniels, chocolate Labradors and wire-haired terriers as accessories. They buzzed like bees around the portable show jumps, Rolex watches and garden furniture.

As the time came for the leading riders to tackle the cross-country course, almost everyone filtered out across the park to stake their claim to the best spots beside the scariest fences. Disregarding the weather, they spread picnic rugs and dug out cameras, binoculars and flasks of coffee. It promised to be a spectacular afternoon of action. As always, the cream of equestrian talent had risen to the top of the scoreboard.

Naturally, people rooted for their favourites. There was the Andrew Nicholson camp and the William Fox-Pitt camp. Others adored Mary King for her humility, intuitive riding and the way she always put her horses first. There were those who argued over whether the Australian, Sam Tide, was better than the American, Stella Blackmore, or if the German, Michael Jung, topped them all. Others vowed they would be Pippa Funnell fans for ever.

When it came to Anna Sparks and Casey Blue, opinion was divided. Many considered Casey to be a flash in the pan. There was no doubt that her achievements were phenomenal but they claimed it was mostly to do with her good fortune in stumbling across Storm, her wonder horse. Casey's devoted followers, on the other hand, insisted she was the most talented British youngster in at least a generation.

The most heated debates were reserved for Anna Sparks. Which side people came down on largely depended on whether they believed in forgiveness or considered her beyond redemption. Either way, they were looking forward to seeing how Incendiary coped with Burghley's unique demands.

The stage was set for a virtual banquet of eventing

spills and thrills. As the clock ticked relentlessly, the tension mounted.

Few in the park were quite so tense as Casey Blue. As planned, she and Storm had begun cross-country day with their own version of eventing's long-format roads and tracks section. Now Casey stood with Mrs Smith, Peter and a British Eventing official waiting for the vet to deliver his verdict on Storm's fitness to continue. A fail would mean automatic elimination.

'Sound as a bell,' he said at last. 'You say that an MRI scan revealed that, like Seabiscuit and Pharlap, the great racehorses, Storm's heart is almost twice the size of a normal horse? Here's why that's a good thing. He's as cool as a cucumber after his morning's work. You'd think he'd done nothing more energetic than stroll over here from the lorry park.'

Casey and Mrs Smith hugged jubilantly. So far, so good.

Peter boosted Casey into the saddle and she rode to the collecting ring with McLeod at her side. It was a sensible precaution but one both viewed as unnecessary. Reassured by the detective, who was of the opinion that the attack on Storm was opportunistic and a one-off, she had put it firmly out of her mind. Her only thoughts were to do with lines and stride counts. She'd walked the course four times and knew it inside out.

'Big and bold,' was how William Fox-Pitt had described it in a television interview. 'It's what Three-Day Eventing is all about. But it tests you mentally and physically. When you walk it, it feels one way. Riding it can be totally different.'

Ruth Edge was more succinct. 'There is no room for error.'

Casey was determined to get a positive start. Setting off tentatively led to time faults. She knew from experience that unless they burst from the D box with intention and intensity, Storm would be in a backwards frame of mind. They had to shave off every available second or finish nowhere. It was that simple. But if they could end the cross-country phase in the top ten or, at worst, the top twenty, there'd be everything to play for on Sunday.

There were thirty-three fences, making thirty-nine jumping efforts in total. As Casey warmed up, Peter and Mrs Smith hurried out to the tenth fence. They hoped that from there they'd also be able to catch a glimpse of Casey at the eighth and ninth and have time to get to the thirteenth in time to see her fly over the fourteenth and fifteenth too.

Casey's father, Roland, and Ravi Singh, his boss and friend from the Half Moon Tailor Shop, were already in prime position at fence twenty-six, the Anniversary Splash. From there they could see the famous water jump. They'd driven up from London first thing that morning and had already seen two dunkings and a run-out.

Provided no one was hurt, watery falls could be amusing, but Roland Blue didn't want any kind of tumble for his daughter. Always anxious when Casey was riding, he grew steadily more nervous as her start time neared.

First, though, came Anna Sparks, Casey's rival. Roland was half-expecting a reprise of her Badminton debacle – a ditching in muddy water, followed by a temper tantrum and a flailing whip. But the girl riding the glorious cocoa-coloured horse looked nothing like the teenage glamour puss he remembered. He had to check the programme to be sure it was her. Anna and Incendiary came pounding down the bank and had cleared all three jumping efforts and splashed out and away before he could blink. The lake was no more challenging to them than a puddle.

'Peter, wait!'

Midway to the ninth, Mrs Smith paused. A wave of agony rippled through her. Despite promising to keep Casey apprised of the most minuscule deterioration in her health, she had not told her pupil that the tablets – even near-lethal doses of them – had stopped working more than ten days earlier. Now when the pain came rolling in it was like a tsunami. It crushed her, leaving her drained.

But that was not the only reason Mrs Smith slowed for a breather. Her heart was racing alarmingly fast. Conscious of Janet's warning about the stimulant properties of the special potion, she thought it prudent to take a rest.

Instantly, Peter was at her side. 'Angelica, what's wrong? Here, lean on me. Are you feeling dizzy? Let me call for an ambulance.'

The pain subsided as suddenly as it had come on. Mrs Smith was so grateful she could have cried. 'For goodness' sake, Peter. You're as bad as Casey. I'm not made of glass, you know. I merely needed to catch my breath. I'm quite fine now. Shall we go? Casey will be starting in a few minutes.'

Peter stood without moving. 'Yes, and Casey would murder me if she thought that I'd allowed you to watch her ride when you were ill and needed help. Please, Angelica. Be sensible. You can watch Casey on TV later. Let me call for the on-course paramedic. That's what they're there for.'

But as he took his phone from his pocket, it started buzzing. The number came up as unknown. Peter answered it without thinking.

'Peter? This is Kyle West.'

Peter was one of the most easy-going people on the circuit, but immediately he was fuming. 'I have nothing to say—'

'This is an emergency, not a social call. I couldn't get hold of Angelica Smith and you are the only other person

I can think of. I found your number on your website. There's this girl at Rycliffe Manor, a junior instructor called Hannah Morley. I've been out of town. I returned last night to find that no one has seen Hannah since Thursday when she went to visit a sick aunt. Her clients are furious.'

Mrs Smith was looking at Peter quizzically. He pulled a face. 'That's fascinating, Kyle, but I have to go. Casey's about to start.'

'Peter, Casey may be in danger. If you care about her, you'll listen to me.'

Peter went cold. 'I'm listening.'

'A few hours ago I asked a friend of Hannah's to check her room in the staff quarters. She found a missing diary belonging to Anna Sparks, piles of newspaper cuttings about Casey with hateful things written on them and a detailed plan of the cross-country course at Burghley.'

'Kyle, we don't have all day. What are you trying to tell me? What's the emergency?'

'My Dad, Ray, he's had a look at the drawings and he's certain Hannah's planning some sort of attack ... I've just arrived at Burghley now, but ... '

A lanky boy in jodhpurs and a sweat-drenched polo-shirt came tearing up to Peter, gasping for breath. 'I've ... been ... looking ... everywhere for you ... Incendiary's groom, Niall sent me ... Message from Anna Sparks. Life and death, apparently. Anna says you need to stop Hannah somebody or other before she gets to Casey and that she thinks she saw her on the cross-country course.'

242

Peter thanked him and gripped the phone. 'Kyle, can you give me a detailed description?'

A minute later he called McLeod. The detective was planning to watch Casey ride from the media centre, where he could see every fence on television.

'Peter, we've run out of time.'

'What does that mean?'

'It means that Casey is on TV right now. She and Storm are on their way to the start. If something's going to happen, there's nothing we can do to prevent it. We can only hope for the best and respond.'

25

*W*HY AM I *doing this?*

That was what Casey was thinking as she waited, reins in hands, poised over Storm's withers, for the starter's countdown. She was supposed to be having fun, but she was terrified. It wasn't that she was terrified for herself. The thirty-three fences that faced her were no picnic, but she trusted Storm to carry her over them safely. He'd never been fitter, stronger or more responsive. But she was terrified for him. What if she made an error of judgement that brought Storm down? What if he broke a leg and had to be put to sleep?

' ... The youngest ever winner of the Badminton and Kentucky Three-Day Events, Casey Blue, riding her own Storm Warning ... '

'Five seconds,' said the starter.

Casey touched the rose brooch in her breeches pocket and consigned every negative thought to the past. Nothing was more important than the next eleven minutes and twenty seconds, the optimum time for completing the course. Mrs Smith's training schedule, though unconventional, had produced textbook results. Storm was as ready as he'd ever be. Tensed beneath her, he was a coiled spring. With a second to go, she squeezed his sides. He surged forward with such power that Casey had to grab his mane to stay with him. The first fence vanished beneath them. The cross-country had begun.

Some riders measured every inch of the course with a wheel in order to plot the most precise stride counts and lines. Casey and Mrs Smith used the old-fashioned method. Four of Casey's strides equalled one of Storm's, and two long strides for her was roughly where Storm would land after a fence. For the most part, though, they relied on strategy. In a race against time the clock mattered most.

Casey cut the corner to the second, a wooden bench. She settled Storm into a comfortable gallop as they approached the third, a big, solid picnic table guaranteed to make him pick up his feet and start thinking. She'd noticed that a lot of horses veered slightly towards the nearby lorry park as they approached it, so she tapped Storm on the shoulder with her whip as a reminder that she was there. It was unnecessary. He never wavered.

After each fence, she pushed Storm on the instant his

245

feet touched the ground. 'Moving on quickly when you touch down can save you fifteen to twenty seconds a round,' Mrs Smith was always telling her. So ingrained were her teacher's words that it was as if she and Casey's mum were riding post, guiding Casey and Storm, protecting them.

Casey glanced at her stopwatch. One minute gone.

That morning, she'd watched Ruth Edge, Michael Edge and a couple of others do the cross-country to see how the fences were riding. Fence four was a Burghley classic, a big rolltop followed, two strides later, by a drop down a steep bank. Casey rode it with Mary King's words in mind. 'The art of riding is to be as quiet as possible on your horse. If you keep changing gears, you're going to use up a lot of energy.'

It was a scary fence and required her to be brave as a rider. If she hesitated, Storm would doubt himself. Knowing that when he landed on the downslope he'd have lots of forward impulsion, she condensed his stride as they approached. Head up and shoulders back, she let the reins slip to allow Storm to stretch and get a good look at the skinny coming up. The last thing she wanted was a run-out. Urging him on with her legs and voice, she breathed a sigh of relief when it was over.

The Elephant Trap, she chose to take at an angle. That way Storm was already in position for the turn when he landed. Hands light on the reins, Casey galloped towards the seventh. The first element was a narrow trunk on the rear side of a ditch – an optical illusion that carried

246

the potential for disaster. Storm wasn't fazed. Nor did he mind the brush fence shaped like a Land Rover. One stride then a ditch, three strides then another brush. The angles were daunting but it rode fairly enough.

It was as she steadied Storm for the Cascade Complex ninth that a feeling of dread came over Casey. She could see, as if she were watching it at the cinema, her silver horse rearing, twisting and overbalancing. She saw herself being crushed beneath him. Her reins slackened. The sky seemed momentarily to darken.

Feeling the contact go, Storm scrambled over the oxer. Casey tried to get her thoughts together, but her confidence had evaporated. The trees that preceded the looming Trout Hatchery were threatening. The jolly, cheering throng lining the ropes offered no protection at all. *They* didn't have to negotiate the pond ahead. That was the thing about riding cross-country. There was nowhere more exposed and few places as lonely.

Casey was not the only person having premonitions of doom. McLeod, Peter and Mrs Smith were each doing whatever they could to find Hannah. Unfortunately, they had little to go on. The description they'd been given was hazy at best and since Anna was not a hundred per cent sure that the woman she'd seen was Hannah, there was no way of knowing if she was even at Burghley.

'She might genuinely be visiting a sick aunt,' Peter said hopefully to the young constable McLeod had recruited to help with the search. They were rushing from fence to fence on foot, trying to spot a five-foot-five redhead. Anna had described her as wearing an olive-green Barbour jacket and navy-blue baseball cap.

'Does Miss Sparks have any idea how many people are in green Barbour jackets and blue baseball caps?' panted the constable as they arrived at the water jump to find thousands of eventing fans packing the edges. 'It's like saying that a suspect at a Manchester United game is wearing red and white.'

McLeod, meanwhile, was hurtling across Burghley Park in a Land Rover. Driving dangerously fast, he only narrowly avoided an escaped Jack Russell and a party of picnicking pensioners. Accompanying him was Kyle West, who'd come rushing up to him and said he had a hunch where Hannah might strike if that's what she had in mind. Burghley security had pointed him in the detective's direction. McLeod took one look at him, made a judgement call and they were in the vehicle and racing across the course before Casey and Storm had left the start.

In the crisis, nobody had thought to mention anything to Roland Blue, sitting oblivious with Ravi Singh at the water jump. And Mrs Smith had been left on her own because there was an assumption that she was neither well enough nor fit enough to join in the hunt. In a way, she was glad. The pain had receded, leaving only its ghost, like a bad memory, and for a moment she was almost at full strength.

Peter and McLeod had both walked the course and knew Burghley, but no one understood it with the intimacy of Mrs Smith. She'd not only watched DVDs of every great rider from William Fox-Pitt to Mark Todd winning there, she'd spent a dozen hours wandering it with intent. Every blade of grass was familiar to her, as were all thirty-nine of the jumps designed by Olympic gold-medal-winning Captain Mark Phillips, former husband of Olympic eventer Princess Anne, and father of Zara Phillips, who'd ridden earlier in the day.

After Peter had sprinted away to join the young constable scouring the course for Hannah, Mrs Smith had felt old again. Useless. No good for anything. But then it occurred to her if there was one thing the cancer could not take away from her it was her intellect.

Distant cheers carried on the wind. She glanced at her watch and realised that they were for Casey and Storm, arriving at the start.

'Think, you old idiot!' Angelica Smith ranted at herself. If someone was going to try something in a place packed with tens of thousands of witnesses, where would they try it? Which fence?

She began to hurry towards the trees that crowded the track before the Trout Hatchery. Because, of course, the best place to bring a horse down at Burghley would not be at a fence, watched live by millions of viewers. The easiest place to do it would be somewhere invisible to the cameras and of no interest to the spectators. A spot where the dappled light danced and the shadows shifted and the rider was, for a second, disoriented.

As Mrs Smith half-hobbled, half-ran, Janet's special potion sloshed through her veins with increasing intensity. Her heartbeat began to increase.

When the sirens announced a stoppage on the cross-country course, Casey did not feel the frustration she normally would have at being halted in mid-flow. In fact, it was a blessing. It gave Storm a breather and allowed her to get a grip on herself before tackling the Trout Hatchery fences.

'Any idea what's happened?' she asked a marshal.

'A fall most probably – not at a fence, strangely, but in the trees up ahead. Saw a Land Rover go tearing in.'

Casey shivered. She wondered if the fall she'd imagined had been a premonition, but about another rider not herself.

An animal scream reverberated from the trees. Storm's head shot up.

'Good grief. What was that?' cried the marshal.

Casey was too busy calming Storm to reply. 'Easy, boy. It's only a bird. Nothing to worry about.' As she spoke, the Land Rover emerged and sped away. Tinted windows hid the occupants.

Shutting both the vision and the scream from her mind, Casey eased Storm into a trot. When the signal came to start, she was mentally ready. Sensing that she was with him once more, Storm felt the same way. He raced through the trees without incident, plunged strongly into the pond, over the Goose Nest and duck and then they were off and galloping.

Ahead were two fences that Casey knew would be a challenge. The first was the fifteenth, a huge white oxer. Walking the course, Casey had measured the back rail and found that it was level with her shoulder.

'It's the type of fence that sorts the brave rider from the less cautious one,' Mrs Smith had told her. 'And believe me, there is a difference. In that way, eventing's come full circle. For a while it became a little disappointing because all the emphasis was on show jumping and dressage. Now the courses are more technical and we're seeing the return of chunky, solid fences that ask the big questions.'

The fifteenth was nothing if not chunky and solid. It was arrived at via a red and white house and a post and rails with a drop. Galloping towards the oxer, which grew more intimidating with every step, Casey concentrated on not getting in Storm's way. He trusted her never to take him over an obstacle he couldn't handle. Now she had to trust him.

As he soared into the air, Casey was conscious of wanting to freeze-frame the moment and hold onto it for eternity. She was no longer afraid. Free of gravity and earthly constraints, she wanted only to savour the breeze in her face, the power and grace of the incredible horse beneath her and the upturned faces of the crowd that willed them on. It was as if she'd stepped through a portal into her childhood dream. Storm was the horse of fire she'd always wanted. A horse with wings.

For the remaining five and a half minutes of the cross-country, she saw everything through that rose-tinted filter. Not that it made the fences any less terrifying. The dreaded Cottesmore Leap, the largest eventing fence in the world, presented itself like an obstacle from a nightmare. As Storm flew over the enormous brush, Casey looked down and saw the ditch that followed – a cavernous expanse wide enough to drive a Land Rover through.

Mrs Smith had insisted that the fence was a 'rider-frightener' – scary to people but not to horses and so it proved. Storm sailed over it with barely a pause but swished his tail crossly on landing, as if to say, 'I can handle that, no problem, but I'm not going to pretend I like it.'

As always, Casey found the water jump more enjoyable afterwards than it was splashing through it with thousands of people waiting (some hopefully) to see if she'd come crashing down in the mud. As they galloped towards Burghley House with a whole ten seconds in hand, Casey couldn't stop smiling. A wall of sound came at them as they swept into the arena. Storm cleared the flower table and leapt through the final arch to ecstatic cheers.

There were many riders still to go so it was not until Storm had been rewarded with treats, hosed down with iced water, massaged, rehydrated and had his magnetic rug put on that it was confirmed that Casey was in eighth place after the cross-country, seven spots ahead of Anna Sparks.

26

AT AN HOUR considered unreasonable even by the standards of the early-rising equestrian community, Casey and Mrs Smith sat wrapped in a tartan blanket drinking chai made with cinnamon and honey. They huddled together watching the rising sun stain the sky with a peachy glow. At the far end of the lorry park there were the first stirrings of life, but here they had only the morning star for company.

'I take back everything I said about the Equi-Flow lorry,' said Mrs Smith. 'I would have killed for a soft bed this week. The sofa in this rented one would have been welcomed in medieval times as an instrument of torture. I've left you some money in my will and I want you to put it towards a decent lorry. No, I don't want to hear any protestations. At the very least buy one that allows you to get a decent night's rest.'

She sipped her tea.

'Whatever happened to Ed Lashley-Jones and Candi and Mandi, anyway? I thought you were being sued for breach of contract.'

'I was,' said Casey. 'But that was before he discovered that Anna Sparks would be riding Casper Leyton's best horse at Burghley and decided that it was the business opportunity of the decade. My lovely lorry has been repainted and Anna's using it this week. I miss the cappuccino machine and the soft bed, but apart from that she's welcome to it. Good luck to her. As far as I'm concerned, not enough great things can happen to Anna Sparks. From what Peter says, she provided the description that helped you, Detective Inspector McLeod and Kyle save us from a horrific fall.

'And Ray helped too, because he was the one who made the link between Hannah's drawings and the likely location of the tripwire. Can you believe that? Ray, of all people. And there I was convinced that Hannah was harmless while Ray was only one step away from being an axe murderer.'

'Like I'm always telling you, never judge a man until you've walked a mile in his boots,' said Mrs Smith.

'Yes, but he didn't exactly help himself. He was sinister and aggressive.'

'Now you know the reason for it.'

'Now I do,' agreed Casey.

She did and not a thing was the way she'd imagined it to be. It was a long and tragic story, but it explained a lot. Ray had grown up as an orphan in a community of travellers, being passed from one family to another and knowing little about his own except that his father had been a horse breeder who'd vanished before he was born.

As a young man he had a tremendous gift with horses, but his brusque manner and disfigured face made it difficult for him to progress as a trainer. In the yards where he worked for peanuts he slipped steadily into alcoholism. His wife abandoned him. But his problems were only beginning. When Kyle was about six years old, Ray hit a child while driving in a whisky-fuelled rage and she later died.

Devastated, Ray vowed never again to touch a drop. Not wanting Kyle's life to be ruined by his mistake, he changed both his own name and his son's and told Kyle to tell everyone he met that his father was dead. To pay the bills Ray retrained as an electrician, but he still dreamed of working with horses. When Kyle started failing his riding instructor course, Ray saw his opportunity. Kyle was blessed with charm and good looks, while Ray had the equine knowledge and experience. Together they made an unbeatable combination.

'It was all working perfectly until the pressure of keeping up the deception caused Ray to start drinking again after fourteen sober years,' Casey told Mrs Smith. 'Added to which, they became victims of their own success. People started to ask difficult questions. Kyle was passed over for the Golden Horseshoe Award because the judges wanted more details on how he went, overnight, from being the worst student on his course to being a star instructor.

'Whisky made Ray aggressive and that's the reason he threatened me on the day I discovered their secret. Apparently, he signed up for a twelve-step Alcoholics Anonymous programme the next day. He apologised to me about ninety times when we spoke on the phone after the cross-country and said he was glad that he could do some small thing to make it up to me. I told him that preventing me from breaking my neck was hardly small, but he was welcome to do it any time.'

'And what of Kyle?' asked Mrs Smith. 'Did you get a chance to talk to him last night?'

'I did. In a strange way, it turns out that being rumbled as a fake teacher may be the making of him. After our fight, he walked out of Rycliffe Manor and got on the next plane to Greece. He needed to get away from everything, to try to find himself again. He rented a cottage in the Pyrenees and did nothing but walk and read for weeks. In the end he realised that what he wants is to be his own man, out of his father's shadow, and to live his own life. He plans to study architecture. Funny, he says he likes horses but prefers houses.'

What Casey didn't mention to Mrs Smith, or Peter for that matter, is that as she'd stood in a deserted corner of the tented village talking to Kyle, she'd realised that there'd always be a frisson of something between them. It wasn't love and it wasn't the overpowering electrical attraction she felt with Peter. But it was chemistry. Walking away, she'd turned one last time to find Kyle still watching her, his sun-bleached hair falling over his tanned face, his blue eyes crinkling at the corners. She'd decided there and then that it was just as well he was changing careers.

'You were saying,' Mrs Smith said meaningfully. She could always read her pupil like a book.

Casey flushed. 'I ... oh, yes, I was about to say that when Kyle went AWOL Ray started teaching his clients because he didn't want to let anyone down before Burghley. To his surprise, people liked what he did. If all goes well with his recovery, he plans to open a small yard of his own early next year. It's not somewhere I would ever visit, but, you know, it works for some people.'

She stopped. 'Tell me again what happened with Hannah. I was exhausted and in shock yesterday afternoon. It was hard to take it in.'

Mrs Smith took up the story. 'When Ray hired Hannah to be an instructor at Rycliffe Manor, he did so on the basis of the sterling results she'd achieved when she qualified. He had no idea that she'd been expelled from her high school for stalker-type behaviour. Once she met Kyle and became obsessed with him, she became fixated on getting him at all costs. That included stealing stuff that belonged to anyone she thought might be a rival,

258

including Anna Sparks' diary, and eavesdropping on Kyle's conversations.'

'That's why she decided to throw Roxy and I to the dogs?' said Casey with a shudder.

'Not the nicest way of putting it, but yes. She overheard Ray telling Kyle that it would take something extreme to bond Roxy to you in a hurry – a dog that frightened the horse and caused her to look to you for protection, for instance. He'd been at the whisky and it was simply the ramblings of a drunk. Hannah took him literally. It's hard to know whether she wanted to scare you off at that stage or grant Kyle and Ray their wish. She made a point of warning you about the guard dogs so you wouldn't suspect her and then padlocked the main gate so that you'd have no choice but to go down the lane. It was sheer chance that Ray happened to be on his way to feed the dogs when he heard them going berserk.

'Unfortunately, Ray's history made Kyle fear that he was in some way responsible for the attack. His world began to crumble. It also made him think that if his father could do that, perhaps he was capable of worse. You see, the question of how Philippa Temple's brakes came to fail, conveniently handing the role of director of the equestrian centre to Kyle, has never been satisfactorily resolved.'

'Does McLeod really believe that Hannah might have had something to do with the crash?'

'He thinks it's unlikely but not beyond the bounds of possibility. Apparently her father was a mechanic. If she was already obsessed with Kyle, she may have had the motive.'

'What I can't understand is why she wanted to hurt me and Storm. I mean, I was only ever friendly to her. What did I do to deserve it?'

'Nothing. She became obsessed that Kyle was falling for you and was eaten up with jealousy. Then when you rowed with him, she blamed you for making Kyle leave the equestrian centre and, more importantly, her. In her head, they had a relationship. She became determined to destroy you. Her notebooks show that she considered giving Storm colic with mouldy grass cuttings, along with other horrendous things. In the end she settled on a tripwire on the cross-country course.'

'She hadn't counted on you parachuting in like Rambo granny,' said Casey with a grin.

'Hardly. I sort of limped up to her, half-dead with exhaustion, and said: "Young woman, do you really think that's a good idea?"

'She sprang at me like a wildcat and would, I think, have strangled me with the wire had Kyle and Detective Inspector McLeod not come roaring up in the Land Rover. Kyle had her pinned to the ground in a trice and Lenny calmly handcuffed her. She was quiet enough until they were helping her into the Land Rover, at which point she let out this eerie howl. It was so inhuman it sent chills through me.'

Casey was quiet for a while. 'How can I ever thank

you? Over the last three years you've saved me from falling more times than I can possibly count.'

'Not half as many times as you've saved me.'

The silhouette of a kestrel appeared in the dawn sky, wheeling and dipping. They followed its twisting flight until it landed, unexpectedly, on a fencepost so close that they could see every detail of its pristine white breast, hooked beak and golden hunter's eyes.

'I was like that once,' Mrs Smith said ruefully. 'A wild spirit.'

Casey gave her a squeeze and tried not to think about how gaunt her teacher had become, all skin and brave bones. 'You still are.'

'No, sadly, I'm not. I'm a bird trapped in the prison of my own body, caged by pain.'

Casey felt a fathomless rage and hurt. How could the sun still rise when the best person she had ever known was slipping away from her, hour by hour. 'On Monday, when this is over, I promise I will search the country – the world if I have to – and find you the finest cancer specialist in existence. If it's humanly possible to cure you, we'll do it. Hey, it's got to be easier than trying to train a teenager who can barely ride to win Badminton on a one dollar horse.'

Mrs Smith laughed. 'If only that was true. No, Casey,

261

you and I both know that one day soon it'll be over. When that happens I want you to promise me one thing.'

'What's that?'

'That you won't be sad.'

Hot tears filled Casey's eyes. 'How can I promise you that?'

'Because, dear Casey, through you and Storm I've lived. Through you I've dreamed. And, most importantly, through you I've loved. I will go from this world more fulfilled and content than any one person has a right to be, knowing that I'd do it all again twice over if I could.'

Casey could contain herself no longer. Sobs wracked her body as she hugged the teacher she adored, and to whom she owed everything. 'So would I, Angelica. So would I.'

27

'ANNA, WAIT.'

A hazy Sunday morning of pinks and golds had given way to a crisp blue autumn afternoon when Anna Sparks heard Casey call her name. She was on her way to the collecting ring. The combination of a superb horse and the praise she'd received for her performance at Burghley had boosted her confidence and there was much of the old Anna in her coiffed hair, stylishly cut show-jumping jacket and the queenly set of her shoulders. She halted Incendiary. 'Hi, Casey. How's it going?'

'Good, I think.' Casey ran a hand through her riot of dark hair. She hadn't yet changed and was still in ripped jeans and a baggy sweatshirt. 'Anna, I wanted to thank you. What you did yesterday – giving a message to

Niall right before you started the cross-country, that was pretty phenomenal. I guess you've heard about Hannah's arrest. If you hadn't sent word to Peter when you did, they might not have stopped her. Anything could have happened to Storm and me.'

Anna smiled, moving easily with her muscled giant of a horse as he jogged on the spot. 'It was nothing. You'd have done the same.' She checked her watch and gathered her reins. 'Have to dash. I'm jumping at 2.30 p.m. What time are you off?'

'Shortly after three. Good luck.'

'Same to you.' Anna nudged Incendiary and they walked away down the track.

'Hey, Anna.'

The hoofbeats continued but she turned to look over her shoulder. 'Yeah?'

It was on the tip of Casey's tongue to say, 'Win or lose, when this is over would you like to go for a coffee some time?' Then reality kicked in. She and Anna could never really be friends. Their values and their worlds were too different. It was easy to be humble when you were down. When fame and temptation returned, as was surely inevitable, and when she was reunited with her cunning, manipulative father and all his millions, it remained to be seen which of the two Annas would emerge stronger.

'Nothing,' said Casey. 'See you on the other side.'

'See you on the other side.'

Casey was on her way to the lorry park when she

264

bumped into Niall, who'd nipped back to collect something. A gangly man in an impeccably ironed shirt and breeches, Incendiary's groom had a permanent air of worry.

'Hope Incendiary goes well this afternoon,' Casey said cheerfully. 'Oh, and Niall, thank you for making such an effort to get Anna's message to Peter yesterday. It helped. You've no idea how much.'

Niall's brightened. 'No problem. Glad to do it. I just feel a bit sorry for Anna who's had it in the neck from Casper. She hasn't said a thing about you, but he watched the replay on the telly and saw that something was amiss at the start. Went ballistic. Says she'd be in contention for the title had she not incurred time faults.'

Casey stared at him, confused. 'But I thought she gave you the message before she got to the D box. Are you saying that the countdown had begun?'

Niall became agitated. 'Look, I shouldn't have said anything. It was only a few seconds. Eleven. It's meaningless in the grand scheme of things. If you lose time in cross-country, you make it your business to gain it back again. That's what Anna did. If anything, it probably galvanised her into trying harder. She rode as if there was no tomorrow. If she jumps clear this afternoon, yesterday will be forgotten. Casper doesn't hold grudges. All he cares about is results.'

At 3.05 p.m. Casey rode Storm into an arena packed to capacity with a crowd high on excitement. Already that afternoon several big names had come to grief, while Anna Sparks, who many had privately hoped would clock up a record number of faults, had ridden a flawless round to shoot up to fourth place on the scoreboard. Sam Tide, everyone's favourite Australian, was currently occupying the top spot, with David Powell and Sarah Evershaw lying second and third.

Up in the BBC commentary box, Hugh McFurlough was reeling off some show-jumping statistics for his viewers.

'The governing body of the sport of horse trials, the FEI, states in its rulebook that there should be fourteen to sixteen jumping efforts, no higher than 1.25 metres and no wider than 1.65 metres. What I find fascinating, ladies and gentlemen, is that the course can be no more than 600 metres long and must be ridden at a minimum of 375 metres per minute. Is it just me or is that not worthy of a gold medal in its own right? I mean, it's not as if a horse comes with a speedometer. I find it hard to keep to the speed limit in my BMW. In case there are any policemen listening, it's difficult but I manage it, okay? But a horse is a wilful creature. I'm reliably informed that a horse in the show-jumping arena has a normal stride of 3.65 metres. Does anyone have a calculator ... ?'

He peered from his window and saw Casey and Storm enter the arena as Andrew Hoy left.

'I must say I'm somewhat relieved to have a diversion, and what a pleasant diversion it is. Casey Blue, the youngest ever winner of the Badminton Horse Trials and Kentucky Three-Day Event, riding Storm Warning, the grey she famously rescued from an East End knacker's yard. Not yet out of her teens – she'll be eighteen next week – Casey has taken the eventing world by storm, if you'll excuse the pun. What's nice is that, in spite of her success, she has remained down to earth and likeable, which is more than I can say for some other young athletes I've met in my time ... but, of course, one shouldn't compare.

'She's also very close to her father, which I think is lovely. Roland Blue designed the magnificent show-jumping jacket she's wearing this afternoon as well as her dressage coat and tails. Quite classy, you'll admit. Roland had one or two troubles in years gone by, but he has since become a tailor of some renown. I have before me a press release that says he'll be launching his own line of tailored performance clothing in the run-up to Christmas. Half Moon Equestrian, it's called. Best of luck to him. I'm sure Casey's very proud.'

Below the commentary box, Storm was cantering slowly around the perimeter of the arena, ears pricked, taking in the vibrantly coloured show jumps, expectant faces and buzz of anticipation.

'And now to the business at hand,' continued McFurlough. 'You don't need me to tell you that one of the reasons you can barely fit a pin between people in

267

the stands today is that everyone who can afford a ticket wants to watch Casey Blue and her wonder horse, Storm Warning. Can they pull off the triple by adding the Burghley Horse Trials to her Badminton and Kentucky crowns?

'The Rolex Grand Slam is worth 350,000 dollars to the winner and is a feat only ever achieved by one rider, Pippa Funnell. Relatively speaking, Casey is a long way back in eighth place. She would have to ride a perfect round, especially since there are several seasoned champions still to go. But we're getting ahead of ourselves. There's the bell now. I don't know about you but my heart is hammering so loudly that I can barely hear myself think. Can Casey Blue do the impossible?'

28

RIDING TO THE collecting ring, Casey had been such a bundle of nerves that she'd dismounted in the shade of a lime tree and stood for several minutes with her face buried in Storm's shoulder. Breathing in his wonderful horse smell and remembering why she was there and what was important calmed her. But after a while, he shoved her with his nose as if to say, 'Are we trying to win this thing or not?'

And Casey had laughed as she mounted him, because although Storm was no longer the skeletal wreck she'd rescued and instead resembled a horse out of a George Stubbs masterpiece, all fire and sinew, he still had the same big heart and unquenchable spirit that had made her fall in love with him in the first place.

'What do I do?' she'd asked Mrs Smith. 'If the impossible happens, what do I do?'

'The same thing you always do,' said her teacher. 'Follow your heart.'

Now, as she cantered around an arena so silent you could have heard a mouse tiptoe, Storm's strength communicated to her as if by osmosis. She felt both peaceful and passionately determined. Victory was within her grasp; she just had to fight for it.

From the first jump, she knew that something special was unfolding. Once show jumping had been Storm's weakest phase. Thanks to Mrs Smith's innovative methods, it had become his second strongest after the cross-country. Creating their own version of the long format had taken the edge off his sometimes frenetic energy, leaving the focus critical for this most unforgiving of phases. Fortunes had been made or lost on the displacement of a single brick. Poised within a whisker of the Grand Slam in 2013, Andrew Nicholson and William Fox-Pitt had both knocked poles to say goodbye to that particular goal.

But for Casey, it was still within reach. With every jump cleared, the tension in the arena increased. In the end virtually every spectator was screaming silent screams, willing rattled poles to stay airborne, praying that Storm would lift his feet.

'I don't know how much more of this my nerves can take,' whispered Hugh McFurlough as if raising his voice might distract the horse from his mission. 'One more jump to go. Is Casey Blue about to rewrite the history books? Oh, my goodness, she's done it. Storm Warning cleared the wall with room to spare. Look at him accelerate – a testament to his racehorse past.'

He craned forward, trying to get a better view, wishing he could leave his booth.

'We'll wait to have the result confirmed but Casey Blue and Storm Warning have moved to the top of the leaderboard. There are still seven riders to come so we can't get too excited, but I think most people would forgive a little premature celebration. This remarkable young lady is within a whisker of the Grand Slam – of walking into greatness. Half the people here are in tears. It's like the second flood here at Burghley and not, for once, due to the weather.'

He pulled himself together. 'Right, next we have the reigning European champion, Scott Davis. Oh, dear, he's not going to be pleased to have kicked out a pole on the first jump ... '

Leaning forward, he noticed with alarm that Casey was surrounded by a thicket of officials. One was gesticulating as if he was conducting an opera. He hoped that there had not been a rules violation of some kind. The rules people could be the most dreadful, boring sticklers for equestrian law. It would be so tedious if they found some draconian rule, invented by a florid huntsman in the fourteenth century, with which to charge her. The impassioned build up he'd given Casey would be ruined. Apart from anything else, he wanted

271

her to win. He was a big fan and not ashamed to admit it.

His producer cut rudely into his thoughts. 'What the devil are you playing at, McFurlough? Do the viewers not deserve an analysis of Davis's round?'

McFurlough glowered at the rider down below. 'Scott Davis is having a torrid time,' he said nastily. 'I can't imagine what he's thinking.'

Casey stood in the cold shadow of the stand, waiting for the remaining two riders to determine her fate. Storm had been taken back to the lorry park by Peter and Mrs Smith and she felt bereft. This week more than any other, she and Storm had been one when they were competing, almost as if their hearts beat in time and the same blood ran in their veins. Without him she felt incomplete.

Meanwhile in the arena the crowd groaned as another pole went flying. Casey's clear round had earned her a place at the top of the leaderboard, but all afternoon she'd been sure that someone would overtake her, beating her into second or third place. Part of her hoped they would, because that would make everything easier.

Anna Sparks came up to her. 'Congratulations, Casey. You must be over the moon. There's no stopping you, is there? It's almost greedy, your list of achievements.'

She smiled but there was a coolness in her tone reminiscent of days gone by.

'Thanks, but I'm not counting my chickens,' Casey said guardedly. 'There are a lot of great riders who'll be trying to win this afternoon. Congratulations on your round too. You rode superbly.'

'Oh, do you think so? I was pleased with the way Incendiary jumped, but not with the overall outcome. Unlike you, I've never been satisfied with finishing anything other than first. Yesterday was an expensive lesson. If I had to do it again, I'd make very different decisions.'

She walked away, leaving Casey open-mouthed. Leopards and spots came to mind.

Next along was Lucinda Green. 'Great ride today, Casey. How are you feeling?'

'Truthfully? I've been better. It's ... well, it's nerve-wracking, all this.'

Lucinda smiled. 'Tell me about it. Been there, have the T-shirt.'

'Do you ever miss it? The circuit? The road?'

'Yes and no. It's such a trip away from reality. You live in a bubble. It's true that you don't go to an office, but it's a different type of grind. Each horse is different and each day is different because an animal is different every day. You're driving through the night and you're working long hours. It's a very hard way to make money. You've had some success, Casey, but nothing's guaranteed. Tomorrow is another day.'

She looked at her watch. 'Gotta run. Take care, Casey. See you down the road.'

Outside, the crowd was at fever pitch. A refusal had knocked the last rider out of contention. They began to chant. 'Casey, Casey, Casey, Casey ... '

Casey forced one foot in front of the other. It should have been the best moment of her life, but it was the hardest. The roar of the crowd and the afternoon sunlight came at her in a dazzling wave.

A British Eventing official put his hand on her arm. 'Casey, you don't have to do this. It's not too late. There is nothing in the rulebook. We've issued no statement to the media yet. We wanted to give you time to think it over. The trophy engraver's having kittens, but apart from that—'

'Go ahead and tell the reporters and the engraver,' said Casey, pulling away. 'Please, it's fine. Really.'

Casper Leyton blocked her path. 'Casey, I've heard what you're up to and I've come to tell you that you're making the biggest mistake of your life. I know the reason for it and I can categorically assure you that it's not necessary. In fact, I'm ordering you not to do it. It's insane. You are not responsible for another rider's actions. You've ridden your heart out.'

Casey smiled. 'Thanks, Casper, but my mind is made up.'

29

IT WAS LATE September, but the air in Burghley Park that Sunday afternoon was so balmy it could have been July. Only a coppery scattering of leaves and the faintest hint of woodsmoke on the breeze suggested that change was on the way.

In the centre of the arena, the show jumps were being dismantled in preparation for the prize-giving. One word from Casey and the world would be hers, delivered on a silver platter.

'Casey, huge congratulations from everyone at the BBC,' gushed Hugh McFurlough, beaming at her from behind his microphone. 'Any chance of getting your reaction on winning the Burghley Horse Trials and, by extension, the Grand Slam? It's a towering achievement that will stand with some of the greatest sporting victories of all time. It brings to mind— I'm sorry, what did you say?'

Casey took a deep breath. 'Hugh, forgive me for interrupting, but there is about to be an announcement that will confirm that I am neither the Burghley champion, nor have I won the Grand Slam. I believe I've finished third behind Sam Tide and David Powell. Sarah Evershaw and Anna Sparks are fourth and fifth.'

The commentator was flabbergasted. Inwardly, he cursed the rules tyrants who had brought about this calamity. 'I don't understand. There must be some mistake.'

'I wish there was, but there isn't. Yesterday, one of the riders was delayed at the start of the cross-country trying to get a message to me – a message that played a part in preventing a serious fall.

'Even without the delay, that rider would not have won the Burghley Horse Trials, but I could not in good conscience take the trophy today knowing that someone lost eleven seconds and incurred a penalty point because of me. There is nothing in the rulebook that covers this situation, but for me it's a matter of principle. I've asked the British Eventing and FEI officials to add eleven seconds and a penalty point to my score. Once that was done, Sam Tide became the clear winner. I'd like to congratulate him now. He's a fantastic rider and a brilliant ambassador for our sport.'

'Yes, but you had a chance to write yourself into

the record books with the Grand Slam,' protested McFurlough. 'What about the 350,000 dollars? That's over 200,000 pounds.'

'Money isn't everything, Hugh.'

'Of course not but—'

Casey smiled. 'If you have a minute, I have another announcement to make.'

McFurlough moved out of shot to mop the sweat from his brow. 'Take all the time you need.'

'As of this moment, I'm retiring from eventing. I know people will laugh because I'm still in my teens, but age has nothing to do with my decision. The past three years have been more magical, more terrifying and more rewarding than I could ever have imagined. I could not have done any of it without my coach, Angelica Smith, or the support of my boyfriend, Peter, and my dad. At the same time, I've learned a lot about myself. When I started eventing I vowed always to put my horse, Storm, and the people I love before everything else, especially fame and success. At a certain point I found that that was becoming a challenge. This is a beautiful life but it's not without its demands and temptations.'

She stopped, struggling to control her emotions. 'But that's not the main reason for my decision. This week Storm Warning was threatened with serious injury or worse. He was put in that position for one reason only and that's because I was pursuing my goals. He's loved competing as much as I have, but now it's time he has a well-earned rest.'

277

'But what will you do?' spluttered Hugh McFurlough, who was feeling overwhelmed himself. 'I mean, you're so young. You have your whole life ahead of you.'

'I'm not sure. I'm going to take some time and take stock. A few months ago, I had the opportunity to do some teaching at my old riding school, Hopeless ... apologies, Hope Lane in East London. It made me think that I'd enjoy helping underprivileged kids learn to ride. I'd also love to open a sanctuary to save horses like Storm. I'm not sure where it would be. Peter is from Wales, so maybe somewhere around there.'

Watching at home, Jennifer Stewart cast a pained glance at the cheque sent by the latest buyer to reject her wayward mare, which lay ripped up on her coffee table. 'As difficult as it is for me to admit it, there's only one owner who's really right for Lady Roxanne and that's Casey Blue,' she said to her husband. 'Horses adore her and when you listen to her talk, who on earth can blame them. First thing Monday morning, let's box up Roxy and dispatch her to White Oaks.'

At Burghley, an official signalled to Casey. The prize-giving ceremony was beginning.

For Casey, it was an odd feeling to stand beside Sam Tide in the place reserved for the rider who finished third when she could so easily have been in Sam's shoes, reaching for the trophy. But she didn't have a single regret. If anything, she felt liberated. She was the luckiest girl in the world to have experienced the joy and exhilaration of eventing, but now it was time to let go.

Sam Tide lifted the trophy and beamed for the cameras as the Burghley crowds erupted. Many spectators would have preferred Casey to win, but Sam was immensely popular and they celebrated his victory appropriately.

'I've dreamed of getting my hands on this trophy since I was a boy,' he said into the microphone, 'and that's why I can't believe I'm going to do what I'm about to do. First, let me explain. The aim of most people who ride or play sport for a living is to be as gracious in victory as you are in defeat. I can tell you from experience that's easier said than done. As Casey said in her interview earlier, demands and temptations come at you constantly. It's tough to always do the right thing.'

He wiped his eyes. 'Gosh, this is embarrassing. I haven't cried since my dog died when I was twelve.'

Laughter rippled around the arena.

'But today I witnessed the greatest act of sportsmanship I've ever known. Casey Blue, who had the chance to stand before you not only as the winner of the Burghley Horse Trials but also as only the second person in history to have achieved the Grand Slam, voluntarily called a penalty on herself to show solidarity with a rider she felt had helped her. Because of this selfless act, I am fortunate enough to be your champion. It is a title I gladly accept. But I would like to acknowledge this astounding act of grace and courage with a gift.'

He turned to the girl on his left and handed her the trophy. 'Casey Blue, this one's for you.'

Don't miss Lauren's brand new book, *The Glory*, publishing in 2015.

Here is a preview of the opening.

1

Dovecote Equestrian Centre, Surrey, England

On a blustery September afternoon as bright as a new-minted coin, a teenage rider cantered towards a jump. Alexandra Blakewood was exercising her eighth horse of the day but there was nothing in her body language to suggest that she was in any way fatigued. She balanced lightly in the saddle as the chestnut thoroughbred cleared the double with room to spare and rocketed towards the next jump.

This was the part where everyone aside from Clare, Dovecote's chief instructor, lost control of him, but Alex used a couple of half halts to slow the horse enough to take the oxer, repeated the process with next two jumps and completed the circuit with only one rolled pole. As she eased him to a walk, her grin was so wide anyone would have thought she'd just won at Olympia.

She rides like an angel, Clare thought ruefully, well aware that in every other area of Alex's life she was anything but. At Dovecote Alex was a model pupil, hungry (almost desperate, Clare sometimes thought) to learn, hard working and the only fifteen-year-old she knew even remotely talented enough or committed enough to volunteer to school seven or eight horses every Sunday, which she did come rain or snow.

But Alex had a recklessness that concerned her. She had a tendency to ride too fast and take too many chances. If she was told off, she became mutinous, although she was careful never to be rude. She knew that Clare operated a zero-tolerance policy when it came to insolence or swearing. From the terse exchanges Clare had overheard between Alex and her mum, she did not exercise the same restraint at home. Far from it. Clare had a feeling that trouble was brewing in the Blakewood household and that when it did it would come with hurricane force.

'Easy when you know how,' Alex said cheekily as she rode up to the gate.

Clare hid her amusement with a scowl. 'Yes, but hard when you don't. He'll never improve his shape over fences unless you spend more time doing lateral work with him. He's weak in all the crucial muscles. As for your position on that last jump . . .'

'Yeah, but . . .'

Alex got no further. Her stepfather's 'winter gold' Jaguar came racing into the car park and skidded to a halt on the gravel. He exited the car at high speed, followed by Alex's mother, her face white and strained.

'I think they're looking for you,' began Clare. But she was talking to herself. Alex was galloping away in the other direction, approaching the first jump dangerously fast.

The hurricane Clare feared had just blown in.

'What is it that we're not giving you, Alex?' demanded Jeremy Pritchard. 'Tell me that. I'd really like to know. So far this year we've bought you a second iPhone after you dropped the first in the bath, not to mention a new laptop and a wardrobe full of clothes and riding gear. Have you any idea what that cost? We've also taken you on holiday to Devon and Tuscany and paid eye-wateringly expensive school fees.'

'And love,' her mother put in. 'We've given you lots of love.'

Despite repeated appeals not to do so, Alex sat with her feet up on the armchair. She buried her face in her knees to stifle a yawn. Her caramel-coloured hair, long and unruly, was still damp from her riding hat. Arguments with her parents always followed the same pattern. Her mum and stepdad would start out clearly furious but doing their best to be reasonable. Why, they'd want to know, had she done whatever it was she'd done. At her last school, the teachers had also been remarkably tolerant. She'd got away with all manner of pranks, including supergluing fifty girls' locks to their lockers. It was the dinner ladies who'd finally drawn the line after live locusts, ordered off the Internet, were set loose in the kitchen.

At her current school they had no sense of humour. The head teacher had taken it very badly when Alex put laxatives in the staff room coffee machine immediately after taping Out of Order signs to all but one of the toilet doors. But the thing that had really caused her to blow a gasket was, to Alex's mind, the most harmless prank of all.

On Friday she'd threaded a piece of string through two Mentos mints – bought online, and suspended them above the liquid in a bottle of Diet Coke she'd found in the bag of the most popular girl in the school. For reasons unknown Olivia had opened the bottle as she was walking down some steps. It had exploded in a sugary fountain. She'd got such a fright that she'd fallen and ended up in A&E. There were stitches in her knee and a miniature cast on one broken finger. Her parents were threatening to sue, claiming it had ruined her future as a possible model or violinist. It hadn't taken the school long to discover the culprit on CCTV. Hence the current row.

'I know you give me love,' said Alex tiredly. 'And I know that I have everything I could ever wish for – apart from the thing I want most, a horse – and, of course, you're the world's most perfect parents, blah, blah, blah.'

'Don't be insolent,' said her stepfather. 'Why do you want to upset me and hurt your mum?'

As always, Alex had the feeling of watching herself from a distance, as if she were staring in at the contents of a goldfish bowl. She saw a girl in black breeches and a baggy V-necked grey sweater hugging herself defensively in a living room straight out of *Country Living*, all oak floors, overstuffed white furniture and artfully arranged rugs and paintings. It was so clean that once a week the cleaner had to spend her whole four hours dreaming up things to do.

On the sofa Natalie Pritchard and Alex's stepfather of two years were rigid with agitation. Jeremy, who was something big in insurance, was in his version of weekend casual – carefully ironed jeans, pin-striped shirt and shiny black shoes.

'I'm sorry,' said Alex. 'What more can I say? I've already apologised a million times. How was I supposed to know that Olivia would get such a shock that she'd fall down the stairs? I had no way of predicting that.'

'No, but you could have not played a cruel trick on her in the first place,' retorted Jeremy. 'You could have focused on your schoolwork like everyone else. If I hadn't known Olivia's dad from the golf club, things could have got awkward.'

Her mum regarded her at if she were a hostile alien. 'Why do you do it, darling?'

Alex stared out of the window at the landscaped

garden outside, every inch of it tamed into submission. Why *did* she do it? The truth was, she didn't know. Partly it was to hide how shy she was and uncomfortable in her own skin. Being a rebel made people who wouldn't normally notice her, notice her. Sometimes even smile at her. The fact that they were mostly the worst kids in the school didn't matter. What mattered is that just for a while she felt less lonely. Just for a moment she felt the way only horses could make her feel. Warm inside. Needed. Worth something.

For a while being a prankster made her feel less angry too, which was good because the slow burning fury that had started as an ember after her father had walked out the door without a backward glance five years earlier now raged in her like a forest fire. Outwardly it didn't show. At school, she was nicknamed Frosty for her ice maiden demeanour. Her parents fretted that she was distant. Cold. Unemotional about things that she should care about, such as exams. Too emotional about things that were unimportant, such as horses.

As if anything could matter more than horses.

'Answer your mother,' ordered Jeremy. 'Why do you do it? I mean, you're nearly sixteen. It's high time you grew up. Why are you always in trouble?'

Alex shrugged. 'It's a laugh.'

Jeremy jumped to his feet, black hair bristling. 'Well, let's see how funny you find it when your riding lessons stop. As of this minute, you're grounded for three months. No, there's no point in appealing to your mum. She and

I have already discussed this. You will not be allowed near any riding school until you learn to behave.'

Alex began to shake. 'No, please, anything but that. I'll do extra chores and study for hours every weekend. I'll work myself to the bone to get As in all my exams. I *need* to ride. I'll die if I don't.'

'Don't be ridiculous, Alex,' snapped her mum. 'Anyway, we don't have a choice. Clare had a word with me while you were collecting your bag from the tack room. I'm afraid you're no longer welcome at Dovecote. She's not having the health of her horses and the reputation of her riding school ruined by a single rider.'

'And that's another thing,' said Jeremy, drowning out Alex's protests. 'Since you've demonstrated yet again that you can't be trusted, we are not going to take you to Paris next weekend. Nor are we going to leave you alone. You'll be staying with Rich and Barbara. You could do a lot worse than to watch how their daughters Chloe and Tiffany behave and try to emulate them.'

It was all Alex could do to stop herself from screaming. Rich was another big tuna in insurance and he and his identikit wife and daughters, all of whom glowed as if they'd been scrubbed with a brillo pad and fed on nothing but organic milk and honey from birth, were the most boring people in the universe.

After failing to persuade her parents to relent either about Paris or her riding lessons, Alex stormed up to her room, where she cried for over an hour. France she could live without but horses were her whole world. They were the first thing she thought about every morning and the last thing she thought about at night. To keep her from them because of some silly prank was cruel beyond words.

As if that wasn't bad enough, she'd been banned from Dovecote Equestrian Centre. It was her mother's fault, she was certain. Clare had always been lovely to Alex. Why else would she have allowed her to exercise seven or eight horses every Sunday? There was no doubt in Alex's mind that, between them, her mum and Jeremy had ruined her life. By taking away the thing she loved most, they'd destroyed the best thing that had ever happened to her.

The room was dark by the time she sat up and dried her eyes on her sleeve. She pulled her laptop out from under her pillow. The screen purred to life, casting a blue halo across the bed. Alex smiled as she opened up Facebook. She'd make her parents sorry. Boy, would they be sorry.

**Collect all of
Lauren St John's books:**

The One Dollar Horse Trilogy

THE ONE DOLLAR HORSE

RACE THE WIND

FIRE STORM

The White Giraffe Quartet

The White Giraffe

Dolphin Song

The Last Leopard

The Elephant's Tale

The Laura Marlin Mysteries

DEAD MAN'S COVE

~~

KIDNAP IN THE CARIBBEAN

~~

KENTUCKY THRILLER

~~

RENDEZVOUS IN RUSSIA

the orion star

★ ★ ★

I, CLAUDIA

By Charity Bishop

Text Copyright © 2013 by Charity Bishop

www.charitysplace.com

ISBN-13: 978-1490954301
ISBN-10: 1490954309

First Printing: August 2013
Printed in the United States of America

For anyone who has ever wondered,
"What happened to Pilate?"

4

Contents:

Chapter One

Mother takes a longer time with her seer than usual.

Normally, she spends less than half an hour in his stinking hovel. She pays him coins, he throws ash onto the fire, tells her what she wants to hear, and we go home.

Today, it is different. I stand at the tent entrance with the late afternoon sun beating on my neck and glance at our Jewish servant girl, Libi. "Go inside," I say.

She shakes her head. "I can't. Father forbids me. You know that."

I push aside the thin curtain and duck inside. The walls teem with jars and shelves; entrails float in green liquid. The hovel smells like death. Our seer sits over glowing embers in a pit with Mother opposite, a stark contrast in her rich tunic from his poor homespun rags. He starts from his trance but as his one good eye falls on me, the half-spoken curse halts on his lips.

"You ask for truth, mistress?" he rasps. Pointing to me with a bony finger, he says, "Here's a true teller of fortunes. Through her lips pours wisdom unrivaled yet it goes unheeded. She'll bear a man to greatness and see him destroyed."

Cold races up my spine and my mother laughs bitterly. "Claudia is of no importance. Your runes lie."

"Belittle her gifts at your peril," he answers, indicating the door. "I'll speak no further to one who doubts my runes. Get out, and never return."

Anger fills her face and she throws her coins at him. He tosses them back at her and shoves us out into the street. His beady eyes follow us down the road. Once out of sight, Mother slaps Libi. "You're supposed to keep Claudia outside!" she snaps.

Libi shuffles her armload of silks and perfumes and whispers, "I'm sorry, Mistress." She shoots me a glance and I shrug apologetically. Her beauty increases by the day and despite her simple garments and head covering, she still draws attention. Male eyes drift over me and linger on her with open interest.

We pass through the gates of Rome and walk toward the vineyards outside the city. My father's is the largest and the light beats off its high white walls as we approach. Catching

sight of us from the gates, a servant runs to meet us. Panting, he cries out, "Mistress, the Fifth Legion nears Rome!"

"Quintus will be with them!" Mother's face brightens. "The gods bless us at last! Your brother returns home!" She hurries inside with Libi on her heels. Rather than accompany them, I walk to the stables. As I enter, I breathe deeply the scent of new hay and horses. Our servant Jacob pitches straw into the stalls.

I lean against the door and watch him, admiring the fervor he puts into it. "Jacob, you needn't work so hard."

A shock of dark hair falls over his forehead as he shoots me a glance. His stern countenance softens slightly at my appearance. "I want to finish before the Sabbath. Is my sister in the house?"

"Yes, but I'm sure she'll be out again before Sabbath begins. Have you heard the news of the legion's return?"

"I did, yes." He scowls and throws another forkful of straw. The horses watch, their ears swiveling forward, snatching mouthfuls.

Stroking my father's stallion, I quip, "You don't sound very happy about it."

"I'm not."

"Don't you want Quintus home again?"

Jacob pauses to look at me, swiping his hand across his brow. "He returns from Judea, the land of my forefathers, where my people live in slavery to Rome. *Should* I rejoice in his return?"

Dust sifts down from the loft above. I perch on the nearest barrel, concerned at his frown. He stabs the hay viciously and my tone darkens as I remind him, "As a *centurion,* Quintus must obey orders."

A snort of disapproval accompanies another thrust of his fork. "He obeys Pilate's orders, you mean."

"Pilate is his commanding officer."

Light dances through the stable slats. Jacob snorts. "You think too highly of Pilate and your brother. You are too young to know what goes on in Rome whenever the legion returns. There will be feasts, wine, pagan sacrifices, and revelry in the streets. It will start as a celebration and turn into an orgy. I suppose you don't know what that is, either!"

My face heats up. "I'm nearly seventeen and I do know of such things!"

He raises his brow. "But you don't disapprove of them?"

"Yes, I disapprove, but Quintus isn't like that."

Leaning on his pitchfork, Jacob studies me with intent, dark eyes. "You don't know your brother. You only see what he wants you to see when he's at home."

At the mare's nudge, I offer her a handful of grain. "I thought you liked Quintus!"

"I did, before he joined the legion and fell in with Pilate. His father, Senator Fidelus, is responsible for the decree over Judea that lets Jews be beaten into submission if the Romans fear an uprising, did you know that?"

Shock catches me off guard but I recover quickly. "Pilate isn't his father!"

"No, he's worse! The Fifth has been in Judea the last nine months! I know all too well what he's done to my people."

Crossing my arms, I say, "You sound more like an insurgent than an aspiring priest."

"Maybe I've learned that actions speak louder than words." He glances at me and his eyes soften. "Priesthood was a childish ambition, Claudia... a dream shared when we were young and believed ourselves equal to one another."

I step closer to him and touch his arm. "We *are* equal. We're both citizens of Rome."

"We're *not* equal! I am a Jew and you are a Gentile. The Romans will crush the Jews under their heel, until we rise up and strike it out from under them."

Dust rises on the road and my heart quickens at the sight of my brother. "Avram won't like you saying such things."

"My father must grow used to it, whether or not he likes it." Shouldering his pitchfork, Jacob leaves without a second glance. I rub Father's horse, bury my face in his mane and breathe in his scent, my heart heavy. Hooves clatter on the road outside and I dash into the courtyard as my brother arrives. With him are a dozen legionaries, most unfamiliar to me.

Dismounting, Quintus catches me in his arms. "Claudia! How you have grown! Where is the child I left behind?"

He smoothes the hair back from my face and I flush with pleasure. "You've been gone three years, brother! You can't expect me to stay a child forever!"

"I can't expect it, but I'd like it! I want this cheerful face never to change!" He kisses me, smelling of dust and sweat, as

the others emerge from the house, my sisters frantically straightening their togas. They eye the soldiers in our yard with approval. Before going to them, he asks softly, "Have the dreams stopped?"

Dread fills me and I shake my head. "You haven't told anyone, have you?"

"No." His hand squeezes mine and he goes to embrace our father.

Pulling back from him, Father says, "We didn't expect you until late! Has the Legion already entered Rome?"

"She has, and Pilate let us disperse. I've even brought him with me!"

My sisters crane their necks to make him out among the others. I saw him the minute he rode into the courtyard. He dismounts, as tall and commanding as ever. Lucilla eyes him appreciatively as he moves forward, but instead he stops beside me and tugs a lock of my hair. "And how are you, little one?" he inquires playfully. He is unchanged, his sharp features still striking, his eyes piercing and blue. His nearness quickens my heart.

"Please tell me you don't still see me as a child, Lucius."

Wonderful, sensual eyes tease me, as they always have. "No, you're a woman now."

Others move around us as Quintus introduces his friends to our father. I walk forward with Pilate. "Have you defended the emperor in all the far reaches of the empire?"

"Yes, although it was never under threat in the first place, Tiberius' throne is safe again." He winks at me.

Father invites him inside. "You honor our house with your presence, Commander."

"Call me Pilate, for a commander shouldn't consort with his legionaries' families." Pilate enters and I wait, allowing the men to precede me indoors.

Mother falls into step with him. "We're glad you make an exception for us."

"How could I not, when I've known such happiness in this house?"

Quintus puts his arm around me and takes me inside. We pass Libi in the hall and she glances at us. His head turns to acknowledge her and a knowing smile touches my lips. "Your taste in women hasn't changed," I remark as we enter the banquet hall.

"You see too much, little sister," he answers, tapping the tip of my nose.

We settle around the low table and a gentle breeze flows through the curtains. Servants bring in the dishes and retreat to a polite distance, ready if needed. Father invites us to eat and his admiring gaze falls on Quintus. "Tell us of your victories, my son."

"Do you want to hear of our adventures in Gaul or in Judea?"

My other sister, Thais, holds up her cup for a refill. Light trickles down her slender throat and shimmers in the gems woven through her hair. "Did you kill all the enemies of the empire?"

"Not all of them, but there's fewer than before! The sand ran red with the blood of our enemies, in spite of warnings to the contrary. Our augurs were in a constant state of anxiety. Some thought us destined for defeat, but we made it as far as the Roman outskirts and the emperor was so pleased with Pilate's legion, he sent us to Judea!"

Servants slip in and out, filling cups. Mother leans back on her chaise and says, "There were many bad omens at first. Even the emperor's augurs feared the legion might be wiped out."

"There was no fear in our house," Thais says. "We had Claudia to reassure us."

Curious eyes swivel toward me and she grins behind a handful of grapes. Irritation burns through me. "I thought we weren't going to speak of that in front of others, Thais," I say sweetly. Her nasty little smirk makes me want to throttle her.

Pilate asks, "What do you mean?"

"My little sister has dreams that foretell the future. She dreamt of your victory in Gaul before it happened."

Heat rises in my face and I sip my wine, pretending not to care. Pilate stares at me intently, his expression unreadable. "Dream seers are rare."

"I don't claim to be one," I answer.

"But if your dreams come true, it makes you one." His eyes linger on mine.

One of Quintus' friends asks, "Have you dreamed lately?"

Memories enter my head of Pilate's hands on me, the touch of his lips on mine. I turn to him and say, "Yes, but not about the legion!" Looking at Pilate, I sip my wine and his expression

changes into curious amusement. We flirt across the table.

Father lifts his cup for a refill. "Fidelus ordered wine yesterday for a banquet honoring your return, Lucius. He must be proud."

Pilate shifts his attention to my father and his eyes harden. "I doubt that."

"Tell us of Judea," Mother encourages. "Is it true, what they say about it? Is it hot and full of heathens?"

Stabbing a piece of meat with his knife, Quintus laughs. "Heathens are what they call us! I have not seen all of it. We spent most of our time in Jerusalem."

"Is it beautiful?" I ask.

Wind stirs the draperies and Pilate shakes his head. "It's a lawless city full of renegades and insurgents. Our governor faces daily riots in the streets over taxes, and the Jews speak often of a new 'messiah' to liberate them from Rome."

Everyone laughs except me. I wait until it dies down and say, "They'd crave no messiah if Rome wasn't so hard on them."

Mother stares at me in horror, her cup halfway to her mouth. Pilate leans back on his cushion. "Is that your opinion?"

"That depends... do I speak before the Commander of the Fifth Legion or a friend?"

His eyes darken, sending shivers down my spine. "Both share the same views, regardless of which sits before you."

"Yes, it is my opinion that Rome is harsh on the Judeans."

Concerned, Father starts to reprimand me but Pilate lifts his hand. "No, let her speak. You assume, Claudia, that kindness toward them would make a difference. It will not. You have not seen the streets of Jerusalem, the land of Judea, or their blatant hatred of our 'pagan' civilization. They scorn our gods, refuse to submit to Caesar, and preach that their ways alone are right."

"Not all of them feel that way."

Smiling, he answers, "Not all of them are like your father's servants."

My face burns and I tighten my grip on my wine cup.

"Pilate is right," Quintus says. "That Rome could change the mind of the Judeans isn't possible. There is only one way to govern Judea—with force. Gratus is a fool and does nothing to command their respect. He constantly submits to the authority

of the high priest."

"I've never known you to be so cynical of the Jews before," Father says, disappointment in his tone.

Quintus swirls his wine and smiles ruefully. "Nine months in Judea has changed my views."

Unease quiets the table and after a beat Lucilla asks, "Have you heard of the new Praetorian Guard?"

"The legionaries speak of little else!" Pilate lets a servant pour him more wine. "Half my men want to be part of the Emperor's Guard!"

Catching his eye, Mother asks, "Will you try for a position, Quintus?"

"They're only interested in the best soldiers. That means Pilate."

Father lowers his cup. "Yes, I did hear rumors about that. Sejanus is impressed with your military success."

"Wouldn't Lucius be of better use to Rome as a general than an emperor's guard?" I ask.

Laughing, Pilate asks, "Don't you want me in Rome, Claudia?"

"I want you wherever you're happiest; *is* that in Rome?"

His eyes dance at me and with a smile, I turn to the guest next to me. After supper, Pilate wanders into the courtyard. Leaving my sisters behind, I follow him. Wind teases my tunic and hair as I approach.

"Your opinions have grown bold since last we met," he remarks, glancing at me.

Gloom closes in around us as we walk together. "Do you want me to be demure and withdrawn?"

"No, I much prefer it when a woman shares her opinion." Pilate smiles and looks toward the distant, rising city, ablaze in the darkness. Hundreds of lights glow against the sky, torches blazing atop the walls. "I'd forgotten how magnificent she is at night."

We enter the shadows under the verandah and I lean against a column. "Will you stay the night?"

"I'd like that, anything to avoid returning home." Pilate steps nearer and my heart quickens. He pushes a strand of hair behind my ear and leans toward me. Footsteps sound on the verandah above and he hesitates, his lips above mine.

Quintus' voice drifts to us through the vines. "I know you're disappointed in me, Father."

My hand rests against Pilate's chest, my body straining toward his as we listen. Every muscle in my body tenses with excitement.

"Why do you think that?"

Leaves rustle. "I saw your face, though you tried to hide it. You aren't pleased with my opinion of the Jews."

Father sounds tired. "Not all Jews are the same."

"And not all of them are like Avram! Judea is a pit of vipers!"

Pilate's forehead nearly touches mine, his hand against my throat.

"Is that your opinion or Pilate's?"

His face moves away from mine as he looks up into the darkness. My fingers curl around the nape of his toga.

Quintus' voice sharpens. "What do you mean by that?"

"He *is* his father's son and you know what Fidelus is like."

Light spills behind us as a door opens. Pilate swiftly pulls away from me and vanishes into the darkness. I feel cold without him and rub my arms as Lucilla appears. Taking in my expression, she asks, "Were you with Pilate?"

"I don't see how that's any of your business." Ducking around her, I enter the house.

She hurries to catch up with me, her face alight with curiosity. "Did he try anything?"

"No!" I quicken my pace and she catches my arm, jerking me to a stop.

Her green eyes search my face. "I don't believe you."

"You wouldn't."

Following me down the hall, she says, "Don't pretend to be so virtuous. You would have him in a minute! I do not blame you! He's the most powerful young man in Rome!"

My dream swirls through my head. I feel his lips at my throat, his hands at my waist. Heat rushes into my cheeks. "Pilate has been around this house since he was old enough to walk. He looks on me as a sister, that's all."

"If he looks at you like he looks at his sister, I'd be concerned about incest. I saw him eyeing you at dinner. You should accept him, if he asks you. It would help Father."

I turn on her. "How would being Pilate's mistress help Father?"

"You know how people look at him since he left the senate. They no longer remember him much less respect him. If you

belonged to Pilate, that would change. It would be advantageous for all of us." Her hand squeezes mine and she rejoins the others.

Footsteps approach and Pilate enters through the garden. "I've had my horse brought up. I should return home."

Disappointed, I tease, "You aren't going to an orgy, I hope."

"Orgies are for legionaries and senators, not commanders." He smiles at me but sadness lurks in his eyes.

Laughter spills out of the great hall and I step closer to him. "You mustn't be hurt by Father. He speaks his mind and didn't know you were there."

"I'd rather he said it to my face, but I don't blame him. My father takes action on his beliefs whether or not others approve. There's no shame in that." Pilate moves toward the door and I accompany him, stepping out into the shadows.

"Father adores you! You're like a son to him!"

Caressing the back of my hand with his thumb, Pilate answers, "Maybe he'll like me better when I leave the Legion."

"What do you mean?"

He glances at me. "Haven't you heard? Sejanus wants me for the Praetorian Guard."

"Is that what *you* want?"

"It doesn't much matter what I want, does it? You and I, we do whatever is best for our families."

Color rises in my cheeks and I start to pull away, but he catches my arm. "How much did you hear?" I whisper.

"Enough." Pilate touches the side of my face. "Becoming a man's mistress is no small thing, Claudia. Is it what *you* want?"

His slightest touch sends tremors across my skin. I shut my eyes as his fingers trace the curve of my neck. His lips brush my throat and I shiver with delight. He tilts my face toward his and I search his gaze. He hesitates, staring at my lips. One finger trails across them and drifts away. "Please thank your family for their hospitality," he says.

Descending into the courtyard, he mounts his horse and rides out the gate. I watch him go and enter the house.

Chapter Two

I have never liked the streets of Rome. They are full of noise and confusion, mingled voices speaking in different languages, heat, flies, and filth. Beggars line the way and hold out their hands plaintively. Children play underfoot, shooed away by annoyed tradesmen. I stay with the others as we pass a long line of silk and wine merchants, perfume vendors, basket weavers, rug makers, and piles of bread to reach the meat market.

Skirting a mud puddle, I catch up to Libi. "Have you spoken with Quintus yet?"

Her face flushes and she sends her father, walking ahead with my mother, a swift glance. "No, but Father won't approve. He wants me to marry a nice Jewish boy from a good family and settle here in Rome."

Laughing, I say, "I know, he views us as heathens!"

She darts out of the way of a chariot, and rejoins me in the center of the street. "You *are* heathens! But I like you anyway!"

We enter the meat market where the flies are worse, slaves standing around with palm fronds to wave them off the hanging carcasses.

"How much will we need this time?" I ask.

Butchers' knives whack into sides of beef and blood spurts into the mud. I see a row of pig heads and steer them away from it. Libi wrinkles her nose and shifts her basket to her other hip. "A lot, if it's to feed all the workers. Your father is generous."

Mother steps forward to haggle with a butcher. Even though I am in the way of the throng of people passing in the square, I refuse to move closer. Someone rudely jostles past, cursing me for blocking the street. Avram pulls me forward. The butcher eyes me, wiping his arm across his face as his son accepts a small handful of coins. It leaves a smear of blood over his brow. A wagon rumbles past, its wheels groaning under a heavy load. Libi pushes me to avoid the hem of my tunic from catching in the wheels and my hands press against the table.

Dread fills me. Mother catches sight of my expression as I examine my bloody fingers. "Claudia, what is it?" she asks impatiently.

I turn and flee. Avram lurches for me, but he is old and

tired; his hand misses my arm. Libi sprints after me, but stops as a chariot and horses drive past. Mother shouts after me to no avail. No one tries to intercept me as I push past. I find a trough and plunge my hands into the water, ignoring the cry of protest from the boy filling it from a nearby well. I scrub until my palms are red with cold.

Trembling, I sit down and try to calm the wild beating of my heart. A mother passes with her children, her garments displaying her humble Jewish upbringing.

I try to find my way back to the others, but in the labyrinth of narrow, winding streets, I lose all sense of direction. The aqueducts loom above me and snake off into the gloom. Crossing the street, I pause at the gate of a house with a courtyard. The walls are in need of repair and water no longer flows in the fountain, full of leaves and dead plants.

"Claudia?" The familiar voice causes me to turn and Pilate looms over me. "What are you doing here?" He looks past me into the courtyard. A hint of suspicion enters his face. Shivers run up my spine. "Do you know where you are?"

Glancing at the house, I shake my head.

"This is an augur's house."

It explains the quietness of the street, why the children avoid the place. Several of them watch us from a distance. There are many augurs in Rome but I have heard Mother speak of the one under the aqueduct.

"Well, now that you're here, you may as well go in with me." Pilate pushes through the gate. It creaks behind us as we make our way across the yard. His usual smile is absent. I rub my arms nervously as he knocks on the door. It sounds hollow inside, as if there is no furniture.

"Maybe he's not in," I say hopefully.

The door opens a few inches, dragging on the stone step. I back up as a hazy gray eye peers at us through the gap. He reminds me of my mother's augur and I shudder.

"I'm told your council is wise," says Pilate.

It opens a bit further, revealing an ancient face, a head of straggly white hair, and a beard reaching nearly to his knees. His rasping voice replies, "Some wouldn't find it so, but you can enter."

He limps away into the house, leaning heavily on a gnarled wooden staff. Pilate enters and with hesitance, I follow. Tallow burns along the walls. We pass into a main hall abused with

time and neglect; branches and vines grow in through the windows, burrowing into the cracks between the tiles. My foot catches on one and Pilate stops me from falling.

The augur descends a narrow flight of stairs into a gloomy room without much of a ceiling. It is full of worn furniture and long shelves extend along the far wall, filled with slots containing rolls of parchment. I trail my hand along them. "You have quite a collection."

"If you steal any, I'll cut your fingers off and throw them in my bone pit."

Pilate and I exchange a glance and I pull my hand away.

A fire burns in a pit at the far end near a rumpled bed. A stench fills the air as the augur returns to disemboweling a rat. "What do you want to know?" he asks.

"Whatever the gods tell you," answers Pilate.

The old man looks at me and a gleam enters his eye. "Knowledge isn't always desired by those with wisdom. It won't be what you want to hear."

"It's a risk I'm willing to take."

Crossing to the fire, the augur rakes out the remains of an animal into the dirt. He takes runes from an urn, shakes them in his hands, and casts them into the smoking entrails. He prods them with his staff. The smell is foul. The augur silently studies them. "Your future is uncertain. Even the gods do not know its final path. Still, there *are* signs."

Shadows lurk around us, moving figures that remind me of my nightmares.

Pilate asks, "What signs?"

"The woman you marry will be a great asset in your journey to power. This power will come and go, if you're careless with it." The augur grows thoughtful, furrowing his brow as he prods the runes. "I see suffering... lust... betrayal... a choice... death... blood... madness."

I feel something watching me. I turn to look behind us, but nothing's there.

"Madness," repeats Pilate.

The augur nods. "The gods reveal nothing except that your name will be remembered." His eyes travel to me and harden. "Do you wish to see?"

"No," I whisper.

Lines crease his face into a cruel grin. "No, for you have no need of runes. You see in your dreams."

Cold flows through me and my hand tightens on my toga. He casts the entrails into the fire. "Go then," he says.

We emerge into the sunshine. I am grateful for the sounds of the city streets. The gate creaks shut behind us and I lean against the wall, glad to draw into my lungs fresh air and not the scent of death.

"So your dreams aren't dreams at all." Pilate takes my arm and we cross the street, approaching the children playing on the far side. One glances at us and says, "You shouldn't go there, the devil lurks within."

"Quiet!" reprimands a woman from a nearby house and the child hurries away with his friends.

We walk through the labyrinth of streets. I drop a coin into a blind man's tin as he sits under an arch. Shadows follow the curve of the houses as they give way to open courtyards. We pass the holding-house of the games. I crane my neck to see inside and Pilate asks, "Have you ever seen a gladiator fight?"

I shake my head. "Why find joy in watching men kill one another?"

Pilate draws me out of the way of a passing chariot. "It reminds us of our mortality."

Darkness creeps in around us as the sun sets. Pilate opens a gate on the other side of the forum and we enter a courtyard surrounding an enormous house. In awe, I follow him inside, hesitating as a girl just past childhood emerges to greet us. Embracing him, she looks at me curiously.

"Claudia, this is my sister, Hermina."

Eying me with interest, she asks, "Can she spend the night?"

"Yes, if it pleases you."

She smiles and takes my hand. Motioning to a servant, Pilate says, "Go to Procula's house and tell him Claudia is safe. I'll bring her home in the morning."

The servant bows and hurries away. Pilate's sister leads me into a large set of rooms full of rich tapestries and furniture. A servant washes my hands and feet, ridding me of the marketplace dust. Hermina pulls careful fingers through my hair to sort out the tangles. Her slave brings gowns for her to choose from and a pale blue tunic settles over my shoulders. It is prettier than anything I own and far less modest. "I don't know if I should wear it," I say shyly, feeling the need to cover myself.

"You look beautiful. I think you should keep it." Hermina

tucks in a final strand of hair and nods. "We have company tonight, Sejanus and his wife."

My heart sinks at the thought of dining with the head of the Praetorian Guard. Smoothing my toga, I follow her into the main hall. When Pilate sees me, he catches his sister by the arm as she passes. "Why did you choose *that* toga?"

"Why, don't you like it?" Her eyes laugh at him as she pulls away.

I feel uncomfortable as the others join us. Senator Fidelus is unchanged from when last we met in my father's vineyards, but his tall, dark-eyed guest fills me with a sudden, swift discomfort.

"Lucius," Sejanus says as he crosses the marble terrace, his sallow wife on his arm. "So the hero of Gaul returns! I hear you improved Judea as well!"

"I'm not sure Judea can be improved, but I did my best." Pilate grips his arm in friendship and hands him a cup of wine.

His father approaches me. "Claudia, isn't it?"

"Yes." I flush under his scrutiny, wishing for more fabric in my toga.

"Pilate says he found you wandering the streets of Rome." His eyes fill with amusement and I laugh.

I accept a cup of wine. "Does your son often bring home strays?"

"No. He rarely invites anyone to the house." Fidelus smiles and glances at me. "I see Hermina has dressed you this evening. You wear it well."

Sejanus' wife glares at me from across the room. Taking a sip of my wine, I answer, "Considering Apicata's expression, maybe too well."

"Women hate beauty in others as much as men hate power." Fidelus puts on a smile and approaches his other guests.

I watch them until Hermina pulls me to a seat beside her. "Horrid old thing," she whispers in my ear, indicating Apicata. "She's haughty and mean. No one likes her, not even her husband. No wonder he takes lovers!"

They settle on opposite sides of the table and Sejanus leans into his pillow. He fixes his intent gaze on Pilate. "Since you've spent a considerable amount of time in Judea, tell me... what do you think of the Jews?"

"They lack leadership but make up for it in passion. There will be small uprisings until we crush them, but they'll never be

a true threat."

Sejanus turns a fig in his broad hands. "So you believe Rome can conquer the Jews?"

"I do."

Dropping the fruit onto his plate, Sejanus says, "You're a man of diplomacy. Like your father, you say what I want to hear, whether it's the truth or not."

"Is there any other way to survive in Rome?"

Wine pours into cups and the slaves keep their gaze lowered. Sejanus shrugs. "You can use power or diplomacy. Power generates fear and if you have it, no one will challenge you even if you say what they do not want to hear. Those in Rome know my opinion of the Jews. It has made me unpopular in the senate. Our countrymen don't want to believe they're a threat to our future prosperity, but from what your father tells me, you believe as I do."

I feel cold in spite of the warm breeze flowing in across the river.

"The reign of Augustus will soon end," Sejanus says softly. "He's old, and his health weakens. When he dies, Tiberius will come into power. He shares our views of Judea. It needs a much stronger governing hand." He lifts his cup and a servant girl fills it.

Pilate asks, "And you intend for me to one day fill this position?"

"You have experience and intelligence on your side. You are a diplomat and a commander, and Rome needs both in its more unstable provinces. Become one of my Praetorians. Mingle with the senate. Draw the attention of Tiberius. Work your way into power." Sejanus looks at me and a meaningful smile touches his lips. "Praetorians can marry, unlike tribunes. As a Praetorian, you will be near Tiberius. Prove yourself to him and he'll appoint you to a position of authority."

Silence descends other than the strumming of the harpist in the corner.

"If you succeed with the Jews, every position in Rome will be open to you."

Turning his wine around in the glass, Pilate asks, "What might I want from Rome?"

"All men want power but few are capable of it. You are one of the few. Join me, Lucius. Rise with me!"

One of the slaves puts fresh bread on the table. I reach for it

and my fingers brush against Sejanus' hand. The shudder that passes over me includes a dark premonition, a strong suspicion that Sejanus will fall. I swiftly sit back and ask, "Isn't it dangerous to plot the accumulation of power? The emperor may see it as treasonous."

Sejanus's voice hardens. "You're the child of a wine merchant, aren't you?"

"Yes." I feel my face grow warm.

He lifts his brow. "Your father is Procula."

Chills tease my spine but I show no fear. I nod.

Sejanus curls his lip. "Your father was in the senate for many years. He had promise but his lack of ambition cost him his place. Now he's a wine merchant."

Lifting my chin, I answer, "You say it as if it's an insult."

"Isn't it?"

"Men tire of ambitious fools but will always drink wine."

Hermina chokes and stares at me in open admiration. Pilate hides a smile.

"Your father knows grapes, but not politics."

I lift my cup. "My father knows how to survive. I wonder, Sejanus, do you?"

The harpist strikes a bad note. Sejanus looks on me in rage. Pilate says, "Certain aspects of the Praetorian Guard do appeal to me."

"Will you join me, then?"

Pilate answers, "Yes. I think it's time I stay in Rome."

His eyes flicker toward me in approval and I smile.

Fidelus says, "I hope your father's harvest is bountiful, Claudia. I'm disappointed in all the summer wines, as the grapes seem sour this year."

"We've let them stay on the vine longer to bring on their sweetness. We start our harvest in the morning. Our workers come from as far as Nazareth."

Apicata's brow rises. "You employ Judeans instead of Romans?"

"We prefer it. They work harder and without complaint."

Pulling a grape from the cluster, Sejanus says, "You could use slaves."

"But then we'd have to feed them all year around. This benefits everyone."

He pops a grape into his mouth. "It also brings Judeans to Rome."

"Rome has nothing to fear from Jews. She's a conqueror, not the conquered." I motion a slave forward and take the wine jar from her. "Will you take more of my father's wine, Sejanus?"

It fills his cup with a rich, dark vibrancy. "You're a clever girl, Claudia," he says. "You know just how far to push and then you pull back. Be careful, for manipulation will not work on everyone. Cleverness can get you killed."

"Cleverness keeps you out of harm's way. *Ambition* gets you killed."

Raising his cup, he answers, "We will see then, won't we?"

"Yes, we will." I clink my cup on his and lift it to my lips.

After supper, I slip out onto the terrace, grateful to leave the others behind. Pilate soon joins me and leans against the rail, studying my face. "You don't like Sejanus much."

"I don't like him at all. I don't trust him." I glance through the draperies at him and frown.

Pilate moves closer to me. "Do you know more than you're telling me?"

"How would I know anything about Sejanus that you don't?"

Catching my hand, he shrugs. "You're the dream-seer."

I pull away from him. "Is that what you see in me, a potential seer? Do you want me to cast entrails into the fire and read your future for you?"

"I thought you dealt in dreams and premonitions, but if you insist..." His eyes laugh at me and my tension fades. "I don't want my future. I want your *opinion*."

Pressing his hand, I whisper, "Be careful, he's dangerous."

"Thank you. That's what I wanted to know."

Voices stir the air behind us and we walk further into the gloom. Rome glitters beyond the walls. Shivering, I lean against the parapet. "It's beautiful."

"You'd be warmer if you had more fabric."

Laughing, I retort, "This is your sister's fault!"

"She has good taste but very little common sense."

Her laughter spills out behind us and makes me smile. "I like her, though."

"I'm glad. Hermina needs people to like her." Pilate glances up at the house. "She's not happy here. No one is. This house inspires unease. It is all its secrets, shut up in its many rooms. Sorrow dwells here, since it's long known only hatred."

"Do you intend to change that?"

Silence curves around us. "How might I do that?"

"Become a better man than your father."

Dark brows lift heavenward. "Do you share your father's opinion of me?"

"He fears Fidelus will bring out the worst in you."

"Do you think I have a 'worst' in me for him to bring out?"

My thin tunic moves in the breeze. "There's darkness in all men," I answer.

"What of the women, does it live in them, too?"

Remembering my premonitions, I shudder. "Yes."

"Is it better to fight it or surrender to it? Which is cleverest, Claudia?"

Light spills out into the courtyard. His nearness sends excited tremors into my veins. "They'll wonder where we are."

"Stay with me." His hand catches mine and lifts my fingers to his lips. My skin tingles as he steps closer. Pilate trails his fingertips across my bare shoulder and lowers his mouth to mine. I let him teach me how to kiss as his arms move around me. His lips travel to my throat.

"Claudia?" Behind us, Hermina's shadow falls across the verandah.

I pull away from Pilate and hurry inside.

Chapter Three

Hermina follows me down the hall. Her red hair bounces against her scrawny form. "Say you'll visit again soon!"

"I'll visit whenever I can." A slave walks past holding a familiar blue bundle. "Is that...?"

"The toga, as I promised. Wear it whenever my brother visits!" She giggles.

I shake my head as we go outside. "You're shameless for someone so young."

"Hermina was shameless the day she entered this world." Pilate offers me his hand and I accept it, walking to his chariot. He notices my expression and asks, "What?"

"It doesn't surprise me you drive a chariot. It is a symbol of power. People move out of your way. You don't have to command them, it's instinctive."

I climb into it and he narrows his eyes. "You don't approve of power plays."

"You're right, but that doesn't mean I won't enjoy the ride."

Taking the reins, he shakes his head. Hermina waves from the top step. Rome stirs beyond the gates as they open to let us into the street. His perfectly matched black horses trot past the aqueducts and I glance over my shoulder at them. We turn a corner and I brush against him. He steadies me.

"Are you thinking of the augur?" he asks.

"It's a lonely life. No one sees him other than when they want something."

"Isn't that how all our lives are?"

Brushing the hair out of my face, I shrug. "It's hard to know something and have no one to share it with."

"You're close to your father."

White walls fade into rich vineyards. Sadness creeps into my voice. "I can't tell him everything."

Pilate's eyes soften as he looks at me. "Then find someone to confide in. Here, let me show you... take the reins."

I grip the long leather straps. They feel warm and alive under my fingers; I sense the power of the horses; a slight tug causes my nerves to tingle. "Life is like driving a chariot, Claudia. You can do it alone and feel every flinch and tug of the lines. You can fight the horses or you can learn from them. It's easier if you have help."

His hands close over mine and our fingers entwine. The wheels turn into a rut and jolt us, forcing Pilate to steady me. His hand lingers on my waist. I look up at him. "Is that what you want, Lucius, to help me drive the chariot?"

"I want you to know you can confide in me, if you need to. The augur chooses to be alone. You don't have to live that life."

We drive through the wide gates into the courtyard. Beyond, the harvesters are hard at work in the vineyard. Quintus emerges from the stables as I step into the dirt. "I see you've brought our runaway home. Why didn't you keep her?"

"I thought your father might want her back."

A disheveled Libi slips from the barn into the house. I eye my brother with suspicion.

"Mother's furious with you," he says. "You may want to stay outside." Pulling a face, I follow them to the watering trough. The horses nudge one another as Pilate lets them drink. Quintus leans against the post. "How fares life in Rome?"

"You know my father. He's moving me to the Praetorian Guard."

Quintus smacks the edge of the trough. "I knew it! I told you that in Judea! You laughed in my face! You said you only ever want to be a soldier!"

"I will be a soldier, just a better paid one."

The side door opens and Libi emerges. Without looking at us, she goes to draw water from the well. Quintus' gaze lingers on her. "You'll be a step away from power. I suppose your father's already chosen you a wife?"

"He has prospects but I'm interested in none of them."

Not wanting my brother to notice my red face, I cross to the well. Libi glances at me as she grips the bucket. "Your father wants to speak with you," she says.

"Did you get into trouble when I left yesterday?"

She is careful not to look at the men. "Your mother blamed you, not me."

I follow her indoors. "Did you enjoy your tour of the hayloft with my brother?"

Libi yanks me into a side room. "You can't tell anyone!"

"Did you—?"

She presses her hand over my mouth. Footsteps pass and she hisses, "No! My religion forbids it! You know that!"

"Religion forbids a lot of things but it never stops anyone."

Lowering the water jug onto the table, she sighs. "I can't be

his mistress, and he can't marry. I told him that."

I pluck a piece of straw from her hair. "Before or after he kissed you?"

"Well, it might have been before *and* after." Her eyes twinkle at me and we burst into giggles.

The door behind us slams into the wall and we jump at the sight of Jacob. He looks on both of us with disapproval. "Claudia, your father wants you. Libi, Servia wants her water. *Go now!*"

He stands aside as we push past him, parting on the stairs. I hurry down the hall, smoothing my tunic and forcing my face into a serious expression. I enter Father's sunlit study, full of scrolls and parchment. He sits in his favorite chair, with Jacob's father at his shoulder. Crossing to stand before him, I fix my eyes on the floor and wait.

Father lowers his scroll and looks at me. "Well, what do you have to say?"

"I'm sorry, Father. I'll never again make such an error of judgment."

"See to it you don't. Your mother came home in tears. The servants searched for you late into the night. Avram hasn't slept and neither have I."

I glance at the Jewish man and he smiles at me.

"Why did you run away?"

"Someone jostled me into the butcher's table."

Avram looks at me in concern. Father pushes back his chair. "Never run from anything, Claudia. Life is full of unpleasantness but you must be strong. There's greatness in you." He touches my face. "Your dreams are a test from the gods. When you conquer them you'll bring honor to us." He embraces me, kisses the top of my head, and says, "Go to your mother."

She is less forgiving and slaps me. Fear lurks in her eyes as she says, "Don't ever do that again! Do you know what happens to girls alone in Rome?"

"Yes, Mother. I'm sorry."

Lifting her chin, she asks, "Did anyone touch you?"

"No, Pilate found me first."

She nods and her face softens. "Your punishment is to help prepare for the harvest feast. Find out from Avram what needs done and do it."

I scrub the household linens until my fingers are raw. I help

the servants move furniture, carry pillows, and transform our sunken courtyard into a sitting area. I toil in the kitchen until sweat rolls off my skin.

The messenger from Rome arrives the morning of the feast. I recognize the royal seal and carry the scroll to Quintus with a heavy heart. His face brightens as he reads it. "The legion departs tomorrow for Judea!"

"But you've only been home a month!" I wail.

Putting his arm around me, he says, "That's the life of a tribune. Pilate put me up for a commendation. I am going to take his place as a commander. It's an honor and you should be proud of me."

"I am proud of you. I just don't want you to leave."

We reach the back door and Quintus pats the side of my face. "I know that, but I must. Now go upstairs and put on that nice little blue toga, the one you said has not enough fabric. Pilate is coming this evening."

"You're as bad as Hermina!"

Laughing, he says, "With me in Judea, someone needs to watch over you, and I'd rather it be Pilate."

I shake my head and retreat upstairs. Libi puts up my hair and I slide new sandals onto my feet and a bracelet around my wrist. Feeling self-conscious in the toga, I mingle with the guests and pretend not to wait for Pilate to arrive. He is late but at the sound of his voice in the yard, I go out to meet him.

Dismounting, he hands the reins to a servant. "Ah, my favorite dress."

"Is it? I thought you'd rather I not wear it."

He grins and takes my arm. "I'd rather others not see you in it, but I never said you shouldn't wear it."

We enter the house and Father turns to embrace him. "Lucius, you must come more often now that my son is to leave us. I understand we have you to thank for his accommodation."

"Your son proved his worth in Judea. I had nothing to do with it."

Raising his brow, Father answers, "I doubt it. You have influence in Rome. That is why Sejanus wanted you in the Praetorian Guard. However, there is a better time for such talk. Tonight, we celebrate another successful harvest! Go and enjoy yourself! Claudia, show him to the tables!"

I take his hand and he trails after me through the guests.

Laughter fills the air, wine flows freely, and all eat with gluttonous delight. Musicians play in the corner and Pilate asks, "Will you and your sisters dance for us tonight?"

"Do you want us to?"

Walking backward, I bump into Jacob. He turns and surprise covers his face; his eyes dart down my front and his brows lift to his hairline. "Sorry," I tell him, laughing, and drag Pilate away.

Thais, Lucilla, and I do dance for our guests. I sway and spin as Pilate leans against a column and watches me. Lucilla takes my arm and twirls me away. I fall out of his line of sight and return to it. Jacob stands beside him. They speak to one another, their faces dark and their voices inaudible over the music. Soon Jacob storms away in anger.

"What is that about?" Thais asks as we pass one another.

He pauses to look at me on the stairs and his eyes rake over me in disapproval. "I don't know. It's not like I'm his sister."

Lucilla ducks under my outstretched arms. "That may be the problem."

Warmth rushes into my face as we finish the dance. Applause rings out and as the music starts again, I make my way to Pilate. "What did you say to Jacob?"

"He expressed disapproval for your toga. I put him in his place." Pilate touches my arm and moves away as Quintus calls to him.

I hurry up the stairs into the coolness of the house. Jacob sits in a windowsill, staring out over the dark vineyard. Sweat coats my palms as I approach. "If you have something to say, Jacob, say it to me, not to Pilate."

"You dress like a harlot."

My cheeks redden and I feel slapped. "You have no right to say that."

"I say what I think and I think your behavior shames your father's house."

Shadows merge beneath us as two figures embrace in the gloom. Jacob curls his lip in disgust. I square my jaw. "It *is* my father's house, and you are his servant. I am not your sister. How I dress isn't your concern."

He stands up, towering over me. "Father would do well to take us from this house, but he stays out of loyalty to your father."

"What are you insinuating?" I call after him as he pushes

past.

Jacob turns at the top of the stairs. "You think I don't know your brother wants my sister in his bed? That Pilate wants you for his mistress! Do you think I am blind? This house is a foul, polluted place and it's no coincidence that you suffer from nightmares!"

"If you hate it so much, why don't you leave?"

Dark eyes snap at me in the shadows. "Someday, I will."

He vanishes down the stairs and I sink to the floor. Lucilla finds me there much later. "Come, we should bid Pilate and the others farewell. Our brother is also about to set out for his garrison."

I follow her downstairs, my happiness vanquished. The slender ribbon of dawn buds across the vineyards. Quintus embraces me. "Nothing in Jerusalem is as beautiful as you, Claudia. I'll remember you in my dreams, little sister."

"You won't be in mine, if the gods will it," I answer, and cling to him.

He and Pilate ride out into the dust. Jacob refuses to speak to me and I avoid him. Libi watches us carefully and asks, "What did he say to you?"

"More than I wanted to hear," I answer. I fold the blue tunic and put it away. My heart yearns for Pilate but he does not return.

Noticing my disappointment when he turns down yet another invitation to supper, Father says, "Sejanus keeps him busy with the Praetorian Guard. They're making arrests this week."

"Procula, your daughter wants to know if she can have the fine wine for her wedding feast." Avram looks up from his ledgers. "I worry there isn't enough of it from last season."

Moving to look, Father says, "She can have what's left. I sold most of it to Fidelus last month. The new wine will be ready soon."

"Why did you agree to the marriage?" I sulk. "Lucilla barely knows the senator's son."

"She likes him and he can provide for her. That's all that matters." Father shuffles through the parchment on his desk. "Go help with the preparations."

I leave the sunlit room and walk down the hall. Servants hurry past with armloads of fabric and cushions. Lucilla glances up at me as I enter, garlands spread out on the floor

around her. "Have you heard the latest of Pilate?"

"No, why?" I drop onto the chaise at her side.

"He dragged a man through the streets on a rope tied to his horse!"

Thais' nimble fingers work flowers into a headdress. One falls and I pick it up, my heart quickening with fear. "I don't believe it."

"It's true." Lucilla leans back into the pillows.

Staring at the floor, I ask, "Why did he do it?"

"Does he need a reason?" Thais drops the headdress on my head. "He did it because Sejanus told him to. He is not the boy you grew up with, Claudia. They fear him in Rome. He oversees all the arrests and floggings in the prison."

I find it hard to breathe. "He's never cruel!"

"He's a *Praetorian*, and Sejanus' favorite. *Of course* he's cruel." Lucilla smirks and continues weaving.

Their voices fade away as I storm from the room and collide with Avram in the hall, leaning on his staff. He is not old enough to need it, but his knees are bad from years of working faithfully in the vineyards. Seeing my face, his darkens with concern. "What is it, child?"

"Nothing," I answer.

He studies my expression. "Did you have another premonition?"

I shake my head.

Glancing at my sisters, he says, "You heard about Pilate."

"Do *you* think it's true?" Fear nudges tension into my voice.

He puts his hand on my shoulder. "Pilate does what he believes is best for Rome, as his father did in his place."

"What *did* his father do? No one will tell me."

Avram softens at the yearning in my face. "It no longer matters, Claudia. I must go to the marketplace. Come with me."

I love the Jewish market. Fine woven cloths fill the stalls along with baskets, tents, gems, perfumes, and all else apart from food. I feel fabric and listen to the people around us. Most conversations are in Hebrew, and I can only understand a few words here and there. We pause in front of a stall and Avram asks, "What news from Jerusalem?"

Glancing at me, the merchant leans closer and lowers his voice. "There's a boy in Nazareth with great wisdom for one so young. He teaches the priests in the synagogue! We have hope,

Avram." He turns to other customers, holding out a brightly dyed fabric to peak their interest.

The streets are crowded and dusty; shepherds drive animals past, carts rumble through the lane, beggars ask for alms. Some are genuine; others are thieves. I give the last of my coins to a crippled boy under an arch and hurry to catch up with Avram. I round the corner and collide with the man standing there. He catches my packages before they fall.

"Oh, I'm sorry, I didn't see—Lucius?"

He grins, holding a package out of my reach. "You're not lost, are you?"

"Fortunately not, and be careful with that—it's perfume."

Giving it to me, he walks with me after Avram. "I hear Lucilla is to marry."

"Yes, do you know him?"

We skirt a puddle. "I know *of* him, enough to approve. He is the son of a senator. My father speaks well of him. It surprises me more to find you here. Why do you come to this market instead of the one in the square?"

"Avram prefers it. He likes to talk to his friends from Jerusalem when they pass through." I move aside to let a woman and her children by and nearly brush against him again. The hand he steadied me with rests on my back.

"Did he speak with them today?"

We round a corner and the scent of warm bread rises from a stall. "Yes."

"What did they talk about?" His tone is innocent, but the question is not.

I stop in the middle of the road, not far from home. "Why do you ask?"

"Why don't *you* want to tell me?"

Avram limps past us and stands at the gate. Pilate considers me with a hint of irritation. I shift my armload and ask, "Are any of the rumors true?"

"That depends on the source and the rumor."

"Do you persecute the Jews?"

"No more than they deserve."

"Have you overseen brutal executions for Sejanus?"

Pilate's blue eyes darken. "Claudia, this is Rome. There is no such thing as a kind execution! It is my responsibility to preside over them. I'm the Captain of the Guard, and that's what the Praetorians do, we investigate, arrest, interrogate,

and execute if they're found guilty."

Repressing a shudder, I ask, "Do you enjoy it?"

"Is that what they say?" Emotion surfaces in his face, either hurt or anger.

Crossing the courtyard, Father catches sight of us and opens the gate.

"That's not an answer."

"It doesn't *deserve* an answer!"

Stepping away from him, I let Father intrude. "Lucius, it's too long since we've seen you! Come in!"

Pilate turns to him with a smile. "I'd like to, but I can't. I saw your daughter in the marketplace and wanted to see her home."

"Considering what happened last time, I don't blame you." Father looks between us with dawning suspicion. "Can't you stay for supper?"

Handing me the rest of my packages, Pilate shakes his head. "I'm afraid not, I must report to Sejanus. He has me on duty tonight."

"But you will come to the wedding," presses Father eagerly.

Glancing at me, Pilate says, "I'll try. Thank you for the invitation."

Father puts an arm around me as we walk home. "Did you argue with him?"

"I might have."

He groans. "Oh, Claudia..."

"Lucilla told me he dragged a man through the streets behind his horse!"

We reach the side door and Libi takes the packages from me. Father stops me from entering. "He's a Praetorian Guard!"

"That doesn't mean he has to be cruel!"

Resting his hand on mine, he says, "Life can be cruel. Sometimes men must be too to exist in it. You have not seen the horrors of the world. I hope you never will. Pilate has. He has been to war. You must trust him to have good judgment."

"You don't trust him! You're afraid he's like his father!"

Surprise crosses his face. "You weren't supposed to hear that conversation."

"I'm not supposed to hear a lot of things." I drop onto the step and put my face in my hands.

Father eases down beside me, winded from the short walk. "I may fear a likeness but I hope against it. I trust him to do

what is right."

"What if he doesn't?"

Calloused fingers grip my hand. "That is his choice to make."

I lean my head against his shoulder and we watch the sun set. Father says no more of it. Dreams torment me in my sleep, of wandering figures and lit torches. I wake when Lucilla shakes me. The light from her lamp burns my eyes. "Claudia, get up! Caesar Augustus is dead!"

Stumbling after her into the hall, I lean against Libi as our father informs us of the news. His grim expression makes him look older than usual. The death of an emperor brings some of the legions back to Rome. Centurions return in the next few days. Crowds of cheering subjects line the streets, throwing flower petals and waving silk scarves. Each day we go out to the gate and watch them pass, only to be disappointed.

Father says, "Quintus is in the garrison in Jerusalem. He won't return."

This saddens Mother and she responds by working us hard. The night before Lucilla's wedding, I collapse in bed with aching feet and tired hands. Sleep descends and with it, a dream.

I stand in a field with Jacob behind me, holding a sword. Blood drips from the end of it into the raw earth. The ground ripples with wheat. As I lift my hands, I find them coated with blood.

What have you done? I ask.

He smears it on my face. *What have you done?*

Stumbling back from him, I fall over a corpse. I scream, and wake to find my family standing over me. Sweat soaks the bedclothes. Father takes my shoulders in his broad, worn hands. "Claudia, we couldn't wake you... are you all right?"

I look past him to the doorway, to Jacob and whisper hoarsely, "What have you done?"

The others exchange glances. Father forces me to look at him. "What did you see?"

"Death," I answer.

Jacob glances at his father and disappears into the hall. I push aside my covers and start after him, but Father stops me. "You must rest! Servia, send the others to bed. There's nothing to see."

Mother claps her hands and the faces disperse. They shut

34

the door behind them and in a small voice, Lucilla asks, "Did you dream of me?"

"No, it wasn't about you."

Relief escapes her in a sigh and she turns over. Soft breathing fills the air. I slip out of bed to walk to the family temple. Lighting a candle, I kneel and pray, "Oh, ancestors, take these dreams from me."

The little statues do not answer me.

I have not much time to consider my dream as Mother busies me with errands. Twilight approaches when she retires to dress Lucilla in her wedding garments. I go to fetch water from the well and see Jacob cross the courtyard under a cloak. He fumbles at the gate. Dropping the bucket, I call his name and he turns rapidly, startled. The setting sun casts a long shadow into the arbor.

"I know what you're doing!" I join him at the gate.

"What?"

Voices carry to us as servants arrange pillows in the courtyard. Glancing at them, I lower my voice. "I saw you in my dream. *Don't do it.*"

"What did you see in your dream?"

Shivers caress my spine. "I saw blood on your hands and mine."

"Then you know nothing." He pulls open the gate.

I slam it shut again. "I know you hate the Romans! I know you hate Sejanus! Whatever you intend to do, do you think they won't kill us if you're caught?"

"I'll do what I must to protect Judea."

Pressing against the gate, I say, "And I'll do what I must to protect *my* family!"

He shoves me aside and I slap him across the face. Jacob backhands me, sending me into the dirt.

Yanking open the gate, he vanishes into the darkness.

Chapter Four

I feel sick as I wait for something to happen—for centurions to storm our gates, for blood to spill into the street, for an explanation for my dream. It is hard to applaud with the others, to dance and drink wine as if nothing is happening. I slip away to sit in the kitchen. Music drifts in from the courtyard. My hands shake as I pour a cup of water and drink from it. My neck tingles.

A figure darts past the window and I race to open the door. Jacob stumbles in, his tunic covered in blood. It seeps between his fingers, clasped against his breast. He staggers into a chair. Through clenched teeth, he says, "Pilate saw me."

Voices carry in the hall. Peering out, I see two shadows merge into one, lips locked as they stumble into the next room. I shut the door and hurry to Jacob.

"I should let you bleed to death," I hiss.

He glares at me.

Ransacking the shelves, I find strips of linen. "What happened?"

"It's better that you don't know."

I cross my arms and glare at him. "Tell me or I won't help you."

"We tried to kill Sejanus in the forum but met too many guards."

Terror grips me. "Was Pilate with him?"

"Yes. He dragged me off Sejanus. How I got away, I don't know."

Scowling, I splash wine on his knife wound and his fist slams into the table. "It serves you right," I tell him. "You may have killed us all!"

"I doubt that. Pilate wants you in his bed, not in a prison cell, although he'd probably take you either way." Jacob flinches as I tighten the bandage with an extra savage yank. His torn tunic lies on the floor at our feet. He gathers it up. "Burn it if you can, if not hide it."

He limps to the back door and peers out into the garden.

"What about your family?"

There is a crash at the gates. Fear grips me.

Jacob says, "Tell them nothing. I'll send word if I can once it's safe."

He melts into the darkness. Clutching the tunic to my chest, I slip into the garden, avoiding the soldiers entering the courtyard. My breath catches in my throat as I see Pilate dismount and follow them inside. The music stops. I hide behind the columns and watch, my heart pounding.

Father rises from his chair, his delight at seeing Pilate changing into concern. Our guests huddle together in the center of the space. Motioning his men onward, Pilate says, "No one leaves the grounds. Search every room and outbuilding and bring all the servants here. Don't harm anyone unless they try to escape."

Praetorians flood the house and Father steps nearer. "Lucius, what is it?"

"You'll know soon enough. I must speak to Avram."

Heart pounding, I crawl to the well. Careful not to let the light fall across me, I shove Jacob's linens into the bucket, pile stones on top, and lower it. I hear furniture tip over and ornaments shatter. The soldiers shout to one another. Taking a deep breath and wiping my hands on the grass, I cross to the other side of the courtyard and enter behind my sisters.

Pilate yanks me behind the nearest column. "Where were *you*?"

I jerk my arm free of his hand. "Why?"

"You *know* why."

A bead of sweat slides down my back. I try not to look terrified. Servants spill out of the house, Praetorians on their heels. Most of them are frightened. Libi joins the others, wide-eyed. I start toward her and Pilate pulls me back. "Where is he? Tell me and we'll have no reason to stay."

I feel cold.

He lifts his hands, streaked with blood. He leans closer and his nearness sends a tremor up my spine. "Claudia, *where is Jacob*?"

Searching his angry, desperate gaze, I whisper, "I don't know."

Loud steps bring one of the guards. "There's no one hiding in the house or outbuildings, and we've gathered everyone here."

Frightened faces surround us, the merriment gone from the occasion. Pilate studies me with suspicion and I avoid his gaze, hoping my guilt is not obvious. "The guests may go. The servants can wait in the main hall. The family will enter their

rooms and stay there until I say otherwise. Procula, come with me."

He pushes me toward the others. Father accompanies him indoors. Our guests, Lucilla and her husband among them, slip into the street, grateful to escape. The rest of us retreat to our mother's room. I watch as our servants enter our father's study and leave when he is finished with them. Neither our father nor Avram emerges. One of the guards brings Libi and she sends me a frightened look before disappearing from view. My hands clench into fists. I sit surrounded by the ruins of our furniture, the floor littered with broken pottery.

"What happens if we're arrested?" Thais asks.

Mother is surprisingly calm, her hand at her throat. "We've done nothing wrong. We won't *be* arrested."

I turn my face away rather than laugh. "This is Rome. Guilt doesn't matter."

Footsteps ring in the hall and a guard enters through the far door. "Pilate wants to see the girl."

The others look at me in concern and my hands shake as I smooth my tunic and follow him along the hall. Scrolls cover the floor in the study. Father sits in a chair with Avram at his side. Libi looks up at me from the corner, in tears. Pilate stands behind the desk. I approach tentatively, my heart racing. Father looks old in the lamplight, his face wreathed in wrinkles.

"Claudia, tell me what you know," Pilate insists.

I look surprised. "What do you mean?"

"Have you seen Jacob tonight?"

My eyes drop to his bloodstained hands. "Is someone injured?"

Father's window overlooks the garden, where Pilate's soldiers search near the well. One leans out to catch the rope. Panic rises in me. Pilate steps into my line of vision, forcing me to look up at him.

"She knows nothing," says Father.

"Tonight, Jacob and a dozen other men tried to murder Sejanus in the forum."

Sweat coats my palms as the soldier pulls up the bucket. I lift my chin. "What does that have to do with me?"

His eyes search mine. "Did you help him?"

"Do *you* think I helped him? Do you think I would turn my back on Rome?"

38

The bucket nears the top of the well. Pilate leans against the desk. "I think you're loyal and would do anything to protect the people you love."

"We have that in common, don't we?"

Lights flicker in the darkness. Pilate says, "I *will* find him."

"*Good.*"

Silence lurks in the corners. Pilate motions to the others. "Avram..." The old man steps forward wearily. My heart drops and I clench my fists. "I have every right to arrest you, but out of respect for your loyalty to Procula and your long service in the house, I won't. The same courtesy won't be extended to your son when we find him."

My eyes close and I breathe again.

"Thank you."

Pilate motions to the guard and leaves the room. The bucket tips into the well as his men respond to his reappearance. I sigh with relief as they mount and ride out onto the road. Behind us, the door opens and Mother appears. "Procula, I thought..."

He takes her hand and smiles. "It was a misunderstanding, don't worry."

Thais joins me as we return to our room. "What happened?"

I feel like I want to faint. "I'll tell you later. Libi, please send a servant to Lucilla and her husband. Make sure they know we're all right."

Pale-faced, she nods and hurries away. I enter our room and stop in dismay at the mess. Thais retrieves one of her favorite togas from the floor. "Remind me to kick Pilate the next time I see him."

"It's a small price to pay for our freedom," I answer.

Sinking onto my bed, I finger the torn netting and try to stop shaking. Mother enters. "I want you to sleep for awhile and then we'll put all to rights. Thais, you can oversee the main rooms. Claudia, see to the courtyard and the garden."

"Did they break anything important?" I ask.

Pausing in the doorway, she says, "Better broken things than broken limbs."

At nightfall, I go to the well, draw up the bloodstained toga, take it into the vineyard and bury it. No one sees me and a fortnight passes without word. It is time to start brewing the wine in barrels. Mother is too busy to bother with household affairs and sends me to the fish market in her place. Even Libi

relaxes as we peruse the stalls, a basket under each of our arms.

"Figs are a nice treat, don't you agree?"

Examining them, I nod and she pays for some. I turn and bump into an older woman. Dark eyes flash at me under her hood. "Excuse me," she says, but grips my hand. I look at her in surprise. In a low voice, she asks, "You're Claudia of Procula's house?"

I nod.

"Then I'm to give this to you. He's safe." She presses something into my fist and moves away as if nothing happened. I uncurl my fingers to reveal a Star of David. I close my hand but not before Libi sees it. Her gaze darts to mine and then focuses on someone behind me.

"Claudia..." she whispers.

Pilate approaches. My breath catches in my throat. "Give me your basket." Dropping the star into mine, I hand it to her. She throws a fish on top of it as he crosses the dock.

"Fish and figs tonight, I see," he says. His eyes are no longer hard, his easy grin returning as he looks at me.

I shift the basket to my other hip. "You should eat supper with us."

"Considering the nature of my last visit, I think not." He walks with me toward home. The wind blows through my hair.

I glance at him. "I understand *why* you did it; I'm just sorry you did."

"And I'm sorry you lied to me."

Fear tickles my spine and I look at him. Pilate stops, forcing me to as well. "You did it to protect those you love. I can respect that."

Biting my lip, I ask, "What did you tell Sejanus?"

"There's no reason to suspect anyone in your father's house, least of all his faithful old servant."

My hands tighten around the basket. "*Thank you.*"

"Claudia, I want to trust you but you make it difficult."

People move around us and pass down the road. Libi waits for me at the gate. Pilate touches the side of my face, his fingers brushing my hair. I cannot meet his eyes and drop them. "You redeemed yourself in Father's eyes."

"I'm glad of it."

Biting my lip, I say, "He's not well, Lucius. He tries to hide it, but a specter haunts him. Don't wait too long to see him."

Weary feet carry me home. Libi joins me. "Is he angry?"

"I don't know. I can't tell."

Pulling open the gate, Libi says, "He likes you."

"That may be, but I can never be his wife. He must marry well."

She turns into my path. "Marrying you *is* marrying well. Claudia, you are a dream-seer. Do you have any idea how powerful it would make him, to marry someone who can predict the future? You're worth ten senators' daughters." I stare at her. Stepping closer, she whispers, "You must marry him soon. Convince him of it. Don't wait."

"Why?"

Her cheeks flush. "It isn't safe."

"What are you talking about?"

Pulling me into the shadows, she says, "Your mother wants to take you to see the high priest. She says they can help develop your dream-seer skills."

"I don't want to develop them! I want to get rid of them!"

She shushes me and glances worriedly into the kitchen. "Then you must marry and make sure your husband beds you!"

"What does that have to do with it?"

Blushing, Libi answers, "Dream-seers must remain virgins. It stops otherwise. Pilate would know this. You must make him desire you more than your abilities."

I cannot imagine a worse fate than being a temple seer. Unlike the augurs in the streets of Rome, seers are isolated and only the high priest may speak with them.

Mother and I set out the next morning for the temple. My anxiety increases as we weave through the crowd mingling on its front steps. Temple harlots peer out at us through the curtains. One does not look much older than Hermina. I have never gone beyond the inner courtyard, where ornate detail covers the pillars and gold decorates the tiles. A boy wearing rich purple robes stops us and once he knows what Mother wants, goes to summon his master.

Footsteps approach and a group of veiled girls pass, their eerie eyes lingering on me. The boy returns to escort us into an inner chamber, the walls heavy with scrolls. "This is the room of prophecy," he says, bowing.

"Come closer," says the high priest. He faces away from us, under the arch overlooking the courtyard. Shutting the door,

the boy moves to a small desk in the corner. "So you think you have a dream-seer."

Mother approaches as near as she dares, dragging me with her. "Yes."

He turns and instinctively I flinch. His milky eyes stare at me so hard I want to sink into the floor. Descending the steps, he circles me. "How old is she?"

"She's seventeen next week," Mother says.

Knobby fingers lift a strand of my hair. "We take them at eleven or twelve."

"But dream-seers are rare and she is untouched."

Those horrible eyes drift over me. "We will test her. Come."

We follow him into a dark room with a fire pit in the center, like the one I saw in the augur's house. A young woman stirs as we enter and her creepy, pale eyes shift to me. The priest shoves me forward. Her hands fall into mine and she leads me to the fire.

"Sit," she says.

I sink onto the pillows.

Muttering under her breath, she casts black powder into the flames. They rush upward, the heat intense. Her eyes seem to glow across from me. "Yes," she says softly, "the spirits are strong with this one."

Rattling something in a jar, she throws bones and runes into the sand and crouches over them, her wild hair making her look like an animal. "They aren't the usual spirits."

The priest moves to look over her shoulder. "What do you mean?"

"Minerva doesn't speak to her."

He glances at me. "Is it another of the gods?"

Prodding the bones, she shakes her head. "It's *a* god, but not one of ours."

Specters are in the room with us. I stare at the dark form lurking over the high priest's head. It revolves into grotesque shapes. "Have you told him about the specter?" I ask.

Mother stirs in the shadows and the woman stares at me in shock. Her black-rimmed eyes narrow.

"Surely you can see it," I stress, indicating the floating shadow.

The priest draws nearer. "What is that you say, girl?"

"You have a death specter hanging over you. But she hasn't told you."

42

The seer rises to her feet, glaring at me.

"Is this true?" he demands, turning on her.

"Lies," she hisses, "all lies! She is not one of us! Send her away!"

I scramble to my feet as she lashes out at me. Black powder explodes in my face, stinging my hands.

"Out!" she screams, "out before I call the gods of death upon you!"

Mother drags me outside, fear in her eyes. "What god did she speak of?"

"I don't know!"

She brings me up short at the gates. "You may have ruined your chances!"

"Good! I'd rather die than go back there!"

Carts lumber past and she jerks me out of their way. "You'll do as I tell you!"

"I won't! I'll leave this place and offer myself to Pilate!"

Mother glares at me. "Why must you defy me?"

I jerk my arm out of her grasp. "It's not my fault that I can see in my dreams, yet you blame me for it! You did that to me, when you paid a sorcerer to make sure you had a son! What did he do to me, Mother? What foul poison did he pour into your womb while I slept there?"

She slaps me. I press a hand to my stinging cheek and blink back angry tears. Mother starts away and turns again, misery in her eyes. "I don't hate you, child. I fear you. You're not the only one who has nightmares."

Glancing back at the temple, I follow her home.

ter Five

Avram sits on the bench at the far end of the garden. His shoulders slump with grief and he looks old in spite of his age. His eyes brighten at the sight of me. Our shadows merge as I sit beside him and gaze over the vineyards. He leans on his staff and watches me. "Did you have a good day in Rome?"

"You know where Mother took me, don't you?"

"Yes."

I glance up at him. "And you don't approve."

"It isn't my place to question your parents' choices."

Making a pattern in the dirt at our feet, I sigh. "I don't want to be a seer."

"You may not be one. You may be a prophet instead." Avram smiles at me.

Feeling the tension in my chest ease, I ask, "What's the difference?"

"Seers seek truth through divination and dark spirits. God speaks to prophets so that they might guide His people in times of great need."

Wind stirs my hem and I lean back. "I'm not one of your people."

"No, but God may speak through you, if it is His desire."

My hand tightens in my lap. "He must hate me to make my dreams so awful. I've never had a good dream, Avram... only terrible ones."

"It isn't for us to question His ways."

The light begins to fade around us and I wipe away my tears. I brush my nose with the back of my hand and lean my head against his shoulder. "I miss Jacob."

"I do, too. His choices are poor but he's still my son."

Opening his hand, I press the Star of David into it. Avram stares at it in shock, and hides it as servants pass behind us into the house. His voice softens. "This belongs to Jacob, where did you get it?"

"From a woman in the marketplace who told me he's safe."

His eyes search mine. "You knew, didn't you?"

I nod.

"Did you warn him?"

"He ignored me."

Avram closes his hand over the emblem and shuts his eyes.

I touch his arm, prompting him to look at me. "He returned injured. I bound his wounds and hid the evidence from Pilate."

"Does he know you lied to him?"

Shivers nip at my heels and biting my lip, I nod. Avram frowns slightly. "I wondered why he let me go."

"You had nothing to do with the attack on Sejanus!"

He smiles and shakes his head. "Do you think that matters in Rome? My son tried to assassinate the most powerful man in the empire. If it weren't for Pilate's love for you, I'd be dead." Pushing away from the bench, he walks toward the courtyard.

I follow. "Jacob knew that. He told me Pilate would not punish us. He didn't want you hurt."

"What if he'd been wrong?"

Feeling cold, I wrap my arms around my waist. "He wasn't."

"He might have been. He hated Sejanus enough to risk all our lives. That is a dangerous kind of passion, Claudia. It's what Pilate has done for you."

I grip his hand. "You must help me! Fight for me! Father cannot let Mother send me to the temple as a seer! Influence him!"

Doubt springs up in his eyes. Mother calls to me from the yard.

"Please!"

He does not answer and his expression haunts me as I hurry home. I kneel in our family temple and pray to our ancestors. Kissing each small statue, I set out bread and wine for them, and retreat indoors.

Father's voice drifts to me through the columns. I look away from the stars and swing my feet to the floor of the verandah.

"Do you never want more gods than one, Avram?"

"One god was sufficient all these years."

They enter the study and a lamp flares, casting a long shadow beside me.

"If you displease him, there's no other god to ask for protection from wrath."

Avram chuckles, "I do my best *not* to anger Him."

I start to enter the room as Father says, "I'm not sure what to do about Claudia. Do you have an opinion?"

Darting behind a curtain, I hold my breath. Scrolls rustle.

"What do you mean?"

Father's chair creaks. "Servia wants to send her to the

temple."

"But you prefer marriage."

Parchment crinkles. "Yes, but to whom?"

"What about Pilate?"

"He's like a brother to her, nothing more."

"Is he?"

"*Isn't* he?"

Avram passes within an inch of my hiding place. "Would he protect this household in spite of the danger if he wasn't interested in your daughter?"

"I don't fancy her as his mistress."

Wind stirs the draperies and flowers scent the air. Father taps his fingers on the desk.

"What about his wife?"

"Could he marry a girl with no station?"

Avram takes down a scroll. "Pilate is the most powerful man in Rome. He will do what he likes. Isn't that right, Claudia?"

Guiltily, I step out from behind the curtain. Father sits back in his chair. "Do you have an opinion on this matter, my child?"

"I'll do whatever honors you, Father."

His kind, dark eyes soften in the lamplight. "Even if I tell you to be a seer?"

"Yes, even then... if it pleases you."

Father snorts and returns to his work. "That's not what your mother said."

I bite my lip to stop from responding.

He waves me aside. "Off you go. I'll think about it."

Entering our room and ignoring Thais when she asks where I have been, I crawl into bed and shut my eyes.

The dream comes in full force this time. I stand alone in a corridor, the wind stirring the curtains on either side. Emptiness fills the house and fearing the worst, I move forward.

Claudia...

I turn but no one is there. A shadow passes through the arch and I follow it into a darkened room. Shivers prickle my arms.

Father?

Movement stirs behind me but my hand touches nothing but air.

Thais shakes me awake, her face pale and streaked with tears. "It's Father, you must come."

He moans in his sleep and burns with fever. I take his hand and sit at his side, listening to my mother's frantic voice in the distance. "Do something!"

"I can't, there's nothing to do," says the physician.

Shadows move around the walls. My eyes follow them, dreading the one that will take his spirit away. Sweat glistens on his brow and I wipe it with a damp cloth. Hours pass and we watch him worsen. I carry the basin out into the hall and rouse one of the servants. "Go to Pilate and bring him at once," I say.

He hurries away. I draw fresh water and resume my tending of Father. I hold back tears as I bathe his face and hands. Footsteps soon echo in the hall and Pilate enters. Mother stares at him and Thais rises from her place. His eyes dart from me to the sick man in the bed. "You sent for me?"

I hold out my hand. "Yes."

His fingers fall into mine and I draw him near. Father stirs and I reach out to wake him. "Father, Lucius is here."

"Lucius," he repeats softly. His eyes struggle to focus on us and soften with recognition. "You should have come sooner, for the harvest."

Kneeling beside him, Pilate nods. "I meant to."

"You're like a second son to me, you know that."

His voice shows his emotion. "I do."

Father motions to me. "Then look after her for me. Take her as your wife."

Our eyes dart to one another and hastily look away. Pilate squeezes my hand. "I will. You have my word, Procula."

We sit with him until dawn when the rising sun takes his spirit. I feel it leave his body. Pilate half carries me onto the verandah. Tears flow, my grip tightening around him.

"I'm glad you're here," I whisper.

Pilate presses his lips to the top of my head. "I'll never leave you again."

Chapter Six

Butterflies flutter in my stomach as Libi lays out my wedding toga. "It's more modest than your blue one," she teases. "But I think he'll like it anyway."

I finish weaving the flowers into a headdress. "Does it look all right?"

"It's beautiful!" Libi takes it from me and brushes my hair. "You'll have to sit still. This is a special arrangement and I've only done it once before." Her careful fingers work my blonde hair into gentle ringlets atop my head. The scent of incense rises from the family temple.

"Mother made her sacrifice."

"Yes. Rub this oil into your skin until it shines."

It fills the air with perfume. "Do you have the bridal sash?"

"It's on the bed." Tucking a final strand into place, she steps back and admires her work. "There, you'll do your family proud."

Turning in my chair, I catch her hand, "Libi, will you come with me?"

"You mean as your servant, in Pilate's house? No, I can't."

Distress prompts me to follow her to the bed. "Why?"

"My brother tried to kill Sejanus! Pilate will never let me in his house." She takes my hands and squeezes them. "You mustn't be sad! This is what you wanted! You don't have to be a seer!"

I try to smile and fail. "That's only if he wants a wife."

"That's why you're drenched in perfume. No man could resist you."

Mother knocks at the door and enters. Libi smiles at me and slips out. Tying the sash around my waist, Mother reminds me, "Only Pilate may loosen it."

"Yes, I know."

She lowers the tunic over my head. "Pilate will show you what to do. He loves you, so he will be gentle with you. Most women aren't so fortunate."

A knock at the door interrupts our talk. Hermina peers around it. "Oh, you look beautiful!" She darts inside and hugs me as Mother quickly retreats. I follow her downstairs. Sejanus is among the first to arrive, his eyes roaming until they fall on me. His expression is unreadable and a chill creeps over me.

"Don't worry about him," Pilate whispers in my ear. I glance up as his fingers entwine with mine. "He may look on in disapproval but he can't stop us." He leads me into the courtyard, where Mother and a priest await. Our marriage happens in a haze, of touching hands and shining eyes. Pilate kisses me, the crowd cheers, and music and feasting begin. I stay close to him as guests congratulate us.

Sejanus steps forward. "You've chosen a beautiful wife, Lucius."

"Thank you." Pilate smiles and turns as his father speaks to him.

Eying Sejanus with dislike, I say, "I'll try my best to curb my tongue."

"Oh, I'm sure you'll find a good use for it. You understand that this is about more than simply pleasing him in the bedroom. As his wife, you are his emissary. You must also please powerful people. Can you do that for him?"

My stomach muscles clench and I nod.

He pats my hand. "Good."

I shudder as he walks away from us and Pilate turns to me. "Father informs me it's time to move the celebrations to our house. I must go. I can't have my wife arrive first if I must wrestle her from her mother's arms!"

"Better my mother's arms than that of a temple priest," I laugh.

Kissing me, he disappears into the crowd. We wait a little while and then set out in a group. Guests, servants, and strangers join the wedding party as we enter Rome. It is not far to his house and we spill into the courtyard armed with torches. Mother walks me to the foot of the stairs and Pilate descends, to a great cheer. Both tug me in opposite directions until he picks me up and carries me inside.

Guests stream into the great hall as I follow him to his room. Mother enters with us. She unhooks my veil and slides my tunic from my shoulders, leaving me in a simple shift. Pilate watches from the far corner, the singing of our guests drifting through the walls. The door closes behind her. Music wafts across the yard and the lamp flames flicker in the breeze, stirring the bed curtains. He touches the side of my face. I lean into his caress, his fingers entwining in my hair. I move closer as he unties my sash. He lowers me onto the bed and his mouth covers mine. His touch is as flirtatious as his eyes,

gently teasing as he sets my nerves to tingling.

"So you didn't want a seer after all," I murmur in his ear.

His tongue brushes my earlobe and he gently nips me. "No, I want a wife."

Dreams descend when passion drifts into sleep. I stand in a great hall alone. White pillars loom overhead as I move through them. The wind teases my tunic and cools my skin. A man sits before me on the throne. Pilate stands beside him and extends his hand. I take it, looking at the emperor with unease. It is not Tiberius. Sunlight drifts into darkness and gloom gathers. I glance around us and when I look at Pilate, blood trickles from the side of his mouth. Horrified, I see the sword protruding from his chest. The centurion behind him draws it out and he collapses at my feet.

No!

My scream echoes in the room, widening the emperor's cruel smirk.

Arms catch me as I fall.

"Claudia!"

I look up into Pilate's face, weary with concern. Our guests are long gone and the house quiet. Dawn creeps into the horizon. My arms go around his neck and he holds me close. He kisses my forehead and smoothes my damp hair. He cradles my face in his hands. "Are the dreams always so violent?"

Flushed and near tears, I nod. "They should have stopped!"

He lowers me into the pillows. "We'll find someone who can help you."

"Avram," I whisper.

Pilate tilts my face back. "What?"

"Father's servant... let them come to me, both he and his daughter."

A cloud passes over his face. Flatly, he says, "Jacob's father and sister?"

"Yes." I shiver in the crisp morning air and he pulls the coverlet higher on me.

"You want me to bring the father of an insurgent into our house?"

"Please? He says it is not a curse, but a gift. He can help me."

His blue eyes soften. "How can I deny you when you look at me like that?"

50

"I'll remember that for the future," I answer mischievously.

When Avram and Libi arrive with their things, I hurry out to open the gate. Libi eyes me ruefully as she enters the house and says, "I underestimated you."

"You underestimated Pilate." I take Abram's hand. "Can you help me?"

Searching my eyes, he says, "I can try."

I fill my days with activities and spend my nights in Pilate's arms. Avram settles into the household and soon arranges my schedule to keep me busy. "Idle minds have more time for dark dreams," he says.

That first dream lingers with me. "Who will be emperor after Tiberius?"

"It'll probably be his adopted grandson, Caligula." Pilate kisses my shoulder and drops back into the pillows, stroking my back with his fingertips. "You'll meet him tomorrow. Sejanus wants to introduce you to the emperor."

"Why?"

He shrugs. "I'm sure he has his reasons."

My dream becomes reality as we pass through the same columns and descend into the main hall. Faces turn in expectation, the women eyeing me with interest. We meet Sejanus at the foot of the stairs and he takes my arm. "Remember what I said," he whispers.

Fear takes hold as we cross the room and ascend to the throne, but it fades when I see Tiberius. His is not the face from my dream, but warm and full of good humor. "So you're Pilate's wife," he says.

Waving away the servant at his side, he shakes out his robes and motions me closer. His shrewd blue eyes brighten in approval. "Beautiful. What's your name?"

"Claudia."

He indicates the chair at his side. "Sit with me."

I sit and his slave hands me a cup of wine. Tiberius sips from his own ruby-encrusted goblet. "I must taste some of your father's wine. I hear his vineyards are the finest in the province."

"You do him honor, Caesar."

"I understand he died recently. I'm sorry."

Sadness dulls my smile. "You're kind."

"Death leaves a mark on us all, sooner or later." His gaze strays to my husband. "Tell me of Pilate. He spends most of his

time with Sejanus."

Conversation drifts around us. The servant offers me grapes and I take a few. "He's a good man, Caesar, loyal to Rome."

"Yes, he does show promise. I only hope Sejanus won't lead him astray."

My hands tighten on the cup. "What do you mean?"

Tiberius turns cold eyes upon me. "Power is what most men covet, Claudia. Does your husband?"

"His first and only desire is to serve Rome." My voice softens with affection.

The emperor looks at me. "I doubt that. He'd be a fool not to desire *you*."

"Pilate is a soldier, as you are. Father told me of your many victories."

Some of his sullenness fades. "I miss it. Rome is full of simpering politics and insipid conversation. I want to go to Capri and leave them to their evil schemes." Bitterly, he beckons to a boy standing nearby. "Caligula, come here."

The dark eyed boy approaches with an intensity that makes my skin crawl. Tiberius puts his arm around him, drawing him to his side. Caligula stares at me and sips from a goblet. "What do you think of Pilate's wife?"

"She's beautiful." His eyes roam more freely than they should and shift to the foot of the stairs, where Hermina stands in a small group of girls. Her eyes sparkle at me and I feel a swift, sudden desire to send her home.

The emperor notices her. "Pilate's sister? I see a resemblance."

"Yes."

"How old is she?"

"Twelve, Caesar."

Caligula asks, "May I go?"

"Yes. Go on."

The boy descends the stairs and stands behind her until Hermina notices. He leans forward and whispers into her ear. She laughs and a shiver captures me. Tiberius bites the edge of his goblet. "He's an unusual boy."

Caligula's is the face from my dream.

Chapter Seven

I do not want to be here. I feel sick standing on the street outside. The smell of blood and incense turns my stomach. Still, I climb the stairs to the temple. The seers have a dark, spectral look, an aura in their eyes that disturbs me. One offers me her hand. "Claudia, come with me, your husband made arrangements."

I follow her into a dark inner room with a fire pit in the center of the floor.

"Sit," she says, motioning to a pillow. Heavy draperies surround us. I sit as instructed and remove my hood. Red embers burn in the pit and stirring them, she asks, "How often do you dream?"

"I can't predict it. I can go months without dreaming."

"We'll try to focus your mind. Concentrate. Think on someone or something and the gods may show you more." She casts a handful of ashes onto the fire. It bursts upward, the flash of heat giving way to a sickeningly sweet scent. Smoke fills the room and closing my eyes, I drift into it.

Pilate...

It is like plunging into an icy stream. I sense cold and darkness... the same darkness as in my dreams, a heavy, oppressive force that fills me with horror.

Screams fill a familiar corridor not far from Fidelus' room. The scream cuts short and a young Pilate rushes past. I follow him into his father's chambers. Fidelus holds a woman by the throat and lets her body drop limply to the bed. Pilate stares in horror. His father glares at him.

Footsteps run along the hall and a servant enters. *Master, what did you do?*

I move toward Pilate's mother, her sightless eyes staring heavenward. Fruit spills over the floor, the result of an overturned table. I see a beautiful child huddled in the corner. Two-year-old Hermina is shaking.

I did what I should have done years ago.

The servant approaches. *Murder is not always a crime in Rome but your enemies may use it against you.*

Fidelus stares remorselessly at his dead wife. *What do you suggest?*

She drowned, yes?

Pilate's head snaps up and hatred burns in his eyes.

You even tried to save her... right, Lucius?

I feel sick as Pilate asks, *is that what happened, Father?*

Yes, and it is what you will encourage your sister to remember.

Her wails fill the air. Pilate passes his father and picks her up. She clutches at his neck and buries her face in his toga. *Yes, Father*, he says, his voice full of loathing.

Good. Take her away.

I want out of the oppressive room; the heat makes me feel faint.

A hand touches mine. *Calm yourself.*

Let me out!

My eyes fly open and adjust to the dark space, full of smoke and flame. I turn to the seer angrily. "You said I'd see the future, not the past!"

"I said the gods might show you *something*. Did they?" Her strange, pale eyes search my face through her veil. Pushing away her hand, I stagger on my feet. She grabs for me. "The gods aren't finished with you! Let them do their work."

"No, I've seen enough."

She follows me through the temple. Incense stings my nose and the stench of raw meat makes me want to vomit. Her hands flutter anxiously. "Please, sit and wait until your mind clears! It's dangerous to enter Rome in a seer state!"

I shove past her out into the brilliant sunlight. Avram hastens to meet me in the street, warning off the seer with a frown. "Be off with you!" His arm wraps around me and he walks me to the litter with disapproval in his face.

"You don't like it," I say weakly, my head spinning.

He sets his mouth in a firm line. "Beware of soothsayers and sorcerers and don't consort with them. That is the teaching of our ways. You know not what evils you wake with such practices. Let this be an end to it!"

It takes hours for my senses to clear and once the haze passes, a headache takes its place. I lie in bed staring at the ceiling and hardly move when Pilate enters. He removes his armor and drops it into a chair. My hand reaches for his and he sits beside me. "Is your sister Sejanus' child?"

Shock crosses his face. "Why do you ask?"

"The rumors in Rome are that he favors you because you're his illegitimate son, but I saw your mother's death today, in the

flames. It is not you, but Hermina! She's his child, not you!"

Darkness enters his eyes and I move closer to him.

"Why didn't you tell me?"

"Does it matter?" Pilate strokes my hand. "You grew up in an atmosphere of love, Claudia. Your father approved of you, doted on you, loved you. Mine hated me because I saw him at his worst—in a blind rage, a fit of jealousy that cost him his career as a general. Oh, the lie flourished, but before long, they replaced him. Mother was foolish to deceive him, but I can hardly blame her." He looks distant. "I heard things growing up... terrible things that no child should hear. She should have left this house but I suppose Sejanus did not ask her. Why would he, when she gave him everything he wanted at no cost to himself?"

Our fingers entwine and I rest my chin on his shoulder. Pilate leans his head on mine. "Since that day, I've waited for death. I know far too much and am a daily reminder of my father's folly. He has every reason to arrange my demise, but my survival protects Hermina, so I haven't made it easy for him."

Pulling my knees to my chest, I ask, "Gaul?"

"He sent me to war hoping I'd die. I returned a hero instead, much to his disappointment, so he pushed me toward Sejanus. He's dangerous and my father hopes that when Tiberius tires of him it'll destroy us both."

Pilate touches my hair, his fingers lingering on my arm.

"What of Hermina?" I ask.

He frowns. "He denies her love yet she's loyal to him. She remembers enough, but not all."

I reach for his hand. "Let me help you."

"You do simply by being here. You give me joy."

Embracing him, I calm the rapid beat of my heart. "I'll help you protect her."

Someone knocks on the door and it opens, a servant offering us a scroll. Pilate takes it. His expression changes as he says, "It is Tiberius' seal." My feet slip to the floor as he opens it. His brows shoot up. "Tiberius appoints me as the prefect of Crete. Did you have anything to do with this?"

"No! He said nothing to me of Crete."

Biting his lip, he glances toward the window. The city thrives beyond our walls and voices drift to us on the breeze. "He's separating me from Sejanus."

"Isn't that a good thing, if he's so dangerous?"

Pilate taps the scroll on his hand. "Maybe but it worries me. Still, a governor is a step up from a Praetorian Guard."

"How soon must we leave?" I take the scroll from him and read it.

On his way out the door, he says, "In a week!"

Hermina is broken-hearted. Not even our promises to write can lift her sulk and it takes an afternoon with Caligula in his chariot to improve her mood.

The voyage is uneventful apart from my seasickness. Libi consoles me, her cool hand sponging my burning brow. I want to die with each toss of the sea. Our first glimpse of Crete is beautiful; the sun beats on the white shore and its line of matching stucco buildings. We drift in with the tide, letting us see the standards of Tiberius fluttering from the ramparts and the heavy military presence on the city walls. There is a gathering of officials to greet us; a man steps forward.

"I'm Demetrius, your Captain of the Guard, Prefect," he says. He helps me from the boat. The air is thick and sultry. I walk behind Pilate and the soldiers form around us protectively. "Crete is different from Rome or even Judea, which I understand you're familiar with. We have few uprisings and our populace is loyal to the emperor. Still, it is not an easy post and I suggest caution. There are many here eager for power hoping for your demise."

"They'll have a long wait," Pilate answers.

A chariot awaits us pulled by two black horses and Demetrius drives us into Crete. Merchants crowd the streets. Pagan temples shine under the midday sun. Fountains flow against white stone terraces. The governor's palace is spacious, built a short distance from the forum. I walk through the garden to the temple and examine the row of ancestor statuettes on the altar.

"I suggest you meet with the priests before doing anything else, and there are several Roman senators waiting for you in the library." Demetrius indicates the way and Pilate accompanies him.

Entering the house, I meet with a line of servants. They examine the floor as I consider them. Motioning to the older man in the doorway, I say, "This is Avram. You will report to him and him to me. Is this understood?"

"Yes, Mistress," is the murmur, but several shoot him dark

looks.

The islands are balmy and the nights never cool. Late afternoon heat drives me indoors. Whenever my husband is not there, I sit in the library. The collection of scrolls is extensive and I happily read the Greek philosophers.

"Do you want me to bring you anything?" Libi asks.

I look up from my scroll and shake my head. Her footsteps fade down the hall. Wind stirs the curtains and draws my attention to the inlet. Sweat drips down my spine and I rise. It is not far to the beach, down the rocky path, and I sit to remove my sandals.

"How much are you going to take off?" Pilate asks from behind me.

Shading my eyes to look at him, I smile. "How is the Roman consul?"

"He's an idiot, like usual." Pilate nudges me with his foot. "You didn't answer me."

Laughing, I stand up. "I can't take off much, what if someone's looking?"

Pilate leans his head against mine. "I'd have to put out their eyes, and since I just ordered another execution, that might not make me popular."

My heart sinks and I ask, "So soon?"

"I'm afraid so." He moves past me along the shore. "I wouldn't have to do it if they'd submit to Rome instead of defying her at every turn!"

Water laps at my feet. "You'd defy her too, if you weren't a Roman."

"No, I'd see the futility in resistance."

Catching his hand, I say, "Swim with me."

"Is that dignified for a man of my position?"

I grin and back into the sea. "No, but it is *fun*."

He catches me around the waist and kisses me, his touch exciting my senses. Footsteps pound along the path and a servant scrambles down the embankment. He shouts, "Prefect, there's a mob at the gates demanding to speak with you!"

Pilate rolls his eyes and returns to the house, gripping my hand. "Stay inside."

The mob presses against the gates and roar at his appearance, shouting against the taxes recently imposed to fund the imperial treasury. Guards stand at intervals around the courtyard. I linger in the doorway.

"I assume they have a list of complaints," Pilate says.

Demetrius hands it to him and he reads it. Rolling the scroll up in one hand, he lifts his arm for silence. The crowd quiets. "For too long, the citizens of Crete have neglected to pay Roman taxes. The last governor saw no reason to enforce this law but I do. Since you benefit from the *protection* of the empire, you should help sustain it."

The mob shouts their disapproval. Pilate watches them in amusement and again motions for silence. "I won't have riots outside my house. Leave before the shadow shifts over the sundial, or I'll arrest every second man in the crowd."

He hands the scroll to Demetrius and I follow him into our room. Pilate pours a cup of wine and watches the mob disperse in the street. I linger at his side and ask, "Is it wise to threaten them?"

"The last governor was too lenient."

My damp garments cling to me as we turn inside. Pilate rifles through the scrolls on the side table. "Crete is a stepping stone. If I prove my worth, Tiberius will assign me to another governorship, one more important. I *want* Judea."

"You make her sound like a woman."

His eyes flicker to me in amusement. "She's the whore of our empire. I want to beat her into submission."

I motion toward the gates. "What if they hadn't dispersed?"

"Then they would be arrested."

Crossing my arms, I ask, "And if they resisted?"

"They wouldn't resist twice." He smiles but it does not comfort me. Feeling nauseous, I feel my way to a chair and sit down. Concern crosses his face. "Are you all right?"

"I'm fine. I just can't seem to shake the seasickness."

He kneels beside me and touches my forehead. "You're hot."

"Crete is hot."

Blue eyes darken and he asks, "Could you be with child?"

I stare at him. "I don't know..."

Squeezing my hand, he says, "We'll find out. Come, lie on the bed."

He arranges me on it and leaves the room. Libi soon enters and sits beside me, holding my hand as the physician examines me. When he is finished, I sit up and he smiles at me. "You are with child... about eight weeks along."

"Is there any way to tell if it's a boy?"

Rolling down his sleeve, he answers, "No! The gods will

58

determine that."

Libi beams at me as he leaves the room and slips out quietly when Pilate enters. He perches on the side of the bed. "So it isn't seasickness, then?"

I laugh and throw my arms around him. "It's a boy. I'm sure of it."

"Since you *are* the seer, I'll defer to you." Pilate smiles and presses his lips to my forehead.

Clutching his hands, I ask, "Will you pray with me, this once?"

"That's not my way, but I won't stop you."

Our ancestors frown at me from their carved niches in the temple. I pray for a healthy child and put out the usual fruits and meat.

Two months later, I wake to find the bed covered in blood. Libi responds to my screams, skidding to a stop as she stares at me, wide-eyed. The pain is unbearable as the tiny body leaves mine.

"Claudia, it isn't your fault." Pilate's hand is on my shoulder as I stare at the sheet wrapped around our tiny son.

I pull away from him, emptiness in my heart.

Then whose fault is it?

Chapter Eight

Our ancestor gods line the altar in the temple. Their faces mock my pain. I strike the nearest one to the floor. It shatters and satisfaction fills my heart. I smack the next one against the altar; its head splits off and rolls away.

Pilate leaves the house and runs toward me. "Claudia!"

I throw the third against the column; it splinters and the pieces fall into the grass. My legs give out and I fall, sobs choking my throat. Strong arms wrap around me and I scream, "*Why*? Why did they take my son? I serve them! I pray to them! I endure their nightmares and still they give me nothing!"

He stops me from lunging at the pieces. I fight him but Pilate holds me close, crossing my arms over my chest. "Claudia, there's no use in raging at gods. They can't hear you; they're only pieces of clay."

Through gritted teeth, I ask, "Why don't you believe in them?"

"Gods must prove their existence to me before I believe them. None have." Smoothing the hair out of my eyes, his face softens. "Gods don't exist. We create them for a higher power to believe in, to blame for our problems and thank in our prosperity. Gods require much and give nothing in return."

Hatred rises in me for the temple. "I want it torn down."

"You don't mean that."

"Yes, I do, I want it destroyed. Send me the stonemasons!"

Their expressions are as incredulous as that of our servants. Glancing at one another, one asks, "Won't the gods be angry?"

"I don't care if they're angry. *Tear it down*." I turn and enter the house.

Avram meets me in the hall, leaning on his staff. "Is this wise, Claudia?"

"Don't you approve?"

Behind us, the stonemasons reluctantly get to work. Avram says, "Your husband is the governor of Crete. It doesn't honor his subjects to remove their gods from his house."

"Let them keep their gods, for they are no longer mine."

Entering my room, I shut the door in his face. Pain causes me to double over and I feel my way to the bed. Libi soon enters with the physician, who touches my abdomen and

frowns. "I want you to stay in bed."

"Why? The child is dead."

He scowls at me. "You may do yourself harm. Promise me."

I nod and he packs up his things and leaves the room. Pilate's soft voice halts him. I see his shadow on the far wall, through the open door. "Is she all right?"

Wind stirs the curtains as the temple pillar falls, crashing into the garden.

"Physically she'll improve but there will be no further children."

I shut my eyes and my hand drifts to my empty womb.

Pilate answers, "I thought as much."

"Give her this if she goes into hysterics. I'll return tomorrow."

Footsteps fade away and Pilate enters. "You're flushed." Sadness is in his eyes, the same sadness that fills my empty soul.

I catch his hand. "I heard what he said."

Another rumble shakes the garden. Pilate searches my face. "I don't care whether or not we have children. I've only ever wanted *you*." He sits with me until I fall asleep. Even before I enter it, I know the dream is dark. Before me is the temple ruin, the broken heads of the gods scattered across the tiles. I kick them aside and picking up a nearby sword, hack the altar to pieces. I only stop when blood trickles down my fingers.

Something strikes me. I flip through the air and slam into the column. It crashes down with me, before another blow sends me careening into the wall. Blood fills my mouth and I choke on it, looking up through the haze as a dark shape drags me up by my hair.

No one turns on the gods.

It has no face, no mouth, only darkness.

My head rebounds off the stone floor with an audible crack. I choke on blood and hear Pilate scream, "Avram!"

The blood is real.

He holds me over the edge of the bed as I spit it up. Shadows dance around us, the flames in the oil lamps flickering as a specter moves through the air. It hisses and coils as Avram hurries to my side. I feel his hands on my face but see nothing.

"What is it?" Pilate asks in horror. "What's wrong with her eyes?"

My body convulses and he holds me down.

"Be gone!" shouts Avram. "Let her be, in the name of Jehovah!" He starts to recite Hebrew words.

I feel like my skin is on fire. Screams tear out of my throat as the devil fights to control me. I thrash and writhe under Pilate's weight. Talons rake my insides and it rips out of my chest, evaporating in a puff of black smoke. Silence fills the house and the pressure on my arms lessens. I open my eyes and the room comes into focus. The bed curtains are shredded. Furniture is overturned. Blood coats my fingers and moistens my throat.

Pilate pulls me into his embrace. His voice breaks. "I thought I'd lost you."

Footsteps bring a terrified-looking servant into the room. "They heard her screams all the way to the temple. The priest wants to know if he may enter."

"Tell him he's not to enter now, or ever again. There will be no more priests in this house." Pilate cups my face in his hands and searches my eyes, worried. The servant backs out of the room.

I drop into the pillows and rasp, "The gods are angry with me."

"That," Avram says, "was no god."

Pilate looks up at him. "Then what was it?"

"A demon, and if you don't want it to come back, you'll let me fortify against it. There must be no more seers, and no more gods."

Tension lurks in the air and at last, Pilate nods.

Avram blesses our house and anoints it with oil. He removes all remnants of the temple and casts the pieces of our gods into the sea. Pilate relaxes his guard when it becomes obvious my dreams are gone. In time, even the hurt of my lost child lessens.

One afternoon many months later, Demetrius brings us a letter from Rome. Pilate reads it and sits down in his chair. "Tiberius wants us to return."

"Is he displeased with you?" I lean over his shoulder to read it. The emperor is not displeased, but offers accommodations. I take the scroll. "He says you've done well here... so why is he sending for you?"

Pushing back his chair, Pilate says, "Judea."

"They say he isn't pleased with Governor Gratus,"

Demetrius says.

Eying him, Pilate asks, "How would you like reassignment?"

"I would like that, Prefect."

Pilate adds the scroll to the pile on his desk. "Good, you're coming with us."

This voyage is without seasickness but my heart sinks as we return home. Fidelus' home is no different from when we left but Hermina is three years older. Throwing her arms around me, she says, "Oh, how I've missed you!"

"No, you haven't," Pilate teases as we enter the house.

She winds her arm through his. "How much do you know?"

"It depends on the topic."

Hermina leans against him. "Tiberius is leaving for Capri."

"Does that mean Sejanus will control Rome?" I ask, exchanging a meaningful look with Pilate.

She drops onto a chaise and her nose wrinkles. "I suppose! There's more than six thousand Praetorian Guards now." Glancing into the hall, she leans toward us and lowers her voice. "Father hates him more than ever. He believes Sejanus is too powerful."

"That may be an opinion shared by many," Pilate answers.

His father soon appears and we rise to greet him. Fidelus is unchanged apart from more gray in his hair. Handing us an official scroll, he says, "Tiberius wants to see you tomorrow. The senate thinks he'll offer you the prefecture of Judea."

Moaning from her chaise, Hermina says, "You just got home!"

"That's what happens with governors, Hermina... we come and go." Pilate tugs on a lock of her hair and makes her smile.

Our drive through Rome the next morning fills me with delight. I had forgotten her winding streets and rising aqueducts. Our chariot passes under them as it carries us to Tiberius' palace. Hermina knows her way around and leads us inside, past columns and inner rooms, guests and marble faces. She goes straight to the emperor and kneels at his feet.

"There you are, my pet! And you bring your brother, too!" Tiberius motions us forward, past the artist sculpting a bust of his face. "Hideous, isn't it? It gives me pleasure to look on beauty again. You are lovely as ever, Claudia. My court is empty without you. But Hermina brings joy to us all."

"That is one of her many talents, Caesar."

He motions her aside and she joins Caligula at the banquet

table. Tiberius rises to his feet. "You won't mind if I borrow your husband, I hope?"

I shake my head and they walk onto the verandah, out of earshot. A familiar sense of dread passes over me and I sense Sejanus at my side. "I see you *have* put that quick tongue of yours to better use. Tiberius is very pleased with Pilate."

"How is your tongue, Sejanus? Is it still hinged in the middle?"

Sejanus laughs and hands me a cup of wine. "I haven't wagged it in your direction in some time. I may have even laid certain rumors to rest."

"What rumors are those?"

His eyes darken. "That you had violent nightmares in Crete."

The color drains from my face.

Circling me, he adds in a soft voice, "They say you're a dream-seer."

"Do you have spies in our household, Sejanus?"

He smirks at me. "I have spies *everywhere*."

Feeling cold, I move away from the door. He follows. "Do you dream of Tiberius?"

"No."

Sejanus searches my face. "Caligula?"

The boy brushes past us, his friends in tow. Hermina laughingly chases them into the hall. I shake my head. He frowns and pops a grape into his mouth. "I don't like that boy, or the rest of his family, for that matter."

"You may want to change that opinion, since he *is* the future emperor."

Leaning against the table, Sejanus says, "Life can be unpredictable."

"Not all of it."

He stares at me. "That sounds like you know something."

I put my cup on the table. "I do know something, about you. Oh, I haven't dreamed your future, but now and again I have premonitions."

"What do these premonitions tell you?"

Searching his face, I answer, "When you fall, you'll fall hard, and you *will* fall, Sejanus. My only concern is that my husband doesn't go down with you."

We glare at one another and he moves away from me as Tiberius returns. Pilate rejoins me and I put my arm through

his.

"My dear, I've made your husband my prefect in Judea." Tiberius sinks into his throne and motions for the artist to continue.

I move nearer to him. "You honor us, Caesar."

"Oh, come now, you'll hate me for sending him away like that."

Leaning against my husband, I say, "I'll go with him."

Tiberius stares at me and silence enters the room. "Judea is full of rebellious heathens. None of our Judean governors have taken their wives!"

"None of their wives are as determined as I am." I smile at them all.

Faces soften toward me and even Tiberius grins. "I can see that. Sit with me."

Servants quickly push a cushion at his feet and I settle on it. "So you summon us to Rome intending to leave for Capri? That is wicked of you, Caesar."

"I see what Sejanus means about your tongue," he laughs. "But in truth, I can't wait to leave Rome. I have never cared for politics, much less senators. I will miss the company of Hermina, though. She's an amusing child."

Pilate drains his cup. "You may not have seen much of her anyway. I am considering sending her to stay with her aunt outside Rome. Her cousins beg me for the sight of her."

My eyes shift to Caligula and Hermina at the far end of the room, their heads together. I sit with Tiberius until he wearies of company and retreats to his room. Rejoining Pilate, I say, "Sejanus isn't the only one who dislikes Caligula."

"Do *you* like him?"

Caligula plays with a lock of Hermina's hair, his dark eyes fixed on her face. I shudder and Pilate guides me toward the door. "You must stand with me on this. Hermina thrives on his attention and she won't like it."

Following us up the stairs at home, Hermina shows me an emerald bracelet on her arm. "Caligula gave it to me. His sister was so jealous!"

I look at Pilate as we enter the main room and he says softly, "They say she and Caligula played certain games a long time after they should have stopped."

My mouth drops open. "What kind of games?"

He puts his hand at the small of my back and says, "The

incestuous kind."

I say, "Hermina, you won't be in Rome next week."

She looks up from her bracelet. "What do you mean?"

"Our aunt wants you to visit her in Capri," Pilate answers.

Her nose wrinkles. "Oh, don't make me go. She's such a bore!"

Pilate crosses the room. "I've told her you'll come on the next boat."

"Then you'll have to write and tell her otherwise, because Caligula and I—"

Calmness enters his voice. "Caligula can curb his disappointment."

Her mouth twists into an unpleasant expression as Pilate looks through the scrolls on the desk. "You don't like him, do you?"

"I don't know him."

The wind stirs the lamp wicks. I lean against the nearest column.

"If you did, you'd find him a kind, thoughtful—"

He looks up. "Is it kind to beat his horses?"

Color fills her face. "No, but—"

"What about his treatment of his servants?"

Hotly, she retorts, "That's different, the boy—"

"So he isn't kind after all," says Pilate.

Bitter silence fills the room.

Her voice is small. "Father won't send me away."

"I've spoken to him and he agrees with me. You leave in the morning."

She glares at him and her hand tightens into a fist. Tears fill her eyes and she cries, "I hate you! I wish you'd never come home!" Knocking scrolls in all directions, she flounces into her room and slams the door.

Pilate shakes his head. "She can hate me all she likes. It won't change my mind."

Chapter Nine

Our first glimpse of Judea is the shoreline of Caesarea. The lights of a thousand windows glimmer against the setting sun. Our ship anchors in the bay and after surveying it with interest, Pilate enters our cabin. I approach Avram, standing at the bow. His hand grips his staff tightly as he stares at the city.

"Is it as you expected?"

His eyes shine in the torchlight. "Judea is the home of my ancestors, the Promised Land! I will see Jerusalem before I die, if God is merciful."

"You can't die yet, Avram!" I laugh, wrapping my arm around his. "I need you. I know nothing of Judean traditions. You must teach me." The ship gently rocks in the waves and I stare at the great city, so different from Rome. I feel a shiver of dread and anticipation.

"I'll do what I can," promises Avram.

Libi steps out of their cabin. "Father, come in and eat."

"What use is food, with such wonders before me?" Avram smiles and goes to her, leaving me alone on deck apart from the few sailors in the rigging. I linger awhile, breathing in the warm sea air, and go below. Supper awaits me in our cabin. I remove my cloak, the oil lamps swinging overhead warming my skin.

"What do the women of Judea wear?"

Pilate looks up from his scroll. "If you wear what they do, you'll die of heat."

"I'll manage. I don't want to insult them." I pop a slice of fruit into my mouth and join him on the bed. "What are you reading?"

Pilate hands me the scroll. "They're reports of the last governor's arrival. I want to announce mine in a way that distinguishes between us. They need to know that I'm *not* Gratus."

"How do you intend to do that?"

Tapping his fingers on the bed, he says, "I'll think of something."

"Did Gratus really fail so miserably in his task?"

He nods. "Judea resists our presence rather than accepts it. It can have its traditions, its Passover, its temple, but I *will* be its governor." Noticing my worried expression, he smiles and

touches my hand. "But never mind, it's our last night on board ship. Let's make it a pleasant one."

I fall asleep in his arms and wake to my first glimpse of the magnificent city in daylight. Ships stretch along the coast, settling under the high walls. Libi helps me dress in a modest tunic and I tuck my hair under a silk covering. "Father sent some of your servants to the palace last night," she says. "The house should be in readiness. You'll go ashore first, and we'll follow with your things."

"Make sure Avram doesn't over-exert himself. I worry about him."

She smiles. "He's excited. His father used to tell him stories of Caesarea and the great city of Jerusalem."

"Quintus is our commander of the garrison in Jerusalem." I watch her as she laces up my sandal, her face flushing. "You'll see him soon."

"Claudia...." Her eyes dart to mine.

I laugh. "It's all right to look forward to seeing him again."

"No, it isn't! I'm a Jewess and he's..."

"A Roman, and centurion, but what does it matter?"

The door opens and Pilate sticks his head inside. "It's time."

I join him on deck and shade my eyes from the sun. A market thrives on the docks and the streets fill with eager faces, many of them lining the streets. Pilate turns to Demetrius and asks, "Have you heard anything?"

"My spies reported to me at dawn. There is no hint of trouble with the locals, Prefect. They want to find out what kind of a governor you are, before deciding whether or not to challenge you."

Ladders lower over the side of the ship into the smaller craft below. Pilate enters first. Demetrius and two other guards accompany us to shore. Shining black horses carry us into the city. The governor's house is not far from the coast and I remove my head covering as we enter.

"We passed a ruin on our way in," I say, turning to Demetrius. "What is it?"

He escorts us past great columns, the sea shining in the distance. "Tiberius' temple; Governor Gratus left it unfinished. He ran out of funds."

Pilate disappears into his office and I survey the line of faces lining the hall. "Which one of you is in charge?"

"I am, Mistress." He steps forward.

"Take me to the kitchens. I want to see them."

Our home is spacious and the kitchens meet with my approval. Avram arrives and I gather the staff in the main hall. "I'm pleased with what I see, but in a Roman household there is always room for improvement. This is Avram. He knows how I run my house. Defer to him in all things. Is this understood?"

"Yes, Mistress," they answer.

I clap my hands and they hurry to unload furniture from our carts. Our room is soon in order and Pilate joins me there at nightfall. I offer him a cup of wine. "Do you find all as it should be?"

Moving out onto the verandah, he stares across the sea. "Gratus did little to improve conditions here during his governorship. It will take weeks to sort out the mess but it isn't as bad as I expected."

"That's fortunate." I lean against the column and gaze out over the city.

He sips his wine and says, "We'll have a visit from King Herod soon."

"I'm surprised Tiberius lets him keep such a title. Isn't the emperor our god?"

Pilate smiles as I join him, wrapping his arms around me. "Herod is a Galilean. Tiberius grants him the title to maintain peace so the Jews feel like they are not entirely under Roman occupation. But from what my men tell me, he's not well liked, too Roman in his beliefs and practices."

"Have you met him before?"

Behind us, servants finish setting out our meal and slip away. Pilate leads me indoors. "I did, in Rome, and I'm not eager to renew our acquaintance."

"What's he like?"

His eyes twinkle at me. "He's fat and insulting."

"Not too much like a Roman then!" I grin and pop a grape in my mouth.

Swirling his wine, Pilate says, "You still have a wicked tongue. Tomorrow, I want you to put it to good use. The high priests of the Roman temple demand an audience and I don't want to see them."

"I'm just as much of a heathen as you are now, remember?"

He pulls meat apart with his fingers. "But you can fake it."

"Very well, I'll do it for your sake."

Entering the temple means nothing to me where once it would have comforted me. I stare at the images of the gods and shake my head. The priests bless and honor me with a sacrifice, read the entrails of a goat, and predict good omens for our time in Judea. I am a curiosity to them, a Roman woman in Judea. Others share their interest. Faces watch from doorways and children approach me in the marketplace, where I sort through fish and figs to give me flowers and fruit.

Demetrius says, "They like you."

"Is that unusual?"

From his expression, I know it is. I return my gaze to the merchant's table and sort through fabric, searching for a compromise between hot, heavy homespun and light, sheer togas. Libi makes my purchases and carries them home. She follows me inside and the tribune standing there turns to us with a smile.

"Quintus, you're here at last!" I embrace him. "You haven't changed!"

He laughs and cups my chin in his hand. "You have!"

Libi stands behind us, her arms full of packages. His eyes soften at the sight of her. "Libi, how does it feel to be in Judea? Your father must be pleased."

"He's delighted and will be even more so to see you again. Does he know you're here?" She flushes slightly.

My brother shakes his head. "I've just arrived."

"I'll tell him." Glancing between us, she retreats. Her shadow passes over a figure standing beside the column. His appearance startles me and Quintus places a hand on my arm.

"This is Germanius, my servant. He's safe enough."

Gentle eyes stare out from a youthful but scarred face. He stays behind as Quintus follows me into the main room. I pour a cup of wine and consider the hulking figure in the hall. "He looks like a Gladiator."

"He's a Syrian and used to fight in the games in Rome but they had a hard time handling him. He cannot speak. I bought him at a slave market. Two years ago, he saved my life in a riot. I offered him freedom but he refuses to leave."

My heart softens toward the giant. "You changed his life."

"I guess I did."

Footsteps echo on marble tiles and Avram enters the room. "Quintus, it's good to see you, my friend!"

Quintus clasps his arm in friendship. "And you as well! I

understand you were at my father's side to the last. Thank you for that."

"It was my honor to serve him and now to serve your sister's household." He indicates the former gladiator. "May I show your servant comfort?"

Nodding, Quintus says, "Yes. Germanius, go with Avram to the kitchen."

They pass down the hall, one an old man with a limp and the other a gentle giant. I sprawl out across a chaise and smile at my brother. "Is it permissible for a tribune to stay at the home of his procurator, or must you go to a stinking barracks somewhere?"

"I'm afraid the latter." Quintus drinks his wine and his expression softens as he looks at me. "You've done well, Claudia. To go from the youngest daughter of a disgraced wine merchant to a governor's wife is no small feat."

Wind stirs the draperies and carries the scent of the sea. "Better a wife than a seer," I answer him.

Pilate descends the steps. "I thought I heard your voice."

"Governor," answers Quintus, rising to greet him.

Laying a hand on his shoulder, Pilate says, "Tell me of Judea."

"Since Gratus' departure, it's quiet. Most are curious about you, but some remember you from when you commanded the garrison in Jerusalem."

Our servants enter with supper and set it out on the low table. Libi pours the wine. Pilate and Quintus move closer to the verandah to speak in peace. I sit and watch them, fingering my cup.

"Then they know what to expect from me."

Quintus half smiles and says, "You should expect some resistance from the new high priest in Jerusalem, Caiaphas. He is more of a politician than his predecessor but also unpredictable. He'll challenge you to see how much control you intend to influence over the temple."

"How much control did Gratus have?"

Looking out over the sea, Quintus shrugs. "He didn't exert much, but things change in Judea. There are now two religious fractions... the Pharisees are the more rigid and the Sadducees tend toward politicizing."

"I see. Maybe we should test them first." Pilate approaches the rail and looks across the courtyard, fluttering with the

Roman insignias. "Jerusalem seems to be the root of all rebellions in this province. Let us remind them it is Roman. Take an extra legion with you when you return with the garrison, and carry the standards of Tiberius into the city."

A silver platter clatters to the floor and Libi picks it up, her face red.

"Neither group will like it."

Pilate turns inside. "But it *will* make an impression on them."

The last of the food is set out and Avram sends most of the servants from the room. I motion for him and he reaches my side. "Why won't they like it?"

His dark eyes are unreadable. "Graven images aren't permitted in Jerusalem. We have one god, and Tiberius is not He."

Chills run down my spine.

"Is that all, Mistress?"

Pilate sits down beside me and I nod. Avram moves slowly out the door. The sound his staff makes as it hits the marble floor is the loneliest in the world.

Chapter Ten

My first glimpse of the caravan is a line of rising dust on the horizon. I lean on the windowsill and watch it approach. "Libi, when is Herod supposed to arrive?"

"His messenger said not until tomorrow." She shakes the pillows and smoothes the wrinkles out of the bed. Joining me, she shades her eyes and watches the caravan move nearer. "Is that him?"

Beneath us, a servant sprints across the courtyard shouting, "King Herod is coming!"

I exchange a knowing glance with her. She makes a face. "I'll tell Father."

My thin tunic ripples as I enter the hall and pass through the small group of men waiting outside Pilate's office. They move out of my way, their arms heavy with scrolls. I enter without knocking and he looks up from his desk.

"What are the architects doing here?"

He indicates the plans spread out before him. "We're starting construction on Tiberius' temple again. What do you think about adding an arch here?"

"Well, it would make more of an impression." I lean against the desk and cross my arms. "Did you know Herod is almost to Caesarea?"

Pilate smirks. "Yes. He always arrives a day early."

Knocking on the door, Demetrius enters. "You sent for me, Prefect?"

"Herod is about an hour from the city. Ride out and escort him." The tribune retreats and Pilate glances at me. "Can you bring the preparations forward?"

"Avram has prepared for every possibility, but it *is* an inconvenience."

Marking out the arch, Pilate says, "That *is* the general idea. He's hoping to catch us off guard, to put us at a disadvantage."

"Well, we'll do our best not to accommodate him then." I kiss him on the cheek and return to the hall, letting in his architects. Bare feet carry me downstairs and I oversee the last minute readying of the guest rooms. "Put fresh fruit in Herod's chamber, he likes it. His horses can have the stall next to Pilate's stallion. You can house his servants here and in the rooms above the stables. If there's more than a dozen, we'll

make other arrangements."

"Should we go to the market and buy more figs? What about fish?"

I nod and the boy dashes off. Libi follows me upstairs. "Which toga?"

"Blue. Herod likes sultry Roman women... let's give him one."

Libi shakes out Hermina's gift and pulls it over my head. She twists my hair into a knot, leaving loose curls around my face. I put on a bracelet and perfume. In the distance, we hear the sound of trumpets as Herod enters the city. I strap on my sandals, take a deep breath, and go to wait with my husband in the entrance hall.

The garrison brings the caravan into our courtyard. We watch from the steps as Herod dismounts from his horse, a servant holding a shade over his head as he ascends the stairs. Intent, dark eyes shine out of a pudgy face tinged with redness. Slaves, servants, and noblemen and their wives accompany him. He grins as he reaches the top step. "Forgive my early arrival, Prefect. The journey took less time than I expected."

"Then you've never been to Caesarea before?" I ask with a smile.

Amused eyes dart up at me before his servant returns his gaze to the ground. Herod's mouth drops open and he stares at me. "Err..."

"Herod, allow me to introduce you to my wife, Claudia."

Fat fingers adorned with rings clasp across the wide girth. "Ah, yes, I heard your wife traveled with you from Rome. Then it is to you I must apologize. I hope our early arrival isn't an inconvenience."

"Not at all, King Herod, we've been expecting you."

The smirk leaves his face as I invite him indoors. He falls into step with me. "I'm sorry my wife didn't come with me. She wanted to meet you."

"I'm sure we'll have many opportunities to meet one another. My servants have prepared a feast for you in the main hall. You must excuse me, I will see to your slaves." I lead him to the door and he passes through it, accompanied by his friends. Pilate winks at me and follows. Avram approaches and I ask softly, "Is everything in order?"

He nods. "The living quarters are arranged and the rooms prepared."

"Good. Thank you. I don't know what I'd do without you." Smiling at him, I touch his arm and return to my guests.

Herod hands me a cup of wine, his dark eyes lingering curiously on me. "You are a topic of much fascination here in Judea."

"Is it so unusual for a governor's wife to accompany him?" I discreetly search for my husband and find him across the room, speaking with Demetrius. Pilate glances in my direction, his usual good humor subdued.

Circling me, Herod says, "Roman wives usually prefer Roman cities."

"Isn't Caesarea a Roman city?" I turn to him, searching his face.

He leans against the table behind us. "Roman in occupation but not at heart; this is a volatile region."

"Pilate intends to change that."

Servants slip in and out, none of them making eye contact. Herod takes a sip from his cup. "He won't do that by sending Roman ensigns into Jerusalem. His being a Roman governor is enough to turn many against him. The rest were undecided until last night, when his garrison reached Jerusalem."

Concerned, I look again at my husband. "What is your interest?"

"I want Judea to stabilize. Insulting them won't accomplish that."

Putting down my wine, I say, "Them? Not you?"

"The Jews don't like me any better than your husband, and they don't respond well to signs of force. This is not Crete. Pilate should remember that." His finger brushes my arm and he returns to the others.

I make my way to my husband. "Herod knows."

Glancing at him, Pilate says, "I'm not surprised."

"What happens now?"

Demetrius retreats and Pilate guides me onto the verandah. "We wait."

"Has anything happened in Jerusalem?"

Guests mingle behind us. Pilate shakes his head. "They'll come here."

"Is that what you want from them?" I ask.

He smiles at me. "I want to see what happens."

Laughter spills out behind us as Herod wipes tears of mirth from his eyes. Pilate's face darkens as he watches the man.

"It'll take at least three days to walk here from Jerusalem. Let's see to it that Herod is gone by then."

"Pilate," says Herod, joining us. "You're building Tiberius' temple?" The night air puts a flush in his cheeks.

"Yes."

"You must show it to me!" Herod slaps him on the back. "I want to see it!"

"If you insist..."

"I do, and you must come with us, Claudia."

Mid-morning the following day finds me in a chariot on a tour of Caesarea. Our first stop is the temple. Stonemasons are hard at work in the heat, cutting stone and constructing the elaborate foundation. I linger in the shade and watch as Pilate's architects show Herod the completed designs. He looks unimpressed. Annoyance flashes across Pilate's face and I take his hand. "He's doing it to get a rise out of you," I whisper.

We drive to the amphitheater. Herod walks the stone steps under the Roman arches and his voice carries to us. "I've never cared for Caesarea's design; it's so ... uncultured. The best architects in Rome designed my palace. You should employ some of them to work on your temple. I'll have my scribe send you their names."

Pilate puts his tongue firmly in his cheek and does not answer. On our way home, as we walk through the gardens, Herod shields his eyes and stares out over the shoreline. "You'll want to fortify the south port as the sea presses inland, or this place will be in ruins."

"Yes, I'm aware of that."

Two days with Herod is more than enough. He appears in unexpected places, insists on sitting next to me at meals, flatters, charms, and drinks. "If he looks at your breast one more time," growls Pilate at supper, "I'll kill him."

"I'll get rid of him," I answer under my breath. When the music ends, I take Herod by the arm and lead him into the hall. "It gave us pleasure having you with us, Herod Antipas," I say.

He beams. "Well, I—"

"We'll be so sorry to see you go in the morning."

The red face stares at me. Patting his pudgy fingers, I stop outside his room. "But we mustn't be selfish and Galilee can't rule itself! You will want to leave early before it gets too hot. I'll make sure you have provisions for the trip."

Hours after Herod leaves, an angry Jewish mob gathers at our gates. Unnerved at their silence, I watch them sit in the street.

"Have they given you their demands?" Pilate asks.

Demetrius hands over a scroll. Pilate reads it and tosses it aside. "They want the emblems removed from your palace in Jerusalem. Should we admit their leaders for an audience with you, Prefect?"

"No."

The next morning their numbers have increased. Children sleep in doorways, curled up against one another. Men stand as long as they are able; others crowd into the wall's long shadow for relief, leaning against the worn stone or sitting in the street. Heavily veiled women bring food in baskets.

"Don't you find their silence unusual?" I ask.

Pilate rises from his desk as Demetrius enters with another scroll. He looks at it and tosses it into the nearest brazier. Flames burst around the parchment, curling it up and melting the wax on the floor. "Tell them no," he says.

Once the door closes, I turn to him. "You must speak with them."

"Unlike my predecessor, I won't give in to intimidation."

Demetrius' voice floats up to us and the crowd stirs. Bodies press against the gates and someone shouts; it starts a cry that echoes in the street.

"Do you *want them* to riot?"

He glances past me out the window. "If they must, I'll let them."

I stare in disbelief. "That *is* what you want, isn't it, an excuse to punish them!" Putting my hands on the desk, I lean toward him. "Force and coercion don't work on these people! You know that!"

"Force is something they must learn if they want to survive."

"It doesn't have to be this way! Show them you're capable of compromise!"

"Rome doesn't compromise and neither do I."

Disappointment floods through me. Speechless, I leave in silence, my sandals clicking on the floor. The shouting continues all night. I lie awake until dawn staring at the ceiling, but the sudden quiet causes me to rise. I push aside the drapery. Guards speak softly to the men at the gates and unlock them. The crowd enters. I pull on a cloak and enter the

hall.

Encountering Avram, I grip his arm. "What's happening?"

"Your husband has agreed to speak with them," he says.

Relieved, I hurry through the house to an upper window. Libi is already there. I take her hand. Shadows stretch before the centurions. Pilate remains at the top of the stairs. "I grow weary of this disturbance."

A fierce-looking man with dark, wild eyes steps forward. "It will continue until you hear our demands."

"I'm aware of your demands. My answer is no." The mob stirs and angry murmurs fill the air. Demetrius glances at Pilate, his hand on his sword. My husband shakes his head.

"You insult us with eagle insignias in Jerusalem! You send in your garrison under the cover of darkness to avoid our protests! Is this how you intend to govern Judea?"

My eyes roam the crowd, tension in my limbs.

"Yes, it is. Who are you to challenge me?"

The man snarls, "I'm Jesus Barabbas!"

"Well, Jesus Barabbas, here's what I've decided. This mob will disperse or I'll have every second man in the crowd killed."

Libi covers her mouth. "He wouldn't... would he?"

"He will," I answer dully.

Avram places a hand on my shoulder, his face grim. I lean weakly against him as the crowd shifts. His friends pull Barabbas back. They speak in low tones and resentfully, Barabbas turns to my husband. "If you won't remove your symbols of idolatry from our holy city, you may have all our lives!" He tears his robe open and falls to his knees. Others drop around him until the courtyard is full of kneeling figures. I lean out the window, shocked. Torches flicker and dawn creeps through the arches. Demetrius climbs the stairs and confers with Pilate. I hold my breath and grip the wall before me.

Pilate is quiet for a long moment and then nods. He turns inside the house as the soldiers remove their hands from their swords and retreat from the courtyard. The crowd cheers and leaps to their feet. Barabbas joins them in celebration and his gaze meets mine. The look in his eyes frightens me. He nudges his friend and points at me.

"Claudia," whispers Libi, gripping my arm.

Her father tenses and I follow his gaze. My heart jumps into my throat. Jacob stands behind Barabbas, half hidden under a

head covering. He turns into the crowd. I reach the stairs first, flying down them and careening into my husband. Pilate is surprised and displeased to see me. Libi stops behind me and the tap-tap of her father's staff meets my ears. Pilate grips me by the arm and moves me aside, leaving them to hurry into the courtyard.

"They won't find him," Pilate says. He opens the door to my room and pushes me in ahead of him.

"You saw Jacob too?"

"Once you've seen a face coming at you with a knife, you don't forget it." Pilate moves aside the drapery, satisfied as the crowd disperses.

I rub my arms to chase off a chill. "Did you mean what you told them?"

"Whatever I say, I mean." He looks at me and his face softens. "Claudia, you're used to your husband, and not a Roman soldier. But here, you'll see both." His gaze returns to the courtyard and the sight of Avram and Libi returning disheartened.

My heart aches for them. "Did you know he'd be here?"

"I suspected. What better place for an outcast of Rome than to hide among those who share Jacob's religion and distaste for the Empire."

"If he's found, what'll happen to him?"

Leaning against the wall, Pilate says, "I don't care. He's the least of my problems."

Chapter Eleven

The Jewish Passover is nearly upon us, and a garrison fills the courtyard the morning we leave for Jerusalem. Avram ignores them as he loads a donkey with provisions for our journey. His hands shake with excitement as he knots the straps. I turn as Pilate descends the steps.

"Do you expect trouble in Jerusalem?"

He glances at the soldiers and his eyes harden. "I always anticipate trouble in Jerusalem."

I climb into my litter and he mounts his horse. Men lift me up into the air, their bare arms already glistening in the heat. Libi hurries from the house, a basket of figs in her hands, her veil streaming behind her.

We move out of Capernaum, half the garrison in front, the rest behind. Others join us in the streets, walking or on donkeys, entire families knowing it is safer to travel with us than alone. Avram's eagerness keeps him at a steady pace.

"What will you do in the city of your ancestors?"

He glances at me and his warm brown eyes soften. "I have wanted all my life to see Jerusalem. Tomorrow, I'll offer a sacrifice in the temple and thank God for letting me behold its glories before my death."

The road is long, the day hot. Travelers camp in the hills, keeping together as protection against thieves. Some are wealthy and ride in chariots; others walk. All rest their limbs at noon and eat. We reach Jerusalem at dusk, along with a steady stream of pilgrims. The crowded road clears as people move out of our way. Faces peer curiously at me and one strikes me with fear.

"Libi," I say, and she hastens her pace. "I saw Barabbas!"

She glances around us and at her father, who stares in awe at the arch as we pass beneath it. "He'll have come for the Passover," she says.

Night descends and torches gleam in the darkness as we reach the Palace of Justice, next to the Jewish temple. I follow Pilate inside, where Quintus awaits us. He hands over a scroll. "Here is a full report of recent events in Jerusalem, Prefect. And Herod will dine with you later this week."

"Is his harlot with him?"

Quintus smirks and follows us into the next room. Oil lamps

tremble in the wind, and a feast awaits us. "Herodias *is* in Jerusalem, but it's a quiet Passover week. I anticipate no trouble. The high priest, Caiaphas, arrived moments ago. He requests an audience. The priests won't enter past the outer chamber; it makes them unclean before the Sabbath." He gestures into the garden, where a small huddle of priests stands near the far wall. Turning over the scroll, Pilate enters the garden.

I move around the column for a better view of the richly ornamented priests. "Which one is Caiaphas?"

"He's the tallest one, there."

Soft footsteps bring Libi into the room. Her eyes dart toward Quintus and away again with a blush as she sets the pitcher of wine on the table and hurries off. I pour us each a cup and we wait for Pilate's return. He is not long, and rejoins us as darkness spreads across the city.

"How is it in Jerusalem since the incident?" he asks.

Quintus settles into the pillows. "Quiet. You made your point, but so did they. I feared more from them but my spies tell me nothing unusual. There is trouble brewing among the Galileans, but that is to be expected. You met their leader in Caesarea, the man who spoke to you from the crowd, an insurgent called Barabbas."

The taste of grapes in my mouth sours.

"But there are no whispers of demonstrations?"

Quintus shakes his head.

"That worries me," says Pilate, tapping on his goblet. "What else have you heard?"

Tearing his bread in half, Quintus dips it in wine. "Many speak of Judea's new prophets. One, by the name of John, never leaves the desert but has a following. He often disputes Herod's marriage to Herodias as incestuous. The other I don't know much of, but he's from Galilee."

Wind rustles the curtains, bringing the temple scent into the house. "Let's hope he's less revolutionary than Barabbas."

After supper, I retire to our room, smaller than in Caesarea but with a balcony overlooking the courtyard. The city is breathtaking at night, with its many lamps shining through stone windows. Feeling a chill, I turn within. The room is dark when Pilate joins me. I fall asleep with his head touching mine.

Shivers wake me before dawn. Dread fills me as I look to my husband, shadows shifting around us. Curtains move in the

breeze. The hair on my arms stands on end. Someone is in the room with us. My hand creeps toward Pilate and he opens his eyes. There is no trace of sleepiness in them. Barely moving, he presses a finger to his lips and slides his hand under the pillow. I tense and stare past him into the gloom as a figure emerges from the dark. Lifting a knife in one hand, he brushes aside the sheer drapery. Before he can strike, Pilate shoves a dagger into his chest. His eyes widen, his mouth gapes in shock, and blood spills from his mouth as he topples backward.

"Guards!"

The door bursts open and centurions stream in. Panic sends them in all directions at the sight. Libi pulls me from the bed, wrapping a tunic around me. Turning the man over with his foot, Quintus says, "I know this man, a Galilean."

Pilate's face frightens me. Running footsteps return Demetrius to us. "Two of our guards are dead in the courtyard."

"So there are no objections to my presence in Jerusalem?" Pilate glares at them. "Both of you come with me... and get *him* out of here."

"Come," whispers Libi, pulling me away.

They carry the body out and servants scrub the floor. Libi helps me out of my blood-spattered shift. Pilate enters his office and confers with Quintus, who reappears first. The smell of sacrifices rises from the temple, thickening the air. He descends into the yard, where his men await. "Twelve of you, come with me," he says.

Pilate appears behind me.

"Where are they going?"

"They go to remind our enemies of their place." He glances at the temple and sudden fear grips me as he continues on his way with Demetrius. My heart pounds in my ears.

"Avram," I whisper.

I reach the street as the screams start. People flee the temple, nearly knocking me over, dragging lambs behind them. I fight my way to the gates. Priests stream out the side entrances as Quintus' men send men thudding to the ground. Blood spatters the walls in red streams.

"Claudia!" A strong pair of hands grips my arm and drags me away from the sight. The crowd knocks Avram's staff out of his hand and tramples it underfoot. He crashes into the wall. I support him as the crowd carries us with it. They jostle and

shove me. I see Barabbas coming toward us. Gasping, I drag Avram away. He cries out and grasps his chest, falling to his knees. His face contorts. I grip his hand as the crowd surges past. I look up; Barabbas is still coming, hatred in his eyes.

"You must get up," I plead.

Horrible silence fills my ears as the screams die away. Avram stares at me, his eyes wide and his mouth gapes. The hand in mine stiffens as with one last convulsion, he dies. Barabbas reaches the edge of the circle of people around us. His hand closes around the knife tucked in his waistband and starts to pull it out.

A man in the crowd touches his shoulder. Barabbas turns on him in anger but seeing the man's face, backs away and flees into the mob. Compassion shines on me out of dark eyes as the man offers me his hand.

"Come," he says.

I let him help me. His palm is calloused and worn. He looks on me far more kindly than the rest. "Pilate's wife," says someone. "He commits murder in the temple, and mixes the blood of men with their sacrifices!"

Anger rises among them but he turns to them. "We must love those who persecute us and forgive those who trespass against us. She has no part in this."

Faces stare at me with hatred and confusion. A priest shoves through the crowd and stops as he sees me. Shock courses through my veins. Jacob looks from me to his father. His mouth opens but no sound emerges.

Heavy footsteps bring the guards. Quintus takes one look at us, and says, "That's enough! Bring him!"

The hem of my tunic drags in the dust as we retreat. I find no sign of the man who helped me, but my eyes fall on Jacob, staring resentfully after us. I feel empty and cold. "Who is he?" I ask Quintus.

"He's the prophet from Galilee, Jesus of Nazareth."

My pace slows as we return to the palace, not wanting to look inside the temple courtyard and see the blood and bodies, to know Pilate is responsible. Women wail in the distance. I pass through our gate, Quintus on my heels. He looks to the guards on either side and says, "I ought to flog you for letting her out into the street!"

Shame burns in their faces as they look away from me. They put Avram on the steps. Libi emerges and her worried

expression changes into one of horror. She cries out and goes to him, cradling him in her arms. Quintus avoids her gaze.

"This is your fault," I tell him.

His eyes harden and he moves away. I enter the house, my breath rapid but without tears. I pace until Pilate returns. He crosses the room and we stare at one another. The tears in my eyes cloud my vision. My hand strikes without thought, slapping him hard. He barely reacts and rage fills me. I move to strike him again and he catches my wrist. I tear it away from him. My voice trembles.

"Avram dreamed his entire life of visiting Jerusalem, of worshipping in the temple. You took that away from him. He died knowing the temple is defiled, that you killed innocent men to save your pride!"

"There's no such thing as an innocent man, Claudia, not in Rome and certainly not in Judea."

Shaking my head, I turn away from him.

Pilate rests his hand on a chair. "I'm sorry for his death. I know you loved him as a father. The only thing these people understand is force. You can't show weakness."

"It isn't weakness to show mercy to your enemies!"

Grief swells up within me and I feel sick. Behind us, the door opens and Demetrius sticks his head in. "Caiaphas wants to speak with you, Prefect."

Neither of them prevents me from following Pilate. I feel numb as I pass through the hall into the garden. The priests turn on us as we approach.

"How *dare you* impose martial law in the temple!" Caiaphas's voice breaks with his rage, his hand tight on his staff. Thin fingers lift it and slam it into the dirt. "You insult us! You insult God! *What have you done?*"

Wind stirs my hair, the air without smoke. The temple is silent. As tall as the high priest, Pilate steps toward them, unnerving Caiaphas. "You're a man of ambition, Caiaphas. Is it in your best interest to question me?"

"In matters of the temple, yes, it is!"

Pilate circles him. "The Galileans support the insurgent Barabbas."

The priests exchange glances.

"I might question your defense of them, if others hadn't convinced me of your dedication to Rome."

Their anger seems to fade and Caiaphas forces a smile. "My

allegiance to Rome is well-documented, Prefect. You need only look at the reports of your predecessor—"

"I read them all in depth. I won't question your allegiance, but the temple seeking to *protect* the enemies of Rome must stop." Fear flickers across Caiaphas' face. Pilate considers him and turns away. "Tiberius isn't kind to his enemies. I may have to elect a new high priest."

"There's no need for that, Prefect!" Caiaphas hastens to his side. "How can we prove our loyalty?"

"On our way here we passed the half-completed aqueducts. Gratus let them languish. I want to finish them."

"You wish us to support you publicly, Prefect?"

"It'll take many years to collect enough taxes to rebuild them, unless we make use of the temple funds..."

My mouth drops open and it takes considerable self-control to shut it again. Caiaphas' eyes nearly pop out of his head. "You want access to the temple treasury?"

"It *is* for the benefit of Jerusalem, isn't it?"

"Yes, but—"

"Good! We understand one another." Pilate enters the house, leaving them gaping after him in disbelief.

I approach Caiaphas. "You have a servant from Rome I want to speak with, a priest named Jacob. Send him to me."

Muscles twitch in his face but he nods. I wait a half hour before Jacob's shadow falls across the garden. He carries his father's staff. "I found it outside the temple," he says.

"You should keep it," I answer. My heart lurches and pain sinks in. It worsens as I find hatred in his eyes.

"I heard rumors of your marriage. You saw what he did this morning, how he defiled the temple. They come to *worship*, not be *slaughtered*." His voice tightens and sparks shoot from his eyes. He twists his fingers around his father's staff until it creaks.

I feel my anguish creeping up on me, threatening to rage out of control. "Your father would want you to bury him."

"He served your husband; he's loyal to a murderer."

Emotion chokes me. "Do it for your sister."

He is surprised. "She's here with you?"

"Yes. Go to her. Comfort her."

For a moment, the old Jacob stands before me, the boy that loved his family above all. He is soon gone again, and his new expression sends a chill through me. "The past means nothing

to me. I have no family. I serve God and the temple. Pilate defiled our holy place. I'll have nothing to do with anyone in his household."

His eyes harden. "Bury your own dead."

Chapter Twelve

Libi's expression reflects mine as she does my hair. Our silence is full of words. Her hand trembles as she finishes. "At least you'll get to meet the infamous Herodias," she says.

I smile at her, my heart full of sadness. "It's not often a man marries his niece, much less his brother's wife. You'd think we were in Rome!"

Pilate awaits me in the courtyard. Our trip through Jerusalem is subdued. Herod's palace is not as central as ours is but still formidable. Three stone towers rise above us as we enter its main arches. Herod greets us, his gaze lingering on me before it flickers to Pilate. He waves a pudgy hand toward the city. "No more riots, I see."

Jerusalem is quieter than usual tonight. It took hours to clean the blood out of the temple. Torches flicker and snap overhead as Pilate answers calmly, "There won't be any more riots for some time."

Herod smirks uncomfortably. "You've certainly made an impression. Come inside, and meet my wife, Herodias."

She approaches from the shadows, a tall, dark figure covered in gold bangles and perfume. Her tunic is more revealing than mine is and her eyes are black and sensual. I can see why Herod likes her. "So this is Lucius Pilate!" Her eyes roam him lustfully. "Claudia, we meet at last."

Music drifts from the banquet hall. She offers me an unwelcoming smile and invites me to accompany her. Leaving our husbands, we move among her guests. A servant hands me a goblet and I taste the wine.

"You must find this place intolerable after Rome. The gods know I do." Her lip curls with disgust as she stares through the window at the city lights. "At least *your* husband knows how to manage the locals. The lunatic in the desert calls me a harlot. Have you heard?"

I nod.

"What would your husband do, if that madman called *you* a harlot? He would arrest him and make an example of him! Pilate is no fool but Herod *likes* this so-called prophet."

"Does he have many followers?"

A servant darts past and she grabs him by the arm. Thrusting her goblet into his chest, she says, "More wine, and

don't make me sorry I asked for it." He scurries away, terrified. "He gains more each day. It shows poor taste to go out to the desert to listen to a demented lunatic in a loincloth, but this *is* Judea after all."

The servant returns with the chalice. His palm shakes as she takes it from him and dismisses him with a wave.

"If he's popular with the people, it may be too dangerous to arrest him."

Her glare chills the blood in my veins. "Who rules Judea? If you let one fool say whatever he wants, you will have an insurrection on your hands. Herod should deal with him by force, as your husband would." She leans in to me and lowers her voice. "He was *upset* to hear of the massacre in the temple, as if he cares for these people! They hate him and always will. He mocks them every chance he gets, but still he feels obligated to defend them against Pilate. Yet, he won't arrest one man in the wilderness."

I ask, "Why did you marry him?"

"Better to be the harlot queen of Judea than a wife in Rome." Wrapping her arm through mine, she guides me to the banquet table. Several people start to approach but stop as she ignores them. "I know why I'm here but not why *you* are. Most prefects leave their wives home when they travel to dangerous outposts. Pilate must be a good lover to lure you from Rome."

I nearly choke on a piece of fruit.

She laughs and the enticing sound causes all the men in the room to look at us. "Herod hates Pilate but there's no reason we can't be friends, is there?"

Hiding my intense dislike for her, I smile.

Half-dressed dancers entertain us during supper. Wine flows freely and music fills the palace. Herod sits me next to him but my attention is rooted on Herodias and my husband. She touches him so often, a fingertip on his arm, a sultry smirk that by the end of the meal I want to rip her hands off.

"How do you find Jerusalem, Claudia?"

Reluctantly, I look at Herod. His beady eyes are full of excitement, his face flushed from too much to drink.

"Her ancient beauty stirs my soul."

He motions for a servant to refill his goblet. "Is she as great as Rome?"

"Each city is uniquely great in its own way."

My skin crawls as he leans nearer. Glancing at Pilate, he

lowers his voice. "Jerusalem is as dangerous as Rome. There, we have politicians. Here, we have rebels. But your husband has a way of..."

"Repressing them?"

He snorts. "*Enraging* them." Rolling away from me, he drinks his wine.

"My king," says Herodias and he stares at her blearily, "Pilate will rebuild the aqueducts."

Herod scowls. "Is that so?"

"It's wonderful! Jerusalem needs water!" Herodias's eyes widen with delight. "You should help him! Let him use our architects!"

Pilate and Herod both look less than pleased. "Yes," says Herod with exaggerated enthusiasm, "they did such a fine job in my summer palace! You must have them. I'll send them around tomorrow."

The air is thick with hatred. The guests near enough to overhear our conversation wait with baited breath. Pilate's stony face reveals none of his thoughts as he says, "Thank you. Let's build them together, for Rome."

Herodias lifts her chalice and echoes, "For Rome!"

As we leave, I ask, "You don't trust him, do you?"

"I trust him to do whatever he can to sabotage me, but it's better to have a lion under guard in the hall than lurking loose outside the gate."

"I half expected the lioness to devour *you*," I say.

He laughs. "They *are* two of a kind."

The streets are quiet, as is our palace. I feel an ache that Avram is not here to welcome us. Another servant is in his place. Pilate accepts the scroll given to him. "I'll be in shortly," he says. He disappears into his office and I into my room. I sit and remove my earrings, dropping them into the hand of a slave.

"Find Libi and send her to me."

She hurries away.

I take off my bracelets and un-strap my sandals. I let down my hair, dropping gems and ribbons into a box. Libi is never late, but the hall is silent. No footsteps approach. Concerned, I go in search of her. She is not in her room or the baths. I look in the dark kitchens but apart from a cook asleep on a cot in the corner, it is empty. Fear creeps through me as I start up the stairs in the dark. I feel my way along and see a flicker of light

ahead. I stop as I hear voices.

"I'm alone now! Everyone is gone... my brother... my father..." Libi sobs.

My hand comes to rest against the wall.

Quintus says, "You're not alone. I'll take care of you."

"You can't."

Her breath catches in her throat.

"I *can*."

Darkness swirls behind me.

"You know what my father would say."

"He'd want me to provide for you."

Shadows creep across the floor. "I won't be your mistress, Quintus."

"Why?"

"You know why. It's against my beliefs."

Fabric rustles and footsteps fall silent.

"*I want you.*"

Her voice softens. "I know."

"No one will be hurt by it."

Silence intrudes until she whispers, "I'm sorry."

I fear she will turn the corner and find me, but she does not. Her step falls away upstairs. The light retreats as Quintus leaves. I emerge into the hall after he is gone and return to my room. Libi never comes to me. I undress myself and climb into bed, wakeful until Pilate returns. A servant helps him with his armor. Pilate puts out the lamp and joins me. "Your face is serious," he remarks. He kisses my shoulder, his hand sliding along my arm. His warmth is comforting after the cold of the stairs.

I lace his fingers through mine. "Quintus asked Libi to be his mistress."

"And...?"

"She refused."

He relaxes. "I told him she'd say no years ago." Pressing his lips to my neck in a final caress, he falls into the pillows.

I turn over, rest my arms on his chest, and gaze at him. "You say it like it's a bad thing."

"Isn't it? She denies her own happiness in order to stay a servant!"

Tracing his scars, I shrug. "Should we always just take what we want in spite of our reservations?" My eyes search his, afraid of the answer. It sends a shiver along my spine.

90

"Yes."

Laying my head on his shoulder, I fall silent.

Pilate's actions cast a somber mood on the Passover. I watch people go in and out of the temple, entering with doves and lambs and leaving empty-handed. The temple fires burn late into the night. When the Passover ritual ends, many go home. Jerusalem is quiet without its travelers and Pilate is pleased since a smaller population means less riots. His attention turns to the aqueducts. Herod's architects spend hours in his office, their voices carrying in the hall. He sends them off to do their work.

"Tomorrow I want a look at them," Pilate tells me. "Come along, the drive will do you good."

Years have passed since the initial construction and a great wall rises above our chariot. Bodies glisten with sweat as men work, clearing away the rubble and making way for new columns. Pilate moves among them, talking to and gesturing at his architects.

"Are you pleased?" I ask when he rejoins me.

Stepping into the chariot, he shrugs. "We'll see."

Our return to Jerusalem at dusk makes us aware of a disturbance in the streets. Climbing the stairs into our palace, Pilate asks, "What's happening?"

"Herod arrested the prophet. There's a small mob forming in protest." Quintus follows us upstairs. From the upper floor, we can see across the city to Herod's palace, lit up with torches. Shadows converge outside his gates. Pilate taps his scroll against the palm of his hand. "Should we do something, Prefect?"

He waves in a sign of dismissal and Quintus departs. I step closer to Pilate, the wind stirring my hair. "I'm sure Herodias put him up to it. She spent half the banquet complaining about the madman in the desert."

Pilate turns away from the view. Our courtyard is silent, the guards in their places. The distant roar of protesters fills the night air. I lean against the balcony beside him and ask, "What did he say exactly?"

"He calls Herod a debaucher, a drunken pretender, and his wife a whore." Pilate's eyes twinkle at me. "I like him already."

Chapter Thirteen

Herodias has satisfaction written into every line of her painted face. She grips my arm and walks me through her palace. "Did you hear of the arrest?"

"I did, and the riot."

She waves her hand in the air. "Judeans riot over everything. Our guards sent them away. But *he* won't be a problem anymore."

The women in the lower room stir as we enter. She ignores them and crosses to a table laden with fruit. The silver bangles around her wrist jangle as she hands me a goblet.

"What do you intend to do with him?"

"I'd love to cut his head off for the lies he tells, but Herod is too afraid of the mob." Maliciously, she grins. "I'll have my way in the end, though. You will see. Come meet my daughter."

Salome's tunic is so revealing it is difficult not to stare. Sweeping dark eyes over me, she arches her brow. "Mother tells me you're from Rome. Have you met the emperor?"

"Yes, several times."

Herodias tucks a strand of hair behind her daughter's ear. "Salome is my greatest accomplishment, with neither the look of her father nor his foolishness."

The girl returns to her friends with a seductive sway in her hips. Struggling to keep amusement off my face, I say, "She does remind me of you."

Smirking, Herodias asks cruelly, "Do *you* have children?"

"No."

False pity enters her face as she guides me across the room to a chaise. "I assumed you left them in Rome." Rather than her intended sting, I feel only dislike. She returns her attention to her daughter. "Children are the one legacy we can leave behind. Men are known by name as much as reputation, but it is not so with us. Our only hope for recognition is through our children."

I swirl the wine in my cup. My response is offhand. "It's a shame you didn't have a son, then."

The beautiful face contorts in anger and eases into a benevolent smile. "Oh, Salome will do well enough."

I endure another hour of her company and retire with relief to my litter. Guards accompany me along the narrow street,

the weight barely causing my servants to hesitate as they climb the stairs. Shouting voices and quick feet bring us to a halt. I brush aside the curtain and ask, "What's happening?"

The servant with me says, "It looks like a crowd in the square, Mistress."

"Go and find out!"

He hurries in the direction everyone is going. The nearest guard says, "We should take you home."

"Put me down."

The litter lands on the street. I step out as people hurry past. Some of them are already shouting.

"It's turning into a riot," warns the centurion. His hand on his sword, he tries to stop me.

My servant reappears. "Pilate is in the square. He wants to speak with the people."

Fearfully, I watch as more figures pass.

"He'd want us to take you home," says the centurion.

Stepping around him, I follow the throng. Someone bumps into me and the guard shoves him against the wall. His homespun cloak falls open. I stare at the club tucked in his belt and my eyes shoot up to his face. He is one of my husband's soldiers.

A desperate hand grips my arm. "Come!"

Bodies cram around me as I squeeze into the arches. Pilate stands a little above the crowd. Armed guards are with him, but I see other familiar cloaked faces in the throng. They scream at him until he holds out a hand for silence. Pacing on the platform, he says, "It occurs to me that you don't understand Roman occupation. If you conform to our laws, we will leave you in peace. But these continuous riots grow troublesome."

A man shoves his way to the front of the crowd. "You dare rebuild the aqueducts with the temple funds?"

"Your own high priest agrees with me that this will benefit Jerusalem."

Angry murmurs spread through the crowd. The man I now recognize as Barabbas points at him. "This is an abuse, an insult to our faith and our god. No Roman taxes on the temple! This is a tax!"

The mob surges forward, screaming in protest. Pilate exchanges a meaningful look with Demetrius. He raises his voice over the din. "This city doesn't seem to understand how

Roman authority works. I must teach you."

He nods to his guard. Cloaks hit the ground. Panic breaks out at the sight of the centurions hidden in the mob. Screams fill the air as clubs strike them to the ground. My guard drags me away, shouting, "I can't protect you here!"

Strong arms shove me into my litter; they hoist me above the crowd, fighting our way to the palace. People flee with us, supporting one another, blood streaming down their faces. I meet Quintus at the top of the stairs. "What happened?" he asks, noting my trembling hands.

"Don't you know?" I shove past him and watch the retreat, the screams dying away into wails. Pilate's absence gives me time to think. Eventually, I hear his voice in the corridor. The door opens and he tosses a scroll onto his desk as he approaches.

"You heard?"

My hands dig into the stone before me. "I saw."

Pilate ascends the steps to the verandah.

"I don't understand how you can be so kind to me, so loving and gentle, yet do so much violence to these people."

"I *love* you." His eyes are hard and distant.

Motioning toward the square, my voice cracks as I shout, "You didn't have to beat them."

He steps closer to me. "I'm here to impose Roman rule. Everyone else failed to bring Judea into submission, but it *will* submit to my authority! The only way to do that is through force!"

I follow him inside, my sandals slapping on the floor. "You wouldn't need force if you used reasonable tactics!"

"Think, Claudia! Why did Tiberius send me here? Why, instead of a politician, did he send *me,* a soldier?"

I feel my way to a chair and sink into it.

His voice softens. "Judea is a humiliation to Rome, the province we can't control, our one failure. It *must* be conquered and who better to do it than a soldier that served Sejanus?"

He hands me a scroll.

I accept it with a questioning look.

"Read it! See what comes of reasoning with Jews!"

Shaking, I unroll it and stare in dismay. Pilate returns my horrified glance with patience. "That is a list of all the men dead because of Judean riots, on both sides. Governor Gratus

did everything but let Caiaphas rule and met with contempt. They riot over taxes. They riot over the Passover. They riot over arrests, trials, and executions. Innocents die on both sides! Tiberius wants it stopped!"

Carrying it to the window, I let it curl up in my hand. "What will happen if you can't control them?"

"Rome will destroy this city and everyone in it."

Ancient buildings stand before us. I imagine the city in ruin and shut my eyes. Disgust wells up in my throat. "So he sends you here to be cruel so they will hate you?"

He takes the scroll. "Not hated... *feared.*"

In this, Pilate succeeds. Even Caiaphas avoids challenging him.

Late summer, with much progress made on his aqueducts, we set out for Caesarea, Pilate riding ahead by two days with the garrison. Quintus stays in Jerusalem and Demetrius rides with me. Our pace is slow and servants walk with us.

Before nightfall, we take refuge in a small town. The innkeeper shows me to their best room. Libi is with me, while the male servants and soldiers stay in the stables.

A girl places a skein of wine on the table and a plate of bread, meat, and goat cheese. I stand at the window and see people hurry past. "What is happening in the street?"

"A teacher walks among us, healing the sick."

My head turns sharply. "*Healing* the sick?"

Shyly she comes to me and nods. Voices murmur below and a boy takes off. "Who is he?"

"I don't know. He's from Galilee."

Dismissing her, I resume my watch out the window. Torches pass in the hands of travelers. Light streams out of doorways as people emerge. Excitement fills the air. I cover my head and go downstairs. No one notices as Libi and I join the crowd. The man I met in Jerusalem slowly makes his way forward. Hands reach out to him, asking for blessings. Gently, he touches each one and speaks softly to them.

I have never seen a man more loved. They look at him with adoration and trust. Others press close to be near him. My hand tingles at the memory of his touch.

"Please," a woman says, falling to her knees, "please heal me, Messiah." Trembling hands reach up to him and he lowers her hood. Her face is deformed; her lips twisted and knotted; her nose askew; her left eye completely white. No one can bear

to look at her, except the prophet. He takes her mangled, terrible face in his hands and gazes into her good eye. He kisses her forehead. She trembles, sobs wrack her thin form and she falls into the dirt, to kiss his feet.

"Rise," he says.

She takes his hand and climbs to her feet. Her face falls into the lamplight, whole and without blemish. She touches her lips in wonder and turns to him. "Thank you," she whispers, "*thank you!*"

Tears flow as others embrace her. The crowd shifts around me, following him into the street. I stare at her until she fades from sight. I saw witchcraft in Rome, but nothing like this.

"Jesus of Galilee," I whisper.

Libi is still at my side, though longingly looking after him. She looks at me curiously. "What?"

I shiver in the night air. "His name, Quintus told me."

The urge to follow him is strong but I resist. She trembles with yearning beside me. "Go," I tell her.

She sprints after them.

I make my way to the inn. Libi returns an hour later beaming. "Claudia, he *is* the messiah. All this time my father told me of his arrival, and I never believed it until now."

Envy fills my heart that she sat with him. I have only myself to blame, my fear of rejection as the wife of Pilate, the governor of Judea, the "butcher," as the insurgents in Jerusalem now call him.

The others sleep but not me. I stare into the patch of moonlight over my bed, thinking of the kindness in his face, the hands that take away pain and give beauty. Yet, he loved her and looked on her in mercy even in her ugliness.

We set out at dawn and see no sign of the messiah. Libi walks beside me with a faraway expression. It is the first time I have seen her happy since Avram's death. It is not many miles to Caesarea but the largeness of our servant-laden caravan causes us to travel slowly and we reach it an hour before nightfall.

I remove my head covering and hand it to the nearest servant. "Where is my husband?"

"He's in his office in council with his architect."

Pushing open the door, I enter. Pilate rises from his chair and comes to greet me. "Tell my wife what you said."

A nervous-looking man motions to the plans spread across

the desk. "We found weakness in the aqueducts' foundation. It appears deliberate." His eyes dart between us fearfully and sweat gathers on his brow. "But I assure you, Prefect, none of my—"

"Oh, it's not your fault, Julius." Pilate taps his hand on the map. "Fix it, but tell no one. You may go."

The door shuts on his expression of relief. I turn to my husband and ask, "Herod?"

"What generosity to send all those architects. Think what might have happened, the outrage set against me, yet another reason for him to file a complaint in Rome."

He hands me an official scroll.

"Do I want to read it?"

Pilate sinks into his chair. "Herod complained, the senate is upset, and Tiberius warns me of less violence in Judea. But still *control it*, mind you."

"You're taking this well."

Blue eyes dance at me. "Herod sees me as a threat but I have more powerful friends than he does. I haven't married my niece, or divorced the daughter of a powerful man, nor have I arrested a popular prophet."

I stroke his shoulder. "What of his architects?"

"I'll send them to him with my gratitude. I don't want to deprive him of them for long." Pushing aside the map, he turns to me. "Did you meet the new prophet on the road?" His mocking tone gives me pause.

"What do you mean?"

"The man from Galilee, we came across him teaching thirty miles from Jerusalem. Let's hope for his sake *he* doesn't accuse Herod of incest like the last one."

I put on a false smile.

Within a week, a messenger arrives from Herod with an invitation to attend his birthday celebrations. "He first denounces you to Rome and then flatters you with feasting and wine!" I laugh.

Pilate reads it without interest and tosses it aside. "Well, provided he's still alive, it may mean our chance to meet the madman after all."

Chapter Fourteen

I climb out of the litter and eye Herod's Palace. Marble arches stretch above us. The breeze stirs his rich purple curtains and brings the scent of water. Pilate takes my hand as we ascend the steps. "Let's hope this foundation is stronger than the one they planned for my aqueducts."

We put on a smile as Herod greets us.

"Your home is magnificent," I say.

Beaming, he puffs out his considerable girth. "My architects are the best in Judea, as you well know. I'm surprised you sent them back to me so soon." His dark eyes glitter with suspicion.

"I didn't want to impose," Pilate answers.

The king leads us through the hall. "Isn't that what Romans do in Judea, impose?" He laughs. "I tease you, as is my right!"

Passing an open window, I see a number of slaves unloaded from a barred cart into the courtyard. Bound and shackled, many of them scarred. My skin prickles and I hurry to catch up.

"Herodias is unstoppable in her plans. Our guests will enjoy ten days of chariot races, gladiator games, dancing, music, acrobatics, and wine."

Pilate and I exchange a glance.

"She must be pleased that you arrested the prophet."

Herod scowls and leans closer to confide, "I like him. He speaks his mind but she doesn't care for it."

Music drifts toward us.

"Well, he did call your marriage *incestuous*." I try hard not to smile. Pilate's eyes twinkle at me.

"Ah..." Herod's pudgy face flushes. "Yes... he rots in our dungeon until I can decide on his punishment."

"Isn't imprisonment enough?"

He laughs again. "Not with Herodias as my wife!" His fat fingers grip my arm and draw me closer to him. I try not to breathe in his heavy scent of wine and horses. "Herodias will be pleased to see you! She complains there isn't anyone worth talking to here, other than me."

Snapping for a slave, he says, "Take Lady Claudia in to my wife and send more wine in to my male guests."

"This way," says the slave boy.

I follow him up some stairs and through an ornate door into

the palace baths. Half-naked women lounge around me as I make my way to Herodias. She stirs from her chair and takes my hands. "Claudia! Sit with me! Kick off your sandals!"

Her daughter, Salome, rests in the bath at our feet. Slaves offer me grapes and I decline. Herodias sips her wine. "How went your journey?"

"Uneventful but then we did have a legion with us."

She laughs. "Will you winter in Caesarea?"

"Yes."

Salome ducks under the water and comes up again, smoothing her hair out of her eyes. She comes out of the bath and a servant wraps a towel around her.

"Pity," says Herodias, "I hoped to see more of you."

I look sad and remind myself to thank Pilate.

Leaning closer, she adds under her breath, "No one likes me here. They speak endlessly of *her*."

I whisper, "Who?"

"Herod's first wife. She went home to her father in disgrace. I hear them plotting. Half the people in this province want his armies to wipe us out."

Biting into a piece of fruit, Salome drips all over the tiles, utterly at ease in her state of undress. Her arms and legs are long and shapely, for she is no longer a child. She asks, "Did you see the gladiators?"

"I did! I'm surprised they're permitted."

Herodias rolls her eyes. "Oh, the Jewish priests complained. They always do, but who cares what they think? I like the look of the big African. I intend to bet on him. He'll be my gift to my husband, if he wins."

From her expression, I doubt it is *his* gift.

Dark eyes look into mine, "What's Pilate's gift to him?"

"A stallion, one of our finest," I answer.

Inviting her daughter to lie with her on the chaise, Herodias nods. "He'll like that. He envies Roman horses. Salome is preparing a surprise for him, too, aren't you, darling?"

"I intend to dance for him."

We study one another with equal distrust. "I'm sure he'll enjoy that."

"Oh, he will."

Self-satisfaction fills her voice and sends a chill into me. "I'm tired. I must rest before the festivities."

Herodias claps for a slave. "Take Lady Claudia to her room.

We'll send for you before the feast begins and tomorrow, we'll have a full day of chariot races!"

She drinks from her chalice and I leave them there. I can feel their eyes following me the length of the hall.

The banquet is a rowdy, drunken affair. Herod laughs until he nearly falls off his lounge. Herodias hangs on him like a snake. Musicians play above the din. Young men crowd around Salome, competing for her attention. Fights break out more than once. Slaves dart in and out with platters of food and jars of wine, dodging the cups and fruit flying through the air. It is a relief to retreat to our room and shut out the noise. Leaning against the door, I ask, "Can't we think up an excuse to go home tomorrow?"

"Not unless an insurrection arises." Pilate unhooks his breastplate. "Herodias does know how to celebrate."

I raise my brows. "Is that what it is? I thought it looked more like an orgy in the making."

"It's the first night. We must expect a certain amount of drunkenness." He sighs with relief as the heavy armor comes off, leaving him in a simple toga. Something crashes in the next room and hysterical laughter rings in the hall.

I drop his wristbands onto the table. "I'm glad it's not one of your vices."

His arms wind around me. "Herod drinks enough for both of us." Kissing my shoulder, he removes his sandals.

Every time I start to drift away into sleep, a guest stumbles past in the hall or shouts into the courtyard. Finally, a few hours before dawn, the palace is quiet. It stays that way until nearly noon, when the bleary-eyed guests stagger out to watch the chariot races. Wine sloshes out of their cups each time the horses pass, as arms lift in cheers or protest. Herodias has a goblet in her hand, but I notice it does not contain wine. She dribbles some on the ground. "Only water," she confides. "Someone must keep their wits about them."

Chariots overturn and men fall, crushed. Horses pull ahead to cross the finish line inches ahead of the other team. Coins spin in the air as gamblers win and lose. I sit with my chin on my hand, longing to go inside. Herod pounds the side of his throne and cheers. Salome leans against the rail and cheers them on. Bangles and gold jewelry hang off her, her dark-lined eyes bursting with bloodthirsty exhilaration. The men look more at her than the races, for each time she lifts her arms and

cheers the horses on, her tunic slides open to reveal her curvy leg.

At dusk, the races end and we retreat indoors. The celebration is no more subdued tonight than before and I send Pilate a withering glance. All of them are too drunk to notice when we leave early.

Listening to them roar with laughter as we lay in bed, Pilate asks, "Do you want to meet the prophet?"

"Can I?"

"Herod as a drunk isn't only amusing but useful. He consented to our seeing the prisoner tomorrow. Though," and his lips press against my hair tenderly, "his words were somewhat less... appropriate."

The next morning the guards make no move to stop us from entering the prison.

"I want to see the lunatic," Pilate says.

The soldier on duty leads us down winding stairs. It smells of earth and blood. The further we go, the worse it stinks of urine and vomit. I cover my mouth and try not to touch the walls.

"Wait here," he says gruffly.

I look around the room of torture, noting the chains hanging from the ceiling and the sharp instruments on the rough wooden table. My stomach lurches. Pilate fingers a mace with interest and turns as the door creaks open and the soldier shoves the prisoner inside. He is wild, with fierce dark eyes under a mass of uncontrolled hair. He lands on his hands and knees, half-undressed, bruises mottling his skin. He spits blood out at our feet.

The guard moves to yank him by the hair, but Pilate holds out his hand. "So you're John."

"And you've come to see the prisoner, have you?" John sits on his haunches, his gaze unwavering. "Am I what you thought I'd be?"

Dirty light shines through the only window, set high in the far wall. Pilate lifts his brows. "What do you think I expected?"

"A madman, a lunatic... isn't it what they call me?"

Pacing the floor, Pilate says, "It *is* lunacy to insult Herod and his wife."

John's lip curls in disgust and he spits out, "His *whore*, his *niece*, his brother's wife!"

The guard hits him hard enough to knock him down. John

laughs as he sits up, wiping blood from his mouth. Pilate tilts his head as he looks at him. "But you're not mad, are you? You know *exactly* what you're doing."

"My purpose is to tell the truth, whether or not others like to hear it, and to prepare the way for the messiah." His filthy hands gesture at the walls. "Herod can imprison me, beat me, take my life, but he'll never silence my tongue!"

Pilate narrows his gaze. "That is unless he cuts it out."

"If so I will write in the sand!"

Glancing at me in amazement, Pilate says, "What is it you have to tell us, then, Prophet?"

"That you must repent, for the messiah is at hand. He walks among men but is not one of us. He'll fulfill the prophecies and bring change in Judea."

My skin tingles and I glance behind me into the hall.

"What manner of change?" Pilate asks.

John points at him. "You fear men, not God! Yes, I know who you are and what you have done. You are concerned with lesser things! You want not the truth but lies! Yet if you want to live, you will listen to him! His voice will be mightier than mine; it will shake the heavens and the earth!"

"What is the messiah's purpose?"

The prisoner rises and stares Pilate in the face, broad-shouldered and thin. "I'm but a voice in the wilderness, a leaf in the wind. If you want his truth, ask him."

Rattling his shackles, he turns to the guard. The man glances at Pilate and at his affirming nod, takes him to his cell. Pilate rests his hand on the table. "Herod may think him mad but I don't. I find him dangerous."

We go up the stairs and into the sunlight. It warms me after the chill of the dungeons.

"Is it wise to arrest him?"

Pilate glances at the prison. "I wouldn't have done it. Prophets in this part of the world are different from common rebels or usurpers. They are not violent so any arrest meets with disapproval. Herod is now in an impossible situation. He can't let him go, or he looks weak, but he can't execute him without trouble."

The shade of the palace is comforting in the heat. From the noise in the main hall, the rest of the guests are up. My voice reveals relief. "He's safe, then?"

"Knowing Herodias, no, he's not safe."

Behind us, the door opens and she appears. "There you are! It is time to start the games! Come along, there's a place for you on our platform!"

Faces line the walls above the courtyard. Pilate sits beside me with Herod on his left. My stomach tightens as two slaves enter the area unchained. One of them is the massive African. The games begin. Salome leans against the wall and screams at them, squealing in delight whenever there is a close blow. One of the men stumbles and the crowd cheers as his opponent's sword slices into flesh. I turn my head away. There is a sickening thud and spatter of blood as the victor slices off his rival's head, to the cheers of the crowd. They drag away the remains, leaving the African victorious.

Salome claps and shouts, "Bring out another!"

I watch men die all afternoon, flinching at each strike of the sword. It sickens no one else but Pilate is quiet, his eyes distant. The skies have mercy on the remaining gladiators and darken. Large drops of rain fall into the bloody yard. It drives us indoors where the celebrations continue. Herodias joins me at the table. "You have no taste for violence?" she asks. "I saw you look away."

She scorns me for it, however pleasant her smile. My hatred for her intensifies. "I'd rather celebrate life than death."

Her eyes darken at the insult. "Then you shouldn't have married Pilate."

My face flushes as she moves away. Pilate puts his arms around me. Softly, he says, "Don't let them see what you feel. Hide it from them." He strokes my arm and kisses my neck. The smug look on Herodias' face turns into a scowl. Moving only slightly, he picks up a goblet.

"I want to go home," I whisper.

Pilate leans against the table. "I sent a messenger to Caesarea in secret this morning. He will return with urgent tidings that draw us away tomorrow. Unfortunately, we'll miss the rest of the week's festivities."

I thank him with my eyes. My heart lightens at the thought of one last banquet. On the other side of the usual debauchery, drunkenness, and bad behavior is the road home. I sit and watch them gorge themselves on food, drink wine until they stammer, laugh until their sides ache. Herod is in high spirits, his goblet never empty, for his wife refills it every chance she gets.

Darkness gathers in the corners of the room and the slaves light the lamps. It casts eerie shadows around us. I recline against Pilate, his fingers caressing my arm.

Herodias silences the musicians. "I want to speak to our guests! Citizens of Rome and Judea, we gather to honor Herod on the day of his birth!" Knuckles rap on the tables in appreciation, and wine sloshes on the floor. Herod waves it off, but his jowls redden with pleasure. "You've given us many fine gifts," she continues. "Horses... chariots... gold cups and adornments... but I have one last gift to give my lord and husband."

She trails her hand across his large front. "In honor of Herod, I present... my daughter!"

Eager faces turn to Salome as she gets up off her lounge. She steps up onto the table and kicks the plates off it. Fruit bounces across the floor and rolls out of sight. Open mouths stare at her as she strips off her Judean tunic to reveal a thin Roman gown leaving little to the imagination. Movement starts in her hips and wriggles upward, a lusty sway that sets my face on fire. Her body moves rhythmically to the music, every gesture intended to seduce. I want to look away and cannot, nor can anyone else. The hand stroking my arm falters as Pilate watches her dance. She reminds me of a cobra glistening in the lamplight, swaying with her hips in constant motion. Chalices tip forward and wine drizzles onto the floor in a crimson stream, all eyes fixed on her. Even the women are fascinated, some with hatred.

I look at Herodias and her smirk turns my blood cold.

With a final thrust, Salome collapses into a bow. Men explode with excitement, pounding on the tables and cheering. Herod stumbles to his feet, his bulging face alight with wine-induced fervor. "Come to me!" he cries. Pudgy hands fall on her bare shoulders and leering eyes devour her with open lust. "Whatever you ask will be given! Do you want half my kingdom? It's yours! Name it!"

Shock fills me. Pilate meets my gaze and lifts his brow.

False modesty forces her to lower her gaze. "You're too generous, sire. I know not what to ask."

"There must be something you want," Herod insists.

She glances at her mother. "Can it be anything?"

My breath catches in my throat.

"Yes!"

Lifting her chin, her dark eyes glittering dangerously, she says, "I want the head of the prophet."

Gasps fill the room. Even Pilate is surprised.

Herod's mirth fades. "It's not an easy gift," he says.

She crosses her arms and pouts. "It's what I want, and a king must not go back on his word."

"A dance isn't worth the rebellion of a nation."

Herodias grips his arm, hissing, "You *promised* her."

I turn to Pilate. "*Stop him.*"

Concern flickers through his face and melts into a half smile. "If Herod wants to tie a rope around a branch and fasten one end to his neck, who am I to object?"

The guests await a response. Herod looks from their expectation to the scowl on his wife's face. Salome puts out her lower lip in a pout. "You *promised*," she says.

Looking to his guard, Herod nods. "Do it."

"I want to watch!" Unease stirs among us. Salome turns to the guard. "Bring him into the courtyard for his execution and carry his head in to me on this silver platter." Dumping a mass of fruit onto the floor, she hands it to him. The man looks wordlessly at his king, who nods. Salome delightedly skips to the verandah.

I press against the wall, feeling sick. Pilate's hand is at my spine, stroking. They drag John out in chains and throw him to the ground. Torchlight reveals his face as he lifts it toward us on the balcony, shifting to his knees. "So the whore will have my head," he says.

Herodias laughs bitterly and drinks.

"You may silence my voice, but you won't silence his! It comes, like a storm from the east!"

Fascinated, the crowd stares at him. The guard unsheathes his sword and looks to Herod. "Do it," he says.

I hear the swish and the double thud. Salome's malicious laughter rings in my ears. Pilate guides me inside, away from the gruesome sight. Soon enough the platter is brought in and presented to her. Salome grips John by the hair and lifts his head, dripping blood across the floor as she carries it to her mother.

"My gift to you, Mother," she says.

Turning my face away, I feel Pilate's hand tighten on my arm. It sets a dark tone for the rest of the evening. Even Herod retires earlier than usual. The guests retreat to their rooms

before dawn for the first time since we arrived. Silence lingers in the palace, burning my ears as I undress.

Pilate watches me from the bed, my hands shaking. "You're angry with me again."

"You let it happen!"

My bracelets bounce off the table.

"Herodias planned it from the start. She got her stupid husband drunk enough to agree to anything and prostituted her own daughter before him. She got exactly what she wanted. I couldn't have stopped it."

I throw my sandals. "You still watched."

"Ah, so that's what upsets you. It's not the injustice but the *indecency*." Pilate catches me around the waist and pulls me into bed. His fingertips trace my collarbone. "Don't be jealous of her, Claudia. You're all I want, all I've *ever* wanted, and all I ever *will* want."

Some of my annoyance fades and I turn my head into his chest. "What will happen now that he's dead?"

Concern is in his voice.

"I don't know."

Chapter Fifteen

Blood stains the courtyard. I try not to look on my way past, Herodias' arm through mine as she walks me to my litter. Her voice scrapes at my ears. "I'm sorry you must go so soon, as I have much planned for the rest of the week!"

Our much-appreciated messenger from Caesarea stands beside Pilate's horse and avoids my gaze. Contempt enters my voice. "You know the Jews, we leave for a few days and there are riots."

She indicates the bloodstain. "We entertained you, though!"

Disgusted, I open my mouth. Pilate steps between us and takes her hand. "Thank you for your hospitality, Herodias. We won't soon forget our visit, will we, my love?" He glares at me.

I put on a fake smile. "No, we will *never* forget it."

She returns to her husband on the stairs. Pilate mounts his horse and I settle in my litter. The servants hoist me into the air as our guard fall in around us. Herod cheerfully waves and takes Herodias inside. Riding beside me, Pilate says, "He's as glad to see us go as we are, but his lack of anger over me returning his architects worries me. I've made arrangements for us to spend some time in Jerusalem."

The people largely ignore our arrival in the ancient city. There is some anger over the death of the prophet, but no riots. "Either they've learned their lesson, or it isn't worth the trip to Herod's palace," Pilate remarks.

Our arrival coincides with a Feast of the Tabernacles, which is not an oversight on Pilate's part. Travelers enter Jerusalem and the city overflows. Other than watching the sacrificial fires from my balcony, I pay little attention until Libi comes to me, breathless. "Claudia, he's in Jerusalem!"

I look up from my needlework. "Who?"

"Jesus! He teaches in the temple!" She falls to her knees and grips my hand. "I heard him speak this morning. He read from the scriptures and taught, even to correct the priests!"

Putting aside my work, I ask, "And Caiaphas?"

"He's furious, my brother too! I thought they'd try to throw him out but they didn't."

Curiosity stirs in me toward this man, who heals and teaches. "Do you know where he stays?"

"Bethany. Tomorrow is the last day of the feast. He may

return one last time to speak." Footsteps pass in the hall and she glances over her shoulder. Her voice lowers. "You should see him."

I laugh. "I can't enter the temple, you know that."

"You can enter the gentile's court!" Her face reddens and her eyes are hesitant in seeking mine. "I want you to come with me, to speak with him if you can." Her face is in earnest.

I ask, "Why does it matter?"

"If he's the messiah, *he can heal you*." Shock courses through me. Libi ducks her head, her cheeks burning.

"I'll consider it." Once she is gone, my hand drifts to my womb. I stir when Pilate returns from his aqueducts but say nothing.

Libi comes for me early the next morning. I wait in my room and draw on a veil as she peers inside. Her face brightens with joy. Silently, we leave through the side gate and cross to the temple. The court of the gentiles is crowded, for everyone is curious. Catching her breath in her throat, her hand tightens on my arm. "He comes," she whispers.

I search him out in the crowd. Jesus moves easily with his people, many reaching out to him in awe and others following on his heels. He approaches the steps to the inner courts and stops as Caiaphas appears. Jacob stands a short distance behind him.

"Since you have such things to teach us," says the high priest loudly, his voice carrying over the crowd, "we ask your opinion on a matter of grave importance." Caiaphas looks over his shoulder and nods. His guards bring a woman forward and shove her before Jesus. She nearly falls, clutching her half-torn garments. Hair falls into her face and she stares at the ground. "We caught this woman in the act of adultery. Moses commands us to stone her, according to the Law. What say you?"

Horror strikes me as I see the stones already in many hands. The crowd is prepared. An expectant silence fills the air. Jesus regards her without expression and kneeling, puts his hand to the dirt. Necks crane around me.

"What's he writing?"

"Can you read it?"

It looks like simple lines in the sand.

Jacob asks, "Should we stone her or not?"

Jesus smiles and keeps writing.

"Answer!" shouts Caiaphas.

Fingers dig into my arm as Libi holds her breath. Her eyes dart to her brother, full of misery.

Glancing up at the priests, Jesus says, "If any one of you is without sin, let him cast the first stone."

Rage fills the face of Caiaphas. His hand tightens on his staff. He turns and sweeps into the temple. Stones fall to the ground as others slip away in shame. One angry looking man stares long and hard at the woman. He starts to step forward and his eyes fall to the dirt. Horror flickers through him. The stone drops and he turns away. The steps clear. Libi tugs on my arm and pulls me into the street. Others hurry past, not looking one another in the face.

"What did it say?"

Her eyes are wide, her hands trembling. "How did he know? I told no one!" Shaking her head and repressing tears, she returns to the palace.

I enter the courtyard and find no one there, but his marks are still in the dirt. I walk around to the steps and stare at them. My pulse quickens.

How does he know?

Jesus wrote "Hatred."

It is my sin.

My skin prickles and I glance into the temple. Then, drawing my veil closer, I run home and burst into the servants' quarters. They scatter out of my way as I open Libi's door and enter her room. She looks up from the bed.

"What did you read in the sand?" Her eyes are wide, frightened. I shut the door. "Tell me!"

"I can't!"

Crossing the floor, I take her shoulders in my hands. "I want to know if you read what I did."

Tears fill her eyes. "Please, don't ask me." She retreats to the far corner of the room.

I let her. "I read 'hatred.' It is true! I hate Herodias for her cruelty. I hate her daughter for her sensuality. I hate Herod as a lecher. I hate Tiberius for sending us here, Jacob for abandoning you, and sometimes I even hate my husband."

Her shoulders shake with emotion and tears fill her eyes. "Quintus," she whispers miserably. "It was his name! Claudia, I..." She sinks onto her bed and covers her mouth. I go to her. Once she finds her breath, she says, "I'd made up my mind to

do as Quintus asks. Father's dead and there's no one to care. My brother abandons me. God took everything from me I love! I want happiness! He *knew*! He wrote it in the sand!" I put my arms around her as she sobs. "I can't do it! Not now that he *knows*."

Holding her until she quiets, I say, "I wonder what sin Caiaphas saw written in the sand?" The laugh half catches in her throat. I wipe her tears away. "We're both shamed today, but tomorrow we'll visit Bethany. You are right. I do want to speak with him... but away from others."

"Is that wise?"

I shrug. "Pilate rides out to see his aqueducts. No one will bother us. Quintus can escort us to Bethany."

Kissing her hands, I return to my room. The next morning I approach my brother with our plan. He listens with patience and says, "Madness."

"As my brother, you can say that, but as a tribune under my husband, you can't criticize my decisions. Either come with us or explain to Pilate where we went."

He rolls his eyes.

"You're off duty today, wear something normal."

Since it is only two miles to Bethany, we walk. I dress as inconspicuously as possible. Quintus forgoes his armor but still carries his sword under his cloak. We pass many coming and going from Jerusalem. He often looks at Libi, who avoids him. She stumbles on the path and pulls her arm quickly out of his hand when he stops her fall. My heart aches.

"Now what?" he asks when we reach the town. "Do you have any idea where he lives?"

Women draw water from the well. I send Libi over to them and they speak for several minutes in low voices. She returns at a trot. "He sometimes stays at the home of Lazarus, off the main square, but they aren't sure he's there. He might have set out for Capernaum."

She leads us to a large house on a narrow street. I hesitate at the gate of the courtyard, suddenly unsure if this is the right thing to do. I glance at Quintus. He lifts his hands and shrugs. "I want no part of it."

Feeling sick, I stare at the house. I decide to go home.

"Can I help you?" A woman holding a water jar views us suspiciously. My mouth goes dry.

Libi steps forward. "We heard the messiah sometimes stays

here."

She stares at me. "Did you come for healing?"

Heat rushes into my cheeks. Libi glances at me and says, "Yes."

"Come in, then. He's not here but will return soon." She swings open the gate and we follow her into the yard. Several children bolt past laughing, nearly sloshing her water. Bare feet pound the dirt as they run.

"Are they yours?" I ask, feeling a pang of longing.

She snorts. "No, but Mary likes to watch them." We enter the house. "My brother welcomes all who seek the messiah," she says, putting aside her jar. "I'm Martha and that's my sister, Mary."

From another room, a curious face peers out at us. Mary returns to her children. Martha motions to us, "Please, sit, and I will feed you."

Eying a crutch covered with dust in the far corner, I sit. Martha notices and says, "It belonged to one of Mary's children. She doesn't need it now."

"Is she...?"

Her blank expression clears. "Dead, you mean? No! You met her in the courtyard!"

Quintus stares at her.

Placing bread before us, Martha considers me. "What brings the wife of Pilate to see our master?"

A shadow separates from the doorway and Mary enters. She is a lot younger than her sister is.

"You know me?"

My brother's hand goes to the hilt of his sword.

"You're recognized in Jerusalem, as is your husband." Martha pours us each a cup of water. "His feelings for our kind are also well known."

Her sister gasps, "Martha!"

"I say nothing that isn't true."

Before an argument begins, I lift my hand to silence it. "I've met Jesus before, twice in Jerusalem. I want only to speak with him, and will tell no one where he is."

"What of your centurion?"

Under her accusing stare, Quintus opens his mouth. From the doorway, a voice says, "What of him?"

Jesus grins and enters, startling us to our feet. My brother grasps his sword and Jesus touches him on the chest.

Amusement fills his voice. "Put your sword away, Quintus. No harm will come to any of you." He steps into the kitchen. Quintus' mouth hangs open. Jesus looks to Libi and she reddens, hardly daring to meet his eye. "There's no need for shame, my child," he says. "You have chosen obedience."

Mary offers him a cup, adoration shining in her eyes. He smiles at Martha and looks to me. "Come with me into the garden." The others remain behind. Setting his cup on the bench, he goes to the far end and reaches up into the fig tree. Branches rustle.

I creep forward. "Do you know why I've come?"

"Do you?" His eyes laugh at me. Sunlight gleams on his dark hair, cut short, like his beard, framing his face.

"I thought I did."

"Your friend brought you for a reason." He gestures toward the house. My face warms. "But what makes you think I'd honor what you ask? You're a gentile and the wife of Pilate."

It hurts and my step falters. He stares at me expressionlessly. "You're not worthy," he says softly.

The earth recedes beneath me; my heart skips a beat. "You might have said that of the woman in the temple courtyard, but you still saved her life."

"I saved more than that, but she's a Jew."

Despite his words, something in him makes me bold. "And by your own laws, she deserves death, yet you spared her, because you're the messiah."

Leaning against the tree, he says, "Am I?"

"It's what they say."

"And what do you say, Claudia?"

I move closer to him. "You show mercy to the undeserving. You love instead of hate. You write in the sand words that mean different things to all who read it... you're the messiah, the one foretold."

"You want me to heal you," he says. Following him across the garden, I nod. He sits on the bench and moves the cup, leaving a space for me. "But what do you want healing *from*?"

My lips part and he holds up his finger.

"Think carefully, Claudia. I can heal the body, but I care more for the soul. I can offer you healing, but what you need is to never thirst again."

Laughing, the children return, burst into the garden and one throws her tiny, fat arms around his neck. Jesus smiles

112

and kisses her round face as she stares at me in wonder. Patting her hand, he asks, "What do you want?"

My eyes stray to the child. She shoves a mass of golden hair behind her ear. Jesus sets her on the ground and she joins the others. I can no longer look him in the eye and stare at my hands.

"Am I evil?" I whisper. Wind stirs the trees, disrupting the silence. "You know what I am, don't you?"

His hand covers mine and I look at him in surprise. "Your demons fled long ago. Not all dreams are evil, my child. Some of them come from our Father."

I search his face and find only kindness. "*Will* you heal me?"

"Yes."

Relief flows through me and I clutch his hand. Jesus smiles at my delight. "But you still have much to learn." He touches the side of my face. "Now go."

Libi looks at me eagerly when I enter the house and I nod. Joy fills her expression as we depart, Quintus still with a perplexed air.

Midway to Jerusalem, the ground shakes. Pebbles dance at our feet. A sound like thunder rumbles in the distance in a cloudless sky.

"What is it?" Libi asks.

A huge cloud of dust rises in the distance.

My brother's face is white. "It's the aqueducts!"

Chapter Sixteen

People flood the streets of Jerusalem. Some pass us as we make our way home; others head for the city gates. Quintus hurries us along, fingering his sword. Unease is in the air, the tension mounting.

"We'll have another riot if it isn't stopped now." He lets us into the palace courtyard. "*Stay inside*, Claudia!"

I pace the floor of our room, waiting for news. When shouting starts in the street, I know Pilate has arrived. I dart to the verandah and see him cross the yard, a dozen men on his heels. Panic rises in me at the sight of his armor and tunic covered in blood.

"Are you all right?"

His blue eyes spark with anger. "I'm fine," he says gently, "it isn't mine."

We enter his office. Pilate throws the contents of his desk to the floor and unfurls a scroll. He points to the main pillar. "You vowed it would hold."

"I thought so, Prefect!" His architect is terrified.

Pilate glares at him. "You promised the damage could be corrected and wouldn't cause a problem! Half of it collapsed, over a hundred Jewish workers are dead, and we have the makings of a riot on our hands!"

"Prefect, we did all in our power to make it sound!"

The silence in the palace highlights the disturbance outside. I glance out the window as the crowd increases. Pilate draws his sword. "Julius, did you betray me?"

His eyes widen. "No, I'd never, Prefect!"

"You didn't conspire with Herod to do this?"

Others stare at him, terrified. His face pales and he whispers, "N-no, Prefect!"

Pilate looks at him stonily. "I don't believe you."

A chill enters the room.

"Creating an insurrection in Judea is a treasonable offense. If I find out you plotted with Herod to destroy the aqueducts and discredit me, I'll have your head." The tip of the sword rests on Julius' chest. Tapping it twice, Pilate says, "Now get out."

Relief floods through the man's face as he stumbles out. Pilate glares at the others. "That means *all of you!*"

Hurriedly, they scatter into the hall. Pilate turns to Quintus. "Have him followed. If he goes to Herod, as I suspect he will, arrest him."

"Yes, Prefect," says Quintus, and departs.

I approach the desk as he moves to the washbasin. Dipping his hands into the water, he rinses off the blood. "I've never seen anything like it. They let the water loose and the middle section collapsed with miles of destruction! Debris flew in all directions, pinning men to the sand. It crushed the centurion standing next to me." He wipes the blood from his face. "I'm starting to hate this cursed place. If it's not a riot, it's a plot, and if it's not a plot, it's a mob!"

Fear tugs at my heart. "You won't..."

"Disperse them like last time?" Pilate smiles grimly. "Not after that warning from Tiberius."

Throwing the towel aside, he goes out to face them. I linger in the shadow of the columns. "Let them in," he tells Demetrius, who signals to the guard. They open the gates and the mob swarms inside. Barabbas is at the forefront. He shouts up at us, "First, you tax us, then you slaughter us, and now you crush us with the vanities of Rome!"

Fists wave in the air and the people roar.

Pilate is unflinching. "Jerusalem needs water."

"And Rome needs better architects!" Barabbas jeers.

Bitter laughter drifts from the crowd.

"Rome also lost men today," says Pilate.

Scoffing, Barabbas shouts, "More Judeans than Romans!" Turning to the crowd, he points at Pilate. "This man brought graven images into Jerusalem! He spat on the sanctity of our temple and filled it with blood! When we protest his use of temple funds to build his aqueducts, he has us beaten and killed in the square! Now, the precious aqueducts we paid for in blood have fallen! Isn't this a judgment from God on Pilate?"

"Prefect," says Demetrius, worriedly.

Silencing him with an upheld hand, Pilate descends. "I don't submit to the authority of your god. I am loyal to Rome. As her governor, it's my duty to improve conditions in Jerusalem." He stops before Barabbas, who glares at him. I move instinctively forward and Demetrius blocks me. The guards at the foot of the stairs are uneasy.

"Does that include spilling Judean blood, Prefect?"

A guard backhands Barabbas. He spits blood at Pilate's feet, who says quietly, "If you care so much for your men, take them and leave. Or maybe you'd rather I repeat the lesson I tried to teach you in the square?"

"Barabbas, come," pleads one of his friends.

He turns away but his hand slips into his toga. I see the hatred in his eyes and cry out a warning. A guard steps before Pilate, taking the full thrust. The man behind Barabbas tries to pull him away but Barabbas turns on him, catching him across the throat. "You're a traitor to Judea," he hisses. With that, his friend falls to his knees and crumples on the ground. Guards send Barabbas crashing to the dirt. He shouts, "Don't surrender to the whore that is Rome!"

The mob riots; rocks pelt the stairs and clang off the helmets of the centurions. They drag Barabbas to the prison. The guards force the people out of the gates. Shutting the crowd out subdues its roar of disapproval.

"Quintus, I want him whole enough for crucifixion."

Nodding, my brother heads for the prison. Pilate looks at me as I shakily descend the stairs.

"I'm all right," he assures me.

Blood pools at our feet. My voice softens as I gaze at the Judean. "He died trying to save you."

"Not me, Jerusalem."

Stones continue to pelt the wooden gates. I feel cold. "Will Tiberius be furious?"

Even though Pilate is unresponsive, I know the answer.

In less than a month, a harsh rebuke and a command for fewer riots and executions arrives. Tiberius is warning us.

"I hope Barabbas likes Roman prison," Pilate snarls, throwing the dispatch onto the desk. "He'll be in it for a long time!"

Jerusalem sees a steady stream of travelers. Libi tells me they pray in the temple for salvation from Rome. "They think the collapse is a punishment for heresy." In addition to the murmurs against Pilate, there are stories of the messiah. He brings a child to life. He spits in the mud, wipes it in the eyes of a blind beggar, and the man receives sight. He teaches and he travels; he performs signs and miracles.

"Five thousand went to hear him preach in Galilee, Prefect... *five thousand!*" Awe is in the centurion's voice.

Pilate dismisses him and his footsteps fade away in the hall,

leaving us contemplating in silence. He drums his fingers on his desk. "Quintus, take a legion to Capernaum. Keep an eye on this messiah."

"We'll leave at once, Prefect."

I approach and ask, "Do you expect trouble?"

"Where large groups gather, it's inevitable."

The streets of Jerusalem are quiet as the year wanes, but excitement is in the air. Even the high priests are not immune to it, and whenever they come to speak to Pilate, they seem uneasy.

One morning I wake and vomit over the side of the bed. My skin is flushed and hot to the touch, but with a thrill of hope, I send for the doctor.

"You're not with child," he says.

The rest of his visit passes in a blind haze. He forces me to drink a potion. I sink onto the bed as Libi approaches with a basin of water. "He healed me! Yet still I'm barren!" Lying in the pillows, I let her sponge my face.

Libi squeezes my hand. "Don't lose hope in him! All things happen in God's time. If he healed you, have faith in him!"

"So I must have faith without reassurance?"

Her eyes darken and she strokes my hand. Pilate enters and she quickly withdraws. He sits on the bed beside me. "The physician says it will pass."

"Yes," I whisper.

Gentle hands dip the sponge in water and press it to my face. "This morning, word came from Herod; his lands are invaded and his armies challenged by a greater military force. Since it is in Rome's best interest for Herod to stay in power, I am sending four legions to his defense. I must go to him. I can't send a proxy."

"What force is it?"

Drops of water slide into my toga. Pilate puts aside the sponge to take my hand. "Aretas, the father of the queen Herod threw over for Herodias."

"How long will you be gone?"

"If all goes well, I'll return in a month. If not, before the Passover." He offers me a scroll sealed with the royal insignia. "In my absence from Jerusalem, Demetrius and you will act as my official representatives. He will appear in public in my place if needed, but will report to you for any decisions."

The door opens and a centurion says, "Prefect, the legions

are prepared to move out on your orders."

"I'm coming." Pilate takes my face in his hands. His eyes soften. "You're a woman of Rome, Claudia. Do her proud in my absence." He kisses me and leaves. I finger the scroll. All I want to do is sleep.

Several days pass before I can preside in his stead. It feels strange to sit behind his desk and read the never-ending list of complaints from the local and outer provinces, to look through the arrest logs, to distribute payment for the legions, and to send regular dispatches to Rome. We must repair the aqueducts and I meet with his architects and spend several hours discussing solutions. Pilate leaves instructions for no judicial trials until his return, so I have nothing to do with the prisons. Due to the imperial ban on further executions, they are full of prisoners: thieves, murderers, and rebels.

"I must speak to you of Barabbas," says Demetrius.

The prison registry is before me, shocking me with its numbers. "What of him?"

"He's causing trouble: spitting at guards, shouting at all hours of the night so the other prisoners can't sleep, insulting his jailers. Our cells are so full we put him in with another man, and he beat him to death with a rock for arguing with him over the Roman occupation. Under normal circumstances we'd have him crucified."

Disgusted, I ask, "Can you isolate him?"

"We can, with some trouble." Demetrius hands me another scroll to seal with Pilate's insignia. "But it won't solve the bigger problem of Barabbas' support in Jerusalem. He's one of the more militant insurrectionists, and his followers want him released."

I read it and drip wax on the parchment. "You want to execute him?"

"Yes, it will put an end to it."

Sunlight falls through the columns. Leaving the desk, I go to the balcony and gaze out over Jerusalem. "But it might start a riot."

"The longer he remains imprisoned, the more dissent we face among his followers. The longer we allow him to criticize Rome and stay alive, the more his reputation as a 'messiah' grows. He *must* be executed."

Shivering, I stare at the temple. Much as I fear Barabbas, I refuse to sentence him to death. "Pilate returns in a few days.

You may talk it over with him."

Demetrius leaves me. I lean against the wall and stare at Jerusalem, stirring only when Libi slips into the room. "My brother is here to speak with Pilate's representative," she says.

"Is Demetrius gone?"

She nods.

"Then he must speak with me instead."

I meet him in the outer courtyard, draped in his finery, his fingers tight around his father's staff. Jacob regards me in open disbelief. "Pilate leaves his *wife* as consul in his absence? I know he doesn't respect the temple, but he might have greater respect for its messengers!"

"Pilate respects you as much as you respect him. You did not come here to insult me. What is it?"

Resentment broods between us. Jacob grinds his teeth and asks, "What have you heard of the messiah?"

I ask, "Which one, Jesus or Barabbas?"

He scowls at me. "Jesus!"

Wind stirs my tunic and casts the scent of oil from the temple. "They say he heals the blind, tends the sick, makes water into wine, and makes cripples walk."

"He also doesn't abide by the Sabbath!"

I walk the edge of the garden with him at my side.

"It's against our laws, yet he heals and performs miracles on the Sabbath! He and his 'disciples' travel on the Sabbath!" Contempt rings in his voice and it deepens into a snarl. "Have you heard what he says of the temple and the high priests? He calls us vipers and thieves! He accuses us of heresy!"

"And this is the business of Pilate?"

Dark eyes burn at me, alight with hatred. "If he speaks against us, it's only a matter of time until he speaks against Rome. You heard of the crowd he amassed on the shores of Galilee, didn't you?"

"Five thousand," I answer, longingly.

"Yes! They wanted to crown him King of the Jews! Pilate makes it clear there is one authority in Judea—Rome! This false prophet and so-called messiah will come here in a few weeks for Passover with his followers. Imagine if he turns the mob against the temple, against your husband!" His hand grips the staff so hard his knuckles whiten.

"From what I've seen and heard of this messiah, he never speaks against Rome." Pausing at the end of the courtyard, I

turn to him. "But I will tell Pilate of your concerns. He returns in a week."

Jacob thanks me with bitter eyes. He sees his sister and hesitates. Libi moves forward hopefully until with a frown he turns and sweeps through the gate.

I find it hard not to hate him.

The palace without Pilate feels empty and I go upstairs to watch his approach from the roof. A garrison rides with him, kicking up a cloud of dust as other travelers move aside to let them pass. Once they enter the city, I go downstairs. My heart leaps as he dismounts, handing off his reins to a servant. I take his arm as we go inside. "Is Aretas defeated?"

"Yes, but he took out Herod's army in the process. His forces are completely humiliated." Pilate washes his hands in a basin held by a servant and dries them on linen. "I trust nothing needs my attention?"

The servant leaves the room.

"Our prison overflows, the high priests are concerned what the messiah may bring to the temple at Passover, and Demetrius thinks we should reinstate executions. But I—"

His mouth covers mine. I lean against him, the dust from his armor rubbing onto my toga. The touch of his fingers against my spine sends thrills through me. Pilate traces the curve of my lip with his thumb. "How I missed you, Claudia."

"It's your own fault for leaving."

Blue eyes dance with laughter and he silences me with another kiss.

Chapter Seventeen

Quintus arrives three days before Passover week, but I remain unaware of his arrival until I see his servant in the hall. The massive man bows his head to me as I enter the office, where Quintus is giving a full report.

"And you met with no violence on the road?"

His helmet under his arm, Quintus says, "No, Prefect. Other than travelers coming for the Passover, it's quiet."

I return my scroll to its shelf. Pilate says, "The temple priests are concerned with Jesus of Nazareth. What do you know of him?"

"He heals the blind, casts out demons, makes lepers clean... they say he can raise the dead. He is not violent, and any suggestion of proclaiming him 'King of the Jews' is met with his disapproval. I saw a mob try it once. He simply disappeared."

Pilate blinks and raises an eyebrow, "Disappeared?"

"Yes, Prefect, there one minute and gone the next. No one saw where he went but by the next day he resumed his travel and the crowd followed him. From what I saw on the road on my way here, many will follow him to Jerusalem. I'd advise anticipating twenty thousand Jews or more."

Shock fills the faces around me. Demetrius asks, "Should we send for another legion, Prefect?"

"Send for *five* legions. I want Jerusalem full of Roman soldiers to dissuade riots. How soon can they arrive?"

"From Caesarea, within a day, but from the outer provinces, it'll take longer... the middle of the week?"

Pilate nods and Demetrius quickly leaves us. The first garrison arrives the next evening, slipping into the city under the cover of darkness to avoid suspicion. Pilate meets with the Sanhedrin to discuss the impending Passover week, leaving me with Quintus.

"This messiah of yours is ... interesting," he says.

Wind stirs the curtains in the hall. I bite into a piece of fruit. "What do you mean?"

"Messiahs are common in Judea yet this one is different. He never speaks against Rome. He claims to come not to liberate men from oppression but make their souls right with God. Unlike the sorcerers in Rome, his miracles are still working

after a week. Lepers are still clean, the blind still see, and the lame walk."

His servant enters the room. Quintus watches him pour the wine and retreat demurely to a corner. "I went to him, Claudia," he says softly.

I look at him in surprise.

"Pilate sent me there to see him, follow him, listen to him; I spent weeks watching him heal, bless, and bring peace to his people and anyone else who approached. He spoke to Jews and Gentiles, men, women, and children. I heard him speak Greek, Hebrew, and Latin."

Footsteps pass in the hall; we wait until it is quiet. Quintus lowers his voice. "Not long ago, Germanius fell ill and the physicians couldn't heal him. Jesus returned to Capernaum. I ran to meet him on the road. I asked him to heal my servant. I fell on my knees before him, and begged for Germanius' life."

I glance at the servant, who is listening to us.

"He offered to visit the house despite it making him unclean. I told him not to, that he could heal Germanius on the road, if he willed it. And do you know what he told me, Claudia?"

Stillness fills the room, sending shivers up my spine.

"That he'd not found such faith in all Judea." Smiling distantly, Quintus swirls the wine in his goblet. "I returned home to find Germanius healed and in the kitchen preparing my supper!" He laughs without humor and looks at me. His eyes soften. "Claudia, he *is* the messiah. He's *their* messiah and yet... he healed my servant."

"Maybe he's our messiah too," I whisper.

Pilate returns and we say no more. I retire but sleep uneasily, knowing more legions enter the city. Morning dawns with an unexpected sharpness, a swelling of anticipation in the streets. Restless, I go out and hunt down my husband in his office.

"My dressmaker is finished with my new toga. I want to pick it up myself," I tell him. His hand covers mine against his chest. I lean over his chair from behind and rest my face against his.

"Take Quintus with you."

I pass Demetrius on the way out and hear Pilate say, "Now, these executions..."

My tailor lives not far from the city gates. Libi walks with us,

now and again glancing at Quintus. Nearly at her door, we hear a loud cheer. People race past us out onto the road. Quintus pulls me out of their way.

"What is it?"

None of us can see over the crowd waving their hands. "I'll go," says Libi, and disappears into the throng. So many are shouting it is hard to make out the words.

"*Hosanna!*"

Children pass carrying palm fronds, fighting their way to the front.

"*Messiah!*"

I look at Quintus in astonishment. "Is that...?"

His hand catches my elbow and pulls me forward. The crowd jostles us as we strain to catch sight of him, and part as Jesus enters the gates riding a donkey, its colt trailing at its side. They throw cloaks into his path and we drift with the crowd along the street. Quintus asks, "Do you see Libi?"

Tearing my eyes from Jesus, I search the eager faces. Libi is not among them but it is hard to see anyone, there is so much excitement. Quintus leads me into an alley as the mob passes. "I must take you home!" I start forward and he grabs me. "This will turn into a riot, Claudia! Pilate won't want you here!"

He drags me away. The chant follows us through the streets, growing louder as the procession goes toward the temple. We force our way through the crowd; the noise is a dull roar when we reach the palace.

Pilate meets us at the gates. "What is it?"

"Their messiah enters Jerusalem."

Sending Quintus a sharp look, Pilate asks, "Will it turn into a riot?"

"I don't know, Prefect."

The shouting intensifies as Jesus nears.

"Do we have men in the square?"

"Yes, Prefect," says Demetrius.

Shouts pass behind the gates and move toward the temple. Pilate motions to his guard. "Watch them but don't interfere unless it turns violent."

At nightfall, Libi returns. I watch for her from my balcony and hurry downstairs as she crosses the yard, but Quintus intercepts her first. I stop in the shadows.

"Are you all right?"

Her face falls into the torchlight as he catches her arm,

123

causing her veil to slip. Her eyes shine with happiness. "I'm more than all right; I sat at his feet and heard him speak!"

"You shouldn't scare me like that!"

Libi glances at his hand and her face alters; she steps back. "You're not my guardian; there's no need to worry."

"I worry because I *love* you."

Fear causes her to look toward the house. The doorway hides me from view. "You shouldn't say that."

"I *must* say it."

She lifts her veil to cover her thick, dark hair, and his hand catches hers. "Don't. Why must you hide from me?" He touches the side of her face and she pulls away.

"Stop it."

Quintus steps before her. "Please, don't leave me. I ask your forgiveness."

Shadows form around them. Libi stares at him. "Why?"

"I wanted you at the cost of your good name. Evil drove me to want you for my mistress, to force you to give up your faith for my pleasure." He lifts her hand to his armor, over his heart. "Forgive me. *Please.*"

"I forgive you," she whispers.

A servant crosses the hall behind me to light the lamps and I dart out of sight. Quintus kisses her hand and says, "My commission will be up in a few years. If you'll wait for me, I will marry you."

"But you're not a Jew." Her tone wavers with hope.

Quintus rests her head against his. "Does it matter to our messiah? Your own high priests dislike him."

"I don't know," she whispers.

"That isn't a 'no,' so I'm content." Quintus moves away from her. "Go to your mistress."

By the time she appears in my room, I lie on the bed staring at a scroll in the lamplight. I put it aside and sit up. "What happened after you left us?"

"He went to the temple and then to a room above an inn here in Jerusalem. I did not dare go inside until Mary, the sister of the woman we met in Bethany, saw me and invited me to eat with them. I listened to him speak, and when it got late and they departed, I hurried home." Taking my hand, Libi says, "As I left, he pressed my hand like this and said, 'Tell her not all dreams are evil.' "

The candle flames sputter in the draft and the hair lifts on

my neck. Her eyes search mine. "Do you know what it means?"

I shake my head. "I haven't dreamt in a long time."

Jesus' words linger in my mind long after she leaves. I ponder them until Pilate enters. "The Messiah certainly frightens the high priests. They are terrified he will disrupt the Passover. I've spent the last two hours warning them to keep order in the temple unless they want me to shut its doors."

"You can't do that on their holy week!"

Dismissing the servant holding his armor, Pilate joins me in bed. "I won't if I don't have to. The mob that followed him into Jerusalem concerns me. They might turn ugly if I refuse them. I've seen it here before, and in Rome." Playing with my fingers, he adds, "Herod arrived in the city tonight, five hours later than he anticipated. The procession held him up on the road! He followed the messiah into Jerusalem unnoticed!"

I shake with laughter. "I'm sure he *hated* that."

He smirks. "I'm sure Herodias hated it, too. I must pay him a diplomatic visit and console him. I would ask you to come with me and save me from Herodias, but my accountants want to see you. You made an impression on them in my absence."

Turning over to look at him, I ask, "Is that all right?"

"If you want to oversee that bunch of conniving, coin-counting thieves, I'm delighted. I'd rather fight a Roman gladiator single-handed than listen to them complain."

Most of them are old and I pretend not to know that they like me as much for my appearance as my mind. Patiently, I listen to their various appeals, concerns, and ideas with interest. "So we *are* low on funds," I say.

"Yes, Mistress," says one of them, bowing. "The collapse of the aqueducts proved expensive, and the temple refuses to contribute to its repair."

Another man says, "Caiaphas is unreasonable!"

Seated on my husband's judicial seat in our inner room, I answer, "It *is* his money, after all."

"It should benefit Jerusalem, not line his pockets." The man flushes under my sharp glance.

I smile. "Still, we must not count on their involvement. Taxes will soon be levied in Judea, can we last until then?"

"If we cease the rebuilding process," he says, "yes. Work stopped in honor of Passover week. We could simply not start up again."

Distant noise comes to us, a faint roar outside. I itch to go

and see what it is and shift in the chair. "It sounds reasonable. What might the fallout be?"

One of the men steps forward. He is younger than the others are. "I doubt any will speak against it. Many see the collapse as a judgment from God. It's difficult enough finding men to work on it, as it is."

The noise continues and several of them look toward the open arches. My fingers tighten on the arm of the chair. "Is that all?"

Glances shift between them and all nod. Darting into the hall, I collide with Libi. "What's happening?"

"I don't know, but it's in the temple!"

Screams fill the air as we go upstairs, to the balcony overlooking the courtyard. It is hard to see through the frenzy of movement; overturned tables, scattered coins, doves fluttering into the air, people fleeing in a panic out into the street. I hear the crack of a whip and flinch.

"Can you see who it is?" I ask, craning my neck.

Her voice is quiet. "You know who it is."

Shocked, I look at her. Guards move uneasily below. A crash returns my attention to the temple.

Everything stops and silence falls in Jerusalem.

Chapter Eighteen

Caiaphas is furious. "He entered our temple! He turned over the tables! He chased out everyone with whips! He called us a den of thieves!"

I know the look in Pilate's eye, one of amusement. "I fail to see what business this is of mine. You've told me many times that it's your god, and not Rome, that governs law in the temple."

"You're the judicial authority in Jerusalem! You must put a stop to this!" Caiaphas bangs his staff on the floor.

Pilate leans back in his chair. "This messiah..."

"He *isn't a messiah*," Jacob hisses.

"This... *man* is a Jew, isn't he?"

"Yes."

"Yet he disrupts the temple in Passover week?"

Jacob scowls. "Yes."

"Then he's yours to deal with, along with your temple guard. I have no authority in religious disputes, since he commits no crime and harms no one. He entered Jerusalem with over a thousand followers. Unless you want a riot that will force me to close the temple, I suggest you leave him alone."

"But Prefect—"

A lifted hand indicates the interview is at an end. With a final seething glance, Caiaphas leads his rabbi out. Pilate descends from his judgment seat. "I've seen enough of the high priests to last for months. Let's hope the rest of this week is uneventful."

Several days pass without significance. The moneychangers and tradesmen return to the temple. I busy myself with the state of our Roman treasury and with organizing our library. Libi helps me. Neither of us says much, other than to remark on the location of important documents.

"Do you feel like something is coming, Claudia?" She stares out the window behind us at the darkening skies. A breeze blows through the curtains, moving them eerily against the columns. The skin on my arms prickles. "I feel it here," she continues, pressing a hand to her breast.

Touching her shoulder, I smile reassuringly and put Plato on the shelf. The feeling leaves neither of us. Her face is uncertain and pale as she serves supper and readies me for

bed. Pilate notices my unusual quiet and putting his arms around me, says, "It'll be over soon."

Sleep descends and I dream. I wander the halls of our palace, pausing to listen for the small cry that tugs at my heart. It is a child's cry and I follow it to the judgment seat. There is no infant, no child. It is empty. I move forward and my sandal tips over a basin, spilling blood onto the floor. It seeps into the hem of my toga, causing me to move backward.

Claudia...

The messiah stands before me, torn flesh covering his body. *Forgive him.*

I lower my hands from my mouth. *Jesus?*

He stretches out his hands. I can see through the nail marks in them. His blood covers the floor.

No!

He smiles at me sadly.

The judgment seat is no longer empty. Pilate sits on it. Water drips from his hands and turns red as it reaches the floor. Emptiness is in his eyes. *Claudia,* he says, without moving his lips.

I feel someone shaking me. Darkness fills the room and the messiah fades.

"Claudia, wake up!"

Strong hands lift me from the damp pillows. My eyes fly open. Pilate leans over me, concerned. I push him away and fall out of bed. He kneels beside me. "Claudia, what happened?"

Choking sobs wrack my body. I shove him away, not wanting him to touch me, to comfort me.

A knock sounds at the door. "Prefect?"

The room feels cold as his hands leave my shoulders. He crosses to the door and opens it. Demetrius says, "I'm sorry to wake you but the Sanhedrin guard arrested the Galilean messiah. I thought you should know."

My heart pounds and my hands shake. Pilate glances at me. "Where have they taken him?"

"He's in the temple courts, on trial."

Dim light shines across the floor from the hall. I reach up and draw the coverlet off the bed, shivering. Pilate considers carefully. "How many know of this?"

"Almost no one, they arrested him a couple of hours ago. Most of his followers fled. There are a few people outside the

temple but not many."

He looks at me again. "Keep an eye on them." The door shuts with a soft click. Dawn colors the east in faint streaks. Pilate returns and pulls me to my feet. I try to push him away and he tightens his grip. "Claudia, look at me. Tell me your dream. It's this, isn't it?"

I whimper.

His eyes soften. "I can't help if you don't *tell me*."

I yank my arm out of his hand. "You'll kill him." Fear enters his face followed by disbelief. I take his hand. "And when you do, his blood will be forever yours. It will ruin us and bring your downfall."

Pilate's fingers slip from mine.

"Don't condemn him," I plead.

Emotion flickers behind his gaze. He turns and leaves the room. I lean on the table for support and then go to the door. My appearance causes our servant to stir from his place against the far pillar. "Send Libi to me, wake her if you must."

I remove my damp clothes and dress. She enters and I tell her what happened. "Go to the temple courts. Stay with his followers. Tell me if anything happens."

The city sleeps and dawn approaches. I pace until footsteps sound in the hall. I accompany Quintus into Pilate's office. He stands on his balcony overlooking the city.

"The high priests want to speak with you, Prefect."

Pilate nods. I follow him into the judgment room. He crosses to the seat. "I see you didn't take my advice, Caiaphas."

"It's in the best interest of Rome, Prefect."

Standing there in their rich robes, I find it hard not to hate the high priests. My eyes move to Jacob's self-satisfied expression.

"I'll be the judge of that," says Pilate.

Tension fills the air. Caiaphas bows his head.

"Why have you come to me?"

Moving closer, the priest says, "This man claims to be the messiah. He's a heretic and must be killed."

"Then do it."

Caiaphas leans on his staff. "Alas, we can't, Prefect, not so near Passover. It will make us unclean."

"I see, so you want me to do it for you." Approaching them, Pilate asks, "What did this man do to merit such a punishment?"

The priests look at one another in distress. "Surely, his professions as the messiah—"

Pilate waves them off. "There's many gods in Rome. What do we care if Judea claims one more?"

"By our laws, Prefect, he deserves death!" Jacob shoves his way to the front.

Recognition glints in Pilate's eye. "And those that defy the laws of Judea deserve death?"

Jacob lifts his chin. "Yes."

"And those who defy the laws of Rome?" Jacob glares at him. Pilate smiles and rests an arm on the judgment seat. "I will speak with him."

"He's in your prison," says Caiaphas.

Nodding to Demetrius, Pilate leaves the room. "Let me come with you," I plead.

He considers me and says, "You won't like it."

The steps descend into torch-lit gloom that is damp and smells of urine, blood, and death. Six steps further we enter a large room surrounded in barred cells. The stench intensifies with the unwashed prisoners. Blood stains the stone floor and tables, where presumably the men are flogged and tortured. Filthy faces turn to leer at me, lips snarling in disapproval.

"Stay away from them," warns Demetrius.

Through an arch, I can see more cells, stretching into the darkness. Only one of them is unoccupied, but when I step closer, I make out the shadowy form in the corner. Demetrius snarls, "Barabbas."

His eyes glower at me. Shuddering, I move forward. Jesus is at the far end. Pilate nods to the guard and he unlocks the door. His face is battered, his lip bloodied, yet he looks calm.

Pilate looks at our guard.

"He entered thus, Prefect."

Stepping in the cell, Pilate motions the temple guards out. Jesus stands in chains. I take hold of the bars. "So you're the messiah."

Jesus searches his face and looks at me. He smiles.

Pilate tilts his head. "That *is* what they call you. Caiaphas is offended by it."

"He's offended by what he can't understand."

Torchlight plays across their faces. Pilate circles him and leans over his shoulder. "It's another name for the King of the Jews. Are you such a king?"

"Is this your own question or did others speak of me?"

From his snort, I know Pilate is impressed. "Am I a Jew? Do I care whom the people of Judea call their savior? No, I'm only concerned with a threat posed to Rome." He stops before Jesus. They regard one another. "*Are* you a threat to Rome?"

Jesus' face softens and his voice is gentle. "I'm not an earthly king. If so, you could not arrest me. My kingdom isn't of this world."

"Then you *are* a king?"

The messiah looks at me. "I came to bring truth to the world. All who love truth recognizes what I say is true."

Pilate asks, "What *is* truth?"

A soldier speaks quietly to Demetrius. He enters the cell and says, "Prefect, there are people gathering at the palace gates. They know he's here."

He nods and returns his attention to Jesus. "You're accused of many things. Do you give an answer?"

Sadness is in Jesus' expression. He says nothing.

Pilate leaves the cell and the guards lock it. I walk with him out of that wretched place. "Let him go."

"I can't, but I *can* send him to Herod." He returns to the judgment chamber and says, "I find no fault in this man. Furthermore, my authority to do as you ask is insufficient. He's a Galilean, is he not?"

Caiaphas flushes with displeasure. "Yes."

"Take him to Herod, then. Since he shares your faith you may find him more willing to condemn an innocent man."

Angry mutters accompany them outside. Motioning to Demetrius, he adds, "Send twelve guards with them. I want four hundred in the city streets. Tell them they are to keep peace but use as little violence as possible. I won't have riots in Jerusalem on the eve of the Passover."

We wait. I sit in anguish.

Footsteps sound in the hall. I tense and look up as Pilate turns from the window. Demetrius enters. "Herod sends him back to you, Prefect. He says he wants nothing to do with his imprisonment or execution."

My heart plummets. I can barely breathe.

"How many of his followers are in the street?"

A distant roar moves with the traveling prisoner. Demetrius' eyes darken. "There's more every minute, and over two hundred in the last hour."

"Bring me Caiaphas *and* the prisoner."

Light shines through the columns. Jesus' chains drag on the floor. Two temple guards flank him on either side. Caiaphas glares at him in disgust and turns as we enter. I remain behind as Pilate crosses to them. He motions to Jesus' bloodied face. "Is it your custom to punish the prisoner *before* his trial?"

"Surely you don't have pity on him!"

Jesus glances at the high priest, who refuses to look at him. Pilate shakes his head. "I see no guilt in him. Even Herod finds him blameless. He's done nothing to merit Roman punishment."

"He's a *pretender*," hisses Caiaphas, his face inflamed. "He claims he's *the messiah*, the King of the Jews. Isn't this against the rules of Rome?"

Quintus enters the room, a scroll in his hand.

"Rome cares little for self-professed messiahs. I'll have him flogged for his insolence, but that's all."

Angry murmurs spread among the priests. Caiaphas shouts, "You can't deny the people their justice!"

Pilate holds out his hand and Quintus gives him the scroll. "In his last imperial dispatch, Emperor Tiberius decrees that in honor of his birthday, one prisoner can be released to the crowd at Passover. Since your people call for justice, we'll let them decide." He nods to the guard and they leave. I hear the gates drag open and people stream into the courtyard. They take Jesus out and Pilate follows. The mob moves uneasily. Demetrius disappears and returns minutes later with Barabbas. He shoves the man to the base of one of the pillars. He is more frightening up close and those nearest the bottom of the stairs shudder. Caiaphas and his priests take their place.

Pilate strides out between them. "I offer you a choice between two prisoners. One will be released: Barabbas, a murderer and thief, or your messiah."

I tighten my hands on the wall and pray.

"Barabbas," says a voice in the crowd. Faces twist to look at him. The cry repeats, "Barabbas! We want Barabbas!"

I cannot breathe. Quintus is as horrified as I am. Even Pilate is shocked. "You want me to release a murderer instead of your messiah?"

"He's not the messiah!" snarls Caiaphas. "He wants an uprising. Better one should die for a nation than all suffer the wrath of Rome!"

The crowd screams in support, stamping their feet. Barabbas leers at them and spits on his guard. Pilate nods and they release him. He looks at me and I feel sick.

"What should I do with your messiah?" Pilate asks.

All my hope is gone. I sink to the floor.

"Crucify him," I hear in a haze. "Crucify him!"

I cover my face with my hands. Pilate says, "An innocent man doesn't deserve death. He'll be flogged."

The crowd roars in disapproval. He turns to my brother. "Quintus..."

"Choose another, Prefect."

The brokenness of his voice causes me to look up, and I see the misery in his eyes. Pilate falters and turns to another guard. "Make it severe, but *keep him alive*." He supports me as we enter the palace.

I hear each blow, each tearing of flesh and crack of the whip. I flinch and look to my husband. Pilate stands at the window staring into grim skies.

"I've ordered many floggings and never regretted any of them before. Why does he torment me?"

Crack!

I cringe. "He's the son of God."

Pilate glances at me. "You can't mean that."

"Can't you see it in him?"

Removing his hand from the ledge, he says, "I don't know *what* I see in him. If nothing else, he is a fool. It is within my power to release him, if he would give me a reason! He says nothing in his own defense! It's as if..."

Thunderous snaps echo across the courtyard. My voice trembles. "As if...?"

His eyes search mine, "As if he *wants* to die."

Quiet enters the house and Quintus returns. His gaze remains downcast. "It is finished."

"Release him," I plead.

Both of them look at me. Pilate says nothing as he goes out to face them once again. I rise and meet a servant in the hall, carrying a familiar basin of water.

"What is that for?" Hysteria creeps into my voice.

The boy shrugs. "The Prefect asked for it."

I close my eyes and listen to him hurry away.

Today, the messiah will die.

Chapter Nineteen

Shock is in their faces, and in mine. My hand covers my mouth, to look upon what the Romans have made of the messiah. He is bloody and bruised, his scarlet robe barely covering his torn flesh, his head bowed in pain but lips silent. Even Caiaphas lowers his gaze.

Pilate motions to him. "He's punished."

"This pretender must die." Jacob pushes his way to the front of the priests.

A voice in the crowd shouts, "Crucify him!"

"Yes, crucify him!" the crowd screams.

His face thunderous, Pilate shouts, "You want an innocent man crucified?"

"Jesus of Nazareth isn't innocent! He must die!" Hands wave in the air in a single forward motion, as they chant, "Crucify him! Crucify him!"

Blood stains the floor under Jesus' feet. Pilate turns to him. "Will you say nothing in your defense?"

Guards beat the crowd as they surge forward. Shields knock people over and the priests move aside.

"Prefect, *give them what they want!*" Demetrius' hand is on his sword, concern written in his face.

Jesus says nothing.

"What is *wrong* with you? Don't you realize I have the power to release or to crucify you?"

The centurions draw swords and shove men aside. Jesus looks beyond Pilate to me and his eyes soften. "You have no power over me not given to you from my Father."

"They want me to execute you!"

A shadow falls on Jesus' face as he answers sadly, "The one who brought me to you has the greater sin."

Pilate looks to me, resignation in his eyes. I lean my head on the column as he turns to the crowd. Wearily, he asks, "Will you have me crucify your king?"

"We have no king but Caesar," says Caiaphas. "If you release this man, you're no friend of Caesar. Anyone who declares himself king is against Tiberius and the Empire, and those who harbor them are traitors to Rome!"

It is all I can do to stay upright.

Pilate says, "I find no evidence against this man. What's

done with him is by your will; I won't be responsible for his death."

"Let the blame fall on us, Prefect," says Caiaphas.

The servant is motioned forward. He holds the basin still as Pilate washes his hands. He tells Demetrius "Give them what they want. Pick two others under sentence and do them as well."

A dull ache fills my spirit as the messiah walks away. I move along the balcony to keep him in sight, until the crowd swallows him up. Jacob follows at a distance. Entering the outer chamber with us, Caiaphas says, "You've made the right choice, Prefect."

Pilate looks at him and narrows his gaze. "I want it written on the cross 'This is Jesus, King of the Jews.' "

"He's *not our king!*" Caiaphas turns red. Our scribe looks between them, pen poised.

Pilate answers, "He is if I say he is. You have your blood. Now take it and *get out.*"

The priests retreat. Outside the palace, the crowd retreats into a dull roar. I move toward the door.

"I forbid it," says Pilate.

Fear creeps over me and I look at him.

"Golgotha is no place for you, Claudia."

The hill rises above Jerusalem. I can see it from the palace, the place where men die.

"I must see it."

We study one another and he looks to Quintus. It is a long while before he nods. I tell a servant to fetch my plainest cloak. Grabbing my arm, Quintus says, "This is madness! Have you ever *seen* a crucifixion?"

The thought makes me sick.

"Do you *know* what happens when men are nailed to a cross and left to die?" His eyes hold as much misery as mine; his voice breaks. He releases me as the servant girl returns.

I tie the cloak around my shoulders with trembling fingers. "If it's too much, I'll come home."

People fill the streets, some of them shouting insults at the three men carrying their crossbeams to the hillside; others openly weep. I fight my way through them to see the messiah, dragging under the weight of his burden. He stumbles and from the fresh blood soaking through his cloak, I know he has fallen several times. Centurions shove the crowds, threatening

them with whips. I hardly have to move; others carry me with them, Quintus struggling to remain at my side. The voices that once shouted "Hosanna, Messiah!" now hurl slanders and mockery.

Tears fill my eyes. He collapses and the beam nearly hits him on the head. The guard strikes him and he stays on the ground. Quintus darts forward, gripping his arm and halting the whip. The Roman turns on him in a rage, sees who it is, and the anger leaves his face.

"Pick someone to help him! He can't carry it alone!"

Quintus returns to my side and puts his arm around me, as the soldiers seize a man in the crowd. Scorn fills his face but as he helps Jesus to his feet, it changes into compassion. Hooking their arms together, the man says, "Come on, we're nearly there."

We fall in behind the procession. I feel helpless. It takes forever to pass through Jerusalem onto the road. From there, many return home, but others, including Jacob, march forward with determination. He sees me and the look of triumph on his face sickens me.

Hearing my name I turn as Libi stumbles over the rocks and falls into my arms. We cling to one another as Jesus collapses on the hilltop. One of the Romans kicks him aside and drags the crossbeam to its place. Quintus begs, "Come away, both of you!"

One of the other prisoners lands on his cross. Libi turns her face into my shoulder. He screams as they tie his arms and drive nails through his hands. I refuse to watch. My gaze falls on one of several women who sinks to her knees as Jesus falls on his cross.

"His mother," Libi whispers.

She never looks away from him, not even when the nails penetrate his hands. I shut my eyes but am incapable of closing out the sounds, the creak of wood, the pounding of the nails, the cries of agonizing pain from the prisoners. They put the plaque above his head and hoist the cross up. It settles into the hole with a loud thump. Blood soaks into the dry, rocky ground. One of the soldiers kicks dirt over it and picks up Jesus' garments.

"Shall we cast lots for the messiah's robes?" He laughs and others join in. I feel a surge of hatred for them. Instinct shifts me forward; Quintus holds me.

The weary voice draws our attention heavenward, as Jesus looks into the skies. "Father, forgive them, for they don't know what they do."

Some of the soldiers' amusement fades. Demetrius glares at them, sending them away. He looks up at the cross and then walks away. Numbly, I watch the others cast lots for his clothing. Many pass on the road into Jerusalem and climb the hill to read the inscription.

"The messiah?" a man mocks, gesturing to the cross. On either side of Jesus hang thieves. "You saved others, save yourself!"

He laughs and his companion shouts, "Come down from there, if you truly are the Chosen One!"

I curl my fingers into a fist as they walk away. "How can they mock him? How can they look upon this and have only hatred in their hearts?"

Dirt and tears streak Libi's face. One of the thieves, a gaunt, cruel-looking man, shouts, *"Aren't* you the Christ? Save yourself, and us!"

The other thief coughs up blood. "Be silent! Have you no fear of the Lord? You and I are thieves! We earned our punishment one coin purse at a time! But this man, this messiah, has done nothing wrong!"

I shiver. Their voices fade into the wind as I turn to the skies. I sense the darkness before it arrives. It closes in and fills us with terror. Those on the road hasten into Jerusalem and many with us on the hillside scatter. It is too dark to see my companions and we cling to one another.

"Light torches!" Demetrius shouts.

Something rushes past me, stirring my hair. Quiet fear pervades us as we huddle together. Panicked footsteps pass and stumble; someone falls in a heap. Flames ignite and reveal the soldiers' pale faces. The man at our side turns over and I recognize him. "You're one of the high priests!"

He looks at me in terror and flees.

They thrust torches into the ground, granting us light. I strain to see the messiah but something hides him from me. Shadows swarm over Jerusalem as lights begin to shine in its upper windows.

A rumble starts deep in the earth. The pebbles begin to dance. Soon the earth shakes so violently it sends all to their knees. The prisoners scream on their crosses and in the

distance, a horrible sound comes from the city, the sound of foundations splitting and columns shattering.

"Father!" Jesus' voice speaks over the earthquake. "Into your hands, I commend my spirit!"

Dust rises all around. I scramble to my feet. No one stops me. Demetrius stands at the foot of the center cross, staring up at the messiah, whose head has fallen to his chest. "Surely he's the son of God," he whispers.

Fear drives the rest away from us; they skid down the embankment toward the road and race for the gates of Jerusalem. Only Jacob remains of the high priests. His face is drawn and pale, his hand curled tightly around his father's staff. "He's *not* the messiah," he says.

I clutch my robes and ask, "Do you say it to convince us, or yourself?"

Resentment hardens his gaze. "It's nearly the Sabbath. They must be dead before then."

Demetrius looks at him in contempt, and nods at his men. One of them picks up a club and strides toward the nearest thief. The sickening crunch as his legs break makes me turn away.

"This man is dead, Captain."

Jacob snarls, "Make certain of it!"

Picking up a spear, Demetrius hesitates and then drives it into Jesus' side. He draws out the tip and water sprays into the wind. It hits Jacob and he screams, clawing at his face. He falls to the ground, writhing. Quintus drops to his knees and pulls free his hands. His palms and skin are red, raw, and blistering. "I can't see!" he shrieks. "I can't see!"

Libi cries out; I cover my mouth in shock. She tries to calm him there, in the blood and sand under the cross. I come to my senses. "Get him to his feet! We'll take him with us!"

"No! Where are you taking me?" Jacob strikes at them. It is all Quintus can do to keep him from reeling down the hill. I retrieve his father's staff from the rocks. Gripping his arm, his sister says, "Trust me, brother! I won't let you fall."

He calms and we find our way to the road. The darkness lifts into gloom. Jerusalem is quieter than ever. No one operates the gates but they are open and we pass into the city. All the windows are closed and I sense a prevailing fear. We see only a few people on our way to the palace, one of them looking behind him as if fearing an enemy will loom up out of

the darkness. Even the temple torches are out. Inside the palace, our servants are nowhere in sight. Two men wait in the judicial court.

Repressing a shiver, I look into Libi's terrified face. "Take him upstairs and tend to his eyes. I will find a physician. Quintus, help her."

Stooped under his weight, Quintus takes him away. I lean the staff against the wall and seeing movement out of the corner of my eye, start. I relax as Pilate emerges from the shadows.

"Jacob got injured at Golgotha." My voice is quiet, distant. "He can't see."

Pilate is surprised but asks nothing as he holds out a scroll. One of the men in the outer room hurries to accept it. "Thank you, Prefect."

"See to it he's buried by nightfall."

Bowing slightly, they disappear into the gloom. I avoid looking at my husband. "I must find a physician."

He catches my arm to stop me and gently, turns my chin to meet his gaze. "Say what you think. Tell me you've never hated me more, that what I did today is unforgivable."

I feel anger but not hatred, anger for those who did this to the messiah. Torches flicker around us. Emotion fills my voice. "When they nailed him to the cross, he said, 'Forgive them, for they don't know what they do.' He forgave all of them, including you. *That* is the man you let be crucified."

His voice stops me in my flight through the hall. "What *is* truth, Claudia?"

I glance at him.

"Rome says truth is one thing, your messiah another. He might have spoken to me, told me his version of the truth, but he remained silent." Pilate moves toward me. "So what *is* the truth?"

"You saw the truth in prison and on the steps, when you spoke with him. The messiah *is* the truth."

He shakes his head. "He is dead. Gods can't die."

"But can a mere man look into your soul and *know* you? Isn't that how you felt when you met him?" I press his palm to my heart. "You *know* the truth, Lucius."

Shadows stir and Demetrius enters the hall. Pilate slips free of my grasp. "Is it done?"

"Yes, Prefect, I gave them the body as instructed."

My husband nods. "Put two guards on the tomb."

Bare feet slip silently along the hall and a servant girl says, "Mistress, will you come? Libi asks for you."

As I pass an open arch, I see the first star in the sky. The bells never rang to announce the Sabbath. Libi awaits me in the corridor outside her room. I send for a physician and he soon arrives. Quintus holds Jacob as the physician pries open his eyelid to look. His eye is milky white and oozes pus. It smells of rotten meat. Jacob jerks away from him and the physician gives me a skeptical look. "You say this happened in the last few hours?"

Offended at his implication, I snap, "Yes!"

"This is an infection that takes *years* to fester."

Lifting my chin, I ask coldly, "Do you call me a liar?"

The physician is not stupid. "No, Lady Claudia, but I'm not sure what I can do to help. He will never see again. The infection is too serious. He may even die."

Passing me, Libi takes her brother's hand.

"I'll give him some ointment but..." The physician shrugs. I motion for him to proceed. Jacob moans as we make a thick white poultice with water and medicine, smear it onto a strip of linen, and tie it over his eyes. He resists the tincture we offer him.

"It'll help you sleep. It'll dull the pain."

"Take it away," Jacob growls.

I hold out my hand for it and the physician leaves. I pass it to Libi and she stirs it into a cup of wine. "Take wine, then, brother," she says. He feels for the glass and drinks. I quietly enter the hall with Quintus.

"I don't understand it," he says. "The messiah wouldn't *blind* a man, surely?" Shadows lurk around us. Quintus looks as tired as I feel. He touches the side of my face. "You must sleep. Try not to think of today."

"That's impossible."

His smile turns sad and I leave him there. My feet grow heavier with each step. Pilate awaits me in our room. Avoiding looking at him, I shut the door and go to the bed.

"What did the physician say?"

Tired fingers unlace my sandals. "He can do little. Jacob may die of infection."

I drop the sandal to the floor and stare at my hands. Pilate crosses the room but avoids touching me. "I'm sorry, Claudia. I

wanted to save him."

"But you lacked the courage."

My eyes lift. I want it to hurt him, and it does. Tormented, Pilate leaves the room. I let him go, not wanting him in my bed, unable to bear the arms of the messiah's murderer around me, not tonight.

I cry myself to sleep.

Chapter Twenty

"Claudia, get up!" Libi shakes me awake in the dawn. I turn over and she throws a cloak at me. "Come with me!"

My eyes are raw and emptiness fills me. "What is it?"

She pulls me from bed and drapes the cloak around my shoulders. "I can't say; you must see for yourself."

I follow her outside barefoot. We meet no resistance in passing through the side gate into the street. Libi takes my hand and leads me into the temple, which is quieter than it should be, without a sign of anyone. She hurries toward the inner chamber.

"Libi, I can't enter there, you know that!"

Her eyes are alive with fear. "It won't matter! Come!"

Fearfully, I follow her inside and stop in shock. A tear divides the curtain separating worshipers from the holy place. It hangs limply, the rich brocade moving faintly in the breeze. I can see past it to the altar. Cracks run along the floor, the braziers overturned, charred marks staining the stone. I drop to my knees.

"I came to pray for my brother and found it like this." Libi clutches her veil as she moves forward. "He's gone, Claudia. Jehovah has gone from this place."

"Where are the priests?"

She touches the curtain. "They must have fled. My brother is not the only one punished."

The room is cold. I muster the strength to rise and grip her arm. "Libi, we must go."

No one stirs in Jerusalem but fear is in the air. It lasts throughout the day and into the night. Passover is upon us and the priests return. Jacob worsens. I sit with him awhile to relieve Libi, listening to him moan and feeling him twitch in his sleep. I put a hand over his heart. The door creaks open behind me. Libi sits a cup of water on the shelf beside him, her eyes red from crying. "You must dress for the banquet."

Each year Jews celebrate Passover and the centurions dine with the governor and his wife. I let Libi dress me and put up my hair. Pilate awaits me in the hall. "You look beautiful," he says.

My hand falls into his but I stay silent, unforgiving.

Our centurions are sullen and withdrawn. We drink wine

and share conversation, none of us in high spirits. The jailer leaves earlier than the rest, after sharing harsh words with a companion.

"Surely this dismal mood isn't for the messiah?" asks another. "One man went to death on a cross! But never fear, my friends, if he *is* the messiah, the Jews tell me he'll rise again!" He laughs and others with him.

I bite into a grape.

"Is that what they say?" Pilate asks.

The centurion holds out his cup for a refill. "Yes, three days after the crucifixion the dead will rise."

"Or the body be stolen in the night," Demetrius says.

Pilate asks, "You posted guards at the tomb?"

"Yes, Prefect."

"Then there's no reason for concern."

I turn to him, "Unless he *is* the messiah."

Downcast eyes stare into cups and hands fall from platters. Even the servants stare at the floor. Pilate considers me at length. "No man can cheat death."

"He's *already* cheated death. They say he resurrected Lazarus when he'd been in the tomb several days, and he breathed life into a little girl in Capernaum."

A boy enters the room and speaks in Demetrius' ear.

"You've seen such tricks in Rome."

Smiling, I retort, "Not that lasted more than an hour. Yet Lazarus is still among us, a year later."

Tension flickers between us and Demetrius slips out the side door. Pilate motions the boy forward. "What happened?"

"Your jailer is dead, Prefect, impaled on his sword."

In shock, we stare at one another.

"How did it happen?"

Glancing at the others, the boy lowers his voice. "He fell on it, Prefect... intentionally."

"You may go." Pilate waves him off and relieved, the boy hurries to his duties.

My appetite is gone. I swirl the wine around in my cup. Pilate says, "I know what you're thinking. It isn't true."

"Your jailer scourged Jesus and died. Jacob mocked him on the cross and fell blind. Take care what you say of him, Lucius." I rise and the men stir. "Thank you, all, but I must say goodnight."

The stillness over Jerusalem stirs at dawn with a second

earthquake. It shakes the house faintly and soon fades into nothing. Shivering, I pull a wrap on and go in search of Libi. My sandals echo on the tiles. I round the curve of the wall and collide with someone coming up the stairs.

I scream.

He catches me before I can fall. "Claudia!"

"Don't touch me!" I kick him and scramble across the stone floor. I cover my face with my hands and he gently pries them free. His hands feel warm.

"Claudia," he says softly, "it's me."

"No, you're ..."

Avram smiles at me. "I'm here now." He kisses my hands. He does not feel like a ghost.

I touch the side of his face. "How has this happened?"

"He cried out to us in the earthquake. The stones rolled free and we emerged from our tombs."

My arms go around him, so tight I can barely breathe. "Tell me this isn't a dream!"

"It isn't. He's arisen, my child... the messiah lives!" He pulls me to my feet. "There are many of us to proclaim it in Jerusalem: the voices of Abraham and David, Moses and Elijah, those who lived and died and serve a greater purpose. In a day our prophecy will be done and we'll return to death, but for now we proclaim he lives!" Cradling my face in his broad hands, he says, "Take me to my son. I must speak with him."

"Do you know what happened to him?"

The wonderful brown eyes soften. "Yes, show me."

We pass downstairs and I open the door to Libi's room. She starts from her chair and backs into the wall, covering her mouth with her hand as her father enters. "Don't be afraid, my child... you'll know all in time."

I put my arm around her and draw her closer. "It's him!"

Trembling hands reach out to embrace him and a sob chokes from her throat. On the bed, Jacob stirs. "Who's there? Who is it?"

His father slides the bandages from his eyes, milky white and unseeing. "It is I, my son," he says.

Jacob half sits up at the familiar voice. "*Father?*"

"Yes."

Hazy eyes widen in horror. "No! What deviltry is this? You're dead!"

"Am I?" Avram grips his hand.

Scrambling away from him, Jacob knocks over the table. He falls in a heap in the corner, holding his hands out before him. "Stay away from me! I don't know how you're here, but it's the work of evil!"

"It's the work of the messiah." Avram kneels before him, grabbing him by the shoulders. He shakes him fiercely. "And you *will* listen to me! This blindness is of your own making! He told me. I heard his voice in the depths of the earthquake. He sent each of us to prophesy to those we left behind. Libi believes in him but you, my son, you spat on him, you hated him, you mocked him... and you're punished by your own guilt!"

Jacob kicks at him. "Let me go!"

"You must endure darkness to find the light! Repent, Jacob! Repent and acknowledge him as the messiah!"

Libi covers her mouth, shivering against me. Avram takes his son's hand and presses it against his chest. "Feel my warm flesh, my beating heart! I live! I live so that you might know that he is God!"

Sunlight pours in the window, falling over Jacob. His expression changes and he touches Avram's face with a trembling hand. "It *is* you, isn't it, Father?"

Their heads rest against one another. Tears flow. "It is I," Avram whispers. "*Believe* in him."

Great, choking sobs wrack Jacob's muscular body. Avram opens his arm for his daughter and Libi goes to him. They embrace and weep together. I leave them and lean against the cold stone column in the hall. Rapid footsteps come along the passage. One of my servants catches sight of me and hurries forward. She shrieks, "They're outside the gates... shouting..."

Catching her hand to calm her, I ask, "Who?"

"Ghosts! The dead walk among us!" She bolts into her room and slams the door. I run up the narrow stairs and emerge in the main hall. From the nearest window, I see eerie, luminous faces pressing against the gates.

"Unusual, aren't they?" I jump at the sound of Pilate's voice. He joins me. "Our servants believe them ghosts."

Guards hurry out to force them away, shoving open the gate to disperse them in the street. They scatter, still shouting in Hebrew. "What are they saying?"

He frowns. "They accuse me of killing the messiah."

145

The crowd disperses and their voices fade. Pilate walks toward his office. "For all their faith in their god the Jews are certainly a superstitious lot—ghosts?" He snorts and rounds the corner.

Avram stands before us. "We're not ghosts," he says. Shock holds Pilate in place. The old man approaches. "You're a man of common sense, Pilate. Even as a boy, you wanted proof. Here, it stands before you. I live for this day because the man you put in the ground, the man we *all* put in the ground with our unbelief, lives."

"What trickery is this?" Pilate looks at me.

"It's not trickery, Pilate. I stand before you. Take your sword and drive it through my chest if you want proof. If I must die again to convince you, so be it."

I dart forward as his hand closes on the hilt of his sword. "Don't!"

Pilate steps forward. "You want me to believe this is the work of Jesus of Nazareth? He is dead. I killed him."

"You had nails driven into his hands but you didn't kill him for he isn't dead. Death has no power over the Son of God. I know you, Pilate. You'll believe whatever lie suits you, such as the one carried on the lips of Caiaphas, who now asks for an audience in your courtyard."

A servant appears. "Prefect..."

"Who is it?"

The boy bows his head. "It's high priest Caiaphas."

"I'll see him in a moment."

Returning his attention to Avram, Pilate asks, "What lie will he tell me?"

"Jesus' body was stolen in the night. He's bribed your guards to lie for him."

I rub the chill from my arms. Pilate does not answer but continues to his inner courtyard. I take Avram's warm hands in mine. "Must you go?"

"Yes, there are others I must speak with." My evident disappointment softens his expression. He smiles and kisses my forehead. Cradling my face in his palms, he says, "Have faith, Claudia. No dream foresees all ends. Now go to your husband."

I enter the courtyard several paces behind Pilate. He and Caiaphas regard one another with contempt before he turns to his guards. Both drop to one knee and one says, "Prefect, we

failed our task to guard the tomb where the King of the—"

"—where *the Pretender* lay," injects Caiaphas, pale and with tired lines under his eyes.

Pilate glares at him and motions to the guard. Staring at his feet, the centurion says, "We stood watch all night but fell asleep before dawn. While we slept they removed his body, leaving the stone rolled aside and the burial garment on the floor."

Silence echoes in our ears. Pilate crosses to his chair and sits down. "Why are *you* here, Caiaphas?"

"Some claim no theft took place!"

Tapping his fingers on the armrest, Pilate asks, "And they say... what, that he arose from the dead?"

Caiaphas scowls. "Yes."

"I see." Pilate indicates his men to rise and approach. "Centurion, did Jesus rise from the dead?"

"No, Prefect, they stole his body in the night."

He nods. "The tongues of Jerusalem wag idly, then?"

The centurion glances at me fearfully. "Yes, Prefect."

Light plays across the floor. Pilate dismisses them. "Caiaphas, you created this outcome when you arrested a popular messiah. You deal with rumors of his resurrection. Don't show your face to me again."

Furious, the high priest storms out. Demetrius steps forward and Pilate says, "Find out what happened at the tomb."

Pilate rejoins me in the shadows. "Do you believe them?"

"No, but I'm not convinced of your side, either."

We walk through the arch into the house. "You've always been a man of reason, Lucius."

"And a man without faith, I might remind you."

I clutch his arm. "Think! He healed the blind! He raised men from the dead! He convinced *you* of his innocence! You felt remorse in having him crucified! Have you ever lamented that before?"

Entering our room, he pours a cup of wine.

"Lucius, he survived a brutal scourging and made it to Golgotha without dying on the way. At the hour of his death, darkness covered the sun. The temple floor split in two and the curtain with it. Jacob is blind and Avram lives! How much more must happen to convince you?"

Pilate looks out over Jerusalem. He moves to the balcony

and I go with him. "Does a god surrender to scourging, humiliation, and crucifixion?"

"This one did!"

He rests his arm on the ledge. Gazing into my eyes, his voice softens, "For what reason?"

I wish I knew.

Taking my hand, he says gently, "Find me one."

Chapter Twenty-One

Herod has changed. The pomp is gone from his strut, the pride from his flabby jeweled fingers. A broken man climbs the steps into the palace. My eyes dart to Herodias in astonishment. She takes my arm and I lead her inside. "Ever since Jesus of Nazareth visited us, he's been in a foul mood," she says. "He doesn't sleep, he won't eat. I haven't been summoned to his bed since!"

I cringe at the thought. "And that... troubles you?"

She scowls at me. "Hopefully Pilate will talk sense into him! He drones on over the messiah! 'Did I do the right thing in sending him to Pilate, Herodias?' 'Should I have set him free, Herodias?' 'What do you think of the rumors of his resurrection, Herodias?' "

Flopping onto a lounge, she covers her eyes with one arm and moans. I recline beside her. "What do you say to him when he asks such questions?"

"I remind him that *he* is the messiah." A servant pours wine and she takes the cup from him. Noticing my repulsion, she leans closer. "Oh, don't look at me like that. You know how we must stroke men's egos. I remind him that *he* is the rightful King of the Jews. If his people call for a messiah, why shouldn't it be him?"

My hair moves in the breeze. "Is that wise?"

"Why wouldn't it be?"

Glancing at the servant, I lower my voice. "If there *is* another messiah..."

"Oh, don't tell me you believe the rumors!" Her laugh grates on my ears. "The man is dead, dead and rotting, like the hideous so-called prophet in the desert! They stole his body from the tomb! That changes nothing! These people search endlessly for a messiah! In another year they'll have a new one!" She shoves her cup out for a refill.

I bite my tongue. "What did he say when brought before you? Did you meet him?"

"I did and I thought him unimpressive. At least John had a certain otherworldly air, a mental insanity to make him *entertaining*. But all men die the same, regardless how it happens." Dipping a long, curved fingernail into her wine, she licks it off. Hatred toward her rises within me and I fight it off.

"Will you stay in Jerusalem or return to Caesarea?" she asks.

I force a pleasant expression onto my face. "Pilate tires of endless appeals from the high priests, so we'll return to the coast in a few weeks."

"It's a shame our palaces aren't in the same place. I find company other than yours tiresome."

We spend all afternoon together. I wave her off with a smile and turn into the house. "How was your afternoon with Herod?" I ask Pilate.

"Interesting. He asked my opinion and spoke well. I underestimated him."

My expression turns wry. "Maybe his hour-long audience with the messiah changed him."

"Yes, he expressed concern. He shares my opinion of Jesus' innocence. In that at least, we agree and may call ourselves friends."

Pausing outside my door, I laugh, *"Friends,* you and Herod? Oh, say it isn't so, husband!"

"Don't worry, he's going home. You will not have to see Herodias until next Passover. We'll leave for Caesarea at the end of the week." He touches my hand. I see longing in his eyes but refuse his kiss.

I turn my face away and whisper, "Not yet."

Disappointed, he leaves me. I enter as Libi prepares the bed. She helps me undress. "Tell the servants to pack our things; we're going to Caesarea." She folds my tunic and puts it away. I drop onto the bed and stretch against the pillows. "I miss the cool night air on the coast, and the sight of ships coming into harbor. It'll do your brother good to walk along the shore."

"We're not coming with you."

Her voice is quiet but still I catch it. I sit up in shock. "What do you mean?"

Libi crosses the room to sit beside me. "Do you remember Martha, the woman from Bethany?"

I nod.

"I took Jacob to see her brother Lazarus today. They spoke for hours. They asked us to join them, to become Jesus' disciples, to live with them in Bethany. In another year, Quintus' twenty-year service to Rome ends. He can marry. I want to stay here and wait for him." Seeing my expression, she takes my hand. "Forgive me, Claudia! I love you as a sister but ... I want to stay with Martha and Mary. I want to learn more of

Jesus. It'll be good for Jacob to have me there."

I free my hand. She looks hurt. "But you're my only friend!"

Her eyes search mine. "You have Pilate."

Pushing her out of the way, I get up and cross to the verandah. Wind stirs the curtains.

"You need to forgive him." Quiet footsteps come up behind me. "Pilate has one link with the messiah: you. Our Lord forgave Pilate on the cross. Can you do less?"

The house is quiet, everyone asleep. My bare feet make no noise on the marble floor. Pilate stirs as I lift the netting and crawl under it. He starts to sit up but I push him down. My hand lingers on his chest as I climb on top of him. I kiss his chest, the scars from battle, gradually working my way to his mouth. It caresses mine, gently and with more enthusiasm as he pulls us together. His hands creep up my spine, sliding under my hair as he gazes at me. We search one another's eyes in the moonlight and take comfort in each other. He strokes my hair, his fingers moving to my arm. He kisses the side of my head, his breath warm against my temple. "What was he like, this Galilean?"

I lay my chin on his chest, my voice quiet. "I found him understanding, and kind to everyone."

"Not to the thieves in the temple, though."

His voice is laden with irony and it makes me smile. "It upset him that they'd trade in his father's house."

Pilate kisses my fingers. "What do you know of him?"

"He's good with wood, a carpenter by trade. I never heard him preach but our servants did. He loves children. They went to him with greater understanding and trust than any who hailed him on the road to Jerusalem."

Drawing his hand along my back, Pilate asks, "And you're convinced he lives?"

My heart quickens. "Yes."

He nods and shuts his eyes. I pray for understanding. I want to love him; I want faith in him.

Libi and Jacob leave the next day. They load a cart and Jacob feels for my hand, leaning on his father's staff. He stares past me, into nothingness. "I'm sorry for the miseries I've caused you, Claudia, here and in Rome."

I embrace him and fight tears. Libi helps him into the cart and turns to me. We stare at one another and she throws her arms around me. Her voice shakes with emotion. "I'll write, I

promise."

Tears stream as she drives away. My heart aches in the emptiness of the house. Our departure for Caesarea gives me a much-needed distraction. Pilate has asked me to be involved in finishing Tiberius' Temple.

"The temple should be finished in a month," our architect promises one warm, late summer afternoon. The skies darken and the scent of rain is in the air.

I stare anxiously at the brewing clouds. "Good. Have them finish early today, to get home before the storm hits."

"Thank you, Lady Claudia." He gathers up his things and leaves with a spring in his step.

I lean against the ledge as Pilate enters through the far door. "I met Arteas in the hall. He certainly looked pleased with himself. What did you compliment him on this time?"

"I liked his plan to add a central pillar to the courtyard." I glance at him and gesture at the fierce skies. "What do you think, should we worry?"

Pilate glances out into the harbor, where ships already bob around on the rising sea. "Are *you* worried?"

I grip the ledge. "I have that feeling of dread like I used to get when waking from a nightmare. Something is coming, Lucius... it arrives on the wind from Rome." Shivering, I turn away from the harbor.

Pilate rubs my arms, concerned. "There's an augur in the city. Maybe we should consult him."

Only one sorcerer lives in Caesarea, on the far side of the forum. The air is heavy as we knock on his door and he ushers us inside. Eerie eyes linger on me in disapproval as I lower my hood. The hovel sends chills up my spine. "Come," he says, and takes us to the fire.

Spirits stir in the house, all of them unseen. The hair rises on my neck. He casts black ash into the flames and smoke surrounds us. "What is it you want to see, Prefect?" he asks.

Pilate's hand leaves my arm. He leans forward, his face pale in the sinister light. "What approaches?"

Rain spatters the roof. Smoke surrounds us. It tries to draw me in. I feel it curve around my mind and then... I hear hissing. Audible murmurs enter the gloom. The torches flicker and the augur looks at me. "You're one of them," he snarls.

I swallow but am silent. Darkness tears at me, the room full of growls. Pilate's face is unreadable. "What do you mean?"

"She believes in the messiah."

It comes out in a dreadful hiss. I see the evil in him and reach for my husband. "Pilate, we must leave."

"No." He leans toward the augur. "Tell me what you see in the flames."

They leap and dance, reflecting on our skin and in his terrible white eyes. Something brushes against me, but nothing is there.

"I can't while she's here," he hisses.

Pilate's eyes gleam with interest. "Are your gods weaker than hers?"

Fury lurks behind the man's sullen face. Something moves in the darkness behind us but I see nothing. He shows his teeth. "You want the truth, Prefect?"

"Yes. Prove to me her god isn't stronger than yours."

Thunder cracks overhead. I flinch. A chill hovers over my thin form. Glowering at me, the sorcerer stirs the flames. His eyes dart to me. "Death approaches... death, betrayal, and insanity. The gods are displeased. What have you done to anger them?"

As he speaks, lightening flashes and illuminates the room. His eyes close and when they open, they glow red, reflecting the embers of the dying coals at his feet. Pilate stumbles back from him and I clutch his arm.

"What is this madness?" he whispers.

The house shakes with the violence of the storm. Rising, the old man points at me. "You," he rasps in an unfamiliar, evil voice, "you who have seen him... you will bring great evil into Rome, a force to consume the souls of all who stand in its path."

He lunges at me. I shriek and throw out my hands. Screams fill the air. Smoke pours around us. Hisses slither across the ground. He grips my head and tries to slam it into the wall. I stare into his face, his madness, the widening of his eyes, the gaping mouth as it opens—and see his spirit leave him as Pilate's sword thrusts through his chest. He falls to the floor in a rush of blood. The shutters slam open and wind fills the house, exploding out into the night.

Demetrius breaks through the door. His eyes fall on the dead sorcerer and dart to me, my hands covered in blood.

Evil leaves this house and enters the storm. It screams and wails overhead as we hurry to the palace; it breaks with rage

against the shore; water surges across the tiles and drains into the pool, which overflows as fire tears through the heavens. Rain beats the columns, not reaching the chamber where I lie. Pilate paces the floor into the dawn, his eyes watchful but his voice silent.

For two days, it rains and blows. When it stops, the silence is terrifying. The city is undamaged but the harbor is full of half-sunk ships; their tattered sails ripple in the wind. I shade my eyes to look at them.

"This will delay the finishing of Tiberius' temple," says Pilate as we watch men drag the ships to shore for repairs. "One of the columns collapsed last night."

His architects walk away, their arms full of scrolls. When I stay quiet, he glances at me. "Do you know what they're saying in the streets? The storm is Caesarea's punishment for welcoming us home. This should do a good deal for our popularity."

"It's superstition. It'll fade in time."

He follows me indoors. "You don't believe that."

"Maybe the storm is *our* punishment." I go to the table and sort through the plans the architects left us.

Pilate moves them aside. "What do you mean?"

"This! The temple! The sorcerer! We build a place of worship to a Roman emperor and consult a seer! Why *wouldn't* God punish us?" I dash the plans to the floor and scrolls bounce into the corner of the room.

Pilate is incredulous. "So we abandon it because you're afraid of punishment from the Judean god?"

"You *know* what I believe."

Gripping my arm, he turns me to face him. "Yes! But it *isn't* true."

"Why is it so hard for you to believe it *might* be true?"

He tilts my face up. "You went to him, didn't you? You sought him out in Bethany and asked him to heal you."

Warmth spreads through me.

Leaning nearer, he asks gently, "Then why are you still barren?"

Shock renders me silent.

Pilate's gaze is cold but I am not the focus of his anger. "Wouldn't a true messiah reward your faith?"

His hand drops as Demetrius comes to the door. "A ship has arrived from Rome, Prefect. Here are the dispatches."

Pilate leaves me on the verandah to read them. I try to calm the thunderous pounding of my heart.

"Claudia," he says suddenly. Numbly, I go inside. Pilate looks at me, aghast. "Sejanus was executed."

I stare at him. "Why?"

"Tiberius accused him of treason, for turning against Caligula, and executed his entire family."

My legs give out and I feel for the nearest chair. I take the scroll and read it, the letters blurring before my eyes. "But Sejanus' daughter is just a child!" Superstitions in Rome claim it is bad luck to kill a virgin. I cover my mouth with my hand. Sensing my thoughts, Pilate says quietly, "Let's hope she didn't suffer long."

"Will their attention turn on you?"

"I may have been out of Rome long enough for our association to fade. But we must be careful." Pilate sorts through the other scrolls and opens one from his sister. He frowns and gives it to me.

My dear brother, I arrive on the next ship, the Marcus. *I bring grave tidings from Rome.*

Chapter Twenty-Two

I stand in the empty corridor of the palace, a goblet of blood in my hand. A scarlet trail reaches into the inner chamber, where a figure lies. I drop the cup and run to turn him over, my tunic turning red as it falls into the crimson pool under his body.

No!

Death nears him, a sword at his side. I cradle his head in my arms and kiss his forehead. *You cannot leave me! Please, do not leave me... I need you.*

Claudia...

Pilate breathes his last. Shadows fall across me and I look up into the face of Caligula. The boy from Rome is gone, and a man takes his place. He has Hermina by the hair and throws her at my feet. *You are all traitors to Rome...* His evil eyes drift over me and turn on the centurion at his side, Demetrius.

Kill them all.

The scream rips from my throat as I sit up, the bedclothes dripping in sweat. Pilate's hand is on my shoulder, his warmth at my side. I lean over the edge of the bed and vomit into the chamber pot. Pilate strokes my arm. "Who is it this time?"

Dawn is in the east and thin tendrils of light creep into our room. "Caligula," I whisper.

He presses me to his chest and I cling to him. He smoothes the hair out of my face, his eyes concerned. "Is this because you must visit the temple today?"

"I don't know."

Tiberius' temple is finished and to honor the emperor, we must attend its dedication.

Pilate rises and I grip his hand. "Lucius..."

"It's all right, Claudia. Your presence is for my sake, not yours. You know Tiberius is no god! But we must please him, and play a farce."

The dream casts uncertainty over my day. My unease increases as I exit the chariot. The high priest bows and leads me inside. Pilate accompanies us. Demetrius stays at the foot of the stairs. Flames flicker around us as we approach the altar. The priest places me on one side. "Stand here," he says. He moves to the other side, lifts his hands, and chants, swaying. Emptiness fills the room and nothing stirs. Frowning, he chants louder. Wind sweeps through the columns and the

flames die. The priests exchange mystified looks. Pilate glances at me. Their temple is an empty building, much like the vacant tomb outside Jerusalem. Shaken, he continues the rituals without the usual mysticism.

Much later, we return to the palace. "At least it's over," says Pilate.

Wind stirs the draperies, tinted with smoke. Darkness covers Caesarea and I look to the west. Flames dance atop the sea. The lines of a ship fall into view as it approaches the harbor engulfed in flames, fire licking up the main beam and burning through the sails.

"Lucius..."

He shouts for his soldiers. The harbor fills with movement as people race across the dock. "If they can't keep it from the harbor, it'll set it alight!"

My fingers tighten on the rail as he leaves. Smaller crafts sail out to meet her, oars thrust against her side in an effort to slow her progress. The beam crashes into the deck and flames spill into the sea; screams echo across the water and dark shapes fall overboard. Timbers crack and splinter, flames spread and die; it drifts toward the dock and the people scatter, shrieking. It misses and crashes into another ship. Men rush to put out the fire, but it spreads too fast. The first ship breaks apart and sinks into the sea, flames licking floating timbers.

The second ship takes longer to burn but eventually it too disappears beneath the waves. Since I can do nothing, I turn away from the smoke. I sleep fitfully, waking every few hours to find the bed empty. Before dawn, he returns. Cold air wraps around me as I sit up and grip his shoulders. "What is it?"

"The *Marcus* burned, Claudia."

Horror sinks into me. "Is your sister...?"

"She's dead."

My arms go around him. "I'm so sorry."

Pilate smiles faintly and places his hand over mine. "I keep remembering how we parted in Rome, how angry she was over me separating her from Caligula."

"You spared her from him, at least."

He pulls away from me and goes to the window. "I may have spared her from Caligula, but not from death in a ship ablaze. And you ask why I don't believe in gods?"

Our conversation haunts me in the next three days. Pilate

finds distraction in the arrival of priests from Jerusalem. "I must see a representative of Caiaphas today," he says, "concerning the latest 'messiah' in Jerusalem."

I help him with his tunic and armor, strapping it on. "What do they know of him?"

"In his speeches he's no different from any of their messiahs, but he *is* open in his criticism of Rome, and my spies tell me he gains popularity." His blue eyes seek out mine. "You see, Claudia, your messiah is forgotten. A new zealot arises."

"Jesus' followers have nothing to do with this man."

He touches the side of my face. "I hope not." Kissing my forehead, he leaves as a servant girl enters.

"Octavia, I want to visit the market today."

She offers me a basin full of clean water. "Should we take a guard with us?"

I shake my head.

The harbor sparkles under the sun. Merchants and tradesmen crowd the dock. The scent of fresh fish and fruit fill the air. I move along the stalls making purchases. Feeling eyes on me, I glance across the way. A man looks on with interest. Our eyes meet and he nears.

"You're Pilate's wife, aren't you?" he asks. Fingering some figs, I add them to my basket. I look to Octavia, who indicates one of the centurions stationed at the end of the dock. The man notices and says, "I mean you no harm. I was sent to speak with you."

I move to the next stall. "Is that so?"

"Yes."

"What do you know of me?"

"I know who you are, and of your dreams."

The centurion passes. I turn my face away, hiding it under the fabric of my veil. Stepping around me, he asks softly, "Is it true you warned your husband not to crucify the messiah?"

"Yes."

His face is familiar somehow. "Then you *are* one of us, as he said."

"Who said that?"

A plump piece of fruit lands in my basket. "*He* did."

Cold cascades over me. "What did he say to you?" I sneak a look at his face as he looks out over the sea. He picks up a fig and pays the stall boy for it. On his way past, he says, "I'm to tell you that dreams are forewarnings of what *may* come, not

what *will* happen. The fate of many can be changed through a single act."

Turning after him, I say, "You're one of his disciples."

"Yes, I'm Peter." Smiling, he disappears in the crowd.

I hand Octavia the basket. She trails after me along the dock. I reach the end and turn to the palace but stop to let passengers disembark from a ship. One of them catches my eye, a lean, small feminine face hidden in a veil. When I run after her and pull it off, Hermina starts in alarm and softens at the sight of me. Her arms go around me and we cling to one another. "We thought you dead!"

"I'm meant to be!" Trembling, she glances into the crowd around us. Her face is pale, her thinness worrying me. She looks ill. "It isn't safe! No one must see us! Go to the palace! Leave your servant so I may enter in secret!" Replacing her veil, she hurries away.

"Go with her!"

Octavia runs after her, weaving through the crowd. My stomach knots and I look around to see if anyone is watching. Returning home I pace until she arrives. She takes my hands in hers. "No one saw me and no one outside of you and my brother, apart from trusted servants, must know that I'm here. He *must* believe I'm dead!"

"Who are you talking about?"

She sinks into the nearest chair. "Caligula! He had me followed, tried to stop me... so many died because I said I'd sail on that ship!" Covering her face with her hands, she takes several ragged breaths.

I pour her a cup of wine. "Octavia, is my husband out of conference?"

The girl tears her eyes away from Hermina long enough to nod. I rest my hand on Hermina's shoulder. "Tell him to come at once."

Hermina accepts the wine.

"Now tell me what's happened." Stroking her arm, I kneel beside her. Hermina looks older than she is, all the childlike innocence gone from her face.

"There's so much to say," she whispers.

The door opens and Pilate enters, stopping at the sight of her. She runs to his arms, bursting into tears. "Our father is dead!" she cries.

"*What?*" Pilate pulls away to look at her.

A trembling hand wipes at her tears. "We found his body floating in the bath, with so much blood..."

Fresh tears appear. Pilate holds her, stroking her hair. "How did it happen? Did he do it himself?"

She sniffs. "Caligula arranged it."

Concern darkens his eyes. "What do you mean?"

I indicate a chair and he leads her to it. Hermina clings to his hand. "Father wanted more control in Rome. Sejanus never liked Caligula, so our father encouraged him to accuse the family of treason! The Praetorian Guard arrested Caligula's mother and siblings, so he fled to Capri. Caligula blamed our father after Sejanus' execution, but Tiberius refused to arrest him. He likes me too much."

Her humorless laugh sends chills through me. "Tiberius is frail and will die soon. Caligula has total control of the senate. Most fear and hate him but know better than to speak against him. I had to leave Capri. I knew once our father died he'd send for me."

Unconsciously, she pulls at her toga. Pilate's voice hardens. "What did he do to you?"

Misery fills her face. Pilate reaches for her shoulder. She stumbles away from him. "Please, don't!"

"*Show me.*"

Hermina glances at me helplessly and lowers the shoulder of her tunic to reveal scarred and rippled skin. "He came to me in Capri. He said he wanted to speak to me. Our aunt was out and I saw no harm in it."

Pilate shuts his eyes, his hand tightening into a fist.

New tears appear. "I fought him, but he was too strong! When he finished, he burned me with one of the lamps for resisting. He bribed my servants to read my letters! He said I'd be his wife, and he'd kill me rather than let me go!"

I put my arm around her. "You're safe now."

"How can I be safe anywhere in his empire?"

Staring out across the harbor, Pilate says nothing.

"Lucius, I know that look." Hermina goes to him. "Promise me you'll do nothing against him."

His hands rest on the ledge. "I can't promise that."

"Caligula is powerful. He'll be the emperor soon!"

Taking her by the shoulders, Pilate says, "Caligula believes you're dead and I'm unaware of the truth. He has no reason to suspect me. This is enough for now. You must rest. Claudia will

show you to a room where you can sleep." He kisses her forehead and turns away.

I lead her to one of our larger guest rooms and leave only after she falls asleep. Returning to him, I ask, "What do you intend to do?"

"I still have friends in what's left of the Praetorian Guard. Sooner or later, Caligula will be repaid."

"Lucius, you shouldn't descend to his level!"

Pouring a cup of wine, he asks, "Does it make me a *murderer*? Did you forget I killed your messiah?"

"He forgave you from the cross! You're pardoned!" My eyes plead with him as he drinks.

"Caligula murdered my father and defiled my sister. I have every right to hate him. What will we do with her?"

"What do you mean?"

Pilate indicates the harbor. "She can't stay here."

"Do you think Caligula has spies in Judea?"

A sad smile crosses his face. "The emperor has spies everywhere. We need somewhere to hide her."

Leaving me on the verandah, he enters the house.

Chapter Twenty-Three

Dawn streams through the pillars in the baths. Servants leave the room as I enter. The doors shut behind them. I remove my robe and slide into the warm water.

"I know where to send Hermina."

Pilate considers me from the far end.

"Send her to Jacob and Libi in Bethany." I swim nearer, searching his blue eyes for resistance.

His head tilts. "Send her to *them*, his followers?"

"Caligula won't find her there."

Water streams across his arm as he rests his hand on my cheek. "Send my sister to the people whose messiah I had executed? Claudia..."

I wind my fingers through the short hair at his neck. "They don't hate you! He taught them not to hate. None of them will harm her."

Laughing, he leans his head against the wall.

My hand falls to his shoulder. "Do you trust my judgment?"

Water laps at his shoulders. "Yes."

"Then trust me in this. Lazarus will help her. Libi will look after her. Quintus and she will soon marry. My brother won't let any harm come to them."

Pilate stares at me. "Quintus intends to marry Libi?"

"He didn't tell you?"

"No, but he knows me well enough not to."

My skin tingles. "What do you mean?"

"I'd forbid it." He moves away from me, toward the center of the pool.

I follow, demanding, "Why?"

Turning to face me, he shakes his head. "I don't want to help him destroy himself."

"Tell me, since when does love end in destruction?"

He snorts. "Quintus has wanted Libi in his bed since she turned fourteen. Love and desire are two completely different things."

"Who are you to decide whether love is true?"

Blue eyes harden and he swims closer. "It won't make either of them happy. He's marrying beneath his station to a woman of a much different background, in a society that neither accepts nor condones such things."

My face flushes. "Haven't we been happy?"

"We're not the same."

"Aren't we? Didn't you marry beneath your station?"

Frustration flickers across his face. "It's hardly the same thing!"

"Isn't it?"

"No! You are the daughter of a wine merchant; she is the child of an indentured servant! And you're not a Jew." He climbs out of the bath and wraps a towel around his waist.

I follow, snatching up my robe. "That's what you dislike, isn't it? You'd prefer him to marry a Roman heathen!"

"Yes, I would!"

Salty air stirs the draperies and I shiver, dripping all over the tiles. "Why do you hate the Jews so much? Is it because they won't submit to your authority?"

"If I liked submission, I wouldn't have married you."

The humor in his voice irritates me. I grab his arm, forcing him to face me. "But you did."

"I did." A smile lurks at the corners of his eyes.

"You *wanted* to marry me."

"Yes."

"Yet you'd deny Quintus the same freedom."

Pilate sighs.

The door opens behind us and a servant, his eyes downcast, says, "Prefect, your messenger has arrived."

"Let him wait in the hall." Pilate waits until he leaves and says, "Claudia, your brother is respected in Rome. Tiberius has taken an interest in him, but if he marries a Jewish servant girl in Judea, his prospects fall away."

Gripping his hand, I say, "Doesn't that prove his love for Libi, if he gives up so much for her sake?"

"Love shouldn't get in the way of ambition."

As he opens the door I ask, "What about my idea for your sister?"

"I'll consider it."

His footsteps fade into the hall and Octavia enters. "You shouldn't stand in the draft, Mistress."

In my room, her delicate fingers comb through my long hair. I play with the fringe on my toga. "Who knows the girl is here?"

"Hardly anyone knows, Mistress."

My senses tingle. "Can you keep it that way?"

"Yes, for a few days."

Pilate only needs twenty-four hours. He comes to me and says, "We'll take her to Bethany. I hope your belief in the messiah's friends is right... for their sake."

We set out at dawn under the pretense of a short trip to Jerusalem. A dozen centurions accompany us. Hermina wears simple homespun and walks beside my litter. For all the men know, she is one of my servants. Midway through the day, I ask, "Are you all right?"

She smiles ruefully. "It's better to walk to Jerusalem by choice than be dragged in a chariot to Rome."

I glance at my husband, riding ahead of us. "We'll stop the night in an inn along the way."

The first one we find has a large enough stable to provide for our men and horses. The innkeeper rushes out to invite us in; his sons unsaddle the horses. "Come, Prefect, sit and eat!" He motions to a table.

Pilate answers, "We'll dine in our room."

The man looks relieved. "Come!" He shows us into his largest room at the top of the stairs. The door shuts behind him as he hurries away promising to bring supper.

Hermina drops onto the bed. "I don't think I've ever walked so far in my life!"

"I'd let you ride but it'd be suspicious." Pilate moves aside a curtain to peer into the street.

When supper arrives, Hermina is asleep. I pull a blanket over her and smooth the hair out of her face. "Is this a life she can handle, Lucius? Can she hide? Can she learn discretion?"

He looks up from his wine. "She's too afraid not to."

I rest my hand on her shoulder and look at her, altered from when we parted long ago. I pray for her happiness in Bethany.

Jerusalem is quiet in our absence and our arrival met without the usual interest. Quintus awaits us at the gate and escorts us to the palace. I step out of my litter and nod to Octavia, who takes Hermina inside. Quintus hands Pilate a scroll. "I've seen to my orders, Prefect. And Caiaphas wants to speak with you on the new plaques in Herod's palace."

"Naturally," Pilate says wryly.

Jerusalem has never felt more dangerous and with relief, we set out the next morning for Bethany. I borrow a simple garment from my servant and join Hermina in the courtyard. Both of us are surprised when Pilate descends the stairs,

looking common in a homespun toga.

"You're coming with us?" I ask.

He shoots me an incredulous look but says nothing. Memories tug at me as we walk the streets of Bethany. I half expect to see the messiah in the courtyard, but Libi runs to meet us, thinner than I saw her last, but alight with joy. "Come, we've prepared a meal for you!"

Pilate considers the house suspiciously and enters the courtyard behind the rest of us. Jacob rises from the table at the sound of our voices. A man moves forward. "I'm Lazarus, welcome to our home." His eyes betray a hint of concern over Pilate. "Please... sit here, Prefect."

Everyone watches as my husband has a seat. I take my place at his side. Lazarus indicates the others. "That is my sister Martha... and my younger sister, Mary."

She smiles at all of us.

"And of course, you know the rest."

Libi invites Hermina to sit and pours wine, passing the bread. Lazarus casts a look at Pilate. "It's our practice to bless it before we eat."

Pilate motions for him to continue.

Turning his hands upward, Lazarus lifts his face. "Our Father, we thank you for these blessings, for the food we share and the new faces at our table. Let what is said and done among us this day honor your son, amen."

Picking up my glass, Martha fills it. Hermina asks, "Aren't you Jews?"

"Yes."

"And you're willing to eat with us?"

Lazarus says, "Our messiah told us to love one another, to bless one another. He ate with others not of his faith and so do we."

I look at my husband. He says, "You speak of Jesus of Nazareth."

"I do indeed."

"The man my centurions put to death."

Quiet fills the courtyard. Everyone looks at Lazarus. He smiles gently. "That is true, but he is not dead."

"Yes, I had heard that."

Martha fills her brother's cup, her eyes darting to me. Lazarus tears off a piece of bread. "You don't believe it."

"I had men guard that tomb. They tell me his body was

stolen in the night."

Dipping bread into his wine, Lazarus asks, "Is that what you believe happened, Prefect?"

"It does seem a more logical explanation."

Lazarus passes a basket of fish along the table. "What purpose does it serve to steal the body and claim he is alive?"

"It encourages belief in your messiah."

His elbows on the table, Lazarus leans forward. "But what purpose does it serve? He *is* the messiah; if not, why pretend otherwise? It is dangerous to say his name in Jerusalem; the high priests forbid it. Those of unbelief persecute us; they even stone us for performing miracles. Yet still we speak it, because he *lives*."

Martha slams the jug noisily on the table. "Brother..."

"This is what Jesus told us to do, Martha!"

She scowls and rips a piece of bread in half.

Pilate refuses any wine. "You believe in *a cause* but I'm not confident this concerns the messiah."

"Would we risk our lives otherwise?"

He smiles. "Barabbas also risked his life, not for the messiah but for Judea. Assure me your motives in speaking of this 'resurrected messiah' are pure and not to secretly start an uprising against Rome. You *do* share your table with an insurgent, after all."

I start to speak and he silences me.

Jacob's face reddens with shame. "I'm not the man you knew in Rome, Pilate."

"Are you the one who shouted for Jesus' death?"

He lifts his chin. "Yes."

"You saw him die yet you believe he lives?"

Jacob's sightless eyes stare into the distance. "Yes!"

"Why?"

He indicates the rest of us. "Who but the son of God could take away hatred and replace it with love in those who follow him? You and I, Pilate, we understand hatred. Yet here we sit, surrounded by those we wronged when we put him to death, those who raise no hand to us, but instead forgive us. How is that not miraculous?"

Wind stirs the branches above us.

"Even if you don't incite violence, such beliefs are dangerous."

Lazarus opens his arms. "As you would die for Rome, we'd

die for our messiah, as he did for us."

"So you don't fear death?"

The man shakes his head. "I've seen it. I spent three days in death, until he summoned me from the tomb. If death finds me again, I'll go to Jesus and not that place of waiting." His face is rapturous and full of longing.

Conversation thrives but Pilate falls silent. I walk him around the courtyard as the others clean up the table.

"What do you think of them?"

Glancing at them, he shrugs. "I don't know."

Hermina shrieks with laughter and his eyes soften. I take his hand. "You can trust them."

Branches sway overhead. Pilate sighs. "I'll *have* to."

Chapter Twenty-Four

Pilate dodges the blow and blocks it with his shield. The massive man opposite sends him staggering with a bone-crunching strike of his club. Pilate rolls out of the way, as it thuds into the sand in the arena, leaps to his feet, and kicks the man's legs out from under him. The gladiator falls with a thud. Pilate's blade lands at his throat.

I descend the steps as Pilate slices the man's arm, a shallow scratch but that draws blood. He throws the shield aside and hands his sword to a servant. The gladiator leaves between two centurions.

"He's undefeated. I bought him for Herod."

"And you couldn't resist trying him out first?"

He smirks.

I rarely see him without his armor. "What if a gladiator kills you?"

"Then I'll be dead, and a fool."

Shaking my head, I follow him upstairs. Wind blows through the columns, scented with salt from the docks.

"Have you heard from my sister of late?"

"No. But Libi writes that she's happy and looks forward to seeing us at Passover."

"We'll not visit Jerusalem this year."

Faltering at the door of his office, I ask, "Why?"

"Tiberius wants me to stay in Caesarea; he worries over the potential Samaritan uprising. They have a prophet of their own now. He also sent me this." He holds out a scroll bearing the imperial seal.

I cross the room and take it. "He orders a removal of the plaques from our palace in Jerusalem?"

"Yes, the Sanhedrin complained."

Pilate pours a cup of wine from the sideboard. I toss the scroll aside. "Is that why Caiaphas wanted an audience?"

"He said the plaques are graven images, but they're names, not likenesses. I refused to remove them, so he went over my head."

Sorting through the documents on his desk, I ask, "Do you think they're still smarting over the death of the messiah and his inability to truly *die*?"

"After several years, you'd think they'd get over it."

The door opens and a centurion enters. Pilate speaks with him and I move out onto the verandah. Ships float in and out of the harbor flying Roman colors. The centurion departs and Pilate rejoins me. "What else did Libi say?"

"She and Quintus are getting married. Will you go?"

Eying the wine in his cup, Pilate shakes his head.

"Can't you support him?"

He stares out over the sea. "You know I can't. But I'll send Demetrius with you for protection on the way."

Two weeks after Passover, we set out for Jerusalem. Our progress halts on the road miles from the city, as a large group crosses before us.

"Where are they going?"

Demetrius reigns in his horse at my side. "They're following a Samaritan prophet. He preaches on the banks of the Jordan."

The last Samaritan moves out of our way and I see the flash of a sword at his side. Demetrius stiffens, but they ignore us as they set out across the grass.

"What does he say, this prophet?"

His eyes narrow as he urges his horse on. "He's a religious fanatic, often speaking of Moses and holy scrolls."

Dirt kicks into the air behind us as we ride on. The palace is empty without Pilate and we visit Bethany the next day. Libi embraces me at the gate and pulls me inside. "You must see the dress Martha made for me!"

She holds it up against her and I admire it, glancing out the window into the courtyard where Hermina takes Demetrius a cup of wine. Libi follows my gaze. "She's happy here. You should tell him that."

My hand falls to the windowsill. "Is Quintus upset?"

"Yes, but he does understand Pilate's objections." Libi folds the gown and sits on the edge of her bed. The room is small but fragrant from the garden. "I'm a servant, after all, and Quintus is a tribune."

I cross to her. "He's a tribune who loves you."

"He *shouldn't*."

Taking her hand, I get her to look at me. "Quintus knows what he wants and it's you. Just accept it."

Her eyes warm and I kiss her hand. "I got you a gift from Rome. I thought you might like it."

She unstops the top and smells. "Perfume?"

"Yes, the finest. Wear it on your wedding night."

Blushing, she smells it again and smiles. I dab it on her wrists and behind her ears. Mary and I comb out her hair and put it up under a veil. We dress her in the lovely gown and put bracelets on her ankles and arms.

Their marriage is a traditional Roman Jewish ceremony. After speaking the words, she and Quintus sit in the lead tent, as the house overflows with guests. Laughter and music spills into the street through the open gate. Everyone in Bethany is present. Martha stays with me until called away to find more wine, then I slip out of the garden. Shadows flicker around me in the silence. I lean against the wall and sigh.

The surrounding houses are quiet, their lamps out. I hear something in the road and turn but see no one. My skin crawls and I start for the gate, only to gasp as a man steps out before me.

"Claudia," he says.

My hand falls from my lips to my pounding heart. He moves closer, his face falling into the light.

Barabbas!

I stumble and his hands are on me, pressing over my mouth as he throws me against the wall. I feel a blade at my throat. "Don't scream," he whispers in my ear, his body against mine. I nod. He removes his hand. Dark eyes glitter at me. "Where's Pilate?"

"He's not here."

The scent of horses and dirt fills my nose. He scoffs, "Not at his brother in law's wedding? You lie."

His blade cuts slightly into my neck. I feel a drop of blood slide toward my chest. "He doesn't approve."

"Something we agree on!" Barabbas glances around as footsteps hurry toward him.

A wide-eyed boy appears. "He's not here!"

Wondering if Demetrius will notice my disappearance, I say, "Pilate isn't at the wedding. I told you that."

"Off you go then, warn the others." The boy runs off into the dark. Barabbas turns to me. "What should I do with you?"

"What did you want to do to me at the first?"

The sneer on his face gives me chills. "You remember that, do you?"

"Yes, and I remember who stopped you."

Barabbas leans closer. I turn my face away, his breath hot on my cheek. "You mean the *dead* messiah everyone in this

town worships? He stopped me that day but is gone now. Your husband crucified him. I wanted Pilate, but you'll do."

Rough stone grinds into my shoulders.

"Will she?"

The voice halts us both; Barabbas looks around as Pilate emerges from the darkness. He releases me and I slide to the ground, spitting up blood.

"So the Prefect did come after all!"

Pilate steps closer. "It's me you want. Let's handle this as men, not as cowards who attack defenseless women."

Behind us, Demetrius leaves the garden. Shocked, he steps forward and Pilate stops him with an outstretched hand. Music drifts over the wall. Barabbas shrugs—and lunges at him. The knife is swift but Pilate ducks under his arm and twists around, causing a snap of bone as he forces Barabbas to his knees. Barabbas cries out in pain. The knife touches Barabbas' throat.

Hatred rises in me toward him, hatred I fight against as I struggle to my feet. Torchlight dances around us as I approach. "Why do you hate us so much, Barabbas?"

Fierce eyes dart to mine, full of resentment. "I hate what you stand for, what you represent: Rome. I once saw that foul place, a haven of debauchery and sin! It will crumble into dust when the *true* messiah arrives."

"Your messiah came, but you didn't know him."

Curling his lip, he sneers, "Jesus the pretender! The true messiah will liberate us from Rome!"

I shiver in the cold night air. Pilate says, "Demetrius."

The guard moves to take hold of Barabbas, leaving Pilate to put his cloak around me. "What do you want me to do with him, Prefect?"

Barabbas laughs. "Judean law prohibits you from executing a prisoner pardoned during Passover. Let me finish what I started!"

"You wouldn't win. I trained with the Fifth Legion."

Other shadows approach out of the night, Pilate's guards. They drag Barabbas to his feet; one of them strikes him in the face. Blood trickles from the corner of his mouth and he spits it out on the ground contemptuously.

"I can't execute you," Pilate says, "but I *can* kill you." He nods to his men and they drag Barabbas away. Putting an arm around me, Pilot leads me into the garden. A haze of guests and dancers swirl around us.

Libi runs across the courtyard to us, beaming. "You did come after all! Quintus will be so pleased!"

"I thought it time to mend our disagreements," Pilate says. Her eye falls on me and darkens with concern. Pilate sits me on the nearest chair and moves toward Quintus. I accept the wine gratefully.

"What happened?" she asks.

Quietly, I tell her. Libi puts her hand on my shoulder. "You're bleeding!"

She takes me inside to tend scratches on my upper back and under my hair. I let her and say ruefully, "I'm sorry! I ruined your wedding day!"

"Barabbas *tried* to ruin it, but didn't." Dabbing at the scrapes, she rinses off the strip of linen.

"Barabbas..." I repeat.

The rag lands in the water basin. "He tried to kill you. You shouldn't feel sorry for his fate."

"I'm not." Her eyes search mine in sudden concern. "Pilate sent him away and I said nothing because it comforts me to know he's dead."

Libi is silent.

"For months, he's worried me and now I feel nothing."

The door behind us opens and a servant girl says, "Peter has arrived."

"I'll be there in a moment." Libi squeezes my hand as the girl darts out. "I don't know what to tell you, Claudia. I wish I had answers for you, but Jesus never promised us a simple life. He, as the Son of God, found it easy to forgive; for the rest of us, it's much harder." Smoothing the hair out of my face, she says, "You look fine. Come outside and sit with Peter. You'll like him; he's one of the messiah's dearest companions."

Others gather around him in excitement. Pilate stands at a distance, arms crossed. Peter notices him and falters but sits at the table.

"Tell us of the messiah," they urge him.

Pilate shifts on his feet. I touch his arm. "Let's go," I beg.

"No, I want to hear this."

Peter smiles and leans toward the children at his feet. "You remember the messiah, don't you? I walked with him, talked with him, fled the night they took him away. I betrayed him. I promised to stay with him, to remain true to him... but I denied him three times, out of fear for my life, as he foretold."

Wind stirs the fabric overhead as Demetrius returns.

"But he forgave me after his resurrection. I denied him and in love, he embraced me as a friend! He told me to go forth and make disciples of many nations, to carry his word to you, and all who never knew him!"

One of the guests shakes his head. "He is dead!"

"He lives! I've seen him, touched him, and heard his voice!"

Passing behind the guests, Demetrius rejoins us. Pilate glances over and he nods. I feel a thrill of horror and guilt. Barabbas is dead.

"He came not to liberate us from Rome," Peter says, "but that we might approach his Father in heaven unafraid! He came not to live, but to die in our stead, so we might have everlasting life! He suffered in our stead, so we might be born anew into a new life of righteousness!"

Flames lick into the darkness. Faces gaze at him in wonder. Moving forward, Pilate says, "I took your messiah from you."

"It's Pilate!"

Whispers fill the crowd.

"It's the Prefect!"

One mother wraps an arm around her child and pulls him away from them. Others show fear.

Peter smiles. "He gave his life."

"Then I didn't kill him?" Pilate sounds amused.

Unease swirls in the air, the guests fearful. Peter says, "All of us are instruments in God's hands. Your blame is no less or more than mine, for he died for each of us equally."

"Only a fool dies for those who don't want his sacrifice."

Patting the hand of the nearest child, Peter says softly, "It isn't foolish to live in hope that a gift, once given freely, will be accepted in time."

Quiet lurks in the courtyard. Pilate narrows his eyes. Taking his hand, I say quietly, "Let's go home."

"Faith isn't hard to find when you seek it," Jacob says. He leans on his staff as he moves toward us. "Tomorrow, I visit the tomb one last time. Will you come?"

Faces turn away from us, guests reaching out to Libi and Quintus before slipping out into the darkness.

"If it's empty, there's nothing to see, is there?"

Smiling, Jacob says, "There's always something to see."

Chapter Twenty-Five

The tomb is empty. I run my hand along the narrow shelf carved into the wall. "So this is where they laid him?"

"Yes." Jacob's staff taps on the ground as he feels his way closer. "He left the burial linens in a heap... he didn't unwind them, simply... escaped them." Years have passed yet his presence lingers. Jacob leans against the ledge. "Peter burned them, not wanting men to make relics of them, graven images of a dead messiah. But he isn't dead!"

"Caiaphas disagrees with you." Pilate ducks as he enters, casting a long shadow across the floor.

Sadness touches Jacob's face. "There's much Caiaphas doesn't understand; he won't admit his mistake or question his judgment. He had a chance to repent when the temple curtain tore but turned away from the truth, as did Barabbas."

"As will I, if you can't convince me, is that what you think?" Pilate asks.

The air in the tomb is fragrant with the scent of wild roses in the garden. Jacob frowns slightly, his hazy eyes focusing on nothing. "I need not convince you, Pilate. You know the truth; you merely wish to deny it."

"Denial is what you and your friends live in, Jacob. Your messiah is dead. His body was *stolen*."

Resting against the wall, Jacob shakes his head. "You want to believe that, but believing it doesn't make it true. You can't deny that strange things have happened... or did you not see my dead father walk among us?"

"I did, though I may have been mad at the time."

The skin at my neck tingles and I look to the burial ledge once more.

"Did madness strike all of us at once?" Jacob feels for Pilate's shoulder and grips it firmly. "You're a man of logic and reason, Prefect. Belief is much easier than denial. Or is it you don't want to believe, in the knowledge that you *may* have crucified the son of God?"

"His life wasn't mine to take, according to Peter."

Jacob's face softens. "Yes, so why do you fear belief?"

"Your messiah said we must be made anew; I want to stay Pilate."

Disappointment floods through me as he walks away. I push

it aside and touch Jacob's hand. He turns with a smile. "Libi said you're planning to leave. Is it true?"

"Yes, Matthew has asked me to go with him."

I take a shuddering breath; he hears it and pats my hand. "He said 'go and make disciples of men,' Claudia. Everyone in Judea has heard his name, but not in the far reaches of the world. I'll be fine."

Pilate steps over a crack in the floor. "Not if you're caught. Rome won't look fondly on the promotion of a single Judean god."

"Then I fear more for your lives than my own."

Footsteps approach and Demetrius ducks inside. "Prefect, I must speak with you."

They pass outside and Jacob turns to me. "I know you are a believer, Claudia. Don't lose faith in him."

"I believe in his resurrection, Jacob... I won't."

He shakes his head. "I speak not of our Lord, but Pilate. A man is not lost until he gives up the fight. One day he must choose between life and death. This much my father foretold, entrusted to him by our messiah."

Light wavers as centurions pass before the door. I clutch his arm. "What else did he tell you?"

"I can't say, but have faith. Guide him, if you can."

Glancing after Pilate, I lower my voice. "My faith is feeble, Jacob. He asks me to love and I find hate; he tells me to seek him out, but I can no longer remember his face; he promised to heal me, yet still I'm without children."

"And I'm without sight, though Peter could have healed me if the Lord had urged him to. What matters is his work in your life and spirit, not your body. You *live*, Claudia! He saves you instead of condemns you! Isn't that enough?"

Tears cloud my vision. I wipe them away as Pilate ducks inside. "We must go. There's trouble in Jerusalem."

Horses await us outside. I lead Jacob to Mary but linger at his side. My voice catches. "Is this farewell?"

"It may be, but only the Lord knows all." He smiles. "Never forget what he's done for you, Claudia."

"Be safe, my friend." I kiss him and let Pilate pull me onto his horse. Demetrius and three centurions ride with us to the city. Jerusalem is quiet but a crowd convenes in our courtyard. Entering through the side door, Pilate meets two bloody tribunes. "What happened?"

"Our legion went to the mountain as you commanded, Prefect, to keep order among the Samaritans."

Darkness slithers into the hall as the sun sets. I feel cold, but from no chill in the room.

"You engaged them?"

Rising at Pilate's command, the tribune says, "Yes, Prefect. Many fought and died. We captured the ringleaders and put them to death as ordered."

"I see... and why does my courtyard overflow?"

The second tribune steps forward. "The Samaritans claim they gathered for religious purposes. They say we incited violence against them for no reason."

"Ah." Pilate dismisses them with a wave. Slapping their fists to their hearts, they depart. He turns to Demetrius. "Have them choose three representatives. I'll see them."

I follow him into the meeting hall and we wait. Soon, Demetrius escorts them in. They bow and approach.

"You find fault in me?" Pilate asks.

One looks up at him angrily. "You attacked an innocent gathering and slaughtered them where they stood!"

"I received information of an uprising."

Another shakes his head. "They didn't intend violence! They met to climb the mountain on a holy journey, to meet our prophet and see the promised scrolls of Moses!"

"Men need arms for a holy journey, do they?"

Servants enter to light the lamps. Faces flush with rage. "Prefect, some of them traveled hundreds of miles! There are thieves on the roads of Judea! Even a Roman man defends his family!"

Pilate considers. Silence enters the hall. Finally, he asks, "How many died?"

"Over a hundred and your men took many prisoners."

He looks to his scribe, who nods. "It's true, Prefect. We took over two hundred prisoners in the riot."

"What did you do with them?"

The man creeps forward. "They're in our prison, sir."

"Question them and if no fault is found, release them." He turns to the others as the scribe hurries away. "I have no quarrel with the Samaritans, only with insurgents. Yet, you expect me to believe this 'messiah' of yours didn't intend to incite them to violence?"

"Our prophet is a peaceful man, Prefect. This is your doing.

You govern with force and teach your soldiers brutality. Even if you didn't order this, they took their initiative from your example!"

Danger lurks in Pilate's eyes.

"You speak of Roman law but care nothing for our laws, our justice, or our ways. You are to be our judicial overseer, not our executioner!"

Demetrius looks at my husband, who shakes his head. "I understand your anger but I must govern with strength in a nation that so despises Rome."

Laughing, the man answers, "You incite riots so you can stop them with violence! Protests are not riots. Religious gatherings are not riots. Since your arrival, you have insulted us, demeaned us, beaten us, brutalized us, used the temple funds and put to death a Jewish messiah. Now you mount an unprovoked attack against the Samaritans!" He points his finger at us. "You *will* pay for this, Pilate! I'll have you sent back to Rome in disgrace!"

"You have every right to complain against me, but you may find the Roman authorities less than concerned. They sent me here to control Judea and that's what I have done."

The man spits at his feet and storms out. Others follow. Pilate motions to his guard. "In the morning, send me four centurions pulled at random from the legion responsible. I want to speak with them."

I return with him to our room, where he sorts through his scrolls. Glancing at me, he says, "Your silence burns my ears. Say whatever it is you're trying not to say."

"The Samaritan is right; you did cause this."

He sinks into his chair. "Yes, I did, and if it comes to it, I'll answer to Rome for it. I don't regret my orders, unless I find them innocent... and I'm not convinced of it."

"But what if it *is* the truth?" I finger the edge of the desk in the lamplight. Night air stirs around us.

Pilate smiles sadly at me. "It wouldn't be the first time I condemned innocent men to death."

Darkness stirs around us and I shiver. "Take me with you tomorrow."

"So you can hate me for my actions?" He shakes his head.

I put my arms around his neck, his cheek to mine. "Don't you know by now I could never hate you? I may be disappointed in you, but I'll never stop loving you."

"But you also want me to change."

Kneeling beside his chair, I stroke his arm. "I want you to be all you're capable of being, whether it's here in Judea or in Rome. If they send us home, I will defend you. Whether or not you're the governor of Judea means nothing to me."

He kisses my forehead. "Let's hope Tiberius shares your opinion of me."

"You'll let me go with you?"

Considering at length, he nods.

The small town at the foot of Mt. Gerizim is quiet, its inhabitants subdued at the slaughter imposed on their doorstep. Blood stains the earth, little left but a ruin since the centurions set fire to it. Pilate dismounts and approaches the smoldering timbers of a former inn.

"They convened here, Prefect," says the tribune. "We ordered them to disband and they refused."

Breaking away from the others, the Samaritan with us says, "That's a lie! You attacked us without warning!" He points to the road. "That's where you cut down an unarmed child!"

A face appears and swiftly vanishes in the near window. I leave my litter and approach the door of the burned out hovel. Shadows slip away from me as I step inside.

"Don't come any closer!" Fearful eyes shine at me under a coat of grime, as the girl holds a knife before her. The room smells of death.

"I won't hurt you. I want to know what happened."

Raised voices continue outside. Her eyes dart toward them. "The soldiers came and killed many of them."

"Did your family come to climb the mountain?"

She barely nods. "Gerizim is our holy place. The prophet wanted us to make a holy vigil on the top of the mountain."

The house creaks as the scorched timbers settle.

"What did the soldiers say?"

The knife wavers and she wipes her tears with her hand. "They didn't say anything."

"They didn't order you to disband?"

Her head shakes. "No, they ..."

Tears fill her eyes and spill onto her cheeks. I show her the emptiness of my hands. "Stay here, wait for me."

I step out into the afternoon sunlight. The days grow cold as winter sets in. Passing behind the arguing tribune and Samaritan, I touch Pilate's arm and incline my head. He

follows me into the building. Fear covers the girl's face.

"It's all right. Just tell him what you told me."

Fearful eyes dart between us. Pilate steps over the broken beam. "Come," he says. Still gripping the knife, she stands before him. "Tell me what happened. You won't be punished."

In a shaking voice, she repeats our conversation. Pilate's face is unreadable. "Do you have others to go to?"

"Yes, I came for our things." Wiping her nose on her sleeve, she motions to a small heap in the corner. He motions for her to leave. She snatches up her bundle and slips outside. He looks around at the ruin and nudges the charred remains with his foot. Our eyes meet and hold.

Demetrius steps inside. "Prefect, we should return before dark."

The Samaritan approaches as we return to the street. "Well, Prefect?"

Pilate says, "Those responsible will be reprimanded."

We travel to Jerusalem in silence. The streets are more subdued than usual. More than a month passes without any change in our situation. Still, I know it is inevitable; I see it in my dreams.

Hermina is distraught when we tell her. "What do you mean you may have to return to Rome? How serious is it?"

Children chase one another around the garden. I watch through the narrow window. Glancing up from his work, Lazarus reminds them to stay out of his fig trees.

Pilate takes her hands, his blue eyes solemn. "The Samaritans accuse me of massacring them without cause. If I'm reprimanded by the governor of Syria, I'll have to go to Rome and defend myself against the charges."

"But that's absurd! You did no such thing!" He glances at me and her confidence fades. "Isn't it?"

"My men did kill them without cause on my orders, and as prefect it's my responsibility to answer for it."

Pulling away from him, she asks, "How could you?"

"I made a bad assumption."

Laughter drifts in from the courtyard. Hermina rubs the chill from her arms. "What'll happen to you?"

"The senate will hear the case."

Shuddering, she grips his hand. "Will they kill you?"

"No, my darling, no... but I may face exile. Whichever way it's decided, I won't be sent back to Judea."

Her eyes fill with concern. "So this is goodbye?"

"Until Caligula's death... yes, but I can make other arrangements for you, if you don't want to stay here."

She squeezes his hand. "They're kind to me. I want to stay with them. And Demetrius will look after me." Remembering his attentiveness at the wedding, I smile. Hermina blushes a little. "I will miss you both."

Crossing the room, I sit beside her. "Have faith there's a purpose in this."

Light plays across her beautiful auburn hair. She ducks her head. "It's easy for you. You knew the messiah as a man! How can I have faith in someone I never met?"

"You've seen him in the faces of everyone around you, in Lazarus and Martha, in Jacob and Libi, and in me. Take comfort in it."

Her voice catches. "I don't want you to go."

"We don't want to go either, but we may have to."

Tears appear but she bites her lip and nods. I hold her until she is finished weeping.

Chapter Twenty-Six

The darkness makes me uneasy. It winds upstairs and slithers through halls. It drifts against the wall and darts up into the arches. It follows me, full of haunting voices, whispers.

Claudia...

My bare feet slap against the floor; I stumble and scrape my knee, blood trickling along my legs. Barabbas haunts me in my dreams. He stands in the upper hall, his head in one hand, the other extended to me.

He will come for you, Claudia...

I shiver. *Who?*

The Destroyer...

He fades away into nothingness.

The vision haunts me the next day as I pace the palace halls. Tired of waiting, of praying, of hoping, I want it to end, for Tiberius to send for us... or reprieve us.

Octavia comes to me. "Your brother and his wife are in the main hall."

Gladness enters my heart. "Tell Pilate." She nods and hurries away. I enter the room and Libi embraces me, swollen with child. I touch her and ask, "How much longer?"

Blushing with happiness, she says, "A month or so."

"Our child may be born in Rome." Quintus leads her to a chair. She sits awkwardly, unused to carrying so much weight in her thin form.

I move a tray of fruit closer to her. "You're leaving?"

"Yes, Thais sent word for me to return. She'll marry soon and the vineyards need tending."

Servants pour out wine. I sit on the divan. "You used to want to go to war, now you return to tend the grapes?"

"Life changes our perceptions." He smiles at me, and turns as Pilate enters. "My friend, how are you?"

"I'm glad to see you but tired of Judean politics."

"They're leaving for Rome," I tell him.

Dark brows shoot up. "So, you're a wine maker?"

"Indeed though I haven't Father's talent for it." Quintus swirls the liquid in his cup. He and Libi exchange glances. "We wondered..."

Sitting beside me, Pilate finishes, "If we'll travel on the same ship? It's likely, since I expect a reprimand from the Syrian

governor by the end of the week."

"Then you *will* be deposed?" Libi is concerned.

He smiles at her. "Tiberius has heard the story from my enemies. I'll be forced to defend myself before the emperor."

"It's fortunate he's fond of you." Quintus' hair moves in the breeze. "You're not popular with the Samaritans."

Pilate squeezes my hand. "He's fond of Claudia, not me, but let's be happy until the official summons arrives. You *will* stay the night, of course?"

"We intended to ride on until dusk."

Libi glances at me and I urge, "Do stay!"

"I suppose we could leave at dawn," Quintus relents.

This lifts our spirits and we sit as the afternoon wanes. A servant enters bowing. "Prefect, a man demands an audience with you in the main hall. His name is Marcellus. He says you know of him?"

"I'll be there in a moment." Darting out again, the servant closes the door behind him. In the ensuing silence, we exchange glances.

Quintus asks, "Marcellus from the Syrian prefecture?"

"Yes and no doubt eager to depose me."

Rising with him, I say, "I'll go with you."

My skin tingles as we enter the judicial hall. Marcellus is a tall, thin man with a severe face and shrewd dark eyes. He turns at our entrance and holds out an imperial scroll. "Your orders are to report to Rome and stand trial before the emperor. I'm appointed to replace you."

I feel sick but try not to show it. Pilate breaks the seal and reads the scroll.

"You have two weeks to manage your local affairs. A ship will await you at Caesarea at the end of the month."

Demetrius stands by the nearest column; I sense by his eyes his empathy for my distress.

Marcellus asks, "Do you accept your orders?"

"Yes."

The man nods. "I want to see your latest reports." His tone softens but his eyes remain hard. Pilate leads him through the far door and I follow. Glancing at me, he says, "So you're the one they say spoke out against crucifying the Jewish messiah?"

"What?"

I hate his sneer. "His followers speak of you, when recounting the story of his death and resurrection. You warned

Pilate against his imprisonment, and had a dream. It's not the first such warning, is it?"

My hands feel clammy. "They speak of me in Syria?"

"Everyone in Rome knows you're a dream-seer."

The color drains from my face. Pilate opens the door of his study and invites Marcellus inside. I part from them in silence and retreat to my room. When Pilate enters an hour later, I cease pacing. He tries to calm me. "Claudia, it's not as bad as you think."

"How did they find out?"

He catches my arm and leads me onto the balcony. "There are spies in Judea, probably among our servants. Your dreams are hardly a secret. They'll think you favored by the gods, nothing more."

"I keep dreaming of Barabbas!"

Concern darkens his face as he follows me inside. "He's dead."

"Yes, I know! You had him beheaded!" Sick amusement creeps into my voice and I shake my head. "He comes to me in my dreams to frighten me... to warn me."

Pilate crosses the room. "Warn you of what?"

"*He's coming for you.* I don't know who *he* is, but if my dreams are known in Rome..."

Silence fills the hall. Pilate takes my face in his hands. "I'll protect you, as I have always done."

"You won't be *able* to protect me. Barabbas makes me think it's someone you won't be able to stop." His blue eyes fill with sadness and his hands drop. I touch his chest over his heart. "We can trust God to protect me. They say my dreams are for a reason... as a warning."

"I'd take them from you, if I could."

Our heads rest together. "I know."

Rather than depart without us, Quintus and Libi wait to accompany us to Caesarea. Her presence is welcome, since I dislike Marcellus. He asks too many questions. We send word to Hermina of our departure. It is too dangerous to see her in person, so I make do with the little twig cross she sends me. I pack it carefully in my things.

"You'll watch over her, won't you?"

Demetrius looks at me and his eyes soften. "Yes."

I take his hand and squeeze it, in silent gratitude. He sees us off without any show of affection.

Our departure from Jerusalem meets with interest. The streets clear out of the path of our legion. They ignore Pilate but call out to me. The roads the messiah traveled fall behind us. Two days later, we are at sea. I spend my time in our cabin trying not to vomit. I drift in and out of sleep, waking every few hours to the sound of hushed voices. I no longer know what day it is, or how long we have been aboard. Dim light peers through the window above me. The curtains move gently in the breeze.

"What do you mean to do?" My brother's voice is low and I glance at him. He leans on the table, scrolls rolling with each motion of the ship.

Pilate throws one into a carved wooden box. "I don't know."

"Surely you intend to defend yourself?"

He smiles wryly. "Will it do much good?"

"Do you think Caligula poisons Tiberius against you?"

"Considering what he did to my sister, I hardly expect a warm reception." Glancing at another scroll, he tosses it aside. "Claudia makes it more difficult. I can't give him any reason to get rid of me."

Quintus steps closer, asking, "Because of the dreams?"

"Yes, think what Caligula could do with a dream-seer!"

Shivers prickle my arms. Quintus' voice lowers, full of concern, "Surely no one in Rome is aware."

"Marcellus knew!" Pilate opens the curtain to look at me. I pretend to sleep. "The messiah's followers are telling the story everywhere they go! If Marcellus knows, Tiberius knows."

The curtain falls into place.

"Tiberius is fond of her, he wouldn't—"

"Our emperor lives for prophecies and will use her if he believes her useful. Fortunately, I still have friends in the Praetorian Guard, Cassius for one. If they rule against me, he will smuggle her out of the city. I won't say where, for your sake if they search for her, but I didn't want you to believe her dead at their hands."

Documents slide across the floor as the ship tilts.

"Thank you for telling me."

A knock on the door brings our supper. Libi dines with us but tires easily and returns to their cabin soon after. I eat a few bites and take some wine before bed. Putting out the lamp, Pilate asks, "Feeling better?"

"Much, but I never want to see a ship again." I slide over to

make room for him. He kisses my shoulder and puts an arm around me. My fingers cover his, entwining. "When did you plan on telling me your concerns?"

His eyes search mine. "I didn't."

"You can't hide that from me."

Pilate props his head on his hand. "I certainly can."

"You trust this man, Cassius?"

Fingertips run up my bare arm. "Cassius served under me in the Praetorian Guard, and in our foreign campaign. I saved his life many times. But I don't want to talk about Cassius." His lips capture mine and I cling to him, the thin sheet straining between us. A knock sounds at the door.

"*Every time,*" Pilate complains.

Laughing, I climb over him and answer it. Octavia takes one look at my disheveled appearance, turns bright red, and blurts, "It's time, Mistress!"

"What, *now?*"

Muffled screams echo in the corridor.

"She wants you!"

Hours pass. I spend them in a darkened cabin holding Libi. She leaves bruises on my arms from gripping me with each pain; it is hot and stifling and the sea air does little to ease her suffering. Before dawn a son is born, screaming. I clean the red, wrinkled baby and place it in her arms. Rather than a sting of jealousy, I feel only joy.

My entrance to our cabin causes Quintus to rise. I grin and say, "Go to Libi and meet your son."

He bolts past and I shut the door behind him. I fall asleep in Pilate's arms and dream. Screams follow me down a long corridor. I break into a run and push through the doors. I collide with Caligula. Strong hands grab me, slick with blood. I look up into his crazed eyes and see a demon, a monster, the darkness of sorcerers.

Let go of me!

Caligula forces me into a room and slams the door. I stumble over a table, scattering jars to the floor. They spin away from me, the poison oozing out onto the tiles. Then, I see his sister dead on the divan. My breath chokes in my throat. *What have you done?*

All earthly goddesses must die to be eternal.

I stare into her sightless eyes, widened in horror. The marks of his hands are still at her throat.

He grabs my ankle and drags me toward him...

"Claudia, wake up!"

I bolt upright, trembling. Lamps sway in the ship's rafters above us, casting eerie shadows on the walls. Pilate bends over me, his eyes full of concern.

A centurion pounds on the door and shouts, "Prefect!"

Night darkens the horizon. Scrolls roll across the floor, following the natural sway of the boat. Pilate goes to the door and exchanges quiet words with the centurion. He returns offering me a cup of water. He tucks a strand of my hair behind my ear, searching my eyes.

"Do you want to tell me?"

Shaking my head, I sink into the damp pillows. Pilate sits with me, stroking my arm. At another, more subdued knock, he says, "Enter."

"We're in sight of the harbor, Prefect."

Pilate avoids his gaze. "We'll disembark at dawn."

The centurion departs. Pilate pulls the covers higher. "Try to sleep if you can. I'll wake you when it's time to go."

Unable to sleep, I prepare to leave and am ready when a Praetorian tribune comes for us. I bid Libi farewell, kiss her son, embrace my brother, and go with Pilate. We disembark in gloom. Rome stands in the distance, quiet under the dawn.

"Cassius," says Pilate to the guard on the dock. "It's been too long, old friend."

"It has indeed." He grips Pilate's arm in welcome, tall and broad, but his voice is weak and high, the result of a scar across his throat. "I'm sent to escort you home, and inform you of the death of Emperor Tiberius."

"*What*?" I step toward him in shock.

His eyes fall on me. "It's been some days, now."

"How did it happen?" Pilate asks.

The tribune's brow twitches. "That depends on who you ask." Removing an imperial scroll from his belt, he hands it to Pilate. "Here are your final orders from Tiberius."

Breaking the seal, Pilate reads in silence. "When will Caligula arrive?"

"Soon, he left Capri last night."

Horses await us and I enter a litter. Home is unfamiliar after the dusty roads of Judea and no one looks at us twice. Fidelus' house is as cold and foreboding as I remember. It sends a shudder through me as I walk its lonely halls. All but

the housemaster and his family fled. He runs to greet us, his sandals slapping on the marble floor.

"So you alone are faithful, Marcus," Pilate says.

Bowing, the white-haired man says, "Yes, sir."

We enter the main hall with Cassius, who removes his helmet. Marcus' daughter offers us wine. "Tomorrow I'll send you to the slave market for replacements."

"News came to us of your sister... I'm sorry, sir."

Pilate places a hand on the old man's shoulder. "Your love for her is known and you served her well. She'd be honored at your remembrance."

Quietly, the servants slip from the room. Cassius sits and takes wine. "I trust she's safe?"

"Yes."

He smiles. "Good."

I make room for Pilate on the chaise. "You helped her?"

"Your husband left her in my charge should anything happen to her father. She came to me and I told her how to evade him. Caligula is a man of obsession. He never gives up until his target is dead."

Fingering his cup, Pilate asks, "What is said of him?"

"He's popular, witty, engaging... intelligent, but cruel." Hardening his face, Cassius stares at the floor. "He's less superstitious than Tiberius but more arrogant. Rumors abound over his relationship with his sisters. More importantly, it's well known that he hates you."

Our servant returns with fruit. Pilate snorts. "Considering my father sent him running to Capri, I suspected that. Will it influence him in my trial?"

"It may, you have powerful enemies in Rome, senators who dislike your handling of the Judeans... but others will rule in your favor. It may not come to a decision from Caligula. From what I know of him, he cares little for the responsibilities of being Caesar, only for its pleasures."

Remembering the impish boy, I am not surprised.

Cassius soon leaves us to the emptiness of the house, to its unpleasant memories... to wait.

Chapter Twenty-Seven

Rome is delighted with her new emperor. He enters in a gold chariot, a self-satisfied smirk on his face. "Hail, Caesar!" they shout. "Hail our new god, Caligula!"

"Would they love him if they knew him as a rapist?"

Pilate rests his hands on the half-wall. "He's their god; he may do as he pleases."

"Who is with him?"

He watches them circle the forum. "It's his sister, Drusilla."

They pass out of sight into the crowd and I follow him into the house. "How long will it be until he sends for you?"

"A week or so, he'll want time to prepare." He returns to sorting his father's scrolls. Mounds of them pile on the floor and the desk.

I finger one inscribed from Alexandria. "Have you decided whether or not to defend your actions in Judea?"

"You make it sound like I shouldn't."

Running my fingers along the tabletop, I stay silent.

Pilate glances at me and lifts his chin. "Claudia, if they decide against me in this, it will end badly. I think of you."

"Then I'll support whatever you decide."

Pilate draws me nearer. "And you won't advise me?"

"I can't. My judgment is impaired."

Wind stirs the scrolls, the distant roar of the crowd fading as the emperor makes his way to the palace. "So you *don't* know what you want me to do?"

"I want you to live, but not deny the truth." Taking the scroll he hands me, I put it on a shelf. Faith is easy when you sacrifice nothing, yet I risk losing all. I *want* to believe. I *want* to give in. I *want* to trust.

Sunlight takes me outside for a walk, to clear my head. Rome rises in the distance, stark against the darkening sky. Pilate must atone for his sins before a man who hates him. How can I believe the Messiah will protect us?

He is beside me in spirit. *Do you have faith, Claudia?*

Tears flow freely. "I *want* faith."

Do you love me?

Speech evades me, so I nod.

Do you love me more than you do Pilate?

Grief sends a fresh wave of misery through me.

If I take him from you, will you still follow me?

Earth rises up to meet me as I sink to my knees. My mind is frantic, filling with memories, with glances, with conversations, with certainty.

"Yes," I whisper.

Yes! He *is* the Messiah. Whether or not I have children, whether or not Jacob regains his sight, whether or not Pilate lives, Jesus *is* the Messiah! *My* Messiah.

Claudia...

It whispers through the columns and catches the wind. Shadows lengthen around me as night sets in across Rome. Pilate puts his arms around me. "You'll get cold."

"I'm fine." I lean into him and we watch the sun set. Our lips caress one another, our arms around each other as night ebbs into day, until sleep claims us both.

Pilate wakes me the next morning. "Let's go home."

"Aren't we?"

Smiling, he kisses my shoulder. "I meant *your* home."

I sit up. "To my father's house?"

"Yes."

The countryside is quiet. The vineyards flourish and the familiar road fills me with joy. Memories of my former life flood over me as we drive into the courtyard. I step out of the chariot and stare up at the house. Libi hurries out the side door. "This is a surprise!"

"A happy one, I hope."

She embraces me. "Yes! Quintus is in the vineyard."

"I'll find him." Pilate hands the reins to a servant and walks toward the stables.

Arm at my waist, Libi takes me inside. Moving a scroll off the lounge, she asks me to sit. A nurse holds the child.

"Have you named him yet?"

Libi takes him and hands him to me. "Judah."

"Not a Roman name, but it suits him." I grin and look up as my sister enters. Returning Judah to his nurse, I hug her. "Thais, I have missed you!"

Laughing, she says, "Liar."

"When will I meet your future husband?"

Servants set out fruit and wine. I sink onto a lounge. Thais shrugs, her dark eyes sparkling with mirth. "He's busy in the senate arguing for fewer taxes."

"He's a true Roman, then."

Warm light falls through the columns behind us.

"Yes! Preoccupied and absent!"

Glancing around the room, I ask, "Where's Mother?"

Libi bites her lip. "She's... not well."

"What do you mean?" My mirth fades.

Waving the servants out, Thais takes my hand. "She's not right in the head anymore, Claudia."

"What? How did such a thing happen?"

"Her visits to the soothsayers increased once you left. She obsessed over a prophecy. She went to a sorcerer a dozen times but he refused to tell her more. She tried other seers with no result. I tried to keep her away from them, but she insisted. She's... changed, Claudia."

My throat feels dry. "May I see her?"

Eying one another, Thais says, "The question is whether or not you *want* to."

Our upper corridor is quiet, subdued. Thais pauses with her hand on the door and turns to me. "Don't expect much from her; she hardly says a word anymore." Inching the door inward, she steps aside.

My heart beats loud in my ears as I enter. The once beautiful room is in shambles. Torn curtains ripple in the breeze. What little furniture remains is worn and splintered.

"Mother?"

She crouches against the far wall and glances over her shoulder at me; the once-beautiful, proud woman is sallow and thin, her eyes sunken and wild. My eyes drift to the walls, to her frantic writing.

Death... murder... madness... crucifixion...

Breath catches in my throat. Thais enters behind me. "We scrub it off and she writes it again, over and over. If we take her ink away, she scrapes her hands until they bleed and uses that."

The garish figure turns to the wall. I step over piles of torn scrolls, full of erratic writing. Kneeling behind her, I touch Mother's arm. She stares at me with haunted, empty eyes. "When did she become like this?"

Thais' skirt brushes mine. "The day night came swift and sure at noon, and darkness covered Rome."

Mother mutters under her breath. I pick up a scroll and cold seeps into my veins.

Defiance... darkness... death...

"Claudia, what do you know of this?"

Mother suddenly grips my wrist her strength inhuman, her eyes wild as she gives a flicker of recognition. "Claudia! The one who brings death to Rome! Death and madness! The one who saw and believed! Because of you, he'll die!"

Fear strikes me. "Who will die?"

"There is only one god in Rome! You bring another!" She wrenches my arm and I cry out.

Thais tries to pry her fingers loose. "Mother, let go!"

"I should have drowned you, the destroyer of Rome!" She lunges at me. Her sharp fingernails tear at my hair, my face and arms. Thais screams. I try to push her off and she follows me, tackling me to the floor. Her eyes are demented, full of rage. "Death! Madness! Murder!" she shrieks.

Pilate drags her off me. She stumbles into my brother, who pulls her away. Pilate picks me up and carries me into the hall. The door slams behind us.

"Are you all right?"

Blood trickles down my throat. The door opens and a tearful Thais emerges. "I'm sorry, Claudia! She's never been violent before!"

A body slams into the door and I flinch.

"Quintus will quiet her, she does better with him."

Libi tends to my injuries—a scraped knee and a gash in my head. Her eyes worriedly search mine. "What did she say to you?"

"I'll destroy Rome with my god and bring death."

She rinses the strip of linen in water, clouding it with blood. "You can't trust sorcerer prophecies, Claudia."

The sorcerer knows what Barabbas knows...

I stare at the bloody water, reminded of Jerusalem. Quintus enters and sits beside me. "You can't let anything she says trouble you, sister... she's mad."

"She mentioned the crucifixion! His disciples are far from Rome. How does she know him?"

No one answers.

"Marcellus may have written Tiberius..."

I half-laugh. "But how does *Mother* know?"

"One of her seers told her? Judean merchants travel to Rome all the time. One of them might have spoken of it."

Doubt clouds the air. Libi catches my hand. "Either way, Claudia, *you* can't destroy Rome!"

"You don't think so?" Pilate asks quietly. We all look at him, as he pushes away from the wall. "Rome is full of gods, from emperors to ancestors. Your messiah says the only way to heaven is through him. Don't you think Romans will take offense at that?" He searches my gaze. "Your mother is right, this *will* destroy Rome. There'll be death... and madness... and suffering."

Heaviness settles over me. "But why blame me?"

"I don't know."

Our return home is quiet. Several days pass before Cassius comes not for Pilate but us both. "The emperor wants an audience with your wife as well."

"Not a hearing?" Pilate asks with surprise.

The Praetorian shakes his head. Pilate shoots me a rueful glance and indicates the door.

Caligula fills his palace with guests and entertainment. Half-naked dancers swirl past as we enter. His thin form sprawls across his throne, his dark eyes fixed on me. "Come, wife of Pilate," he says, "sit beside me."

His sister glares and moves aside. Pilate remains at the foot of the stairs. Caligula's head tilts as he stares at me. "I know you."

"We've met before, Caesar, in your childhood."

Those eerie, disquieting eyes flicker with recognition. "I remember. Hermina spoke of you. Shame she died. I might have made her my queen otherwise." A nasty sneer tugs at his lips. I feel cold inside. Exchanging a smirk with his sister, he says, "Tell me of the Galilean Pilate executed in Jerusalem."

"Why, Caesar?"

"I'm curious. They say you warned him not to do it."

"That presumes much, doesn't it?"

His eyes narrow. "Then you *didn't* warn him?"

"What you've heard is probably not the whole truth."

Leaning against his throne, he smiles. "I heard the 'messiah' claimed to be a god. I heard the Judean authorities arrested him, and you had a dream that so disturbed you, you warned Pilate not to deal with him. Is that the whole truth?"

Cold ripples over me but I fight not to show it. "Yes."

"You have a reputation for such things in Rome."

I try not to knot my hands in my lap. "Do I?"

"Yes..." The creepy eyes flicker over me curiously. "But no matter, we're here to deal with your husband." He motions

Pilate forward. "You return in disgrace, Prefect. The senate wants you arrested and tried for... what, Gracchus, crimes against the populace in Judea?"

Nearby senators exchange glances.

"Yes, Caesar, he massacred a group of Samaritans." One of them holds out a scroll and he waves it aside.

"What reason had you for this slaughter, Pilate?"

"Uprisings are common in Judea, Caesar. Any large, armed gathering is suspicious."

Twitching a gold sandal against the floor, Caligula asks, "Did they intend to riot?"

"We'll never know, since he slaughtered them!"

Caligula grins. "What do they say?"

"He killed a religious sect intent on climbing their holy mountain." Gracchus moves as near as he dares.

The emperor curls his lip. "Ugh, religion... another prophet, I suppose?"

"Yes, Caesar... there's one every five years or so." Pilate reveals nothing in his tone, his eyes distant.

An aging senator I recognize steps forward. "Caesar, it caused much distress in Samaria; our Syrian governor..."

"Sent word for Pilate to return to Rome, yes, I know, but Tiberius is dead and the matter rests with me, right, Julius?" Under Caligula's glare, the senator falls silent. Caligula thrusts out his hand and a servant hastily hands him a goblet. He considers Pilate over the top of it. "Do the Samaritans worship me?"

"No, Caesar, they worship the God of the Judeans."

The skin on my neck tingles. I glance at Caligula, noting the thinness of his golden hair. His sister sulks in her corner.

"It's the duty of a Judean governor to maintain order. If the Samaritans intended a religious riot, isn't it within the Judean governor's rights to maintain Roman authority?"

Horrified, Gracchus says, "But Caesar, we've permitted Judea its own religion since our invasion. The Samaritans have the same rights as the Jews!"

"To not display our emblems and such, yes, I know. The Judeans have too much leniency; our governor puts up emblems, they riot; he uses their temple funds to build an aqueduct, they riot. Their religion is treasonous if it contradicts Roman rule." Caligula drums his fingers on the arm of his throne.

Another senator says, "Sire, the only way we have peace in Judea is to let them have their religious rights."

"But we don't have 'peace,' do we? We have riots over standards, over emperors, over messiahs, over taxes, over aqueducts, over governors..." Drusilla leans against his throne. He smiles at her. "I *may* choose leniency, considering Judea *is* a rebellious outpost."

This shocks me as much as the rest of them. I feel cold.

"The Samaritans won't like it, Caesar."

Pulling a face, Caligula tosses the empty cup at a slave. "They never like anything."

"Caesar, should this be your first act as emperor, to pardon Pilate against such grievous charges?"

His eyes straying to the gyrating dancers, Caligula shrugs. "It isn't a pardon, for I see no fault."

The senators eye one another and stay silent.

"What, doesn't my leniency please you?"

Julius scowls. "Tiberius reprimanded Pilate twice! He deliberately took violent actions despite Tiberius' orders for more benevolence toward the Judeans."

The emperor turns to me, catching me off guard. "What do you think, Claudia? My senators thirst for blood. Should I punish your husband?"

"Isn't your disapproval punishment enough?"

Caligula considers, tapping his finger on his chin. "Why was he reprimanded?"

"He tried to install Roman emblems in Jerusalem."

The hand falls. "And...?"

"He beat rioters who objected to the aqueducts."

Delight fills his expression. "I see!"

Gracchus approaches. "Do you, Caesar? Pilate is highly unpopular in Judea! Not to punish his behavior—"

"It sets an example of Roman authority, that our decisions aren't swayed by the disapproval of the Jews."

Silence fills the room; the dancers pause. Caligula motions for them to continue and the music resumes. He leans closer. "Tell me, Claudia, what did you think of the Judeans?"

Though repulsed at his nearness, I smile. "I'm intrigued by them."

He indicates Pilate. "Is your husband fond of them?"

"No, Caesar."

"And he governed with... unnecessary brutality?" His

excitement at the thought disgusts me.

I glance at Pilate. "The Syrian governor believes so."

"If I wanted the opinion of the Syrian governor, I'd ask him. What's *your* opinion?" Impatience taints his voice. Drusilla sits on his armrest. His hand goes to her knee, sliding up the fabric to find bare skin. I struggle to keep an approving smile.

"My opinion is whatever yours is, Caesar."

"Ha! More than just your dreams make you wise. This is true diplomacy, Senators; take heed of it!" Snapping his fingers for the scroll, Caligula tosses it in the fire. He stares at my husband. "You do look like Sejanus."

"Who overstepped his bounds as well," Julius says.

The smirk returns. "We'll see."

"Caesar, what will we tell the Samaritans?"

Staring at the ceiling Caligula says, "As our official representative in Judea, Pilate's actions bore our consent. Let that be an end of it."

Scowls pass between senators. Caligula stands and taking his sister by the hand, turns to leave. He pauses at the foot of the stairs. "I'll find another use for you, Pilate." His lips turn in a malicious sneer and he leaves.

"The gods side with you today, Pilate," snarls Julius, "but you'll not always be so fortunate!"

I descend the stairs to his side. "Is that the end of it?"

"Oh," says Pilate, "I doubt it."

Chapter Twenty-Eight

My favorite place in Rome is not the slave market and Pilate knows it, which is why when he hands me a purse, he says, "Think of it as rescuing them from a harsher master."

I stay away from the gladiators and search instead for a house slave to run errands for us. I find one and eye him. "Where are you from, boy?"

Gentle, dark eyes gaze at me. "Syria."

"He's strong," the slave trader assures me. "He works hard! He's worth a fine price!"

I shrug. "He's too young."

"He's young enough for guidance, old enough to not need to learn it!" The man grins.

A crowd merges around me. "How much is he?"

He names a high price. I decline it and walk away. He runs after me, lowering it. I shake my head. "For you, Mistress, I lower the price to fifty gold pieces!"

The boy looks at me searchingly and I nod, handing over the coins. "Take him to the house of Pilate."

"You're Pilate's wife?" His face lights up in excitement as his hands are unbound. "Then you..." Dark eyes dart behind me and hit the dirt. His happiness fades. I feel a shiver and turn to find Caligula, without his usual entourage.

"Bit scrawny, isn't he, for a house slave?"

Guards move around us, Cassius among them. I smile. "I wanted to leave the best for you, Caesar. There is a fine Greek across the way. He speaks six languages!" I wave Marcus and the new slave away.

Caligula walks with me across the courtyard. "How many do you speak?"

"Three, but only two of them well."

He gazes lustfully at a dark-haired slave girl. Nodding to his purser, he walks on as the fat man waddles forward to pay for her. I feel sick. "Your husband has many enemies in Rome."

Others move out of our way, faces craning for a better look at their handsome young emperor. I sense the envious eyes of women following me. "He's fortunate you're not one of them, Caesar."

"Having him around infuriates Gracchus which gives me great joy." He stops to eye another pretty slave girl. "Yet, his

parentage is..."

Hoping for her sake he moves on, I answer, "Oh, but those are rumors, Caesar! We only *assume* Sejanus' affair with Pilate's mother. For all we know, Pilate's father is a wine merchant."

Caligula laughs and walks on. "You're one of the few clever people I've met. Most think they're clever but few actually are."

"You'd know, Caesar, being so clever yourself." Even though I want to gouge out his eyes, I smile.

He returns to his chariot. "I may make him a senator. Fidelus' seat is empty and there's no evidence he *shouldn't* have it."

My skin crawls as he drives away. I return to the house and the boy hurries to open the door for me. "You," I say, turning on him, "what did you start to say to me in the marketplace?"

His cheeks flush and he drops his eyes. "I'm honored you bought me, Mistress. That's all."

"No, you meant something else... *what*?"

Looking at me, his face warms. "You *saw* him, the messiah. You spoke to him! You fought for him! They all speak of you!"

Fear grips me. "What is it they say exactly?"

"Your dream foretold his death." Shadows flicker along the hall. I enter the next room and he follows on my heels. "When my stepfather sold me to the tradesman, I cursed this place. I cursed Rome. I never thought He would lead me to you, to one of *us*! God is merciful, Mistress!"

"Listen to me carefully." I pause as a servant passes and lower my voice. "You can't speak of me to *anyone*."

Misery flickers across his face. "Yes, Mistress."

"How old are you and what do they call you?"

The thin frame straightens. "Silvanus. I'm twelve."

"Go to the kitchens. Tell them I want you to eat well."

He hesitates. "Did you meet him?"

"Yes, several times."

Blushing furiously, he asks, "How did you find him?"

"Jesus was gentle and strong, compassionate but not tame."

His grin is infectious and he runs off, his bare feet slapping the tiles. Pilate enters the room and puts his arms around me. "I send you for a lion and you buy a lamb."

"He'll turn into a lion, one day."

Silvanus is my shadow, trailing me by day and sleeping in the hall at night. Scrawny and kind to all things, he is the son I

might have had. After he proves his worth, I let him go to the marketplace. He returns one afternoon in a rush. Shouting "Mistress!" he skids into the room and slides to a stop on seeing Pilate.

Looking at him in amusement, Pilate says, "Continue."

He comes to me. "I saw the emperor in the forum."

"That's not unusual." Pilate returns to his scroll.

Crouching at my feet, he says, "I followed him. He went into the temple to visit one of the seers."

"You mean one of the prostitutes?" Pilate smirks.

The boy shakes his head. "No, the high sorceress; he asked to see the one that spoke with *you*, Mistress."

Pilate sends me a sharp glance. I pat Silvanus' hand. "Thank you for warning me. You have done well. Go on, to your duties."

Once he leaves Pilate asks, "How much does she know?"

"It depends on whether she's a true seer or not, but she'll remember me. She tried to kill me."

Pilate goes to a meeting with his fathers' friends in the senate a week later. I go for a swim in the bath and when I emerge, Silvanus awaits me outside the door. He averts his boyish eyes from my damp robe. "You're wanted in the main hall, Mistress."

A servant helps me dress and untangle my hair. I emerge to find a Praetorian guard awaiting me. "Caligula sends for you."

Tension floats in the air. Silvanus follows and the guard stops him. "Her husband entrusts her protection to me," he says. "I'll be beaten if you don't let me go with her!"

Frowning, the Praetorian permits it. Silvanus being there comforts me, though he cannot enter the main rooms of the palace and must wait in the hall. The Praetorian lets me into a large bedroom full of lavish furniture. My stomach clenches.

"Ah, there you are!"

Caligula enters through the far door, draped in a rich blue toga, a golden cup in one hand. His eyes flicker over me as I show him the proper respect.

"You sent for me?" I force a smile. "Are you in need of my cleverness for your amusement, Caesar?"

He takes my hand and draws me toward the bed. My heart quickens, pounding in my ears. "Amusement... yes, I need amusement. You intrigue me, Claudia. I could have your husband killed with one command, yet you don't fear me."

Throwing the cup on the floor, he shoves me onto the bed. His fingers slide up my arm and across my leg. "But I'm more intrigued with something else." Putting his mouth at my ear, he says, "The *dreams*."

I flinch as he grips my chin, forcing me to look at him. "I wondered why Sejanus' son chose a common girl out of the vineyards instead of a senator's wife. Now, I know." He straddles me. "I considered what to do with you," he says, his hand at my throat. "One idea appealed to me but I'm told rape can destroy a dream-seer. Pity, you *are* so lovely." Long, cold fingers drift lower. "That wouldn't do. Dream-seers are so rare, after all."

He licks my throat. "Tell me, Claudia, have you dreamed my future?"

"No."

Dark eyes penetrate mine; a nasty smile curves his lip.

"She's lying." The voice comes from the other side of the room, and the temple seer emerges from the shadows. Darkness enters with her, swirling over her head and glowing in her face. I shudder as it touches me.

Sharp fingernails dig into my arm. "Remember me?"

Panic threatens to overcome my calm. She goes to the lit brazier and throws something into it. Black smoke enters the room with a heavy scent of incense.

"Don't, please..." I try to twist free.

Caligula pins my hands to the coverlet. "Tell me of this Judean messiah," he says. "You wanted him pardoned. Why?"

"He committed no crime."

The seer snorts and tosses powder in the fire.

Blonde brows shoot toward the ceiling. "Innocent? He called himself the son of god, *a* god! There is only one god in the Roman Empire! *Me*!"

My senses drift; I fight to keep hold of them.

"Tell me!" Rage fills his face, blossoming into redness. I stare at him in terror. "Tell me what you've seen! Make her show me, witch!"

She forces something bitter into my mouth; I choke on it and spit up blood. The witch takes my head in her hands. I scream as pain shoots through me, a thousand splinters exploding behind my eyes. "Show me," she whispers.

Blackness descends; a terrible pit of darkness where I drown; struggling, fighting toward a distant surface. I feel her

reaching into my dreams, drawing them out.

"She is resisting me!"

Caligula snarls, "Get them from her! I want to know!"

Blood clogs my throat. I thrash and twitch.

"I have never felt anything this powerful before!" Fear touches her voice. I am not fighting her; something else is, far more powerful than either of us, a force that swells up inside and growls at her.

Someone screams. It is not me.

"You cannot stop!" Caligula shakes me violently. "My augur warned me of her threat! Find out what is in her mind! Tell me her dreams! Tell me of this god, this Judean messiah!" His eyes penetrate the blackness, cold and furious, full of terror and rage. The witch has removed her hands. He glares at her. "Do it! Do it or I'll have your head!"

Trembling fingers touch me again. The world implodes. Light chases screaming shadows away. The witch shrieks and releases me. Caligula's face comes into focus above me. He stares into the far corner of the room in shock.

You are not a god, Caligula...

My body relaxes. The fire goes out.

The emperor snarls, "I am! I'm a god, as my forefathers were before me!"

There is but one god. It is I. I am the Alpha and the Omega, the beginning and the end. I am Yahweh. I am Jehovah. I am El-Shaddai!

Swirling light moves toward us.

"What deviltry is this?" Caligula tightens his hand on my throat, his eyes fierce. "What do you unleash, witch?"

I no longer feel fear.

You asked for me. I am the Messiah!

The emperor's face contorts hideously. "You are no messiah! You are not the king of the Jews! You're not a god!"

Blood drips from his nose. He looks astonished. His eyes fall to the witch, dead on the floor.

Fists pound on the door. "Caesar!"

Caligula stumbles off me. I run to the door and find it locked so I rattle the handle. Silence falls in the room as the light fades. The door opens and Silvanus spills inside. Cassius shoves in past him. "What have you done?" he asks in horror.

The emperor grins as blood streams down his front. He steps forward, a look of fear crosses his face—and he falls to

the floor. Cassius turns him over; unseeing eyes stare at the ceiling. "Get her out of here! No one can know!"

I stagger against Silvanus. "One of the guards knows."

"He won't when I'm finished with him. Now go, before anyone comes! Take the side door!"

The boy drags me through it and we stumble down a flight of stairs. It leads us out into the street. Behind us, voices cry out in alarm and footsteps race toward Caligula's rooms. Silvanus all but carries me to the river. We follow it until the house comes into sight.

Pilate meets us in the main hall. "What happened?"

"I don't know! Caligula took her!"

Strong arms catch me before I fall and Pilate carries me to our room. Gentle hands draw damp hair out of my face. "Claudia, what did he do to you?" His voice is cold, tense, but without a hint of volume.

I clutch at his hand. "He sent for the sorceress... she tried to read my dreams."

Dampness rolls over my lip. I lick it and taste blood.

"I will kill him for this."

My head throbs; the incense still burns my lungs. I shake my head. I can barely speak. "Don't."

"Claudia..."

Tightening my hold on him, I say, "Promise me."

"No!"

Blood chokes my lungs. "Be a better man than he is!"

Fear enters his eyes. "Silvanus, fetch a physician! Go!"

Sandals pound the marble as Pilate turns to me. I convulse, lean over the edge of the bed, and vomit blood.

I know little after that. Voices sound garbled to my ears. Faces fade in and out. I fight to stay conscious and slip into darkness. Dark and light bleed together into nothingness.

Claudia...

Hands touch me.

She drank poison! I cannot do anything to help her!

Gloom closes in. I am lost, enveloped in nothingness that fills me with contentment. Life ebbs away from me. Though death arrives, fear eludes me. Life leaves me slowly as the darkness merges into light. I want it to go faster, to take me to the Messiah. I sense His presence all around me...

Claudia! A cry from Pilate's heart reaches me. He is distraught and clutches my hand. *Do not leave me!*

I cannot stay! Warmth draws me closer to my Lord.

Messiah...

This is not my voice, but his.

Forgive me. Forgive me!

Wet touches the side of my face. He holds me close. His tears are not for me.

Jehovah, save her.

The light blends into grayness.

I believe, Messiah... I believe...

Death releases its hold. The room comes into focus. Pilate embraces me. His breath is ragged in his throat. "I thought I lost you for a moment!"

Our foreheads rest together.

You did.

Epilogue

They say the emperor went mad. He believed himself to be a god. He erected statues of himself in all the temples in Rome, and commanded one for Judea. Marcellus, the new governor, refused... nicely.

We are far from Rome. My spies say Caligula never looked for us nor mentioned the day he met the Messiah. They say he murdered his sister, so she could be a goddess. Others claim she died of a fever. Rumors circulate that Cassius killed Caligula in the end. He insulted him one time too many, or maybe it was out of loyalty to Pilate.

It is fitting in a way, for madness does not suit a god.

After giving birth to my son, my dreams slowed and now that he is older, have ceased. The healing Jesus gave me that day in Bethany was real and his timing perfect. Fleeing from Rome with a small child would have been far more dangerous.

"Paul is here!" our son calls out. Silvanus runs to greet him. He will want to go with Paul when he leaves. Since he is no longer a slave, nothing holds him back.

I rise and go to meet them, winding my arm through Pilate's in the hall. I do not miss the armor or the Roman man I married. A change has come over Pilate, as it has us all. The Messiah has changed Rome. He did it, not with a sword, but with a cross. We both played a part in his death and now play a part in his resurrected life.

My greatest hope is that all who witness the Messiah in the lives of his followers will believe.

Character Index

Avram: trusted servant in Procula's household, father of Jacob and Libi.

Barabbas: insurrectionist against Rome, sentenced to death but freed by the people in exchange for the Messiah.

Caligula: Roman Emperor from 37-41 AD. Contemporary historians present the first six months of his reign as noble and moderate, followed by cruelty, extravagance, and sexual perversity. His assassination was led by Cassius, a member of his own Praetorian Guard. *

Caiaphas: High Priest of Judea during the Messiah's life.

Cassius: a member of the Praetorian Guard, responsible for the murder of Caligula. He endured endless mockery at the hands of Caligula over his high-pitched voice, the result of an injury in battle. He serves as one of Pilate's friends in the Praetorian Guard. He was executed in 41 AD.

Claudia: the wife of Pilate, a dream-seer, and sympathizer to the Christians.

Demetrius: a Centurion of Rome, first met in Crete, who accompanies Pilate to Judea as his trusted "first" among his personal guard.

Fidelus: a former Roman general and current senator. Father of Hermina and Pilate. His wife was suspected of having an affair with Sejanus, so he murdered her, leading to his fall from popularity.

Germanius: Quintus' trusted manservant.

Gratus: Prefect of Judea from 15-26 AD. He appointed Caiaphas as High Priest.

Hermina: younger sister of Pilate, suspected daughter of Sejanus, and desired by Caligula.

Herod: ruler of Galilee during the time of Christ. He divorced his first wife in favor of Herodias, his brother's wife. Responsible for the death of John the Baptist. Herod was exiled in 39 AD by Caligula after facing accusations that he plotted against the Emperor Tiberius with Sejanus.

Herodias: a Jewish princess of the Herodian Dynasty, granddaughter of Herod the Great, and half-sister of her husband, Herod Antipas. Her "incestuous" marriage was criticized by John the Baptist, leading to his death. She accompanied her husband later into exile in 39 AD.

Jacob: son of Avram and brother of Libi. A servant in Procula's household until his violence against Sejanus sends him in exile to Judea. There, he becomes a Priest in Caiaphas' temple.

Jesus: the Messiah, whose trial and crucifixion changed history forever.

Lazarus: one of Jesus' friends who arose from the dead. His sisters Mary and Martha are also included.

Libi: sister of Jacob, daughter of Avram. Trusted friend and faithful servant of Claudia. Pursued romantically by Claudia's brother, Quintus.

Lucilla: Claudia's oldest sister, newly married.

Lucius Pilate: Prefect of Judea (26-36 AD), known for his brutality toward the Jews, for attempting to complete the Jerusalem aqueducts, for the massacre of the Samaritans, and for crucifying the Messiah. He was sent to Rome to answer charges by the Samaritan governor. After 36 AD, there is no further record of him. He is the suspected illegitimate son of Sejanus and an early high-ranking member of the Praetorian Guard.

Marcellus: friend and lower official of the Governor of Syria, who served as temporary Prefect of Judea following Pilate's dismissal.

Peter: one of the twelve apostles of Christ, and the one who "denied the Messiah three times." Peter was martyred in Rome around 64 AD.

Procula: Claudia's father, a wine merchant.

Quintus: son of Procula, older brother to Claudia. A Centurion in Rome and in Judea. He is the commander of the Garrison at Jerusalem during the time of Christ. He seeks Libi as his mistress or wife.

Salome: daughter of Herodias and stepdaughter of King Herod, who danced for the king and asked for John the Baptist's head as a prize.

Sejanus: commander of the Praetorian Guard from 14-31 AD. He reformed the Guard from mere bodyguards into a powerful branch of the government. He influenced Emperor Tiberius and during Tiberius' withdrawal to Capri in 26, Sejanus became the *de facto* ruler of Rome. Sejanus' plotting against Tiberius and Caligula led to his denouncement and execution in 31 AD.

Servia: Claudia's mother, usually referred to simply as "Mother." Servia is fascinated with seers and oracles.

Silvanus: the Greek name for Silas, companion of Paul and leader of the early Christian community. A slave in the Roman household of Claudia.

Thais: Claudia's older, spinster sister.

Tiberius: Roman Emperor from 14-37 AD. One of Rome's greatest generals, but a dark, somber, and reclusive ruler unloved by the people. He died in 37 AD.

* The Praetorian Guard: an elite group of bodyguards whose sole purpose was to protect the Emperors. Sejanus expanded their power and influence in Rome during his brief period as their prefect.

5989779R00115

Printed in Great Britain
by Amazon.co.uk, Ltd.,
Marston Gate.